BACK TO THE MOON

BAEN BOOKS by TRAVIS S. TAYLOR

One Day on Mars
The Tau Ceti Agenda
One Good Soldier

Warp Speed
The Quantum Connection

The Science Behind the Secret (nonfiction)

with John Ringo:

Vorpal Blade
Manxome Foe
Claws That Catch

Von Neumann's War

BACK TO THE MOON

Travis S. Taylor
Les Johnson

BACK TO THE MOON

This is a work of fiction. All the characters and events portrayed in this book are fictional, and any resemblance to real people or incidents is purely coincidental.

A Baen Books Original

Baen Publishing Enterprises
P.O. Box 1403
Riverdale, NY 10471
www.baen.com

ISBN: 978-1-4391-3405-4

Cover art by David Mattingly

First printing, December 2010

Distributed by Simon & Schuster
1230 Avenue of the Americas
New York, NY 10020

Library of Congress Cataloging-in-Publication Data

Taylor, Travis S.
  Back to the moon / Travis S. Taylor & Les Johnson.
      p. cm.
  ISBN 978-1-4391-3405-4 (hc)
  1. Space flight to the moon—Fiction. 2. Manned space flight—Fiction. 3. Space rescue operations—Fiction. I. Johnson, Les (Charles Les) II. Title.
  PS3620.A98B33 2010
  813'.6—dc22

                                                2010039852

10 9 8 7 6 5 4 3 2 1

Pages by Joy Freeman (www.pagesbyjoy.com)
Printed in the United States of America

Dedicated to Emily Jo Howard,
my friend, mentor and first employer
at The Book Rack in Ashland, Kentucky.
—Les Johnson

Prologue

Standing on an airless, desolate plain flanked by boulders the size of houses and by mountains taller than eight Eiffel Towers stacked atop one another had a way of leaving a man humbled and feeling just how fragile a human so far from home truly was. Gene squinted in the bright sunlight, pondering what to do next. He and his two colleagues were near the end of a decade-long journey; the three days of travel from the Earth to the Moon followed by three amazing days on the lunar surface were only the most recent portions. The journey of Apollo 17 was the culmination of the most technologically advanced endeavor mankind had ever attempted. With the majestic, stark, and absolutely unforgiving Moon soon to be only a memory, a fleeting moment from his glory days, Gene reached behind his spacesuit as best he could to point the camera toward the vehicle that would soon take him from this place and put him on a journey back home. Gene realized that it would be a while before humanity felt the spark to return. Humanity's candle had burned exceedingly bright for a decade, but it just couldn't maintain such a vast level of effort. Going to the Moon was a major endeavor that took the full focus of an entire nation driven by the desire to defeat another great nation. Americans had won the race, and Gene, along with the rest of Apollo 17, was the final flicker of that bright-burning candle.

At a distance of about one mile, the camera would capture his moment of liftoff and transmit the video back to Earth. Or, if something were to go terribly wrong, the video might be useful in reconstructing how he and his partner might have met their untimely demise on the distant lunar surface. The camera, mounted on the lunar rover that had served them so well during their all-too-brief visit, provided a needed connection to mission control back on Earth. Gene didn't want to leave so soon, but at the same time, he was anxious to go home.

After making final adjustments to the camera, he again paused. Then, ever so slowly and with the appearance of great clumsiness due to the limited movement granted by the inflated spacesuit, he kneeled down to the surface of the Moon and scratched three letters into the lunar dust. Satisfied with his work, he stood up, brushed off some of the dust from the lower half of his suit, and began Moon-bouncing back toward the Lunar Module.

It was a short walk, but Gene was nonetheless huffing and puffing by the time he arrived. Working against the inflated suit required strength, aerobic conditioning, and endurance all at the same time. Despite the technological prowess required to send him to the Moon, the bulky, awkward, and oh-so-heavy spacesuit required considerable effort to use—even in one sixth of Earth's gravity.

Gene stood by the Lunar Module knowing it was his time to make a historical last statement for the bold and ever-decreasingly budgeted American space program. He uttered what were to be the last words spoken from the surface of the Moon for over a half century.

"Bob, this is Gene, and I'm on the surface; and, as I take man's last step from the surface, back home for some time to come—but we believe not too long into the future—I'd like to just say what I believe history will record. That America's challenge of today has forged man's destiny of tomorrow. And, as we leave the Moon at Taurus-Littrow, we leave as we came and, God willing, as we shall return, with peace and hope for all mankind. Godspeed the crew of Apollo 17."

With that, Apollo astronaut Gene Cernan climbed the ladder

to join his crewmate and friend, Harrison "Jack" Schmitt, in the Lunar Excursion Module. They would then let their training take over and begin all the prelaunch preparations required to get them off the surface of the Moon and on their way back to the only place in the universe known to contain life—Earth.

The next day, with the camera recording nearly every detail, the LEM named *Challenger* lifted into the blackness of space, carrying two brave men back toward home, leaving the Moon lifeless once again.

Humanity had left its mark on the Moon six times, impressions of twelve feet, and two of those feet had been Gene's. But he had left more, a more personal mark. Etched into the lunar dust, probably to remain undisturbed for several human lifetimes, or more, were the letters *TDC*—the initials of Cernan's daughter.

"Shh, Mommy! They're leaving the Moon for good!" Bill gave his mother a stern shush as the precocious five-year-old kept his eyes glued to the small black-and-white television in the family room. He leaned in and squinted at the screen as if that would help him see more details of the spaceship and the Moon. All it really did was accentuate the large phosphorus pixels of the old black-and-white picture-tube technology.

"Don't sit too close to the TV, honey—it will hurt your eyes," his mother said.

"Oh, mom."

"So, you think the spacemen are neat?" Bill's father smiled proudly at his son.

"Yeah, I like the Moon. I'm gonna go there someday." To Bill, the statement was simply the fact of the matter. He *was* going to go to the Moon someday.

Chapter I

As famously depicted in the movie *2001: A Space Odyssey,* the movements of objects in space did appear to be choreographed like those of dancers. With grace, precision, and painfully slow forward motion, the two-hundred-eighty-two-thousand-pound Earth Departure Stage, or EDS, and the four-person Orion capsule moved closer and closer to each other. From the Orion capsule's point of view, it was moving toward the EDS, with its attitude-control thrusters firing in quick "bang bang" succession. As the distance between the two spacecraft decreased from kilometers to mere hundreds of meters, the glorious blue and white Earth moved quickly beneath them only a hundred or so miles away.

The latest test flights of the vehicles that would hopefully carry people back to the Moon for the first time in over fifty years moved toward completion. The present tests were an important step even though no people were onboard either of the vehicles.

The vehicles were on autopilot, testing the "new and improved" automated docking and rendezvous system that NASA had been working on since the space-shuttle days. Gone was the day of the astronaut "rocket jockey" controlling every spacecraft movement with a throttle and stick. Of course, the "rocket jockeys" themselves didn't agree with the move, and the general public typically liked the notion of the superheroic space-pilot astronauts. However, the guys with the software had won the technical arguments and determined that having the pilot "out of the loop" was by far a safer approach. Or so their calculations indicated.

The massive aluminum-and-composite EDS had been launched just hours previously by the mighty Ares V rocket. Measuring over ninety feet long and containing enough fuel to carry four people, a lunar lander, and all the supplies needed for a week's stay on the Moon, the EDS appeared to be dead, floating effortlessly two hundred and ten kilometers above the Earth. The over-one-hundred-forty-ton behemoth moved around the Earth at nearly seventeen thousand miles per hour. The Orion was closing in on it, moving with about the same speed, adding only enough velocity to catch up with the EDS in order for the two spacecraft to dock.

And the distance was closing—rapidly. Too rapidly. The first warning bell sounded in mission control at 2:58 p.m., local time. Nobody was particularly alarmed by the bell.

"Bill, we've got an anomaly with the Orion's close rate on the EDS," Marianne Thomas said calmly from her console near the back right corner of Constellation Mission Control at the Johnson Space Center in Houston. The anomaly had been simulated in training, but she hadn't expected it to happen during the test. But that was why they trained. "Orion's laser ranging indicates they're closing faster than programmed and faster than the onboard computer says it's going." There was only objectivity in her voice and not a trace of the anxiety that she was starting to experience in her gut.

"Roger that," Mission Commander and Blue Team's Flight Controller Bill Stetson responded automatically—again, thanks to the training. "Do we have confirmation of the closure rate from GPS?"

The onboard differential GPS system was supposed to be able to resolve the relative positions of the two spacecraft and calculate relative motion based on successive position measurements. Stetson was set to command the next flight—the one that would actually carry people to the Moon—and was in charge of this portion of the final flight test. Up to this point, everything had gone fairly smoothly, and this was just fine with Bill Stetson.

"Bill..." Thomas hesitated, a pause that was noticed by all in the room, including Stetson. "Looks like we have no data from GPS." Her eyes were scanning the display in front of her, desperately trying to find out why there was no data and simultaneously not believing that she would be the one with the flight anomaly. She pursed her lips and repeated her last words for clarity. "We have no data from GPS. I'm trying to find out why."

Throughout mission control, those on console were verifying and reverifying the data scrolling across their screens, hoping to have some bit of information to provide that would help all in the room understand the situation. Only a minute had passed since Thomas' announcement, but to those responsible for the success of the test flight, it seemed like an eternity. Finally, the technician monitoring the Orion's propulsion system saw something and spoke up.

"Orion propellant is showing lower than predicted," the console tech said. He then hesitated a moment before continuing. "It's not enough to trigger an alert, but it is lower than it should be." The technician, known to his comrades and friends as "Stubborn Stu" due to his alleged inflexibility in virtually all things, might also have been called "Meticulous Stu" for his attention to detail. Whatever the nickname might have been, when he spoke, his colleagues always listened.

"Roger that, Stu." Bill thought about the data briefly. He knew that less propellant in the tank could mean that more propellant was being used than predicted. And that could account for the Orion moving too fast. If the engines were burning for even a fraction of a second too long, then they would consume more propellant. And if they were consuming too much propellant, then the spacecraft was accelerating faster than expected. That wouldn't be good.

Of course, there could also be other explanations. In this case, the specific reason why the propellant was low was not of immediate concern. But Bill was certain that the fact the propellant level was too low was all the confirmation he needed to conclude what his next step ought to be.

"Marianne, what rate does laser tell us we're dealing with here?"

"Hold on." Thomas tapped some keys on her console without hesitation and then replied. "According to laser, we now have a delta-vee excess of slightly over five meters per second and accelerating. No confirmation from GPS."

"Sheesh," Bill muttered to himself. Five meters per second was just a little more than fifteen feet per second. All in the room understood the implications. The Orion and EDS were designed to soft dock with one another. In other words, their rate of closure would gradually decrease to only a fraction of a meter per second when they finally made contact. If they were to collide moving tens of feet per second, not only would the docking maneuver fail but it might result in a crash, with the loss of both the Orion and the EDS being a real possibility. And that was simply not acceptable to NASA, mission control, or Bill Stetson.

"Abort options?" Stetson hated to ask the question, but mission procedures gave him no option. A safe abort and potential retry in a few orbits was simply the right course of action to consider. Lives were not at stake, but billions of dollars and months, perhaps years, of schedule were. And Bill Stetson didn't want a test-flight failure to set back the date for his flight to the Moon. Who knew how the press would handle another NASA failure? The evening news report of a disaster in space might be enough to halt the Moon mission altogether.

The technician who reported the excess propellant usage had on his screen an algorithm that constantly told him what propellant would be required to perform an abort and an estimate of the trajectory and time required to recover from the abort so that another attempt could be made. Bill knew that the console tech was ready for his question.

"Well, Bill," Stubborn Stu started, "if laser ranging data is correct and we have to perform a burn to take out that velocity and then fly around a few orbits to try again, we will be at the minimum propellant margin for the rendezvous. But it still won't meet mission-success criteria. The EDS will have been on-station too long. Propellant boil-off will exceed TLI commit."

Though never actually uttered, virtually everyone in the room heard the expletive that Stetson thought to himself. Bill pulled his headset free for a second and adjusted his thinning hair while making a motorboat sound with his lips. Not being able to do a TLI, or Trans-Lunar Injection, burn of the rocket engines would mean not going to the Moon. The longer the EDS had to wait, the more propellant would evaporate—reducing the total burn-time possible for the engine. They had to fire before too much had boiled off.

The EDS was powered by one of the most energetic rocket fuels known—liquid hydrogen. When combined with an oxidizer, in this case the ultimate oxidizer, liquid oxygen, the combustion produced the rocket thrust that would propel the EDS toward the

Moon. It was these same propellants that powered the three main engines of the old space shuttle, producing much of the cloud of steam that was the hallmark of a successful launch.

Unfortunately, to keep hydrogen liquid, it had to be kept cold. In fact, the temperature had to be kept to about minus four hundred twenty-three degrees Fahrenheit. To do this, the huge hydrogen tanks in the EDS were kept wrapped in the best thermal insulators known and placed in the vehicle so as to minimize the heat they might receive from the sun and that reflecting back into space from the Earth. It was, in effect, a large thermos bottle in orbit. It was also an imperfect thermos bottle; some heat inevitably would always get through to warm up the hydrogen. As the volatile gas warmed, it boiled and evaporated and then vented into space. Hence the phrase "boil-off."

Engineers designed the EDS tanks and propulsion system to have enough liquid-hydrogen propellant remaining—after boil-off—to complete the mission even if the craft had to remain in orbit for a few days before beginning its trip to the Moon. If its time in orbit exceeded the design limit, then there would simply not be enough fuel remaining to complete the mission. Since there had been some minor glitches before this one, the allowable time in Earth orbit was close to being over, and a further delay would mean that the burn to send the Orion to the Moon would not happen—at least not on this test flight.

"Oh, well," Bill Stetson responded with an audible sigh as he readjusted his headset. He then straightened himself in the seat and barked, "Release the automatic docking system to manual control. Give me real-time data from the laser ranger and don't give me any more data from the damned GPS!" This, too, they'd practiced in training. A manual docking was something the astronaut corps had insisted upon since the Shuttle-Mir program of the 1990s. This was what the pilot and mission commander *lived* for. In an instant, Stetson decided to assume control of the Orion instead of asking his pilot, Charles Leonard, to do so. It was his call and he made it. Leonard heard the call and, though disappointed, accepted the decision and made himself ready to step in should he have to do so.

Switching views on the monitor in front of him and seeing the requested data feeds appear on the secondary monitor to his right, Stetson prepared to take manual control of the Orion.

Forgetting about the paperwork that would be required should he be successful, and the probable reprimand should he fail, Stetson gave the order to release the vehicle to manual control.

"Alright, give her to me," he said.

To a detached observer, it would have appeared that Bill Stetson was beginning to play a video game. With a controller that looked like the technological cousin of a PlayStation game controller and an LCD screen with a simulated 3-D rendering of both the Orion and the EDS, he assumed manual control.

At first, he saw no discernible effect from his efforts. He'd begun by firing the thrusters on the Orion that were responsible for making a rendezvous possible. But he didn't fire them to accelerate the craft; rather, the opposing sets of thrusters were used to slow it down. Newton's laws are unforgiving. Every action has an equal and opposite reaction. To speed something up, you fire rocket engines. To slow that same something down, you fire rocket engines that point in the opposite direction. And it takes the same force to accelerate to fifteen feet per second as it does to slow down by fifteen feet per second.

"You should be seeing something. The propellant in the tanks is starting to drop rapidly," Stubborn Stu said calmly. "You still have plenty remaining, but I'm definitely seeing it." He, like just about everyone else in the room, was starting to perspire. It was a stereotypically hot Houston afternoon in a room with stereotypically cold Houston air-conditioning doing nothing to prevent the perspiration from coming. It just made the sweat feel uncomfortably cold.

The sweat starting to bead on Bill's forehead glistened in the control-room lighting. He kept a watch on the laser-ranger data, and finally the velocity numbers began to decrease. The velocity dropped from an excess of five meters per second to four. Then to three and finally to a closure rate that should permit safe docking. This happened not a minute too soon—as Stetson fought to bring the closure velocity down, the distance between the Orion and the EDS continued to dwindle. They were now only a hundred meters away from one another and in desperate need of fine guidance for the final rendezvous. This, too, was a maneuver that the team in mission control had practiced manually, and their training not only took over for these last few minutes of the rendezvous, but it alleviated the stress and allowed the heart rates of the console techs to fall back to normal.

"We have manual docking in three...two...one." Marianne Thomas provided the countdown. Bill could tell from the tone in her voice that she was grateful he had overcome the problem and that it wasn't something she'd done. He figured that the engineer already was beginning the mental construction of a fault tree that would help the mission-review team find out why the automated system had failed and why the GPS data was suddenly blank.

"Phew," Stetson said, relieved at completing the docking maneuver successfully. He then declared, "We're not finished here yet, people. Need I remind you, we've got a vehicle that needs to be checked out and sent on its way to the Moon. No dinner and bar just yet." And he knew that he was correct. If nothing else went wrong, the flight was supposed to continue to the Moon, with the EDS lighting its engines to escape Earth's gravity in just a few hours.

The two concurrent failures still needed to be explained and corrected. While the GPS measurements would be useless at the Moon—which had no Global Positioning System satellites—the onboard computer that was supposed to make sense of the laser-ranging data would be used again when the Altair lunar lander returned from the surface of the Moon to rendezvous and dock with the Orion in lunar orbit, allowing the crew to transfer back to the Orion for their trip home. Yes, this was an unmanned test flight, but the systems nonetheless had to work or the launch of the actual mission would be postponed indefinitely until the problem was resolved. The public and political pressure was mounting to kill the space program, and having to scrub so close to launch could be a public-relations nightmare. Bill hoped to circumvent all that.

The decision to continue the mission or not would have to be made within hours or the liquid-hydrogen supply would boil away uselessly into space. That would give the ground-support team at least a few days to troubleshoot the automated rendezvous and docking system, and its computer and software, to find the source of the problem and hopefully fix it. At least, that's the logic Stetson was using when he made the decision that only he could make.

"All right, everyone, we're go for Lunar Orbit Insertion unless and until I say otherwise. We'll get this problem fixed and patched before it's needed again. Let's stay the course." In his unflappable way, which was one of the reasons he had been selected to be the commander of the first human lunar return flight, Stetson both committed the mission to the next phase and reassured all in the room of the can-do attitude that was so crucial to past mission successes, had been missing at NASA for decades, and, while on his watch, was absolutely crucial to the current mission—his mission. Bill was going to go to the Moon or bust.

Chapter 2

The cause of the rendezvous and docking failure was still unknown, but virtually every member of the team that developed the system and its flight computer were called in to begin working on understanding the failure and figuring out how to fix it. Rocket scientists and engineers in Houston, Texas, and Huntsville, Alabama, found out that they wouldn't be going home on time. A flurry of cell-phone calls, e-mails, and text messages to spouses or significant others went out explaining that they wouldn't be home for dinner. Take-out pizza would be the most common meal of the day.

Thirty-six hours later, the command was given for Lunar Orbit Insertion. In typical NASA fashion, the media were told that all systems were "nominal," thereby guaranteeing that the viewing public would be put to sleep by the whole event. To those engineers engaged in making it happen, however, "nominal" would not be the word that first came to mind. It certainly wouldn't be the story they told their families and friends later in the week.

Upon receiving the command, the EDS fired up its single J-2X cryogenic engine, which began to burn two hundred twenty thousand pounds of hydrogen and oxygen, accelerating the hundred-ton Earth Departure Stage to greater than the twenty-thousand-miles-per-hour velocity required to escape the pull of Earth's gravity.

If not for the incredibly cold liquid-hydrogen fuel circulating through the pipes wrapping the outside of the J-2X engine, the hellish six-thousand-degree heat produced by the burning of the hydrogen and oxygen in the combustion chamber would have almost immediately melted the nozzle. The fuel circulated through pumps and around the exterior of the rocket-engine nozzle and then back into the engine, where combustion would take place. The hydrogen and oxygen burned together and forced superheated and pressurized gasses out through the throat of the nozzle to its exit and then into space with a pure bright orange and white fiery glow.

The J-2 engine originally flew on the second stage of the venerable Saturn V rockets that carried the Apollo astronauts to the Moon. The J-2X was an upgraded version for the new generation of Moon rockets, and it was designed to complete its job in just less than seven minutes of burn time.

Throughout this acceleration, the Orion continued to perform what was known as the barbeque roll, so-called because it resembled the process of slow-cooking a pig on a spit over an open fire, slowly turning the pig so as to not overcook one side from the intense heat of the flame. The Orion performed this slow roll for the same reason—so as to not cook the ship by having one side of the vehicle continuously exposed to sunlight and therefore becoming a barbeque in space. After all, nobody likes their rocket overcooked on one side and raw on the other, especially not the astronauts inside it.

In addition, the delicate solar arrays that would power many of the onboard functions, previously unfurled like origami, were rotated so they would continuously point toward the sun. The solar panels were crucial in maintaining the electrical power required to keep the Orion's systems functioning.

All of these pointing-and-control maneuvers were controlled by onboard computers. And all of the onboard computers that performed this function had within them a board manufactured by Alcoa Electric Corporation. This same board was used to control the automated rendezvous and docking maneuver between the Orion and the EDS.

"Bill, I think we've got one of the problems figured out." Stetson, without having to look up from what he was doing, recognized the voice at the door as that of the chief engineer for the rendez-vous and docking system. It had been almost two days since the nail-biting Earth-orbit rendezvous of the Orion with the Earth Departure Stage, and no one was really expecting the engineers to figure out the cause of the problem so quickly. Not that Bill Stetson would appear to be surprised by anything.

"Come in." Stetson looked up from his desk and motioned for the seasoned but ever-eager Rick Carlton to take a seat at the small conference table across the room. Bill rose from his chair and strode to the table, the alpha male in the room by the way he carried himself and his purposeful stride to the chair adjacent to the one Carlton had just occupied. "What have you got?" he asked.

Carlton, no lightweight by anyone's standards, was intimidated by the astronaut's presence. Bill could tell, but then he hoped the man would get over it because Bill didn't go through life trying to intimidate people. It wasn't his style. He wasn't trying to be intimidating—he just was. Asking him not to take control over just about any situation in which he found himself would be like asking the sun not to shine. Bill was just one of those people who demanded attention and he usually got it.

"Uh," Carlton began his explanation, nervously shuffling the papers he'd brought in with him, "the glitch appears to be in the flight-computer software. You know the software was the tall pole leading up to this flight, and I am surprised the IV&V didn't catch it long before now." The NASA Independent Verification and Validation team had the task of approving all flight software. The team's job was to be another set of eyes to review all the software, line by line, just to make sure it was correct and that there wouldn't be any major flight-system failure from faulty computer code.

"Really?"

"Yeah. The computer is supposed to take all the sensor data from the Orion and route it to the systems that need the information to function. It's supposed to take data from the laser ranging, the GPS, the sun sensors, and just about every other sensor on the vehicle and make sense of it. Sort it and then funnel it out to the elements that need it next. In our case, however, that didn't happen." Carlton paused, and Bill could tell that the pause was not only to take a breath, but also for effect.

"Why not?" asked Bill, looking at Carlton expectantly but not impatiently.

"Well," Carlton began again, "the software got to the computer all right, but the code added the position-error function to the data twice, making its actual position appear to be incorrect, thus causing the ship's thrusters to overcompensate in an attempt to get it where it was supposed to be—which it already was, at least the first time. Since it didn't know where it really was, it appeared to be where it was at an earlier time. The thrusters fired to move it to where it was supposed to be, and then the lag happened again. The ship appeared to have not moved or moved only slightly. The thrusters then fired again, making the Orion move faster than it was supposed to in an effort to get to where it thought it should be when, in fact, it was already there." He began to wonder if his wordy explanation was making any sense.

"Hmm." Bill nodded.

"Are you following me?" Rick Carlton asked, but Bill Stetson was not just following him; he was ahead of him in his thought processes.

"So, the Orion, thinking it was sitting where it used to be sitting, fired its thrusters to get where it thought it was supposed to be when in fact it was already there. And then it got stuck in this loop, making the ship accelerate when it should have been slowing down. Correct?"

"Yes." Carlton, who seemed pleased that Stetson had understood him, nodded and continued. "And then there is the matter of the missing GPS data. Shortly before Earth departure, the data started appearing again. The only thing we can figure is that there is some sort of short in the system. We've isolated the problem to a particular circuit board. A loose connector or a lead that wasn't well potted could have caused it. We still don't know exactly, but . . ." He trailed off, lost in thought or perhaps unsure of what he should say next.

"But what?" Bill asked.

"Well, the same board is used in several pieces of hardware throughout the Orion and some in the Altair." *Altair* was the generic name of the lunar-lander craft, not the name given to any particular lunar lander. "We believe there is a quality problem with this one board, and that's it. But there is a chance the problem isn't isolated. If it's a generic problem with the board's design, well, then we have a big problem."

Stetson knew what that problem would be. If the board's design was at fault, and it had to be replaced wherever it was used in the entire system, then America's return to the Moon would be on indefinite hold until a replacement was designed and the entire system assessed for any unforeseen changes that might result. It could mean a mission delay measured in years.

"Good work, Rick." Trying to reassure himself as much as Carlton, Stetson added, "Let's take it one step at a time. Since we can't look at the board until the Orion returns from the Moon, let's not sweat it too much. Once the team gets it in front of them on a workbench, they'll be able to make that call."

Carlton stood up, picked up his papers, and started to walk out the door. He almost made it before Stetson called out his name and asked another question.

"Rick, what other hardware might be affected?"

"Uh . . ." Carlton frowned and looked toward his feet before answering. "Lots. The Orion attitude-control system and solar-array pointing system, the Altair attitude-control system, both communications systems, and just about every other piece of hardware that has to be concerned with pointing in one direction or another. It's all over the place."

"Okay. Thanks," Stetson responded. The tone of his voice conveyed both concern and that the discussion was over.

"I guess I've been dismissed," Bill overheard the man mutter to himself as he hurried out the door and down the hallway toward his office. Bill paid it no mind at all. He had more important things to deal with.

Elsewhere, the now-docked Orion and Altair lunar-lander vehicles, thousands of miles away in space, separated from the EDS and began the remaining part of their journey toward the Moon.

Chapter 3

"**W**here's Bill?" Astronaut Jim England was looking for his longtime friend. England was a tall, lanky man with a noticeable "hillbilly" accent that he seemed able to turn off and on at will depending upon the situation. Presently, his pronunciation of "Bill" would make listeners swear it was a two-syllable word. He'd known Stetson since their first flight to the International Space Station together back in the shuttle days and had immediately become a part of Stetson's inner circle of close friends. England never seemed to meet anyone he didn't like, and almost everyone responded to his warm personality by counting him as a friend.

"Hi, Jim." Stetson's secretary looked up from her computer screen at the astronaut. She had been Stetson's secretary, or, to be politically correct, his management support assistant, for almost five years. Married for over thirty years, with a grandchild on the way, Millie Lawford was cordial, worldly wise, and very good at her job.

"How're things?" England asked. "You look perplexed."

"Bill's calendar." She grunted as she tapped at her keyboard and then clicked her mouse several times. "It's a frustrating experience that I'd say is more like herding cats while being overrun by mice than trying to actually schedule adult professionals in the same place at the same time." She managed a smile for England.

"Ha." Jim laughed out loud. "Try tuna and milk."

"He's in the office. Shall I tell him you're here?" She started to rise from her seat.

"No, that's okay," Jim said. "I'll go on in. Unless you think I shouldn't?"

"No, I'm sure it's fine. Go on in." She looked back at her screen, forgetting about Jim, and immediately frowned. "NASA just has too many meetings," she half muttered to herself. "How the heck is he possibly supposed to be in all these places in one short ten-hour day?"

"Good luck." England shook his head. Taking her inattention to him as dismissal, he walked up to the closed simulated-wood-grain door to Bill Stetson's all-too-government-issue office. He knocked on the door and reached to open it in one quick, fluid motion. If Stetson were doing something that he didn't want anyone to see, then he would certainly be caught by surprise.

Fortunately, Stetson was simply sitting at his desk looking at his thirty-inch computer monitor with a mild grin upon his face. He looked up and motioned for Jim to join him on the other side of the desk.

Stetson, though an astronaut and commander of the next flight to the Moon, the first flight "back to the Moon," was still only a civil servant and subject to civil-service rules regarding office space and accoutrements. The simulated-wood-grain desk and generic cream-colored filing cabinets were the primary features of the room. On the walls were framed pictures of a shuttle launch, the International Space Station, Stetson floating in the U.S. Laboratory Module of the ISS, and many, many pictures of his wife and two children. In the family photos, there were none that didn't have Stetson surrounded by the satellites that were his family. And in all of them, his wife and children wore great big smiles.

Jim rounded the corner of the desk and heard a voice talking from what sounded like a deep well. The audio was crackly. He knew what he was listening to an instant before he saw the screen and had his guess confirmed. From the speakers came ". . . forged man's destiny of tomorrow. And, as we leave the Moon at Taurus-Littrow, we leave as we came and, God willing, as we shall return, with peace and hope for all mankind. Godspeed the crew of Apollo 17." The voice of Gene Cernan trailed off as Stetson pressed the pause on the touch screen.

"Watching Apollo 17 again?" Jim smiled and shook his head

at the same time. "God, how many times have you watched that video? A hundred times?" He reached behind Stetson and pulled forward a chair. Though good-naturedly teasing his friend, he didn't really take his own eyes from the screen as he sat down. After all, no modern astronaut had ever made it higher than a few hundred miles above Earth. Cernan had walked on a body about two hundred and forty thousand miles away. What astronaut wouldn't be in awe of the Apollo-era groundbreakers?

"I have no idea what you are talking about, Jim. This is the first time I ever saw this," Stetson replied with a smile. He pulled himself to an upright position and turned to face his friend.

"You know how long it has taken us to get here. Jesus, what took so long?" Jim said. "You know, I've been thinking about the Moon since I was a twelve-year-old kid listening to Reagan announce that NASA was going to build a space station. To think that man walked on the Moon just a year or so before I was born is almost bizarre."

"Hell, Jim, I was five the first time I saw this, and it was live. If we wait much longer I'm gonna be too freakin' old." Stetson pointed to the frozen image of the lunar surface. "I'm ready. I've never been more ready, and I'm getting impatient."

"'Amen,' shouted somebody from the choir," England replied. They'd had this conversation, or a variant of it, many times before, pretty much as long as they had known each other.

"Mankind just does stuff in fits and starts, historically. We went to the Moon for a grand total of three years and then stopped. We just stopped! We took apart the greatest machines ever built by man and put them in museums. Heck, one of them is standing up as a marker for the Alabama/Tennessee state line. Can you believe that?" There were Saturn V rockets in the museums across the country and the Saturn IB at the Alabama Welcome Center.

"Been there. Seen 'em." Jim could tell what sort of mood Bill was in. He'd also heard this part before.

"Did you know that that SOB Nixon decided to kill the Apollo program before Armstrong ever set foot on the Moon? I guess he just couldn't stand the thought of Kennedy getting all the credit. What a vindictive sonofa—"

"Whoa, just a minute here." This direction for the conversation was a twist on the usual one. "This is a new one, Bill. What the hell are you talking about? Nixon?" Though they had talked about how the lunar missions should have continued so that today they'd be having this discussion about going to Mars, and not back to the Moon, Nixon being an SOB had not come up before. At least not in *this* context.

Stetson stood up, unconsciously (perhaps) putting himself into the mode where whoever was around had no choice but to listen to what he had to say. Jim was used to it and wasn't intimidated in the least. He knew Stetson too well for that; he was just curious about what his friend was going on about.

"Think about it. Yes, Apollo was expensive and there was the Vietnam War going on. Those were tough years, with riots, assassinations, protests, and all that crap to contend with. But Tricky Dick could look past all that and see what mattered to him, not the good of the country or future generations—just to good old Tricky Dick." He reached down and picked up from his desk his model of the Apollo lunar lander.

Holding the lander in his left hand and motioning at Jim with his right, he began again. "Nixon was president of the United States—the highest achievement that anyone can aspire to. He'd done it. He'd beaten his adversaries and was riding high. And every time there was a new story on television about the upcoming Moon landings, what did he see?" Stetson paused for effect, not really to allow Jim to answer his somewhat rhetorical question.

"Okay, I'll bite. What?" Jim didn't really care to offer his own opinion, since he wasn't sure what might tweak his friend too far at the moment.

"He saw another president getting all the credit. He saw John Fitzgerald Kennedy standing at the podium over at Rice University saying, 'We choose to go the Moon in this decade and do the other thing....' He saw or heard JFK whenever or wherever the Apollo program came up. And that simply burned him. And do you know why it burned him?"

Jim decided to just keep his mouth shut. He leaned back in his chair and slumped a little to relax. Politics never seemed to help the space program, and bitching about it was almost as fruitful. He decided to just ride the storm out.

"Do you know who ran against John Kennedy in the presidential election of 1960? That election was the closest election in modern history—until the election of George Bush in 2000, that is. Do you know who he beat to become president?"

All England could do was shrug. He knew his American history fairly well, but keeping a mental log of who lost presidential elections was not among the facts that he'd memorized in order to pass the public-school history exams.

"Well, and the kicker, there was controversy about some ballot-box stuffing throwing some doubt on the election outcome even!" Stetson sat the lander back on his desk, thinking to himself, *Houston, Tranquility Base here. The* Eagle *has landed.* He smiled inwardly and then answered his own question. "Richard Milhous Nixon. Kennedy beat Mr. Nixon for the presidency, just barely, in 1960. Nixon even made a statement saying something about the country didn't need the turmoil of an investigation into the election at that time."

"I don't recall ever hearing that in school," Jim said with a raised eyebrow.

"It's true. Look it up. So, what do you think Mr. Nixon thought about when *he* was president at one of the greatest moments in human history and the guy who beat him, perhaps questionably, almost a decade previously—a guy who had been dead for years—was getting all the credit? Do you think that made the man who kept an enemies list happy? No way! The SOB must've seethed at the thought, and I am convinced the old man had neither sympathy nor remorse for ending the Apollo program. He probably said good riddance." Stetson walked a few steps to his window overlooking the complex of the Johnson Space Center. "And that's why we're just now going back to the Moon instead of Mars."

"Ha, ha!" England guffawed. "Bill, that makes some crazy-conspiracy sense, but I cannot imagine that's how it came down. The cost of the war, the civil-rights movement, and the Cold War—NASA just became too expensive, and people lost interest. It got boring."

"Well…" Stetson, still looking out at the mid-day sun, seemed to have his sails deflated by his friend's comment. Jim was just glad that it seemed to be calming him down.

"Come on, Bill," Jim said. "The U.S. was slipping into a recession then, too. Science fiction movies made space look sexier than the astronauts could. It was a whole bunch of forcing functions in a very complex dynamic system that caused the Moon missions to stop. Apollo 13 was preempted on television during primetime, and that was long before Cernan and Schmitt's flight. I don't think it was Nixon at all."

Stetson said, "Yeah. All those things are true. Once you've gone to the Moon, what else can there be? How do you top that? NASA was given a tough act to follow—its own."

England said, "Think about it. James T. Kirk was going to other star systems and hooking up with hot green chicks. All those Apollo guys ever did was bring home some rocks. The public got more out of the price of a movie ticket or a television show than NASA was delivering with their publicly perceived giant budget."

"And you and I both know that NASA's budget is tiny compared to most every other entitlement program or congressional boondoggle."

"True."

Stetson continued. "Only NASA can make the most complex and challenging endeavor in the history of humankind seem dull. Maybe we should've hired George Lucas or Steven Spielberg to do our marketing. Sure, we had great coverage for the last shuttle flight, with lots of legacy stories about the successes and failures of the shuttle program. Though if I'd had to see that video of the *Challenger* exploding again, I think I'd have puked."

"No hot green chicks," Jim interjected. "We need some hot green chicks. I think they were called green animal women slaves from Orion or some such thing. Yep, we need 'em."

Bill ignored the comment and kept on going, "Yes, it was a tragedy, and yes, mistakes were made, but we've got to get over it someday and move forward. Think how insulting it must be to the thousands of engineers who made sure that those other one hundred and twenty flights were flown safely. What about the video that shows their successes?"

"Uh, people like a train wreck," Jim reminded him.

"Humph." Bill was on a roll and wasn't ready to relinquish the floor just yet. "And what about the first manned flight of Ares I? The press was there with cameras rolling to see the rocket fly, but I think they'd have been just as eager to see it crash. They probably had their commentaries written for that before they even arrived at the Cape . . . and the astronauts' obituaries, too. We were lucky the second flight made the news at all. If it hadn't been for the Chinese having a launch failure the week before, I doubt we'd have rated high enough to report on.

"So, now we've flown over a hundred space shuttle missions, circling our tails in Earth orbit for decades. We've built a space station that people have been living in for fifteen years with the public's perception that they were just floating around twiddling their thumbs and having fun eating floating globules of liquid astronaut food. We're rebuilding a capability to go the Moon that we had—we *had,* mind you—when I was a child and then threw away." Stetson almost looked angry as he turned to face England. Jim hated seeing his friend getting so worked up.

"Water under the bridge, buddy. Now, if we can manage to find some of those green animal—"

Bill cut him off with a very Spock-like raised eyebrow that told Jim he was about to push a little too far. "Jim, we've wasted fifty years since Neil Armstrong walked on the Moon. Yeah, we've done some science, and we've supposedly learned about how people will ultimately survive the trip to Mars. I'd never say it in public, but we've wasted the legacy of Von Braun and all those engineers who put us on another world before you were born. I want to get back to the Moon and prove to the American people that space exploration is worth it. That going to Mars is doable and worth it. And that going to Mars should not wait another fifty years. Going to the Moon is the first step toward that, and it is what I'm *meant* to do."

"Me, too, Bill. Me, too." Jim smiled at his friend because he didn't doubt his last statement for an instant.

Chapter 4

Retired Navy pilot Paul Gesling paced in the waiting area outside the office of Gary Childers, president of Space Excursions. Gesling, who was too tall to qualify as a NASA astronaut, looked more like a recently retired professional basketball player than a soon-to-be commercial space pilot. His forty-one-year-old frame was covered with muscle, and his piercing green eyes and coal-black hair gave him the appearance of being some sort of wealthy playboy—at least to the ladies whom he frequently found himself in the company of. And they seemed to like it—and him.

He grew tired of pacing after a while and sat on the plush green couch in the waiting area. Being one of those people who was uncomfortable just sitting around without something to read, he absentmindedly picked up one of the brochures that described the company's history.

The Space Excursions headquarters in Lexington, Kentucky, was everything one would expect of a company founded, owned, and managed by a man who had made his billions in coal. Rich, thick carpet and high, ornately carved ceilings adorned every room in the twenty-five-story building that served as the global headquarters of both Space Excursions and Coal Tech, Inc. The glass and steel building might not be the tallest in town, but it was certainly one of the most striking. A French architect, whose name no one could recall without resorting to looking it up online, had designed the building and reserved the top floor for the company founder and CEO's pet project, Space Excursions. A dedicated elevator running up the north side of the building served to remind all visitors that they were leaving coal country and entering the twenty-first century.

Gary Childers, having lived through sixty revolutions of the Earth around the sun, as he liked to put it, was a genuine space geek. Born and raised in Kentucky, he had made his fortune in coal. Of course, having started with a smaller family fortune certainly helped. He made his money and career in mining, shipping, and selling coal, but his heart was always in space. His interest became his business after the success of the first commercial human space flight back in 2004 with the launching of the Paul Allen and Burt Rutan project, SpaceShipOne. While other companies were forming to send people to Earth orbit, he decided to do them one better and offer a commercial ride around the Moon. Space Excursions was born.

He hired the best and brightest engineers and scientists from America and around the world to make his vision a reality. With a manufacturing facility in Nevada near the Las Vegas Commercial Spaceport, Space Excursions quietly took the lead in the next step of space tourism. Over a thousand people had now paid over two hundred thousand dollars per person to make suborbital flights with his competitors, and several millionaires had paid the Russians to take them to orbit. Now it was his turn. Five people had paid twenty-five million dollars each for a seat on the maiden flight of *Dreamscape,* the flagship of Space Excursions. Twenty-five more had made deposits for the next flights, the first of which was scheduled to occur within six months of the first. It had taken a little over fifteen years to get to this point, and Childers had selected Paul Gesling to be the pilot and commander for the first flight.

Thumbing through the rest of the brochure, Gesling saw the usual corporate mumbo-jumbo marketing and financial statements as well as some pretty pictures of the Space Excursions Nevada facility, at which he had practically been living for the last three years. He glanced over the section called "Company at a Glance" and saw listed the other two divisions of Space Excursions that sold their wares to either NASA or the Pentagon. He didn't have anything to do with those operations. Commercial space was his sole interest. The NASA work was done mostly at the Nevada facility. The work for the Pentagon was performed just outside of Albuquerque, New Mexico.

Gesling was still thumbing through the brochure when Childers's door opened and the company president waved him in. He tossed the brochure back into the stack and entered the office.

And what an office it was. First of all, it was large. It had the usual corporate furnishings of desk, meeting table, and bookcases, plus obligatory corporate photos along the walls. What made it stand out were the models. Models of virtually every piece of space hardware that had been flown by the United States, the U.S.S.R. or Russia, China, Europe, a few from India and even Iran. They were everywhere. Suspended from the ceiling was a model of the International Space Station flanked on each side with Russia's Mir space station and the U.S. Skylab. Along the north wall were models of each of the rockets that had carried humans into space. The east wall was graced with models of rockets that carried only satellites and unmanned spacecraft. The south and west walls were the windows that made his corner office, and high above each window, just out of direct line of sight, were hanging models of spacecraft—well over a hundred of them.

Gesling took the seat directly across from Childers, and both men sat down at about the same time.

"So, to what do I owe this pleasure?" Childers began. "Your text said it was important but not urgent. I don't get many of those. Usually *everything* is urgent and important." Childers, with his full head of closely cropped salt-and-pepper hair, looked the part of a corporate executive. He could have been the CEO of any large business or a Wall Street executive. He had "the look"—the look of a man with money and power.

"Well," Gesling started. "Gary, you know I am dedicated to this flight. I've worked my butt off getting ready. I've been with you for seven years, helped you make the pitches to the board and the regulators, faced the media, and I even took that low-blow interview for *60 Minutes* that made us—both of us—look like fools eager to part with our money. But I've just about had it up to here with some of the pantywaists we're taking to space." Gesling quickly moved his right hand to his forehead as he completed the last sentence and then dropped it back down to his side.

"I'm a pilot, and a damned good one. I flew for the Navy and faced hostile fire more than I'm supposed to admit. That 'police action' near Indonesia just about became a war between China and us, and let me tell you, for those of us in the planes, it sure felt like war. I've been chewed out by the best the U.S. military has to offer. *You've* given me a few that I'd just as soon forget. Dodging missiles is a piece of cake compared to what you've asked me to do—and I am not talking about flying *Dreamscape*. She'll be a pleasure. It's the damned customers that are driving me crazy!"

"You've got to be kidding" was all Childers could manage to say. Gary Childers was not usually a man at a loss for words. From the look on his face, he seemed frustrated with Paul. Paul couldn't understand why.

Looking exasperated and more desperate than a Navy fighter pilot should ever appear to be, Gesling directed his gaze downward to the floor and then back to Childers's face.

"I am not kidding," Gesling told him. "Take Matt Thibodeau, for example. First of all, he showed up for the survival training late. While he was there, he kept taking calls on his satellite phone and basically tuned out most of the time. He won't work with his seatmate—says she's 'too bossy' and will hardly give her the time of day. He's not yet been able to seal his pressure suit correctly and insists it's everyone else's problem but his own. He doesn't have a clue how to share the emergency air supply and shows absolutely no interest in learning. On top of that, he pukes every time we fly parabolas in the trainer and refuses to acknowledge that it is his responsibility during the flight to clean up his own mess. I cannot and will not clean up this arrogant customer's puke when we are on our way to the Moon!" Gesling gritted his teeth behind his pursed lips. His jaw muscle tightened tensely.

"And then there's that Sudanese guy, Sharik Mbanta. Who does he think he is? Sure, his father is filthy rich, but that is absolutely no excuse for him trying constantly to sleep with my trainers. Sharon and Tara are good at what they do, and, yes, they are both pretty good-looking. They are also both very married, and Tara has two kids! But that doesn't stop Mr. Mbanta. Oh, no. If he propositions her one more time, he's liable to end up with something removed from his anatomy and stuffed in his mouth by an irate Mr. Tara. I could go on...." Gesling's voice trailed off.

"Ha." This time Childers's laugh was genuine. "So, the unflappable Mr. Gesling doesn't like his job as babysitter-in-chief?"

"Damn right I don't" came the clear and unequivocal response.

"Believe it or not, I understand. But that doesn't mean I can or will do anything about it. What you need from me isn't action; you need me to be your counselor. You probably want me to tell you to suck it up and be a man. But I won't." Childers sighed and leaned back in his chair before he continued. "Yes, Thibodeau is an ass. He has a reputation for being selfish, self-centered, and an all-around difficult person to work with. He's also well connected, and if he takes the flight and enjoys it, I suspect at least five others from his circle of friends will sign up for a future flight."

"Money, Paul. Money." Leaning forward for effect, he intoned, "That's one hundred twenty-five million dollars." Once again leaning back in his chair, he continued. "Mr. Mbanta is a special case. He doesn't have many friends eager to fly in space. But there are many filthy-rich Africans who have spoiled family members eager for that next thrill that will be lining up at our door once Mr. Mbanta gets home and the African press runs with his story. I cannot do anything about his overactive libido other than offer your trainers hazardous-duty pay."

Paul was taking it in. He knew he had to suck it up, and he knew that it took money, lots of money, to go to the Moon. But he was not sold yet. Gary Childers rose from his seat and walked around his desk to stand by Gesling's chair.

"Paul, I'm the president and CEO of a Fortune 500 company. I don't just deal with contracts, the futures market, and keep up with the latest green-energy legislation. I find that I spend over half my time managing people. The buck stops here on everything in the company. We recently fired an employee for selling sensitive corporate data to a trading company that was actually owned by a Chinese sovereign investment fund. The guy is now under investigation by the FBI, yet he sues us for some alleged prejudicial misconduct. It seems the man is also a member of some offbeat religious cult, and he claims we singled him out because of it. I can't tell you how many meetings—how many hours—that's taken. And the list goes on. I simply do not have time to whine nor to hear my key people do so."

"I am not whining. I'm just used to dealing with people who take orders and, most of all, take their mission seriously. Out of the five passengers you've given me for the first flight, three are okay. The other two I'd just as soon see kicked out of line and replaced with their backups."

"Kicked out?" An incredulous tone appeared in Childers's voice. "*Captain* Gesling, that is simply out of the question. Let me remind *you* that I have a backup for you. This is a business—not the military—and these are paying customers. They are paying us millions of dollars for this trip, and unless I determine that one of them is a risk to the flight, they will all, by God, be flying. So, and I said I wouldn't say this, but by damn, suck it the hell up, Paul! Stop your damned whining and do your job. Make it work and quit involving me at every hiccup!" The tone in Childers's voice went from incredulous to borderline anger, and it was clear that he wasn't going to put up with much more of Paul's whining. Gesling really hadn't thought of it as whining until just then.

"Yes, sir!" was all Gesling could say at this point. He was used to following orders, and that was exactly what had just happened. He had trained too long and too hard to let Thibodeau and Mbanta cost him a trip to the Moon. It was all he could do not to stand at attention and salute. Given Childers's mood at this point, doing so might have cost him his job—and a chance to go to the Moon.

"Damn right." Childers's tone returned to a more businesslike one as he retraced his steps back toward the other side of his desk. "Was there anything else?"

"No, sir."

"Very good. Now, I've got that personnel matter to attend to. If you will excuse me?"

Taken aback at how this informal "chat" had nearly cost him his job, Gesling arose uncomfortably, but quickly, and walked back toward the office door. As he neared the exit, two models on the rocket table caught his eye. Clearly visible on a simulated lunar landscape were the Apollo lunar lander and the new Altair lander that NASA at this moment was commanding into low lunar orbit as part of their unmanned test flight.

"Yeah," he muttered as he opened the door. "I envy those guys...."

Chapter 5

Mission Specialist Anthony Chow awoke with a start. He turned his head and saw the red LED numbers gleaming on his clock radio, seemingly taunting him as they informed him that it was 2:45 a.m. He looked to his left and saw the slumbering form of Paula, his wife.

Thank goodness I didn't wake her up again, he thought to himself. This was not the first time he'd been awakened by that recurring dream. Merely thinking about what he'd been dreaming caused him to shudder.

Carefully and ever so slowly, he pulled back the covers and eased himself out of bed. Remaining in the bedroom only long enough to pull on a pair of socks, Chow moved toward the hallway door and then down the hallway and stairs to the kitchen. A late-night cup of hot tea and then a few minutes with the newspaper were becoming a ritual that he'd just as soon not become a habit. And it was all because of that dream. *The* dream.

"Tea. Earl Grey—hot," he said with his best English accent as he stood solidly and looked at the microwave just before it beeped. He pulled the teacup from the appliance and halfheartedly chuckled to himself. "Replicator's a little slow tonight. Gonna have to get Mr. La Forge up here to have a look at it." He smiled to himself and sat at the kitchen table.

After sipping the tea and perusing yesterday's headlines, Chow once again became drowsy enough to fall back asleep. He put down the teacup and padded his way back up the stairs and into bed. Paula's regular deep breathing was not interrupted as he pulled the covers up over his shoulders.

"Good. I won't have to tell her that the dream came back." Chow was asleep in minutes.

As usual, Chow began his day with a 5:30 a.m. run around the neighborhood. He was forty years old, in excellent physical condition, and intended to remain that way. The average age of a payload specialist was forty-two. He still had years of his astronaut career left if he took care of himself. He focused on his breathing and took in the sun as it started to rise. The reds and oranges cast rays across the sky that made getting up early worth it. It was going to be another glorious day with clear blue skies and not a cloud as far as he could see.

His MP3 player finished his five-mile playlist just as he reached the front porch of his house. He shut the device off, pulled the headbuds from his ears, and eased open the door, uncertain if Paula was awake or not. As he started up the stairs, he passed Paula as she came down them and moved toward the kitchen.

"'Morning."

"Good run?"

"About the same as usual. I need a shower." He smiled at his wife.

She was dressed and ready to begin her day at Oak Park Travel. She was a "travel consultant" for one of the more success-ful travel companies in Houston. The sight of her slight figure and long blond hair falling seemingly haphazardly over her left shoulder was always enough to remind Anthony why he'd asked her to marry him.

"I'll leave breakfast on the counter behind the stove. I've got to go in early for a meeting. I hope the landing goes well. Will you be in mission control?"

"No, but I'll be watching from the conference room. We'll be listening to the chatter from the control room and seeing what they see on the monitors. The next best thing to being there..." His voice trailed off as the unintentional humor of his own words registered in his brain.

"Sounds exciting. Good luck. I love you." The words came naturally, though hurriedly, as Paula rounded the corner into the kitchen.

Chow briefly paused to rethink whether or not he'd put away the teacup and newspaper from last night's "calming session." He was sure that he had. With that, he continued up the stairs and into the shower.

"Standing room only?" The conference room was crowded when Chow arrived. "And I'm here two hours before separation," he muttered to himself. Two large monitors hung from one wall of the room while a dozen or so computers lined the conference table, each showing something different on its screen. Seating was not ad hoc. Even here, in a secondary conference room, one could not simply pop in to observe. Each person in the room was supposed to be in the room, and that included Anthony Chow.

As he entered, he looked around to take a mental note of who else was there. He didn't like being surprised.

Today Chow would be an observer. With a doctorate in bio-physics and a medical degree, there wasn't really much for him to do on a test flight with no humans aboard. Engineers would be monitoring the detailed information from the systems and subsystems of the Altair—power, propulsion, communications, and navigation. Unless there were questions about human health or relating to the planned crew health experiments that they were to undertake during their upcoming manned flight, Chow would have the pleasure of watching history from the inside with nothing to do.

He stood there and psychologically fed on the energy of the people in the room. Given that level of energy and sense of purpose, one would think that this modest conference room holding almost four dozen people was actually mission control rather that simply a room down the hall from it.

"Tony! Come here a minute, would ya?"

Chow recognized the voice as that of Helen Menendez, the other mission specialist who would be going to the Moon with him as part of Commander Stetson's crew. He respected Helen and trusted her implicitly, but he couldn't say he really "liked" her. At times she could be downright antisocial. But she was good, very good, at what she did. Not only was she near the top of her field, geology, but she was cross-trained in all things mechanical. If a moving part was on the Altair, you could bet Helen knew where it was and all about how it worked.

Chow rose from his not-yet-warm seat and moved down the table to lean over Menendez's shoulder as she stared intently at the computer monitor in front of her.

"Tony, are you as excited as I am? What's it going to be like? Leaving the Orion and all of us going to the surface in the Altair? We've been training for years, but seeing it happen on the screen in front of me with no crew seems kind of creepy."

"Hmm." Chow thought about it for a moment and rubbed his fingers through his hair. "Helen, I honestly don't know. It doesn't strike me as creepy. It just seems, well, wrong. Empty. People are meant to be there. What's the point if it doesn't happen with people?"

She said, "Wrong. Yeah, that's it. Wrong."

"Uh-huh." He hesitated. "Is that all you wanted?" Having all-work-and-no-play Helen Menendez call him over for what amounted to idle chitchat at a moment like this was simply not normal.

"No, not really. I'm just excited. That's all." That and the fact that her blunt approach to just about everything at work and outside of it had alienated a sizable fraction of the people in the room. "I just thought you, of all people, might be able to understand. Never mind."

With that, Menendez reverted back to the business at hand. And that no longer included off-topic conversation with Anthony Chow. He immediately regretted his reaction to her overture.

Chow returned to his seat and reviewed the mission-summary reports from the previous thirty-six hours. With only a few minor exceptions, all had gone according to plan and all systems were working nearly flawlessly. Only a few hours previously, the Altair lander had used its engines to accomplish the Lunar Orbit Insertion (LOI) burn, slowing the vehicle down so that it could be captured into orbit around the Moon. Depleting about forty percent of the fuel in its tanks, the Altair was now poised to burn the remainder in its descent to the surface.

Having separated from the Orion a few hours previously, the Altair was about to perform a totally automated descent and landing on the surface of the Moon. The more Chow thought about it, the more he regretted his response to Menendez.

She is right to be excited, he thought to himself as he felt his own heart rate increase. *We should be there.*

Chow looked up at the monitors in the front of the room. The one on the right showed various camera views from the Altair. One was toward deep space, with what appeared to be the Orion as a point of light in the distance, barely resolvable as more than a point in the sky. The one to the left showed the interior of the lander. Finally, the bottom portion of the screen showed the gray and brown landscape of the surface of the Moon moving rapidly beneath it.

It was this view that caused Chow to relive the most vivid portions of his recurring nightmare. He lost touch with what was happening around him in the crowded conference room and remembered how it played out in his dream....

It was always the same. He was not with his crewmates and colleagues on the surface of the Moon. Instead, he was alone. He was standing in the crew cabin of the Altair, looking across the desolate lunar surface and feeling afraid. Afraid because he'd just learned that the ascent engine that was supposed to loft the top portion of the Altair, called the Lunar Ascent Vehicle, was not functioning. The ascent vehicle was supposed to carry the crew back into space for a rendezvous with the Orion and the trip home. But, at least in his dream, the engines did not light. He was trapped. Alone.

In the dream he could hear the voice of his wife telling him that she loved him and would miss him. He recalled hearing the voices of his friends and family tell him similar things as he frantically sought a way out of being trapped on the lunar surface to die. And the people who spoke to him on the radio included his now-dead parents, both of whom told him how much they loved him and what a hero he would be. In the dream he wept, and, in many cases, he awoke from the recurring dream with tears running down his face.

Alone. Trapped. Facing death. No way out.

No way out. Nowhere to run except out the airlock and across the barren and very dead lunar surface.

It was a nightmare he didn't dare to tell anybody other than his wife. And he didn't tell her about most of them. There was no need to give a shrink any reason to ground him from the mission.

He was sure he was having just a private moment of inward

reflection, but when he snapped out of his stupor for a moment he was positive that everyone in the room had noticed his lapse. As he looked around, however, he discovered that no one was paying him any particular attention. They were either focused on their individual data streams or engaged in conversation with others nearby.

"Whew," he sighed. Relieved, he resumed scanning the status reports. To himself, he asked, *Am I ready for this? Do I need to see a counselor? Will the dream ever go away?* Another part of himself answered silently, *Suck it up, wussy. Give up a trip to the Moon? What, am I nuts?!*

Thirty minutes later, the command was given and the Altair's four liquid-hydrogen and oxygen engines fired for the second time, slowing the twenty-two-ton lander and causing it to move closer to the lunar surface. The onboard radar and extensive lunar-terrain maps were correlated and cross-checked as the lander began its descent.

The landing site for this practice run was to be near the lunar south pole, though not nearly as close to the Aitkin Basin as was thought to be the leading candidate for the next flight—the one with people aboard—the one that would be his.

The descent to the surface would take only twelve minutes, and to those in mission control and in all the conference rooms throughout NASA it would seem like hours. Since 2004, tens of thousands of engineers had been working for this moment, and most were now glued to their televisions and computer monitors, holding their collective breath.

"Landing in three minutes," came the voice from mission control. All the chatter in the conference room now died down to nothing—all would be listening for the proverbial pin to drop.

"Landing in two minutes." Still no one in the room with Chow spoke.

"Landing in sixty seconds."

With that, Chow averted his eyes from the big-screen monitors at the front of the room and scanned the faces of those in the room with him. He had always been more interested in human emotions than machines. Though he'd always been fascinated by all things space, he'd never considered the traditional engineering fields. They were all about the toys—he wanted to understand the people who went to space. He was eager to experience the Moon and not worry so much about how he was to get there.

Menendez's eyes were fixed on her own screen, and she seemed totally oblivious to the images coming back from near the lunar surface being returned by the Altair's imaging system.

Though many others in the room were similarly transfixed by the raw data, most had now placed their attention squarely on the monitors as the lunar surface loomed closer and closer, yet a quarter million miles away.

"Ten seconds, nine, eight, seven, six, five, four, three, two, one....We have touchdown!"

The room remained silent for another minute as all who had held their breath released it and erupted in smiles. Spontaneous applause broke out and then almost everyone in the room stood up so that they could clap even louder.

"Alright!" Chow heard one of his colleagues a few chairs to his right proclaim. "America's back on the Moon. No more boring robotic landers and ridiculous rovers. By God, we're going to put boots in that dirt!"

Chow smiled and nodded in agreement but was lost in his own thoughts at the moment—his boot steps would be among the first ones back there. His feet would be on the Moon sometime within the next year. The bad dream didn't even cross his mind....

Chapter 6

"**P**aul, come in." Gary Childers sat back and propped his feet up on his desk. The Bluetooth earbud on his left ear was blinking. Gary touched the side of the apparatus and motioned for him to wait a second and to have a seat. Paul Gesling looked around the office and saw the video-teleconference monitor was on. The familiar red hair, horn-rimmed glasses, and ever-cheerful face of Caroline O'Conner was smiling back at him from the other side of the digital screen. He smiled and waved back.

"Hi, Paul. Looking forward to seeing you two out here tomorrow," she said.

"Right. I'm taking my trainer out this afternoon and should fly in sometime tonight." Paul sat down and angled his chair where he could see both Gary and Caroline. Caroline was the media-relations liaison, public-relations expert, and general all-around marketing guru for Space Excursions. "What's this about?"

"Not sure. He called this a bit ago, but my BlackBerry doesn't show a subject for the meeting." She shrugged.

"Okay. I guess we wait." Paul turned and watched Childers, who was rocking back and forth in his chair and talking a mile a minute about buying something short. Paul guessed there was a broker on the other end. Finally, Childers tapped his earbud and hung up the phone.

"Paul, glad I caught you before you left for the airport." Paul grunted and nodded. "Caroline, is everything set up for the press conference tomorrow?"

"Yes, sir. No hitches as far as I can tell."

"Very good. We need to talk about our demeanor tomorrow. Not sure if you two have had time to watch, but NASA just did the automated landing on the lunar surface." Gary looked over at Paul and then at Caroline. Paul guessed it was to judge his reaction. As far as Paul was concerned, he didn't really care. If he had sixteen billion dollars a year, he was certain that he could land a pickup truck, a marching band, a full-fledged circus, and a swimming pool equipped with synchronized swimmers right in the middle of the Sea of Tranquility. He wasn't that impressed. Apparently, his expression showed it.

"That right there, Paul. That expression! You can't make that face when NASA and the Moon missions are brought up." Childers didn't frown at him, but he didn't smile, either.

"I understand what this is about," Caroline said. "We've talked about this, Paul. No matter how you feel about NASA and how they are performing their mission, we must show unified and enthusiastic support for it. We cannot afford to look like nay-sayers, pessimists, or anti-space in any way. It will hurt us and everything we've worked for."

"What? I wouldn't say anything."

"Paul, just stop. We're not accosting you for your opinion." Gary held up his hand and started in. "Hell, I agree with you. The best success NASA has had since Apollo has been unmanned. Oh, sure, the shuttles were successful, at flying up and down and round and round in low Earth orbit. The public doesn't really care, or we'd still have shuttles. And all these stupid little robotic controlled rovers rolling around on Mars? Give me a break."

"Gary," Caroline said, "The *Pathfinder/Sojourner* was a great public relations success for NASA. We studied it in graduate school. The thing had over a million hits a day to the mission Web site for the first couple of weeks."

"Nonsense." Gary laughed.

"It is a fact, Gary. You can look that up."

"Oh, hell, I know it is a fact. The nonsense part is that the million hits meant a damned thing. How many kids are in the public-school system in the U.S.? Hmm? Do you know that statistic?" Gary tapped his knuckles on his desk when he asked.

"Uh, no, Gary. I don't." Caroline looked perplexed, as if she didn't see the relevance.

"Well, I do. I've studied this industry long and hard. The public doesn't give a damn about the robot rovers. The so-called success was due to every science teacher in every public school having the fifty-four million students in the U.S. log on to the Web and write a homework essay about it. That is how the thing got so many hits. And clearly, less than one fiftieth of the students managed to do this. But the fact that the hits lasted a couple weeks probably accounts for a lot of them." Gary wrapped his knuckles against the desk with each point he made.

"I agree with Gary on this. And look where they chose to land!" Paul finally joined in. "They landed in the desert, for God's sake. You know what the official NASA mission description for the rover mission was? Rhetorical question. Don't answer. I can tick them off one at a time. Let's see . . . Number one, to prove that the development of faster, better, and cheaper spacecraft is possible for a cost under one hundred and fifty million dollars. Number two, to show that it is possible to send a load of scientific instruments to another planet with a simple system and at one fifteenth the cost of the Viking missions. Those damned things were just under a billion dollars back in the seventies. And number three, to demonstrate NASA's commitment to low-cost planetary exploration by finishing the mission with a total cost of under like three hundred million dollars or so, I forget the exact number. Oh, and that was including the launch vehicle and mission operations. Do you see anything exciting in that? Oh, and by the way, land in the desert so there will be no way that anything exciting will be found."

"This is good stuff, Paul. What else? What about the desert?" Gary asked. Caroline just shook her head at the both of them.

"Well, they landed in the desert, right? What do kids want to find in space? What do old people want to find? What does everybody want to find? Aliens! Everybody wants to see aliens, dammit all to hell. Don't lie and say you don't."

"Uh, Paul," Caroline muttered.

"Let him finish, Caroline."

"So, nobody really believes we'd find aliens on Mars, but what about life? We might find life. At least water, which everybody wants to believe is the key to finding life. Any kid with a good pair of binoculars can look at Mars on a clear night and tell you where you should land your spaceship if you want to find water." Paul looked around to see if they understood him. The businessman and the marketing major didn't seem to get it. So he told them. "The polar *ice* cap. There is an ice cap on Mars. Oh, some of the planetary guys will tell you that it is all dry ice, but others will tell you that it can't be all dry ice. Some of it must be water. The odds are at least better that we'd find water at the edge of the ice cap, where it meets the desert, rather than in the middle of the bone-dry desert! The Mars Reconnaissance Orbiter, the *Phoenix*, the *Opportunity*, all of them saw evidence of water. The MRO took pictures of what looked like lakes, the *Opportunity* took pictures of puddles of water, and the *Phoenix* actually had water drops form on it and the camera sent back images of the droplets running down the structure on the thing. But how many people in the general public know that? NASA's PR people suck."

"You about done, Paul?" Gary smiled at him. "If you need me to, I can get Burt Rutan on the phone, and you and he can go off on NASA and how they screwed us out of going to space. It would be therapeutic for both of you."

"What?" Paul was surprised. "I thought you were on my side."

"Paul, I'm on the side of my company making a whole bunch of money," Gary said, not really tongue-in-cheek. "And if it means we need to cheerlead for NASA for a while, then that is the side I'm on. I don't really care if they have done what they should've done in the past. They are what they are, and they are the nation's space agency. We are a space company. Therefore, all things space are good! Sis boom bah! Rah rah rah!" Gary waved his arms like he was wielding pom-poms.

"So, what are we saying?" Paul asked.

"Don't be so slow, Captain." Caroline smiled at him. "This is marketing, Paul. We have to market ourselves positively. Negative campaigns are never as successful as positive ones. All things space are positive. They must be. From now on."

"You understand us, Paul? I let you vent for a while. That's good sometimes. But it must be done in private. Now, forget about all that and start studying the cool things, the unique things, the amazing things that NASA has done and is doing. They *are* sending four people to the Moon within a year from now. That *is* pretty damned amazing."

"I see," Paul said, still not really seeing.

"Make sure you do, Paul," Caroline added. "Thinking about the cool things when you discuss NASA will change that expression on your face."

"You don't get it yet, Paul," Gary said. "Focus on the good NASA is doing overnight, and then you'll see. Have a safe flight out. I'll see the both of you tomorrow."

Chapter 7

Paul Gesling was glad to be back in Nevada and away from his metaphorical near-death experience at the hands of CEO Gary Childers in Kentucky. The desert was familiar territory and one in which he felt perfectly at home. And he also preferred being on the "engineering" side of the massive facility and not the "passenger training" side. He wasn't due to be there with the whiny rich brats, aka customers, until tomorrow.

Gesling, like most Americans, had watched the moderately publicized landing of NASA's Altair the day before with a mixture of amazement and disappointment. Amazement at what humans could accomplish when challenged and that we were finally on our way back to the Moon. Disappointment with the time it took for America to get back to where it was in 1972. Overall, the landing was flawless—except that there were no human astronauts on board. That in itself was a big enough flaw to keep people from tuning in. Americans, hell, the rest of humanity, could not care less about another robot probe sending back video images of a place that it seemed nobody would ever set foot on. On the other hand, playing it up as the precursor to the very near manned flight did spark some optimism around the country. At least it boosted Paul's flagging enthusiasm about what he and his crew were soon to accomplish themselves. They were about to take five paying customers on nearly a weeklong fly-around of the Moon. It was to be their own Apollo 8 moment.

He was on his way to a press briefing. The NASA unmanned Moon landing had boosted interest in all things space related, and Space Excursions was high on the list of many reporters for that "next day" follow-up story.

Gesling walked into the conference room that had been modified to accommodate the press and was immediately startled by the number of reporters there. He had expected maybe ten or twelve, most of them local, but the room was packed with what he quickly estimated to be fifty or more. There was standing room only in the drab tan-paneled makeshift press room. He recognized the big names like CNN, Fox News, and the networks, but there were others: *China Daily,* the *London Times,* and the *Times of India,* to name a few.

Already at the podium stood Gary Childers and Caroline O'Conner. Kentucky had come to Nevada. Although he wasn't late, Gesling was the last one to arrive, and he hoped it didn't leave a bad impression with Childers. He and Childers were on shaky enough ground as it was. Paul walked briskly to the front of the room and stood behind and to the left of his boss.

"So, as we can all see," Childers said, "our brilliant captain has arrived, and so I'll turn this over to him." Childers motioned at Gesling to step up to the podium.

"Ahem." Paul cleared his throat to buy some time so that he could remember what he had planned to say. "Good morning. Thanks for your interest in Space Excursions. I'm sure we all saw NASA put on quite a show yesterday by landing the Altair on the lunar surface." There were sounds of affirmation, some heads nodding, but there was little in the way of enthusiastic applause—typical reaction from a press corps only interested in drama to sell advertising time.

"We're very pleased with our nation's success and look forward to seeing the test flight successfully completed. That said, we're gonna beat 'em to the punch. And"—Paul paused for his own dramatic emphasis—"we're gonna do it with people. Real live human beings who are customers who paid to train and become astronauts." Despite what some bloggers had to say, Paul and Childers and the rest of the company did not view the government's space endeavors as competition, and he only wished them well. Hell, Childers had originally begged NASA to sell them a seat on their mission, but NASA had for all its existence resisted sponsorship and commercialization. The original space tourists used Russian flights. The Russians understood capitalism, or at least commercialism, better than NASA. That was a funny bit of historical irony in Paul's mind. But in the end it came down to dollars. Space Excursions was in the business of making money and commercializing space. It was the government's job to explore and do the costly endeavors of space science. It was industry's job to follow and turn the public investment into profit through commercialization wherever it could.

"So, you're all here to learn about our company, Space Excursions, and we're here to answer whatever questions you may have.

"As Mr. Childers said, I am Captain Paul Gesling. I'm a former Navy pilot, and thanks to Mr. Childers I am proud to have been chosen to be the captain and pilot of *Dreamscape* for its maiden voyage to the Moon."

"There isn't a person I trust more with my ship than Paul Gesling," Childers interjected. From the press's point of view, these two appeared to be more like brothers separated at birth instead of a boss and his employee—especially not a boss and employee just past a rough patch in their working relationship.

Childers then launched into a short history of the company. He explained why he had founded it and how it was going to revolutionize and commercialize space exploration. He took a couple of questions and then gave the floor back to Gesling. "And now, I'll let Paul explain a little bit about *Dreamscape* and how he's going to get our customers to the Moon and back again. Paul?"

Gesling stepped back to the podium and promptly picked up the telescoping aluminum pointer Caroline had made sure was ready for him. Though not technophobic, Gesling very much preferred the solid aluminum pointer to its jittery laser cousin. He never trusted that those darned things were eye-safe. He then picked up the remote control from beneath the podium and turned on the projection system.

Immediately behind him, the projection wall came to life with an image of the *Dreamscape* on a runway. The camera's view was from a helicopter that circled the parked space plane to allow viewing from several angles. Paul tapped the screen, pointing out parts of the spacecraft as he talked.

"*Dreamscape* itself is the reusable-spaceship part of a two-stage-to-orbit rocket. The first stage of the rocket is a supersonic combustion ramjet, or scramjet. Based on the technology work conducted by NASA through the early 2000s, Space Excursions picked up where NASA left off and perfected the technology. Lifting off from the Nevada spaceport, test flights of the scramjet first stage reached upwards of twelve times the speed of sound, flying to successful landings at Space Excursions' alternate landing site in Australia in just under two hours. Instead of carrying both rocket fuel and oxidizer, as do most conventional chemical rockets, a scramjet scoops oxygen—hence the term *oxidizer*—from the atmosphere to mix with the propellant to make the rocket go. Without having to carry all that heavy oxidizer, the rocket is much lighter and very, very efficient."

The image behind him came to life with a video of the *Dreamscape* flying indescribably fast from one end of the frame to another. The video appeared to have been shot from a chase plane that was quickly left behind by the supersonic *Dreamscape*.

"Instead of having to be carried to a high altitude and using rockets to achieve high airspeeds before the scramjet begins operating, as was the limitation of the NASA design, Space Excursions found a way to throttle the engine at low airspeeds. Our design begins flight as a conventional jet aircraft, starting its journey from a dead stop in the Nevada desert. Once airborne and above twenty thousand feet, the scramjet fires and our ride to orbit begins."

Another video began to play at this point. Clearly an animation, the video showed the separation of the *Dreamscape* from its scramjet first stage and its ascent into space.

"This is where the fun begins." Gesling was clearly in his element and enjoying every minute at the podium. "At an altitude of about twenty miles and a speed of Mach *twelve*, the rocket engines on the *Dreamscape* will ignite, pulling the passenger-carrying rocket away from its scramjet first stage and into a trajectory that will take it to a three-hundred-mile low Earth orbit. That's just above the altitude of things like the International Space Station and low-flying satellites. Following in the footsteps of Virgin Galactic and doing it one better, we've already taken flights not only into space, but also into orbit—a much harder task. Getting into space is comparatively easy. Accelerating to the orbital velocity of seventeen thousand miles per hour is another task altogether. And *Dreamscape*'s two stages accomplish this nicely."

The animation continued. Seemingly floating high above the Earth, the *Dreamscape* maneuvered close to a large cylinder that was also in Earth orbit. As Gesling resumed speaking, the two were moving close together.

"Once in Earth orbit, the *Dreamscape* docks with a fuel tank launched by an unmanned rocket to refuel. After tanking up, the *Dreamscape* again lights its engines and begins its journey to the Moon."

The video at this point shifted to the interior of the vehicle, showing a computer-animated crew cabin and then the small passenger compartment. Sitting in what appeared to be tailor-made and very comfortable seats were five passengers eagerly looking out the windows and into space. One of the passengers unclipped from his seat at this point and pushed off to experience zero gravity.

"Well, I think we need to tell our passengers they cannot float around while the engines are firing. I don't believe Newton would be too happy. I'm sure our movie animators will be trained better if they ever get to go on a flight." The remark received a few chuckles, but some of those chuckling didn't really understand why it would be funny—just that floating around while firing rocket engines was somehow bad and that it had something to do with rocket science. "There will be ample time for our passengers to experience weightlessness during their six-day trip to the Moon and back.

"Our trajectory will put us on a course to pass around the far side of the Moon and then return to the Earth. We'll come within sixty-five miles of the Moon. And our passengers will have one heck of a view!

"From that distance, this is what the Moon will look like to them. And as they swing around the Moon, this is how small the Earth will appear." The video showed animated craters and mountains in amazing computer-graphic detail. In the distance was a small blue and white beauty—Earth. The video then shifted to more scientific details and illustrated the Earth-Moon system, showing the *Dreamscape*'s trajectory as a dotted line from the Earth, around and behind the Moon, and then back to the Earth. The final frames showed the ship entering the Earth's atmosphere and gliding to a landing at the Nevada Spaceport, changing almost seamlessly from the in-space animation to video shot of an actual *Dreamscape* landing.

Gesling placed the pointer on the podium, still fully extended, in case he needed to pick it up again during the question-and-answer period. He picked it back up but then realized he was fidgeting with his hands. Flying in space didn't make him nervous at all. In fact, it pleased and excited him. The damned press, on the other hand...

The reporter from CNN was the first with his hand up. Paul nodded to him.

"You are charging your customers twenty-five million dollars per seat—that's only one hundred twenty-five million total for the trip. Yet NASA is spending billions of dollars for its landing mission. Why such a big difference? How are you able to do so much yet charge your customers so little?"

Childers motioned to Gesling and O'Conner that he wanted to answer this one, and he stepped up with a smile on his face.

"Well, there are really two reasons for this. First, the American dollar has rebounded in the last decade from the economic recession of the decade before. Had we done this ten years ago, the price would have been double or maybe triple the cost. And because we're using technology that NASA already developed, we don't have to pay as much to develop our own. Did I say two reasons? Okay, really three. The first few flights don't have to make money. It is no secret that I have money. Lots of money. I'm rich, and I choose to spend my money underwriting the company and its bottom line. We've got a solid business plan that will result in us making back my investment and then some. It just won't happen during the first few years of operation. But in ten years, when we are ready to make our first landing on the Moon, charging one hundred million per seat, we'll be turning a hefty profit for our major investors—and that is mostly me. So you see, I plan to make more money off this little adventure."

"Mr. Childers! Mike Mahan, Fox News. What about the risk? NASA is conducting a robotic test run before sending any people. So far, it looks like it is going well. Aren't you taking a big risk by not doing something similar? What if you lost a crew?"

"We will have one more test flight. It will be orbital. We're going to go through all the steps up to departing for the Moon. But the real answer to this one is directly related to the first question. If we were to make *Dreamscape* robotic, not only would Captain Gesling be out of a job, but it would have perhaps doubled our development costs. No, we've flown people to orbit and kept them there for longer than this Moon trip will take. We know how the ship will respond, and she's well designed. We also know that we will take advantage of something called 'Lunar Free Return,' which will pretty much guarantee that the ship and her passengers will come home—just like NASA did on Apollo 13. We're managing the risks, and my customers will be safe and have one fantastic vacation—providing the laws of physics remain as they always have." Childers spoke with confidence and authority and a tinge of humor in his voice. And he believed what he was saying as he said it through a toothy smile.

The next half hour or so of the press conference was filled with questions about the training of the passengers and the various regulatory hurdles Space Excursions had had to overcome in order to send people to the Moon independently of any government. Childers fielded most of them, leaving only the technical questions for Gesling to answer. Near the end of the allotted time, the reporter from the *China Daily* raised his hand.

"Mr. Childers. Mr. Childers, please. Does not your company do business with NASA and the U.S. Department of Defense? Is not the reason you're not concerned with making money because they are, in fact, paying for this mission as part of an American attempt to secure the Moon and the mineral resources there for itself? Are you not a front for the American government under the guise of commercialism?"

Childers, Gesling, and the unflappable Caroline O'Conner were all taken aback by this one. They weren't certain if the man was serious or some sort of nut. Both O'Conner and Gesling looked to Childers to respond. And respond he did. Paul smiled at the fire in his boss's voice.

"With all due respect, my company is *my* company. Yes, we do business for NASA and for other agencies within the U.S. government. They, like the *Dreamscape* passengers, are my customers. All of this is public knowledge, and I am proud of what we do and for whom we do it. Yes, I have government contracts. But they don't come close to paying for this spacecraft. Hell, the government cost me more damned money in legal issues than building that space rocket!"

He calmed down a little and continued. "There is no conspiracy surrounding what we do nor with this trip. It is what it is. I'm in business to make money and give my customers one hell of a ride. I hope that answers your question, and, as far as I am concerned, this news conference is over."

With that, Childers walked from the stage, still clearly agitated by the last question. Childers was more agitated, in fact, than Gesling would have thought possible.

"Damn," Paul leaned toward O'Conner and whispered. "What's up with that?" Gesling was surprised that a question most in the room would consider balderdash would get such a response from Childers—perhaps giving it more credibility than it deserved.

"Search me," O'Conner responded with a shrug as she moved toward the podium to more formally close out the news conference. "I don't know, but I need to wrap this up on a more positive note or that will be the question everyone here will remember—and we clearly don't want that being the sound bite on tonight's news!"

I dunno, I kinda liked it. Shows we've got balls, Paul thought to himself. If he'd been holding the pointer, he could have smacked it in his hands like a billy club for effect. He stood sternly anyway and glared with a slight grin at the press members—the boss's enforcer. He decided then and there that he liked Childers and had every intention of keeping his job and his boss happy, no matter how annoying the passengers got.

Chapter 8

During the tour, while Caroline O'Conner was charming the four dozen or so reporters and their accompanying camera crews with her knowledge of Space Excursions, *Dreamscape,* and space exploration in general, Gesling's telephone buzzed in his pocket, almost startling him. Somewhat annoyed, he took a deep breath and then fished it out of his pocket. Paul thumbed the center key and then the number key to unlock the thing, and then it dinged at him, saying that he'd received a text message from Childers.

The message read: AFTER THE TOUR, MEET ME IN MY OFFICE ASAP.

Gesling was used to getting boss-grams and didn't really give it much thought. At that point, he couldn't imagine that the text message and Childers's reaction to the question asked by the reporter from the *China Daily* were related. But he was soon to discover that, unfortunately, they most certainly were. He plopped the phone back in his pocket and ignored it for the time being.

Completing the tour and seeing the reporters to the heavily monitored exit from the Nevada test facility took about another hour and a half. Pual's stomach croaked at him a time or two and then started in with a full rumble. He had skipped breakfast and by now was ravenously hungry. He debated whether or not to grab a bite before hotfooting it off to Childers's office. He opted to grab a candy bar and a soda from the break room first. The candy bar at least quieted, if not appeased, the rumble in his stomach. The soda helped, too.

Gary Childers's Nevada office was not nearly as spectacular as the one in Kentucky. A desk, credenza, and table were the only furniture pieces, and only a few deep-space photographs adorned the walls. By the time Paul got there, he saw that a meeting was already taking place. In the room were Mark Watson, Space Excursions' chief of security, Helen Jones, the "IT Lady," who kept the computer network operational, and David Chu, the lead systems engineer for the *Dreamscape* itself.

It took only seconds for Gesling to determine that everyone in the room was agitated about something. They were all seated at the meeting table and all looked up when he entered the room. He couldn't tell if they were upset with him or were welcoming an interruption to their apparently intense discussion. Paul was beginning to feel agitated himself, because he didn't have a damned clue what all the hubbub was about.

"Come in, Paul. We've got a problem." Childers motioned for him to take a seat at the table next to him. Paul took the last sip of his soda and dropped the can and the candy-bar wrapper in the garbage can by the door. The IT Lady sneered at him as she looked back and forth between the garbage can and the recycle bin beside it. Paul bit his tongue to prevent him from saying the word *hippie* and ignored the sneer as he sat.

"Sure. What's up? You guys look like we've lost the vehicle or something."

"Well," Chu commented, "in a manner of speaking, we have."

"What?!"

This time, the IT Lady picked up the discussion. "Paul, we've got a major security breach. One of my team began to suspect something was up last week when he noticed an uptick in outgoing data volume from e-mails, file transfers, et cetera. You know, the usual stuff. But this uptick wasn't from any particular user or at any specific time. It was about a twenty-percent increase in everyone's data usage. When we looked more closely, we saw that every single file being transferred was statistically larger than it should have been, given our past few years of data."

"Really?" He leaned forward.

"When we moved from looking at the overall system level and began looking at specific outgoing messages, we saw that each and every message had some additional data encoded and attached to it. Sort of a hidden attachment, as it were. Then we noticed that messages were also being cc'd to an additional e-mail address. And not the same e-mail address—hundreds of different ones, not one being the same. In a matter of a few days, the extra data volume that went out of here was over a terabyte. And that was before any flags had really been raised. Had a single user been sending that much data, we would have shut him down immediately."

Gesling was not an information-technology expert, but he was pretty smart, and what she was describing sounded deceptively simple. Almost too simple to be possible.

"What data was being sent? Financial? Technical?"

"Good question." Chu was quick to respond. "Technical. Whoever did this got most of the *Dreamscape* design and a lot of performance data."

"That's the way it looks now." Jones continued her explanation. "Yes, it was technical. Somehow, a Trojan software program was latent in all of our computers until it was activated last week. Once it turned on, it began to systematically carve up and send out selected data files from every computer in the office. It found our engineering drawings, customized software design tools, parts specifications, test reports, everything. You name it. We haven't found a single computer that wasn't compromised."

"Goddammit all to hell! I can't believe we let this happen!" It was Gary Childers's turn to add to the tempest.

"By the time we realized what was happening and cut off our access to the outside world late last night, it was too late," Jones said decisively.

"Hundreds of e-mail addresses?" Gesling asked. "Is there a common link? Do we know who we're dealing with here?"

"China" was the answer from the IT Lady. "I asked Phil."

Phil was on Helen's team and was well known by just about everyone in the company as the guy you called when your system went down. He seemed to be able to fix anything. He was also an ex-hacker. When he was in high school, he was expelled for hacking the school's computer system. When he was in college, he was arrested for hacking a computer at the U.S. Environmental Protection Agency. There was a story about how he'd managed to get out of jail time, but Paul had never heard it.

Phil had always said it was because he did it just for the sake of doing it—sort of like the answer people gave when asked for their motivation in climbing Mount Everest—or for going to the Moon. He never tried to take anything or cause any problems, he just had to prove to himself that he could do it.

He never graduated from college, but that hadn't kept Helen Jones from recognizing his talent and convincing the company to pay him enough that he would not consider climbing any more Mount Everests while employed by Space Excursions. Phil was good at his job and had outside connections that could help him in situations like this. Helen didn't want to ask who some of these outside connections were.

"Phil nosed around some. He said that we were getting IP port probes on a regular basis now and that the packets that left here went where the probes are coming from. He thinks it all went to China."

"Do we know how our systems were compromised?" Mark Watson asked.

"Uh, well," Jones responded. "Mark, look at your cell phone. Where does it say it was made? Check yours, too, Paul. Gary, flip over that laptop and tell me where it was assembled."

Childers picked up the laptop that was sitting idle in front of him and read from the back.

"Assembled in China."

"Same here," Watson replied.

"Mine, too," said Gesling.

"Of course they are." Knowing that she had their full attention, Helen Jones continued her explanation. "All of the computers in the facility were either made or assembled in China. The company name on the outside is as red, white, and blue as you'd ever want. But the lure of cheap labor is too much for the CEOs—present company excluded, Mr. Childers. We've outsourced almost all of our computer-manufacturing base to China.

"I believe our computers came with some additional software embedded in the operating system. It was then triggered or turned on by someone who knew what we were doing here."

"Wait a minute." Childers leaned forward in his seat. "Are you telling me you've figured all this out since last night?"

"Oh, heavens, no," Jones responded. "No, at this point it is just a theory. The idea wasn't mine. It was Phil's. It seems this is an active discussion among the hacker community and pretty well known there 'unofficially.' There have apparently been other incidents that Phil knew about. When we started looking into our problem, he told me about them."

Watson could contain himself no longer.

"Folks. Are you aware of the implications here? Yes, we've lost some expensive and important technical data. *But what about the rest of the country?* We aren't the only ones who own this brand of computers. What about the banks? Other defense contractors? The government, for God's sake. If her theory is correct, then we could have a security breach of national importance!"

"Alright, alright, let's settle down a bit." Childers took back control of the meeting. "All in good time, Mr. Watson. We need to ascertain the degree to which we've been compromised, fix the leak—no, stop the leak—and then we can figure out who to report it to. And we will report it—but not just yet. First, I need to understand what this means to us.

"I need to know something for absolute certain." Childers looked at Gesling and Chu as he spoke. "Is there anything someone can do with this data that will compromise our flight? We have a manifest of paying customers and a launch date. I need to know if this leak will force a delay."

"Gary, if all they did was copy our files, then we should be okay," Chu said. "But are we sure that's all that happened? What if this Trojan program did more than copy the data? What if it changed something in the procedures or, God forbid, in the specifications? Paul might be halfway to the Moon and a bad command dumps all his fuel. We'd better make sure none of these systems are connected to the wireless on the ship."

"God, a wrong requirement could vent the cabin to vacuum," Paul added.

"Or God knows what else," Chu said. "What we need is more work at this point. I can't tell you about the launch or the safety of the vehicle until my team has had time to review the files and compare them with the backups. How do we know they weren't compromised, too?"

"The backups appear to be okay," Jones said. "They're stored on external drives and isolated from the computers here in Nevada. Before we bring any of them up, I want to have my team check the machines that host the backups and make sure they don't have the same bug." She carefully placed her cell phone on the table in front of her as she continued. "Gary, this scares the crap out of me. I've never seen anything like this—all of our computers had the Trojan embedded in the operating system. The OS is propagating the program *everywhere*. We've got to tell someone."

"Hmm." Childers rose from his seat, pushing the chair back with deliberate slowness. "I hear your concerns, and we will report it. But we'll do it quietly, and we certainly won't talk about it to the media. As of now, whoever *they* are—the Chinese, whoever—they don't know that we know about the leak. Computers go down all the time, and this just might be one of those times. Who knows?"

"Gary, hold on a minute." Gesling, remembering the numerous counterintelligence briefings from the years he spent in the military, had an idea. "Let's follow your suggestion and inform the FBI of the breach. I suspect they'll want us to resume normal operations, leaving the software in place. That way they might be able to better track the e-mails back to the source, or perhaps they might want to use us to send specific information that they know will be received and acted on. This might be like some of the black ops the British did back in the Second World War with the captured German Enigma coding machine."

"You want to play spy versus spy with our systems?" Watson asked. "Paul, you've been reading too many books. I want this place locked down and secure as fast as possible. We need to let the government know about what happened—sooner, rather than later—but we also need to secure our systems and make sure that nothing else is lost or damaged."

Paul watched Childers, who had begun pacing during this last interchange. The CEO had reached a decision. Paul could tell by the expression on the man's face.

"Okay. Mark, I want you to call the FBI and let them know what happened. Helen, you need to first make sure this bug is cleaned out of our systems and then bring them back up online. From this point forward, we will work only from the backup files. They are the only ones we know aren't tainted.

"David, before we use them, I want you to double-check the files from the backup server to make sure they *are* accurate, and then get them to those who need them. Just tell the engineers that some data was corrupted and they'll be okay working from the backup files. Please, please, please do not tell anyone else about the leak. And we will fully cooperate with any official investigation. Let's move out, people."

Chapter 9

One week later, the Altair lunar lander was being prepared to take off from the surface of the Moon. Poised on the barren and scorched lunar surface was a robotic emissary from Earth, lifeless, peopleless, but controlled by people back on Earth.

Chow was once again sitting in the same conference room at the Johnson Space Center facing down his own demons from *the* dream, which had recurred four out of the last seven nights. The team's sense of optimism was palpable. So far, all lunar-surface operations had gone flawlessly, and their confidence in the lander was growing daily. All that remained for it to do was lift from the surface of the Moon into low lunar orbit. There it would rendezvous with the Orion for the trip back to Earth.

Taller than a three-story house, the massive Altair would eventually be the home away from home for four astronauts who would be two hundred forty thousand miles and at least three days' travel from the nearest park, coffee shop, or hospital. Built for functionality and not comfort, many would question it being considered a home away from anywhere. But to the astronauts who were going to live in her, she was a beauty, a masterpiece.

Perched atop the Altair was the ascent stage. The entire lander would not make the return journey into space, as that would require too much fuel. Newton's First Law, force equals mass times acceleration, governed everything regarding rocket propulsion.

To get something, the mass of the rocket and its passengers, moving, meant accelerating it. And that acceleration required a hefty force. The greater the mass, the greater the force required to get the acceleration. The lander, which at the time consisted mainly of empty propellant tanks that were depleted during the landing, was simply too massive to lift back into space. Too much fuel would have been required to get the acceleration needed to escape the gravitational pull of the Moon. Instead, a small portion of the lander, the ascent stage, would be lofted by a single modified Pratt & Whitney RL-10B engine. That engine produced just under twenty-five thousand pounds of thrust.

Had Chow and his colleagues been in the lander at that moment, they would have been standing shoulder to shoulder, anxiously awaiting engine ignition. Not only was there not enough room for chairs in the stage, but also the chairs would have mass. And, again, from Newton's First Law, any increase in the mass of an object to be moved would require a commensurately greater force. Standing was a small price to pay for being among the first people to walk on the Moon in half a century.

Chow arrived well before the scheduled liftoff, wanting to have plenty of time to look over the mission briefings and to be part of the camaraderie that inevitably came with being where the action was. And the action was, most certainly, right there.

Above the conference room's wall monitors were two clocks. The first showed mission elapsed time, begun at the moment of liftoff from the Kennedy Space Center in Florida. The second was a countdown clock, now set to count down to the moment when the Altair's ascent stage engine lit—it was stopped at twenty minutes and had been stopped there for more than an hour. It was a scheduled hold in the countdown and did not indicate any serious problems.

Chow saw Menendez was there, busily scanning engineering data and mostly ignoring his presence just like she had during the landing. He noticed she occasionally looked up from the screen and scanned the room before returning to her busyness.

Bill Stetson appeared in the doorway. He looked around the room and seemed relieved when he caught Chow's eye. Dodging various people milling about, Stetson made his way over across the conference room.

"Tony, I came to get you and Helen. I'd like for you to be with me in the control room for ascent."

"Is there something wrong?"

"No, I just think it would be a good thing for my team to be with me. We've also got a better view. Charles is already there." Stetson grinned. He was totally correct. Mission control was outfitted with an entire wall of huge flat screens showing in high definition what was happening on the Moon—both inside the Altair and outside looking back at the lunar lander.

"Get your stuff together while I go get Helen. We're coming off hold in about fifteen minutes, and I need to get back. This is my pee break." Stetson slapped Chow on the shoulder.

While Chow picked up his laptop and other belongings, he noticed Stetson talking with Menendez and her enthusiastic response—packing her things fast enough to meet Chow at the door as they left for mission control.

Nine hundred miles to the northeast in Lexington, Kentucky, Gary Childers was also watching events unfold on the Moon. In his typical fashion, he was also multitasking, reviewing various financial reports, answering e-mails and wondering when he might be able to sell tickets for a moonwalk. After all, flying around the Moon was pretty cool, but not nearly as cool as walking on the Moon. And he knew there would be a very large customer base interested in walking on the Moon if they could get there and back safely. The company's current projections showed that happening in less than ten years. How much less was the big question.

An exhausted-looking Mark Watson entered his office with a small stack of papers in hand.

"Gary, we've looked at the entire database and nothing was changed," he said, looking over the papers. "They only copied data. We don't see any sign of tampering."

"Good."

"The FBI's been mostly quiet about what they know, but Helen's hacker is certain the data went to China. I'm glad he's on our side."

Gary Childers was not easily fazed, but the breach in *his* security certainly came very close to doing so.

"This really pisses me off. I convinced NASA and the DoD to let us have the scramjet designs. We improved them and found a way for the whole thing to work from takeoff through getting

Dreamscape into orbit. And now the Chinese steal the plans—making us look like rank amateurs and giving the people who wear stars on their sleeves in the Pentagon an excuse to not share technology with us or anyone else in the future.

"I just hope the press doesn't get the story. The last thing I want to do is damage control. We're about to make history and, by the way, money." He was definitely not in one of his better moods.

"Understood. So far, the only people who know about the breach are us, the FBI, and, of course, the Chinese."

With that, Childers looked up from his desk and, with his head slightly tilted, gave Watson what he thought of as an "evil eye." Without saying another word, he let the engineer know that now wasn't the time and he didn't want to discuss it any further. Watson slunk from his office, leaving Childers alone with his paperwork.

Five thousand miles away, in Beijing, China, a room of highly decorated military leaders sat in a room watching news coverage of the pending launch of the Altair from the surface of the Moon using flat-screen monitors nearly identical to those being used in Texas—made by a Chinese manufacturer, of course. In fact, it was the same Chinese manufacturer as the one that made the monitors at the Johnson Space Center.

The senior official in the room, to whom all others present expressed extreme deference, watched the screen without reaction. He turned to the man on his left and spoke so that all could hear.

"The president is anxious to see us launch on schedule. Are your people going to be ready? He is not happy that the Americans may beat us to the Moon, and I am not optimistic after reviewing the latest test reports."

"Yes, sir." General Xiang Li, the chief designer of China's lunar program, nodded. Xiang, an MIT-educated engineer with multiple technical degrees, was responsible for China's impressive buildup toward their own lunar mission. It seemed to him that his entire life was a movie script, with him playing the role of the great hero, destined to lead his country to the Moon. And by placing a Chinese flag there he could show the world that China had a place on the world stage as a great power. And—that the Moon was *theirs.*

"Are you certain?"

"Yes, sir. We will be ready for launch as scheduled. I've personally reviewed the test reports, and the engineering team has a plan to fix the problem with the landing system. When our taikonauts are ready to land on the Moon, they will have a one hundred percent functional system to do so." Though his words were bold, his heart was not in what he was saying. The test reports were actually not good, and there was not a consensus that the planned technological fix would even work. But the schedule had to be kept, lest Xiang lose his reputation and his job and, likely, his life.

"Very well," was the simple reply from his boss, who then turned his head and focused intently on the television screen as the countdown clock resumed counting down from twenty minutes. As that clock ticked, the American test flight would be in its final phase, leaving them nothing to do except the real mission with a crew. And all in the room knew that China had to get there first.

The resumption of the countdown clock was met in mission control with muted approval. The time for celebration would be after a successful liftoff, not before. Not one second before.

Unlike the conference room, mission control was filled with engineers who monitored their data not simply because they could, but because they had to. The success of the robotic dress rehearsal depended upon them and their ability to think on their feet. The system was designed to be mostly autonomous, but everyone knew that if something were to go wrong, it would be quick-thinking people who would make the difference. And they could not forget that there was about a second-and-a-half delay between the Earth and the Moon due to the speed of light and data-relay loops, so they had to be extra careful, cautious, and expedient.

Menendez, Chow, and Leonard stood near the back wall, not wanting to get in anyone's way. After all, they were last-minute observers and not part of the team currently on shift.

Stetson was sitting on console just behind and to the left of the Green Team flight director. Stetson was flight director when Blue Team was on shift. This time the Green Team was on console and Stetson was in the room as an observer. Not being in the flight director's chair was tough on Stetson, but he knew he couldn't be in it twenty-four hours a day nor for every critical mission event. This was a *team* effort. But it was still tough for him to not be in charge.

The Green Team flight director spoke up at T-minus fifteen minutes.

"Okay, folks. We're fifteen minutes away from getting this bird off the surface and back into space. The last time we did this was 1972—before some of you were born. Let's show Commander Stetson and his team that we know how to give them a good ride, because the next time it'll be *them* on the screen, sweating real sweat and looking to us to get them home." With that, the entirety of the room looked at Stetson, Chow, Leonard, and Menendez along the back wall. He concluded, "Now, damn. Let's fly this thing!"

Stetson couldn't help but grin at his team. Chow and Leonard accepted the attention by smiling, but Menendez only nodded curtly.

The countdown was flawless. As the clock reached zero, the camera inside the Altair began to shake—slowly at first, and then with greater intensity. The external cameras also started to move, but with much less apparent jitter than their interior counterparts due to the stiffness of their mounting hardware.

Slowly, the lunar surface began to move away from the rising ascent stage. The base of the lander was now clearly visible on the view screen, battered but basically as good as the day it was manufactured. A few pieces of insulation were torn open and blasted by the rocket exhaust, but otherwise there was no obvious damage being caused by the ascent stage as it rose into the perpetually dark lunar sky. The lifeless and gray lunar surface began to dominate the camera's view as the Altair gained altitude and its shadow began to move laterally across the surface, diminishing in size.

Instead of the cheering that many might expect to hear with a successful liftoff, the team in mission control was dead silent, holding their collective breath. As it became apparent that the vehicle was not going to be stranded on the surface, nor was it about to crash, people began to breathe again—and a few did begin to clap their hands.

When the stage reached an altitude of ten miles, all of the

screens abruptly went blank and numerous red lights simultaneously appeared at the workstations throughout the room.

"Holy...!" the Green Team's flight director heard. "We've lost
all telemetry."

"Ditto that, no signal at all—not even the carrier." Another
confirmation that something had gone dreadfully wrong came
from a worried engineer monitoring the health of the communications system.

Seemingly instinctively, but actually resulting from years of
training and simulation, the Green Team went to work trying
to figure out what was going on. With no data coming from the
Altair during ascent, there was no way of knowing if the vehicle
had exploded, gone off course, or was performing as it was supposed to.

Stetson's mind raced, running through what he would do if he
were in the flight director's chair at this moment. But he wasn't,
and there was no way he was going to do anything other than
speak if spoken to. Green Team was good, and they were doing
everything they could to regain contact with the Altair. His mind
was racing nonetheless.

From Houston to Lexington to Beijing, all ears were listening
to the voice of NASA's mission control as the obviously flustered
commentator tried to fill the otherwise dead air with calming
words and speculation about what was actually happening to
the Altair—two hundred and fifty thousand miles away. No one
in mission control had the time or inclination to provide the
commentator with up-to-the-minute information, so he had to
wing it. All things considered, he was doing an adequate job.
After all, the Green Team in mission control didn't know what
was going on, either.

"Bill." Looking at the harried Green Team doing its job with
extreme professionalism, Helen Menendez leaned forward and
spoke to Stetson quietly at first. Then a little louder. "Bill, the
Altair is on autopilot, and if it is working correctly, we should
see it on the Orion's exterior cameras any minute now." She spoke
loud enough to be heard by Bill Stetson, Charles Leonard, and

Anthony Chow, but not loud enough to be heard by anyone else. She was as sensitive as Stetson regarding their role as observers and observers only.

"Roger that." Stetson nodded in affirmation. "That's what I'm counting on." As he spoke, his gaze shifted to the second screen from the right on the front wall. On the screen, which held his gaze, was the view through the Orion's window of the lunar surface passing peacefully beneath the vehicle. If one could focus on the nose of the capsule and not be distracted by the sight of the lunar surface scrolling by below or the majesty of the myriad stars visible directly through the upper part of the frame, the docking ring that would attach the Orion to the Altair would be clearly visible. It was to there that the Altair was programmed to return—if it was still in one piece.

"There!" Seemingly on cue, a voice called out from somewhere in the room. "I see her! We've got a visual of the Altair from Orion!" Now all eyes in the room focused on the image from the orbiting Orion. There, in the distance, was a tiny glint. A spot of light only a few pixels in size on the monitor. But it was there, and it was growing larger. A few seconds more and the spot grew into more of a small disc as the Green Team watched breathlessly. After a few minutes it became apparent to all that the spot of light was, in fact, the incommunicado Altair, performing its automated rendezvous maneuver as it was designed and programmed to do.

"Hot damn!" Bill couldn't contain himself any longer.

"I'll second that" was all the Green Team's flight controller could manage as he and the rest of the team began to prepare for the lunar-orbit rendezvous of the Altair and the Orion. Pictures and telemetry were coming from the Orion just as they should. The Altair remained totally silent.

Weeks later, after hundreds of engineers had a chance to review data from the voyage, it would be discovered that telemetry was likely lost due to a poorly potted connector in the primary communication system, stopping communication with the Earth but not stopping the flow of engineering, position, and velocity data between it and the Orion. The important data, that which was required to complete the rendezvous, was never disrupted. The backup communications system didn't activate, because the primary system's fault-detection software never detected the problem—after all, the Altair and the Orion never lost communication. Only the dirt-bound humans in mission control were cut off. The software routines never deviated; they assumed all was well with the data transmission and that nothing more needed to be done. Shortly thereafter, a bright console engineer would realize that he could have simply relayed the data from the Altair through the Orion feeds and then to mission control. Instead of getting egg on his face and making a big thing of it, he wrote an e-mail about it to the fault-response team that was duly noted and stored away.

Despite the success of the mission, that type of fault was one of the worst kind—two separate and distinct failures in the same system had caused a failure of the primary and backup communications systems. Fortunately, the double failure happened in a rather benign system and didn't imperil the mission. Had the failure resulted in a loss of communications between the Altair and the Orion, then a successful rendezvous would have most likely been impossible. That is, since there were no humans aboard either spacecraft. Bill's craw got all tied up in knots every single time he thought about it. Every system, step, procedure, and control had been automated to the point that pilots could do very little during the test program to show that the mission could still succeed even if one or more of the automated systems failed. He kept to himself the thought that decades of flying in low Earth orbit and only sending out robotic probes had sucked the adventure out of his colleagues.

"Damn it all to hell," he muttered to himself. "This could have halted us by a couple of years."

Chapter 10

Barely six weeks later, glimmering in the unrelenting Nevada sun, sat the *Dreamscape,* engines running with a loud rocket noise right out of a science fiction movie. It was just barely audible to those in the observation stands. The reusable spaceship was poised to make history, just waiting for the pilot to begin its maiden journey to Earth orbit. The unmistakable power of the vehicle was obvious to all onlookers as crisscrossing lines of exhaust poured from the thruster nozzles. But the restrained explosive beast was kept in check by its human masters.

To the pilot, Captain Paul Gesling, the moment was anything but serene. Despite the air conditioner in his pressure suit running at maximum, Paul was sweating profusely—he barely noticed the cold air or the sweat. Instead, he cursed happily.

"Hot damn!" he shouted over the spacecraft's interior noise. He was elated to be in the pilot's seat, even if it was just a test. He eyed the various status touch screens displayed on the iPhone-like LCD display that had replaced the old-fashioned gauges and dials of spacecraft and aircraft from previous generations. Then one of the icons turned from green to yellow and then to red. He uttered another stream of epithets. "Damn! Damn! Damn! Hell!"

"Warning, ACS fuel pressure approaching critically low level," the onboard computer voice, aka "Bitchin' Betty," announced over the ship's internal communications system.

"Control, what's up with the helium repress?" Gesling said not quite calmly into his microphone. Hoping for a positive answer from the lead engineer in the control room barely one mile away, he reset that status display and pressed the attitude control system status icon one more time, hoping that the low pressure reading would go away, clearing *Dreamscape* for its first orbital flight. The gauge showed that the pressure in the fuel tank that fed the ship's attitude control system was low. That was a critical function. It contained the subsystem that would allow the *Dreamscape* to remain in a stable orientation while in space—in other words, keeping it from spinning in random directions. There would be no flight unless the problem was resolved. The spin could induce too much of a g-load on the structure and tear the ship apart. Of course, that would be after the crew had either vomited themselves into oblivion or passed out.

"Hold on, Paul, we're looking into it," was the reply from the engineer in the Space Excursions control room.

"Warning, ACS system failure imminent."

"Well, check it faster!" Paul replied.

Unlike their NASA counterparts, Space Excursions had no big control room full of specialized engineers. Instead, their mission control consisted of five people, each cross-trained in multiple engineering disciplines. At this time, all five were working frantically at their computer stations, looking at their status screens and a large replica of Paul Gesling's screen prominently displayed on the wall at the front of the room. They saw what Gesling saw in addition to the next level of detail, available at the touch of a button. Having only five people running the mission saved the company a lot of money. And the automated systems now monitoring the health of the vehicle, though costing the company a load of cash to develop, were working flawlessly, reporting the status of every major and minor system to mission control. Any significant issues that could affect the flight were flagged and brought to the attention of the people who controlled it.

"I'm still waiting." Gesling tapped the red icon on his screen again.

"Warning, ACS system is offline."

"Oh, shut the hell up," he shouted to Bitchin' Betty.

It seemed to him that an intolerable length of time had passed, but to the flight controller, and to any external observers not impatient for a launch, barely three minutes had gone by. Paul chewed at the inside of his mouth, certain that he would have to wait a bit longer, quite a bit longer, before *Dreamscape* would make its full-scale test flight to space and back.

"Damn."

"We have a technical problem with one of *Dreamscape*'s systems that I am sure will be resolved momentarily," Gary Childers said to the VIP guests in the room with him. He scanned the readouts of the test from an observation room just outside his personally funded, high-tech, and oh-so-expensive mission-control room. Not that he understood all the data—Childers was a businessman. What he understood was that delays cost him money.

Childers was clearly impatient, yet at the same time he remained firmly in charge. In his mind, VIP stood for "valuable investment people." Childers had invited several potential investors to attend the test flight, with full expectation they would be so impressed with his operation that they would commit to helping him fund his next entrepreneurial space endeavor—a charter cruise to the surface of the Moon. Once *Dreamscape* was making routine flights *around* the Moon, Childers's marketing surveys indicated that many of the world's ultrarich would be willing to put up at least one hundred million dollars each to actually walk on the Moon. And he was ready to offer the service.

Despite his sizable wealth, even Gary Childers didn't have the money required to finance the construction of a spacecraft that could take people to the Moon and back. After all, the same mission was costing NASA *billions* of dollars. He had invited ten of his most promising investors to the test launch; seven accepted. And now he was in the position of having to explain to them what was going on and why the launch had already been delayed two hours.

"Folks," he began, nodding and smiling, "we're experiencing some problems with one of the *Dreamscape*'s many systems, and my team is telling me that the launch will at best be delayed another hour or so.

"I'm needed in the control room for a few minutes. Ms. O'Conner will take care of you until my return," he said as he motioned for Caroline O'Conner to join him. As he moved toward the door, he lowered his head and softly said to O'Conner in passing, "I just hope it isn't longer than that."

"The wolves look hungry," she whispered back to him. Gary only raised an eyebrow at the comment and hurried to the main control room. The *real* control room.

Childers entered the room just as Gesling's voice once again came over the loudspeaker. "Control, the pressure is starting to drop again. We need to scrub. This whole thing is going the wrong way."

Not uttering a word, uncharacteristic of Childers in a business meeting, seemed entirely appropriate as he waited to hear the response from the experts, his experts, hired at considerable expense to make this whole venture happen.

"Paul, we concur. Prepare to save onboard systems and stand down" was the only reply from the engineer responsible for the test flight.

"Damn!" This time it was Gary doing the cursing. "Shit!" He promptly turned on his heels and began walking back to the VIP room. Now he had to explain this mess to his potential investors and hope that they would be willing and able to hang around until the problem was resolved and the *Dreamscape* could take flight. Childers was too smart to ever try to overturn a technical decision from his team. They were the experts; he paid them to make technical decisions, and he trusted them completely. That didn't mean, however, that he was happy with them or the situation.

But when he had started out on this venture, he had hired a company to complete an extremely detailed analysis of the space industry and why NASA was not economically viable. The space shuttle program had been designed to offer cheap access to space but turned out to be a money pit. The analysis showed that when NASA managers started putting pressure on the program to fly more missions to improve the cost efficiency of the shuttles, that was when the major accidents had occurred. Gary hadn't paid heavy for the analysis just to ignore it. That was their job. He'd just have to find a way to make the day's lemons into lemonade. *That* was *his* job.

Aboard *Dreamscape*, Paul Gesling began the ground abort procedures with the skill of a trained pilot, always glancing at the checklist of required tasks and procedures as it scrolled across the LCD screen, checking each item off as required. In the back of his mind, he was frustrated. But he was a professional, and professional pilots knew that procedures saved their lives—taking out his frustration would have to come later. He was thinking about a bottle of scotch and a punching bag.

The press was having a field day. Soon after Childers returned to take charge of his guests, Caroline O'Conner had the unpleasant task of going to the press observation room and telling the assembled reporters that today's flight would not happen. She didn't yet know when it would happen, and she didn't exactly understand the reason for the delay, but she knew enough to provide the media with the immediate facts.

O'Conner took up her position behind the podium and microphone at the front of the room and said, "May I have your attention, please?

"Today's maiden orbital flight of the *Dreamscape* has been scrubbed due to a pressure leak in one of the ship's propulsion systems. Our experts are looking into the problem, and we will let you know soon when the next attempt will take place." O'Conner, as usual, sounded knowledgeable and self-confident as she made the announcement.

"Ms. O'Conner, Ms. O'Conner!" shouted the reporter from *Space News,* the major online news outlet covering all things space. "How will this affect your schedule? Your schedule shows that you'll be taking paying customers around the Moon in just a couple of months. Do you expect to keep the schedule?"

"At this time, we don't know. The engineers tell me that the problem should be easily fixed, but I can't say how the delay will impact our first commercial launch," she said in response.

"Ms. O'Conner!" shouted another reporter.

And so it continues, thought Caroline to herself before pointing to the next anxious reporter. *They really do seem like a pack of wolves circling the injured animal, waiting for the feast....*

Chapter II

"**G**o, baby, go!" was all Gesling could utter as he alternated looking out the window at the landscape of Earth receding below him and the LCD display that showed the status of *Dreamscape*'s onboard systems. After fixing the faulty sensor on the fuel tank two days previously, the restarted countdown for the launch of *Dreamscape* had gone flawlessly. Now Gesling was nearing the point at which the scramjet first stage would separate from the vehicle and the powerful onboard rocket engines would fire, giving him the final acceleration needed to attain the seventeen thousand miles per hour required for orbit. Escape velocity was just one stage away.

He felt his pulse quicken in anticipation of the stage separation, and he waited for the five small explosions that would soon sever the bolts holding the two parts of *Dreamscape* together. The explosive bolts had to fire within milliseconds of each other or the resulting unequal forces acting on the vehicle would tear it apart. Gesling knew the bolts had been tested, retested, and tested again, but that didn't stop him from being anxious and replaying the catastrophic-failure simulation movies in his mind as the clock on the display counted down to zero.

"Just fly the plane," he told himself. The foremost thing all pilots trained themselves to do was to learn to fly the plane no matter what the instruments were saying or whatever else was going on around them. *Fly the plane.* He gripped the controls and swallowed the lump in his throat, forcing it back into his stomach. The stage-separation icon flashed, and the Bitchin' Betty chimed at him.

"Prepare for stage separation in ten seconds. Nine, eight, seven..."

He felt only a small bump, and then the green light indicating successful stage separation glimmered before him. Seconds later, the *Dreamscape*'s rocket engines ignited, pushing Gesling back into his padded chair on the flight deck. The *Dreamscape* picked up speed.

The first stage, now fully separated from the rocket-powered *Dreamscape,* began its glide back to the Nevada desert. Operated by onboard automatic pilot and with constant monitoring by engineers in the Space Excursions control room back at the launch site, the first stage was on target for a landing back at the location from which its voyage had begun. Onboard computers were sending a steady stream of telemetry back to the ground so the flight engineers could reconstruct all phases of its flight should the worst happen and the vehicle crash. Although the ship had black boxes on board, they were a redundant system at this stage. All operational data was immediately sent to the ground as long as the *Dreamscape* could get a communications link to a ground station or one of the orbital relay satellites that Childers owned time on. But once they were on the way to the Moon, the data rate would drop to the point that the black boxes would be the main system for flight-data storage and retrieval.

On the ground, the Space Excursions computer was busy receiving, interpreting, and storing the data while Gary Childers was excitedly explaining each element of the flight, as it was happening, to his potential future investors—all of whom had decided to wait the extra two days it took to recover from the aborted launch and to this successful one. It was turning out to be worth their while.

"As you can see, the *Dreamscape* is now under rocket power and accelerating as it approaches its three hundred kilometer orbital altitude. Once there, pilot Paul Gesling will shake her down during a minimum of ten orbits before he will rendezvous with our tanker satellite and test the refueling system," Childers explained. Feeling more confident by the minute that his investors were becoming interested, he continued, "After that test, Gesling will begin the reentry process and bring the spaceship back home—landing only a few meters away from where it began its journey. Just future orbiting rides like this we can sell at ten to twenty million a pop and use them as training rides for the Moon missions. We might even consider building a copy of the *Dreamscape* just for that purpose."

Childers assessed the reactions of the seven multibillionaires in the room. They alternated between listening to his explanation and tuning him completely out as they surveyed the status board and the onboard-camera feed that showed them the same view as that being experienced by Paul Gesling. The view was difficult for Childers to compete with. The beautiful blues and whites that stretched across the Earth were quickly becoming a fixture at the bottom of the screen, and the dark blackness of space was growing in prominence. In low Earth orbit, the curvature of the Earth was clearly visible, but spectacular in a different way than the "blue marble" made so famous by the Apollo astronauts. That view would have to wait until Space Excursions' customers were on their way to the Moon.

What the heck, thought Childers, gazing at the view screen along with everyone else in the room. *I think I'll just shut up so we can enjoy the majestic view.* Sometimes the best sales pitch was not pitching at all and just letting the product pitch itself.

Fifteen miles away, perched on a small mesa, a Honda minivan was parked in the blazing Nevada sun. The motor was running and the air conditioner was at full blast to keep the occupants and their computers cool and safe from the unrelenting heat of the desert. Inside were three men, all Chinese, and all were watching their computer screens as the data they were collecting from the antennas mounted on the roof came streaming in.

"And they didn't even bother to encrypt the data?" asked the eldest man among them. He was incredulous, given that his last assignment was to intercept data from an American antimissile test rocket flown over the South Pacific two years previously. The encryption on that data had taken them months to break, and they still weren't sure if they understood all of it. Without understanding how the instruments were calibrated, there would always be some uncertainty around the accuracy of the data intercepted.

Zeng Li almost grinned at his colleagues at the thought. He had years of experience with his country's foreign-intelligence community, for many of which he had been living in America working as the representative of a Chinese import/export bank. His other missions had proven much more difficult to acquire data access alone, and that was nearly as tough as breaking the decryption keys. This assignment seemed absurdly easy, and that made him nervous.

Li and his team were charged with monitoring the flight of the *Dreamscape* and collecting copies of all its telemetry during the test flight. The team had modified the Honda van and turned it into a mobile communications center, though the only external evidence of this was the antenna. Perched on top of the van was a small dish antenna, clearly designed to receive satellite space communications. Had the profusion of home-entertainment systems with satellite television not become commonplace in homes throughout the remote portions of the American southwest, the antenna might have stood out suspiciously. But satellite TV was ubiquitous, and almost every home and camper had the required hardware. Their van, therefore, looked no different than the many others who simply used their satellite communications system to watch *Sunday Night Football*.

"It looks like they are about to successfully achieve orbit," said another of the men as they keenly watched the data scroll by on the computer screens.

"I could have told you that," said the third man, who was watching the whole event live on Fox News, CNN, MSNBC, and the Science Channel.

No one paid any attention to the van or its occupants as they collected the data that would enable their colleagues at home to better understand the *Dreamscape* design recently stolen from the computers at Space Excursions.

"*Dreamscape* is in orbit," declared Paul Gesling. Though he had been in space several times piloting the suborbital rockets that preceded *Dreamscape*, this was the first time he would actually circle the globe. Gesling was now euphoric. He was whizzing around the Earth in a 186-mile-high circular orbit at 17,253 miles per hour. One trip around the Earth at that altitude and speed took ninety minutes almost to the second. The mission plan included a total of ten orbits, which meant that he would be in space for the next fifteen hours. A lot of that time he would be busy, but there was enough of it to allow the occasional gaze out the window.

"Control, now preparing for orbit-orientation burn," he read right off his checklist. "OOB in forty-five seconds."

"Roger that, Paul. Preparing for OOB."

At the *Dreamscape*'s circular orbit, the ship was still in an airplane-like flight path. That meant that the nose was forward and the planet was underneath the belly. It would be easier to fly and maintain a steady spacecraft orientation if the ship was rolled over and flying ass-first just like the old space shuttles used to. The view would be better, too. Paul toggled the OOB (pronounced "oh-oh-bee") and the forty-five-second clock started to count down. The countdown allowed the onboard computer systems to interrogate the global-positioning data, the inertial-navigation units, and the exterior star trackers to determine the exact orientation of the ship with respect to the Earth and space. Then it calculated the appropriate sets of burns to safely rotate the ship into the upside-down-and-backward flight configuration. The clock hit ten seconds, and all the calculations showed complete.

"Warning, orbital-orientation burn in three, two, one." Paul instinctively raised an eyebrow at the sound of the Bitchin' Betty and gripped his restraints in preparation. The burn fired.

Several small cold-gas rocket thrusters fired on exterior of the ship, flipping it over and rolling it. Then the thrusters fired again to stabilize and stop the flight path. Burns, very small ones, would be needed over time to maintain the proper orientation of *Dreamscape,* but they would be so small they would barely be noticeable compared to the OOB.

"OOB is complete," Paul announced as the Earth filled the view in all the windows. "All systems look good, and to quote John Glenn, 'Oh, that view is tremendous!'" Gesling had been trying to think of something historic to say, but the best he could do was rob from history. The sentiment perfectly fit the moment as it stimulated the memory and feelings he had the first time he had heard that scratchy radio recording from 1962 when American astronaut John Glenn made his first journey into space—years before Gesling's birth. Even though he had heard it as a rerun, it had instilled in him something amazing. Looking out the window now, he understood what it was. How Glenn must have felt that first time he looked out the window and saw that beautiful world beneath him...Paul felt the same way now.

"Roger that, Paul," Childers replied from his own control-room link. "You'll have to let me tag along for the ride sometime."

"I'll bring you up anytime you want to pay for it, Gary," Paul replied with a chuckle.

A checklist icon turned yellow on his monitor. The changing color caught his attention, which was why it was designed that way. The icon told Gesling that he needed to begin preparations for the rendezvous with the refueling satellite, now only eight orbits away. That was about twelve hours—he had plenty of time.

Slowly but surely, Newton's laws were guiding the *Dreamscape* and the refueling spacecraft closer together. Once they attained the same orbit and were separated by only some tens of meters, the most difficult part of this flight would commence. *Dreamscape* would gently bump into the orbital gas station, lock on to its docking ring, secure a connection, and demonstrate how fuel could be transferred from one vehicle to another. Without the extra fuel, the *Dreamscape* would not be able to go to the Moon. While no fuel would actually flow this time, they would test out every system so that when the actual Moon flight occurred, they would be reasonably sure that no problems would keep the transfer from happening.

Again speaking only to himself, Gesling said, "If NASA can do it, then so can I."

About that time an icon labeled ISR Payload turned red, showing that it had priority in the mission timeline at the moment. Paul tapped the monitor and brought up the checklist for the Intelligence, Surveillance, and Reconnaissance package. Step one was to activate the system. This he did by tapping the appropriate key sequence. On the Lunar mission the ISR package would be controlled by the person in seat number 2B. It could be controlled by any of the seats, but the future occupant of seat 2B was the person who had trained for the ISR job. The job consisted of turning on a very nice twenty-inch commercially available telescope system.

The telescope was a Schmidt-Cassegrain type with real-time

digital-color visible video and false-color infrared video cameras. There was a full zoom capability and pan and tilt controls, all software-driven from the touchscreen on the back of any of the seats. With the planned ten-mile closest flyby altitude of the Moon, called the orbit's periapsis, the system could resolve an inch or two on the lunar surface. It couldn't read the license plates on the moonbuggies (if they had them), but it could give a pretty good image of the thing. At *Dreamscape*'s 186-mile-high orbit above the Earth, it could resolve, at best, about fifteen inches per pixel on the camera—assuming there were no atmospheric distortions in the way. In other words, the smallest thing the camera could see was the size of a beach ball. Although the system was designed for fun viewing of the Moon and for finding potential landing spots there in the future, Paul knew that the company had funding from other, more terrestrial, sources for flying future rapidly deployable spy missions. The *Dreamscape* was, in essence, a quickly deployable spy satellite that could be maneuvered to "locations of opportunity." Paul also understood that Gary Childers liked money, *Dreamscape* needed lots of it, and the U.S. intelligence community liked the product they had, and they had plenty of money. Space Excursions had gotten contracts for undisclosed amounts from various DoD and three letter agencies to try out the system while in orbit around the Earth. Childers planned to create a fleet of these things that could be used for Moon missions, Earth-orbit tourist missions, and DoD missions; based, of course, on when the customers could pay.

Paul ran the ISR telescope through its test sequence and then played around with it for the allotted thirty minutes he had available in the mission timeline. As he rolled around the planet, he could see Florida coming into view. He zoomed in on the Cape at the launch pads there and could see the Ares Vehicle Assembly Buildings. He could see motion around the pads like a flurry of ants on an anthill. A few minutes later he was over the Atlantic Ocean and couldn't find much to look at. He put the system on auto and closed the icon on his screen. To close out the checklist for this item, there was only one other thing he had to do. He unstrapped himself and practiced floating back to seat number 2B, where he checked that he could control the ISR system from there. All was well. *Check.* He floated his way to all the seats and ran through their operation.

After the basic ship checkout and the occasional fun full backflip, he made his way back to his seat up front. It was time to start prepping for the rendezvous with the fuel depot. All the motion through the ship had made him a little dizzy, and he needed to strap himself in and focus to keep from getting motion sick. Microgravity was fun to him, but Paul knew to be careful until he was well adjusted or it could lead him down a dangerous and gut-wrenching path.

At launch plus fifteen hours, the *Dreamscape* had completed ten orbits, docked with the refueling satellite, separated, and was preparing to fly home. Childers was ecstatic. The *Dreamscape* had performed flawlessly. In just a couple of months, if this landing went smoothly, he would be sending his first paying customers on a trip around the Moon.

His soon-to-be partners were reassembling in the VIP area after a celebratory dinner and an abbreviated night's rest to await the dawn landing of *Dreamscape*. Childers had already gotten verbal and e-mail statements from all seven investors of their excitement and plans to invest in the company. He would soon nail down the dollar figures and the paperwork, but it looked as though all seven in attendance would fully commit to the Moon-landing partnership, giving him and his company the money needed to begin work on Space Excursions' next venture before the first one was even complete.

Looking out the windows, Childers, O'Conner, the VIP entre-preneurs, and the press gazed expectantly at the sky. The sun was barely above the horizon when they caught the first sight of the *Dreamscape* winging its way back from space. Applause broke out everywhere, even in the control room, though there the applause was brief due to there still being much work for them to do.

The vehicle glided onto the desert runway and bounced only once before rolling to a complete stop. As the air temperature began its daily rise from simply uncomfortable to totally unbear-able, astronaut Paul Gesling opened the doors of *Dreamscape,* and awaited the portable stairs that would allow him to walk again on terra firma.

Childers didn't rush to greet his pilot; he was too busy chatting up his new partners, taking their enthusiastic congratulations with appropriate modesty, deflecting credit to his engineers and to Gesling. Childers was an expert at working a crowd, large or small.

The Honda van on that mesa fifteen miles away was also bustling with activity. The roof antennas were being retracted and the hardware fastened down for travel. They had miles to go that day and a mountain of data to organize and send to their faraway homeland. As soon as they got to the local cyber café, their mission would be accomplished. Li was glad. He preferred cloak-and-dagger missions to require at least a cloak, if not the dagger, too. This was just too easy.

Chapter 12

Launched twelve months previously on an Atlas V unmanned rocket, the thirteen-thousand-kilogram Lunar Mapper spacecraft had been doing its job of mapping the Moon with quiet precision. Flying just fifty kilometers above the lunar surface in an orbit carrying it from pole to pole, the spacecraft's high-resolution cameras photographed most of the lunar surface. Multiple overflights of the same terrain at different times during the lunar day, and with a slightly different viewing angle due to the Moon's slowly changing orbit, allowed stereoscopic images to be created of most of the lunar surface. With Earth-based processing, a 3-D map of the Moon was created.

The scientists at NASA's Ames Research Center in Mountain View, California, had been studying the images for weeks as they worked to narrow down the landing-site options for Bill Stetson and his crew. They knew the landing would be somewhere near the Moon's equator, selected because it was easier to reach this region of the Moon than the higher latitudes, and because that was where the Apollo missions had explored. They knew that it could be done, so doing it again would be the best and safest way to begin the return of NASA's astronauts to the Moon. For NASA's critics, it would just be another example of NASA's inability to do anything new and different.

On this day, the site-selection team was preparing their final recommendation for NASA Administrator Calvin Ross. Ross had been appointed by the President and had the distinction of being the only former United States senator to be appointed as NASA Administrator. The President had not made NASA a priority, and appointing his former colleague in the Senate, one who had recently been defeated in his reelection campaign, was a signal that he was not taking the direction of America's space program seriously. Ross was neither an engineer nor a scientist. Before becoming a senator, Ross had been an attorney at a prominent Billings, Montana, law firm. Many viewed Ross's appointment as a simple payback for some previous political favor or favors. Few in NASA appreciated his political savvy, and fewer still realized how hard he fought for the agency.

The lead scientist for the site-selection team, Dr. Henry Morton, was standing before a wall-sized mural of the Moon made from images returned from the Lunar Mapper spacecraft. He was wearing 3-D glasses and studying carefully no less than six potential landing sites.

Morton was a career scientist from the prestigious Lunar and Planetary Institute in Houston. He began his career in the late 1970s, when exploring the Moon was no longer "hot." In fact, at that time, studying the Moon was considered career suicide. Funding for lunar research had dried up with the death of Apollo, and Morton kept his interest alive by winning small research grants and by convincing his management to keep his work funded, although at an embarrassingly low level. Morton had quietly waited in the wings until interest in the Moon resurfaced in the mid-2000s. He then quickly rose in prominence to become America's leading expert on all things lunar. It helped that he was also virtually alone in the field. Without consistent funding for lunar science, there simply weren't many others around. It was easier to be a big fish when there was a small pond. And the pond for lunar science had been very small indeed.

"You'd think that since the 1950s we'd have developed a better way to view 3-D than by wearing these god-awful glasses," said Morton to no particular member of his team. They were all assembled and themselves looking at the wall mural. And, without surprise, no one responded directly to his comment. He was prone to complaining about the glasses.

"I'm just amazed that we can see Surveyor and all of the Apollo sites," was the closest thing to a response. The comment came from one of the junior members of the team, Saul Britenstein. He continued. "Look here. As I've been saying, if we land near the Apollo 17 site we can show continuity with our last mission, and maybe even bring back the picture Cernan left on the surface. Wouldn't that be cool?"

"And the science benefit is what?" asked Mariam Upchurch, senior member of the team. Morton had heard that she had begun her career as a *lunatic*, as lunar scientists were sometimes called, back in the early 1980s, when even the International Space Station was yet to be built. Upchurch was interested in the science return of Project Constellation, not the cool technology and the "fun" things that the astronauts might accomplish there. She also had absolutely no inhibitions about sharing her strongly held opinions.

"We've been through this all before, people," said Morton, quickly losing patience with the continuous disagreement among his team about where the Altair should land and where people should again walk on the surface of the Moon. Morton showed his visible frustration by entering what many had come to call his "lecture mode." To an outside observer, his demeanor would have appeared astonishingly similar to that of a parent lecturing a recalcitrant teenager about the dangers of having unprotected sex.

"We know we have to be near the equator. We know we want to be near one of the Apollo sites because we want to bring back a piece of hardware to assess how being on the Moon affected it. And Apollo 11 is out of the question. It will be a historical landmark, and we aren't to mess with it in any way." Morton broke out of the lecture mode to ask a real question. "Saul, other than the picture, what's the benefit of going back to Taurus-Littrow and Apollo 17?"

Morton considered Britenstein to be brilliant. In fact, the twentysomething scientist from the University of Arizona was on Morton's short list of future recruits for the Lunar and Planetary Institute. Britenstein was tall, frighteningly thin, and certainly not among the most attractive half of the human species. Morton more than once wondered how such a brilliant and obviously awkward young man had managed to marry the quite attractive medical student that was his wife. But Morton didn't want to be distracted by *that* thought at the moment.

"Well," began Britenstein, "it was from this area that Schmitt found the rocks that gave us the best history of the Moon to date. I think there is more to be gained from going back here and collecting more samples for comparison. I've shown you the data, and most of the selenologists agree. If you want to better understand the formation of the Moon, this is the place to start. Or, restart, as it were." It was not Britenstein's most eloquent response, but they had all seen his data before. There was no need to repeat it to this group.

Morton, still peering through his 3-D goggles, was looking closely at one of the few lower-resolution images on the Moon mural. Though the Lunar Mapper had been in orbit about a year, there were still a few areas on the Moon that had escaped multidirectional imaging. Some of the gaps were caused by one-of-a-kind mission anomalies; others were caused by the vagaries of the Moon's orbital rotation rate and the slow evolution of the spacecraft's orbit around it. The portion of the image at which Morton was staring was one of those low-resolution areas that would soon be corrected with an upcoming flyover of the spacecraft.

"Look at this," said Morton. His tone was inquisitive, and this drew more of a response from his teammates than his frequent, though never really negative, wry comments and complaints.

"It almost looks like there is another lander here. See the odd shape of this rock? The reflectance data I just pulled up doesn't match a natural rock formation. It looks more like the remains of a spacecraft. But the image is simply too poor to make it out. I looked in the catalog, and there are no known missions that landed near here, neither Soviet nor American. And if the Europeans or Japanese had done it in the last several years, then we would know about it. Very odd."

"Hmm," Upchurch responded, "do you think we've found a crashed flying saucer or something? Hardly likely. More likely another 'Face on Mars' that will go away when we get the better imagery. I'd recommend you forget about it for now."

"Probably not aliens, you think?" Britenstein laughed. "If the data rate were higher, we could watch the Altair land on the surface almost as soon as it actually happens. The cameras on this bird might even be able to resolve Stetson as he takes his first walk across the surface. Now *that* would be cool."

"Mariam, you're right. With only low-resolution data, we cannot recommend the site for a landing anyway. Too risky...Too bad," Morton added. "Now, back to the task at hand. We have two excellent choices that meet all mission criteria. Which shall it be?"

The debate resumed, and the remains of China's failed attempt to land a robot on the Moon remained undiscovered.

Meanwhile, some 240,000 miles away in lunar orbit, the Lunar Mapper spacecraft was following its slowly repeating trajectory around the Moon. Its camera was working flawlessly after nearly a year on the job. If someone had been there looking around, they might have noticed a glint on the horizon, occasionally captured by the spacecraft's primary camera. The camera was pointed toward the lunar surface, and not out into deep space. The glint was photographed a few more times over the next several minutes as the images were sent back to the Earth in nearly real-time by the spacecraft's onboard telemetry system. Data analysis was not conducted in real time, so there was no one looking when the small projectile collided with the Lunar Mapper spacecraft at a relative velocity of four kilometers per second. While the projectile was traveling at less than half the velocity of a spacecraft in low Earth orbit, it was moving eight times faster than a bullet, packing sixty-four times the destructive energy. The collision obliterated the little mapping spacecraft.

Only after the data stopped did anyone look at the last few images sent back to the Earth from lunar orbit; it was then that the "glint" was observed and the idea put forward that the Lunar Mapper was victim to either a piece of space junk or an errant meteorite. Both were incredibly unlikely events, but the reality was something so unlikely that no one even considered it.

The Lunar Mapper spacecraft, set to continue taking high-resolution images of the Moon for at least another half a year, was the victim of a piece of depleted uranium deliberately sent to collide with it. The uranium projectile that impacted the spacecraft had been launched several days before from China. The launch was hailed by China as a lunar flyby mission that would use the Moon to slingshot the spacecraft toward the sun for future solar-weather observations. But unbeknownst to the rest of the world, the real goal of the mission was stopping all high-resolution mapping of the Moon for at least the next two years. Building upon their demonstrated capability to destroy a satellite in Earth orbit, which they did in 2007, China had quietly developed a capability to intercept and destroy any spacecraft in the Earth-Moon system. Lunar Mapper was the first target; no one in China asserted responsibility for the attack or even acknowledged that an attack had taken place. And though analysts in the National Reconnaissance Office later suggested in appropriately classified memoranda that China was responsible, no one at NASA had a clue.

Chapter 13

Calvin Ross was alone in his top-floor office at NASA head-quarters in Washington, D.C., when he received a text message from his friend and former Senate colleague, the Honorable Karen Anderson of Texas. It was just 7:30 a.m. and most NASA workers were still in the middle of their morning commutes. Ross had arrived in the District early and worked out at his favorite gym just down the street. He was in top physical and mental condition, working out each and every morning for at least forty-five minutes before reporting to work.

First running his hands through his full, though now graying, hair, Ross picked up his BlackBerry from between the picture of his wife (whom some called a trophy wife because she was fifteen years his junior and looked great in a tennis outfit) and the digital frame scrolling through twenty years of family pictures.

The message was blunt:

NEWSOME TO REQUEST NASA CUT TO PAY
FOR EDUCATION BUDGET INCREASE.
FIRST MOON FLIGHT TO BE LAST?

"Ha!" Ross laughed out loud. "So, Newsome is going to pay back the teachers unions by killing the one thing that might inspire some of America's kids to become interested in science and technology."

NASA's eighteen-billion-dollar budget was very visible, though very, very small compared to the overall government budget of just over three and a half trillion dollars. But it was considered "discretionary," meaning that it wasn't part of Social Security, Medicare, or National Health. As such, the politicians were free to grandstand and make claims of saving the taxpayers money by cutting it. The reality was stark. If all of NASA were canceled, the money saved wouldn't even pay for the annual growth in spending of the Medicare program, and the unemployment that would follow would create extreme recessions in many states across the country—at least ten of them. Unfortunately, though it made little difference in the overall federal-budget situation, NASA's visibility made it a ripe, juicy target. Ross shifted in his seat, pondering which hotline to activate and which political favors to call due. After, of course, he got the full story from the NASA Legislative Affairs Office.

Though he had no technical background, and certainly no lifelong interest in space or space exploration, Calvin Ross was nonetheless going to protect his budgetary turf. NASA was his to manage, and he was going to manage it, and its full budget, using every skill he possessed and every political maneuver he could manage. For Ross, it was a matter of personal pride to keep the agency under his care from being cut. He was playing "the game," and the rules said that he would be a winner if he kept others from eating his pie. He liked this game and was considered to be good at it, even if his former constituents didn't recognize and reward him for it with reelection.

He had lots of friends in the Senate, and he was about to enlist their support—and that of the legion of Washington lobbyists who had an interest in keeping lucrative government contracts funded and pumping money into their sponsors' coffers.

Ross looked at the message again before responding. OK. IF IT IS A FIGHT HE WANTS, THEN WE'LL GIVE HIM WATERLOO. Satisfied with his somewhat dramatic response, Ross sat back in his chair to once again run his hands through his hair.

"He won't kill us without a fight!"

That night, instead of being alone in his office, Ross was in the company of ten others. Five were aides to senators with NASA facilities in their districts. The other five were the dreaded aerospace lobbyists, present to help preserve the pieces of the budgetary pie that they thought were rightfully theirs. All were discussing the proposed NASA budget cut.

Ross had laid out the scenario to the group shortly after they arrived, some still sporting the remains of a hastily eaten dinner on their carefully pressed Oxford cloth shirts. One of the staffers looked like he'd just been awakened from a night's sleep. Or perhaps he looked like he hadn't slept at all.

Another, a vivacious and piranhalike aide to the Honorable Senator from Texas, looked like she was ready for a night on the town. Dressed totally in black to match her jet-black hair, the neckline on her blouse dipping into dangerous territory due to too many buttons not fastened, she was the kind of staffer Ross had successfully avoided throughout his tenure in the Senate—though it had taken every ounce of willpower he possessed.

The meeting was a classic Washington business meeting with the usual cast of characters. Calvin Ross was in his element, and, of course, he had a plan. He *always* had a plan. Sometimes the trick was in the implementation part of the plan.

"Ahem!" Ross cleared his throat and raised his voice. "Now that we know what the son of a bitch wants to do with the NASA budget, we can stop him. We all know that head-to-head we will lose in any public fight over spending between NASA and Education. Our kids are failing, right? They were failing when I was in school, and they are still failing, despite billions of dollars and decades of patience. No, if the public has to choose between going to the Moon and their little Johnny learning to read—as ridiculous as the choice would be—we will lose.

"No, we can't win that way. But we can convince some of our colleagues that the aerospace jobs in their districts will evaporate if our budget is cut." Nodding to the exhausted-looking staffer, Ross commanded, "Ned, pass out the data you collected earlier today."

Ned, far from being asleep, leapt to his feet, opened the backpack carelessly slung over the back of his chair, and began passing out a neatly stapled set of charts that clearly showed where each and every dollar of NASA's budget was being spent. The first page was a map of the United States with each state highlighted. Typed within each state was a dollar figure—the amount of money in NASA contracts that flowed into that state in the last fiscal year—along with the names and thumbnail images of its two senators. On the next fifty pages were enlarged images of each state, broken down by congressional district; again, within each district, was a dollar figure. And beside each congressional district was a thumbnail image of its representative.

No senator would come away without knowing how much money was at stake in their state. No congressman would remain ignorant of how much money poured directly into his or her district. This was the political game played with its most basic currency—cash.

The last two pages of the handout contained a summary of NASA's Constellation program, describing exactly how they were about take Americans back to the Moon for the first time in over fifty years.

Ross, ever prepared, had read the history of Apollo. He knew very well that the decision to cancel Apollo had been made before Neil Armstrong ever set foot on the lunar surface. The politicians in 1968 decided to pull the rug out from under NASA at the height of its success, and a half century had passed before NASA was able to rebuild the capability it had before most of the people in the room were even born. Ross was not about to let history repeat itself on his watch.

If Bill Stetson or any member of the technical leadership at NASA had been in the room, they would have been apoplectic. For them, seeing over a decade of technical work and planning, the product of thousands of highly trained engineers and scientists working overtime, reduced to less than two pages in a set of over fifty charts would have been simply too much of an insult. This was especially true since only one person in the room even bothered to take the time to look at them. All the rest were too busy looking over the dollar amounts on the various pages. Ross had briefly considered having the NASA Chief Engineer be part of this closed-door meeting, and as he watched the people in the room, he knew he had made the right choice in not inviting him. He would have had a seizure and/or bored the living hell out of the staffers with rocket-science talk while all they wanted to know about were how many votes they were buying.

Ross, sensing that the assembled were now aware of exactly what was at stake, dug in deeper. "In the committee, we can count on at least thirteen of the sixteen votes we need to kill Newsome's amendment to the budget. All thirteen in our column are either real supporters of space exploration, God bless 'em, have a NASA field center in their district, or at least have a major contractor working on the Moon program in there somewhere. It's the other three we have to worry about."

Glancing up from his notes, seemingly unaware of the large ketchup stain adorning the collar of his designer shirt, the aide to the senator from Florida chimed in. "Senator Booker needs support for this year's farm bill. His state has a lot to lose if the subsidies for making corn-based ethanol are cut. I'm sure a few senators could voice their support—after we let him know why he's getting it." Mr. Ketchup pulled his eyeglasses down to the tip of his nose, tilted his head forward and spoke directly to Ms. Piranha. "That would mean your boss would have to eat a little crow and ease off on her comments about pork spending in the farm states."

"I'll see what we can do" was her only response.

Ross watched and inwardly smiled. He knew that her boss would do what it would take to get support for NASA. Her state simply had too much to lose if the money for the Moon contracts stopped flowing. Losing thousands of jobs just before one's six-year term in the Senate was about to be over didn't do a lot for one's reelection chances.

In every group of lobbyists, there was always one who looked the part. In this case, it was Dr. T. Rathbone Smythe of the Aerospace and Aviation Advocacy Committee, or the AAAC, as it preferred to be called. Smythe could have been forty, fifty or even fifty-five years old—old enough to convey experience and authority but not too old as to appear out of touch. With carefully groomed salt-and-pepper hair, and only a hint of a receding hairline, a finely chiseled face and an ever-present tan, Smythe was the type of person who inspired confidence. Living up to his aristocratic-sounding name, Smythe was also a smooth talker and was comfortable making small talk with just about everyone. He was an equal with the elite and a paternalistic supporter of those with lesser social status. Smythe could play the game at all levels. He cleared his throat and entered his opinion into the conversation.

"I can get the other two votes. Senator Lipman is running short on cash for his reelection campaign, and I think our members can step up to the plate to make sure his coffers get refilled."

Smythe looked at the handout showing the funds being spent in a certain Northeastern state—the one which the senator in question called home.

"Good." Ross nodded.

"It would help if these numbers were a little higher." Smythe aimed the comment directly at the NASA Administrator.

"I guess it would." Ross smiled, slightly bemused. "Mr. Smythe, there isn't anything I can do about that. Believe it or not, the career civil servants who make these sorts of decisions are usually quite honest in their reviews, and I could go to jail if I were to try and influence the peer-review process.

"In addition, as you are well aware, contracts are awarded in a competitive process that sometimes takes years from start to finish. Even if I could influence the process, there simply isn't time." Ross didn't want the conversation to go in this direction, especially with so many potential witnesses in the room. He had to shut down that line of discussion before it went places that he didn't care to go.

"Calvin, I wouldn't dream of asking you to do anything unethical. I'm just saying the tasks themselves need more money." Smythe made a convincing response. He took Ross's hint and moved on. "The other vote, well, let's just say I think I can convince another member of the committee to oppose the amendment." He took a long pause before continuing. "Let's just say that a favor is owed."

Ross, again running his hands through his hair, looked around the room at the faces of the aides and lobbyists gathered there. *Washington's finest,* he thought to himself before speaking out loud his final thoughts.

"Let's do it, then. The amendment will be offered sometime next week. Can we get the support to kill it in place by then?"

One by one, heads in the room nodded—all of them. When compared to the overall federal budget, NASA's budget was small. But when put on an individual or corporate level, its eighteen-billion-dollar annual appropriation was still enough to make many people rich, and it was simply too much to be ignored by anyone with half a brain. And these people, and the ones they represented, certainly had more than half a brain when it came to the dog-eat-dog of politics.

)　●　●　●　(

One week later, the amendment offered by the Chair of the Senate Appropriations Committee, an amendment to reduce wasteful spending on a boondoggle program to explore the Moon and to channel the money instead into Education for the nation's vulnerable youth, went down to defeat. The Honorable Senator Newsome, the author of the amendment, was not pleased.

Watching from the gallery, NASA Administrator Calvin Ross *was*. He had protected his turf and shown that he still had what it took to be a player in Washington.

Chapter 14

Stetson heard the news from his Houston office, as he was reviewing the latest landing-site recommendations from Dr. Morton's team. Like most in his generation, Stetson was an expert at multitasking the inflow of information. Instant messages, e-mail, tweets, texts, and a customized space news feed scrolling across the lower portion of his computer screen and cell phone were simply part of his everyday life, and he didn't seem fazed by the constant flood of often-irrelevant data. One headline scrolling across his computer's news bar did catch his eye.

SPACE RACE HEATS UP AS CHINESE LAUNCH
UNMANNED MISSION TO THE MOON

He glanced away from Morton's charts and clicked on the headline.

> Following in America's footsteps, the Chinese government today announced the successful launch of their own unmanned mission to the Moon. The spacecraft, said to be identical to the one that will carry Chinese taikonauts to the Moon in the future, will be controlled robotically. The Chinese Minister for Space said that the mission would test all of the systems required to send a

crew to the lunar surface. "This mission will be the final dress rehearsal before China is the first country in over fifty years to have its citizens walk on another planet," the minister said. There is not yet any official reaction from Washington, but independent experts widely believe America will win this new race to the Moon despite the recent technical difficulties with NASA's lunar dress rehearsal and the rumors starting to circulate that the launch scheduled in two weeks may again slip.

"What the hell?" Stetson cursed before picking up his cell phone and calling Jim England. At first, he didn't think his friend was going to answer. The phone had just started to roll over into voice mail when he heard the familiar Southern drawl of his colleague. "Yeah-us, hello?"

"Jim, this is Bill. Did you hear about the Chinese launch? It's on the ticker now."

"Yeah, I heard. I haven't gotten anything through channels, only what I've seen on the Net. Looks like we're going to beat 'em— but not by much. I doubt they can turn around another launch before you go. If they hadn't decided to play it safe with a test, we'd be looking up at a Chinese Moon in a few days."

"Luck, all right. I really don't like the idea of us being second to anyone in space, and this is all just too close for comfort. And can you believe that Senator Newsome? We're not even on the Moon yet, and he tried to pull the rug out from under us. I wonder if he will say anything about the Chinese." Stetson could barely contain himself. As he spoke, his voice grew louder and his posture stiffened.

"Well, try not to let it get your goat, Bill."

"I'd like to get that senator's goat and barbecue it. Maybe we should send him to China for a few years. That would teach him about how their politicians and people feel about space and space exploration. Over there the astronauts are treated like heroes and the public demands more of their space efforts, not less."

"Yeah. And I guess I have to give Ross credit for saving us on that one. Did you see his testimony in Congress? He really stepped up and made a compelling case for exploration—how could they have voted for that cut after they heard from him about all the technical benefits we'll get from going to the Moon?"

"Yeah," Stetson reluctantly agreed. "You're right, you know. I originally thought Ross was just another politician who didn't give a rip about NASA. But he did come through for us. It was nice to see rationality win on that one."

"Bill, I'm gonna switch gears on you, buddy."

"Go."

"Space Excursions is launching next week—on Monday."

Stetson's posture relaxed, and he leaned back in his chair. He had a lot of admiration for Space Excursions. They'd come out of nowhere and built an impressive system for taking tourists into space. And they'd done it all in about ten years. He didn't know Gary Childers personally, but he respected him nonetheless. He thought to himself, *That man is a leader. Why isn't he running NASA?* And then he answered himself. *Because he makes a lot more money running his business than he would working for the government.* This all happened too fast for England to notice that his friend's thoughts had wandered.

"Jim, I wish them all the best. The Chinese haven't even sent anyone to fly by the Moon and an American company is about to go. That means not only NASA will beat them there. A bunch of lunatic, freewheeling, money-hungry capitalists will get there ahead of them, too! I'm all for it. God bless America!" Stetson said, very animated.

"Bill, the press is all over this. You really need to read the blogs more often. They're all about how this guy Childers is going to the Moon for a fraction of what it cost us—and the taxpayer—and how we should just turn over all of NASA to private industry."

"And, you know, sometimes I think they're right. This whole thing *has* taken too long. We should have been there years ago!" Bill replied. Stetson could tell it was time for his friend to get agitated. These two had this discussion, or one very similar to it, at least five times a month. It wasn't boring; they loved it. But before, it was just hypothetical. This time real people were about to fly in real rocket ships to the Moon. One ship was going to carry tourists on a joyride around the Moon. The other was going to carry scientists to its surface. And the latter was much more complicated, and expensive, than the former.

"Jim, we've had this discussion before. What they're doing is a piece of cake compared to going to the surface. You and I both know that. Don't sell them short, though. It is still dangerous as all get-out."

"Bill, yes, *we* know that. But the public doesn't!" England was emphatic. "Sometimes I wonder why we care so much."

Stetson was unprepared for that one, but it did ratchet down the emotion and the volume of the discussion. Everyone involved in the space business, government or private, had probably asked themselves that same question at one time or another. Some asked it many times. "Why do I care about it so much?" For Stetson, the answer was simple. Because it was there, and that meant that someone, and it might as well be him, needed to go "there" and explore.

He knew how Childers would answer if he'd been on the phone and asked the question. Stetson was confident that Childers would talk about how there was money to be made on the Moon and how he was going to be the one to make it.

Not realizing he was mumbling out loud as his thoughts once again wandered, Stetson said, "You can't argue with that." He was, of course, talking about Childers's likely motivation for going to the Moon, though England had no way of knowing that.

"Huh? What's that you said?" asked England.

"It was nothing. Spaced out on you for a second. I wonder why we do care so much sometimes."

Gesling heard the news just after he crash-landed the *Dreamscape* in the Nevada desert. During this latest simulation, the vehicle experienced a complete loss of pressure during reentry, followed by a premature deployment of the landing gear—at twenty thousand feet. The result was a pretty messy landing, without gear, at the Nevada Spaceport. The passenger cabin remained in one piece, and the sensors indicated that at no time did the g-forces cross the line into "fatal." If this had been real life, and not a simulation, Space Excursions would have been very glad they had a good team of lawyers.

As Gesling extricated himself from the pilot's chair, which was not an easy task for someone of his height, he heard the voice of Caroline O'Conner chatting on her cell phone just outside the *Dreamscape* simulator. She was fairly excited and asking whomever she was speaking with to e-mail her the complete details of whatever they were discussing. He liked Caroline, not in a romantic sort of way, but as a friend and overall decent person to be around. He always looked forward to spending more time with her. Perhaps he was beginning to enjoy her company too much....

"Paul!" He was roused from his musings by her voice calling his name. As he hesitated to respond, she raised her voice. "Paul! Over here! You'll want to know about this."

Gesling was finally free of the harness holding him and his bulky pressure suit to the pilot's chair. Though he couldn't yet exit the simulator because of the numerous to-do items remaining on his checklist, he did motion for Caroline to step inside.

"Hey, Caroline. What's up?"

"The Chinese just launched their complete lunar system. They're conducting a robotic test run end-to-end. The news is saying this means they may be on the Moon within a couple of months."

"Are they flying a *Dreamscape*?" asked Gesling, sarcasm dripping from every word.

"Ha!" O'Conner cocked her head backward and looked down her nose at Gesling, which was difficult since he was easily eight inches taller than she. "No, they aren't *yet* flying a *Dreamscape*. But the Moon is going to be crowded these next few weeks. The Chinese test flight began today. We launch next week, and NASA is supposed to fly the week after that. We haven't been to the Moon in half a century, and now everyone will be going—within a few weeks of each other. We couldn't have planned it this way if we'd tried. Gary is gonna be ecstatic!"

Gesling was hearing her words, but for some reason he was distracted by the way she raised her right eyebrow as she looked "down" at him in her best schoolteacher manner. It really accented her green eyes and high cheekbones. Before long, he wasn't even hearing her words anymore.

"...Lunar surface trips for Space Excursions." Caroline paused, wondering why there had been no reaction from Paul. "Paul? Are you in there?"

"Oh, yeah, sorry about that. I was just thinking about the simulation," he lied. "What did you say?"

"Sometimes I wonder about you!" was her first reaction. She then said, "Gary told me this morning that he's signed a deal with investors to begin our own lunar-landing effort. He's going to announce it after you return from the Moon. I think he wants to tell you himself, so please don't let on that I already told you."

Gesling was not totally surprised; he and Childers had spoken several times about what the next step would be for Space Excursions. He just hadn't expected it to come so soon. He at first thought he should bolt to Childers's office and give him every opportunity to break the news. Then he remembered the post-simulation checklist and procedures. But even that took second place to finishing the conversation with Caroline. Yes, he would definitely have to make more time for talking with her.

The U.S. military took notice of what the Chinese were doing as well. Before the media knew of the launch, the U.S. Space Command was already on top of it. Headquartered at Peterson Air Force Base in Colorado, Space Command had been informed in advance of the Chinese plans and had the appropriate air and space assets in place to monitor all aspects of the launch and its early flight. Thanks to excellent human intelligence from within the China National Space Administration, American intelligence and the U.S. Space Command were watching as the Chinese version of the American Ares V lifted off from central China on its way to the Moon.

Pictures taken from the Pentagon's low Earth-orbit spacecraft could literally read the lettering on the side of the rocket as it passed on its way to Trans-Lunar Injection. Additional spacecraft in geostationary orbit were retargeted to make similar observations as the vehicle accelerated away from the Earth. The launch was flawless.

The Chinese had opted for a lunar orbit rendezvous approach. Like Apollo, they were going to launch the entire vehicle, including the crew and the lunar lander, on one rocket. Unlike the United States, whose lunar missions would use two rockets, one for crew and the other for all the hardware required for reaching the Moon, the Chinese opted for just one. They had no International Space Station to service with the crew-launch vehicle, so the idea, and cost, of building two rockets was simply out of the question.

To those monitoring the flight and listening to all the telemetry and voice chatter from the Chinese ground controllers, this seemed to be a full dress rehearsal for the real thing. As far as anyone could tell, the Chinese were treating this like a crewed launch and dotting all their i's to make sure it went according to plan. Signals-intelligence stations were even picking up mock-up voice-data channels going back and forth between the ground and the rocket.

As good as American intelligence was, they still could not decode in real time all of the telemetry coming back from the rocket. The encryption was too good, and it would take some time to decipher. The data was passed off to the supercomputer center at the National Security Agency with top priority for decryption. The code-breaker wizards there would figure it out soon enough. Unfortunately, it would not be deciphered for at least a week, because there was already a priority cipher in the queue—and a few surprises would have been avoided had they been able to decode it just a little bit faster.

Before the press knew what was going on, appropriate phone calls were made to the White House and the Pentagon about the Chinese launch. Within an hour, Calvin Ross was aware of the flight and had called the manager of the NASA Public Affairs Office, asking him to be prepared to take the inevitable questions from the media. And once the story broke, the phone calls started coming in.

In China, when the news broke, the public was euphoric. Spontaneous rallies broke out at China's major engineering universities, with the students carrying homemade banners extolling both their space agency and their political leaders. Schoolchildren began writing letters to the taikonauts who, they were told, would be taking the first piloted journey in just a few months. Companies that had made hardware for the flight convened "all hands" meetings of their employees, allowing them to take time off to watch televised replays of the rocket launch and the animations of what the rocket would be doing in space during its voyage to the surface of the Moon.

For China, it was a day of national pride and anticipation. Anticipation of the next step, expected in a scant few months, that would carry three Chinese taikonauts to the Moon and show the world that China had "arrived."

Oddly enough, the public in archrival India celebrated as well. The world's largest democracy, though much poorer than its Western cousins, had made tremendous strides in space exploration over the previous decade. India itself was only a few years away from sending vyomanauts into Earth orbit. Seeing another formerly backward country be on the edge of accomplishing what only one of the last century's superpowers could attain was a cause for celebration. Engineers were jealous. Politicians were eager to use the moment to promote India's growing technological prowess. And the average Indian looked forward to their own day on the Moon.

In America, few noticed and even fewer really cared. And fewer still understood the technical implications and political ramifications. In America, it was just another day and another headline about something happening "over there somewhere."

Chapter 15

"This is it!" Paul Gesling said into the camera that transmitted his image from the cockpit of the *Dreamscape* to the five passengers strapped into their seats behind him in the crew cabin. "In a few days, you'll be the first people since the Apollo astronauts to go to the Moon and back. I know the training has sometimes been less than fun, but what we're about to do will make history and give you something to tell your grandchildren about. You are going to get your money's worth—and then some!"

Not wanting to be distracted from his preflight checklist any longer, Gesling turned back to the forward view screen and instrument panel. With the press of a virtual button on the touch screen, he turned off his audio but left the video feed on. Gary Childers insisted that the paying customers have a chance to see what the hired help was up to in all stages of the mission.

The *Dreamscape* was certainly living up to its name. Perched on the Nevada desert runway like a large and beautiful bird, it was about to take flight. The engines were running, producing the telltale heat exhaust, causing the air behind the vehicle to distort light in unusual ways, making objects appear to ripple in the heat of the mid-day sun. Crisscrossing orange and red plasma streams poured into a billowing exhaust cloud of puffy white steam. Emblazoned on the front of the spaceship was its name, the corporate emblem of Space Excursions, and a big American flag. Gary Childers was in business to make money, but he was also a proud American.

Within the vehicle, hundreds of sensors were measuring electrical current in numerous subsystems, fluid temperatures, and the mechanical status of anything and everything that had to move or rotate in order for *Dreamscape* to make its upcoming voyage.

As the passengers waited anxiously in their seats, the shrill whine of the jet engines increased in volume as one of the last preflight tests was run to completion.

Gesling was pleased. So far, all systems were operating as they should, and the launch countdown was proceeding on schedule. In just another few minutes, he would ease off the brakes, throttle up, and begin the journey down the runway. *Piece of cake,* he thought to himself.

Now it was time for Gesling to examine the crew in the last of his preflight checklists. This checklist was not one that the FAA required; rather, it was one Gary Childers mandated. First, he was to look over the vital signs of each passenger, as relayed to the display to his left inside the cockpit. From here he could monitor their heart rate, blood pressure, body temperature, and virtually every other organ in their bodies. Each had been benchmarked against their physiological profiles during training, and the current results were meticulously compared with their earlier results by the onboard computer. If any were out of the anticipated bounds for this, the real thing, then Gesling was authorized to have them removed from the vehicle. The Moon was nearly a quarter million miles away from the nearest hospital, and under no circumstances could the health of any passenger jeopardize the mission (or its profitability and good press coverage).

The second part of the Childers Checklist was highly subjective. Paul was to look over the faces of each passenger and determine if any looked like they were about to panic or faint. Again, this could be cause for removal—but Paul knew that if he exercised this option and the passenger turned out to be okay, his future piloting opportunities with Space Excursions would be limited indeed.

The *Dreamscape* was designed with seats much like those of a commercial jet. There was one pilot seat up front in the middle of the cockpit. Behind the pilot seat was the "aisle," and on either side was one seat. Each passenger therefore had an aisle and a window. The seats were numbered in rows and lettered for the side of the aisle they were on. Seats 1A and 2A were on the left side of the aisle. Seats 1B, 2B, and 3B were on the right. Where seat 3A would have been was where the docking/boarding hatch was located. And behind seat 3B was the bathroom and storage-container wall. Each of the seats was designed for full reclining to allow for sleeping on the long lunar flights. But at present all the seats were upright and filled with occupants.

Paul looked at Matt Thibodeau in seat 1A. The arrogant SOB looked calm enough. He was in his seat, glancing around the cabin, out the window, and then down at the status screen on the back of the chair in front of his seat. If it weren't for the pressure suit, he would look like any other bored businessman taking an airplane flight to some other city for a business meeting. Gesling didn't much like Thibodeau, but there was no obvious reason to remove him.

Next, he glanced at Maquita Singer, the millionaire owner of South Africa's Singer Luxury Hotels, who sat in seat 1B. She was definitely nervous, her eyes darting around the cabin, not remaining on any one spot for more than a few seconds. Paul examined her vital signs again and saw that they were elevated but absolutely normal for someone about to accelerate from a dead stop to over twenty-four thousand miles per hour, leave the bounds of Earth's gravity for the first time in their life, travel nearly a quarter million miles through deadly vacuum to orbit the Moon, and then travel back to land here in the desert. No, this wasn't to be a normal day in the boardroom of a luxury-hotel chain.

Paul rolled his eyes when he looked at Sharik Mbanta in seat 2A. Mbanta was staring to his left, across the aisle, directly at Singer. The man who tried to bed every woman on the training staff apparently wasn't thinking about going to the Moon. To Paul, he looked like he was thinking about how he could join the "More Than A Mile High" Club with Ms. Singer. Aloud, Gesling muttered, "I can't believe this guy." But his vital signs were also normal, and Paul really had no firm basis for ejecting him from the flight—other than extreme dislike.

Bridget Wells in seat 2B looked as cool as she had in all phases of the training that led up to this moment. She was blond with only a little gray, in her mid-fifties, and in excellent physical condition. A mother of two from Marshalltown, Iowa, she looked like just about every other soccer mom one might expect to run into at the supermarket. By looking at her, one would think there was no way she could come up with the money to pay for a trip to the Moon, but Paul did know and understand why she had so eagerly paid millions to have a seat on *Dreamscape*. She was a believer.

During training, Bridget had told Gesling her story. She was born a couple of years before Neil Armstrong walked on the Moon and had no memory of watching it happen—she was too young. When Bridget was about twelve, she discovered science fiction and became hooked. She read all the classic science fiction writers, including Robert Heinlein, Arthur C. Clarke, and Isaac Asimov. She didn't have a math aptitude, so she didn't go down an engineering path for a career in the space business. But she never lost her interest. She had written more than eight screenplays for science fiction movies that had turned out to be blockbusters. It was from these movies that she had earned her millionaire status. Early in her training she told Paul of watching the NASA TV channel for hours at a time, wishing that she were the one in space. *Dreamscape* gave her the chance to live her dream and aboard her she sat, grinning like a kid in a candy store, ready to go to the Moon. All her vital signs were normal, and Paul was hoping that she, more than all the others, would have the trip of a lifetime.

Finally, there was Dr. John Graves. Graves, too, was in his mid-fifties, but he was not nearly as trim and fit as Bridget, nor, for that matter, as any other passenger. In fact, he almost didn't get to fly due to his weight. If he hadn't lost the required forty pounds, someone else would be sitting here rather than him. Even so, no one would say he looked "fit and trim." Graves was an engineer and vice president at a major computer company, and, like Bridget Wells, he was a believer. The big difference between him and Ms. Wells, other than his sex and overall physical condition, was his attitude. Graves treated the flight as something he deserved. Though he was never quite rude, Gesling knew that in Graves's eyes he was merely the bus driver. Graves sat stiffly in his chair, his body rigid and his head unmoving as if afraid the *Dreamscape* would suddenly take off with acceleration sufficient to rip it off his shoulders. His vital signs were elevated, but still within the bounds of what the flight computer considered normal for a passenger at this point of the trip.

Gesling made note that the passenger assessments were complete and focused back on the prelaunch checklist and the status screens. He told his flight controller that *Dreamscape* was ready for takeoff.

The United States Federal Aviation Administration had long-since cleared the sky for miles around the Nevada Spaceport. Otherwise, there would have been the inevitable stray airplane or errant news reporter wanting to cover the *Dreamscape*'s flight from too close to the launch site.

Thousands of spectators were present, filling the highways around the spaceport. Reminiscent of the earliest of the rocket flights of the 1960s, the mood among those gathered to watch the launch was akin to that of groupies at a rock concert or hard-core partiers. And party they did. This was a big day for anyone who ever thought they might want to go into space. *Dreamscape* was about to take five everyday people (aside from the fact that they were rich enough to pay for the flight) to the Moon. For many, this was the unfulfilled promise of Apollo and NASA, and it was about to happen for real.

"Okay, we're going around the horn," Paul announced over the intercom. "I want a thumbs-up, a smile, and your name and status just like we've trained." Paul toggled the screen to show five sections. Each split-screen section had a corresponding seat number and occupant name above it.

"Seat 1A, status?"

"Matt Thibodeau is A-OK!"

"Seat 1B, status?"

"Maquita Singer is A-OK!"

"Seat 2A, status?"

"Sharik Mbanta is A-OK!"

"Seat 2B, status?"

"Bridget Wells is A-OK!"

"Seat 3B, status?"

"John Graves is A-OK!"

"Roger that. *Dreamscape* crew is good to go." Paul gave them all the green light and returned the thumbs-up and smile. "Control, our checklist is clear, and we are all systems go."

"Roger that, *Dreamscape*. All systems are go for launch."

In addition to the space enthusiasts, the Honda minivan was back, antenna deployed, positioned to monitor the *Dreamscape* launch from its chosen observation post fifteen miles away—the occupants doing their jobs for their country. That didn't stop them from also reveling in the moment, for they, too, harbored an interest in going to space. Watching *Dreamscape* start to roll down the runway was just as exciting for them as it was for all those at or near the spaceport. They just wanted to make sure that there was enough data captured for their countrymen to someday duplicate the feat.

The acceleration pushed Paul back into the webbing that secured him to his seat. He could feel the skin on his cheekbones being pulled back toward his ears. He could hear his heartbeat and feel the kick to his abdomen as the *Dreamscape*'s scramjet engaged at a little over twenty thousand feet. The whine of the engines was only momentarily loud before the cabin's active soundproofing kicked in and diminished it to something just short of a deafening dull roar.

Just a few feet away from Gesling and the five passengers, *Dreamscape*'s engines began running in ramjet mode, with the airflow into the engine traveling at something less than the speed of sound. As velocity increased, so did the speed of the air coming into the engines.

All systems were working as they should, and Paul saw no warning lights. He watched the *Dreamscape*'s velocity steadily increase from Mach 1 to Mach 2, and, in just a few short seconds, to Mach 3, then 4. At Mach 8 the engine switched from ramjet to scramjet mode as the air flowing into the engine's inlet became self-sustaining at hypersonic velocities. Now the vehicle was truly hauling ass and accelerating toward its top airspeed of Mach 12.

While Gesling was focused on the vehicle, the passengers were taking note that the Earth now appeared to be rather small, with noticeable curvature. The "ah ha!" moment came first to Maquita Singer, and she couldn't help but voice her observation, "It's a planet after all. Where are the borders? It's just one planet. This is truly amazing!" Her comment elicited a grunt from Thibodeau and a nod from Dr. Graves.

"It's called the overview effect," Bridget Wells commented knowingly. "Since the sixties, many astronauts independently made the same observation once they got up here. There've been books written about it—I read them all doing research for the last television series I was writing for."

Another grunt came from Thibodeau.

Gesling and all the passengers felt the hard slap of the first stage separating. The scramjet first stage had done its job and propelled the *Dreamscape* to twelve times the speed of sound. It was now time for it to fly back to the landing site for refurbishment and repair.

A fraction of a second later, the upper-stage rocket motor ignited, once again pushing everyone back sharply into their seats. The rocket continued accelerating the *Dreamscape* as it left the last remnants of Earth's atmosphere and entered interplanetary space.

The passengers, now astronauts, stared out their windows at the spherical blue Earth beneath them. The thin haze that was the atmosphere enveloped the globe, and sunlight glinted off the now-useless wings on the right side of *Dreamscape*. Above them was pure darkness until their eyes grew accustomed to it and they were then able to see the stars.

Gesling saw all this, and more. But he didn't have time to appreciate the beauty and grandeur. He had a job to do. So far there were no warning lights, and all systems appeared to be working as designed. A few minutes into the checklist, the onboard Global Positioning System locked on to four satellites, the inertial-navigation unit spun up, and the exterior star trackers started mapping their orientation. The amalgam of the three systems input data into the ship's computer, which in turn calculated *Dreamscape*'s exact orbital position and orientation with respect to the Earth and space.

"GPS acquired," Gesling said. "Computer: nav-lock to depot." He didn't often use the computer's voice-recognition program, but in this case he made an exception. A few moments later, projected on the heads-up display as if written by a ghostly unseen companion, the trajectory the computer plotted between his current location and the nearly co-orbital refueling station appeared before him. Relieved, Gesling spoke to his ground controllers. "I've got the trajectory to the depot plotted and am about to engage. We're right where we're supposed to be, and we should rendezvous in less than three orbits."

"Roger that, *Dreamscape*."

"Control, we're ready for OOB in forty-five."

"Roger that, *Dreamscape*. Clock shows OOB on schedule."

"Warning, prepare for orbital orientation burn." The Bitchin' Betty's voice chimed throughout the little spacecraft. "In three, two, one."

The thrusters fired, rolling and pitching the ship over to the upside-down-and-backward flight configuration. The ship jostled a bit and then settled down as the thrusters halted the ship in just the right position so that the occupants could get a really good view of the Earth from their side and overhead windows.

Only then did Gesling have time to check on his passengers' physical status. He glanced to his side at the cabin view screen and pretty much saw what he expected. Thibodeau had opened his visor and was puking his guts out into the low-pressure barf bag attached to his seat. The low-airflow suction attached to the bottom of the bag kept the liquid from floating around the cabin as the system pulled it into the onboard sewage tank.

Maquita Singer and Sharik Mbanta were both green at the gills, and hearing Thibodeau lose his lunch was about to send them over the edge also. Space sickness was very common, and almost everyone going into space experienced it. There was no good reason for one person to get sick and another not. It just happened. Gesling was pleased that Thibodeau was among those afflicted.

Bridget Wells and the stuffy Dr. Graves were unaffected. They glanced somewhat nervously at their stricken colleagues and then promptly looked back out the windows.

Gesling assessed the urgency of the situation and decided that it wasn't too bad. Their training had prepared them for space sickness, and it appeared that they had paid attention to that lesson.

"Matt, Sharik, and Maquita, I would recommend you do your best to reset your inner ear with the exercise we trained on. If you need meds, let me know." Paul did his job. He looked at the five-sectioned monitor reporting on each of the crew members. Those who were sick began shaking their heads madly, to reset the balance system in their inner ears. Astronauts had learned that trick from watching cats fall out of trees—or at least that was the story Paul had heard. "We're going around the horn. If you can make it, I want a verbal and a thumbs-up."

"Matt?"

"Uhm, good, *gulp*," he groaned from around the barf bag and gave a thumbs-up.

"Maquita?"

"Good." She gave a thumbs-up and seemed to be locking her jaws to keep from being sick again.

"Sharik?"

"A-OK," he got out before having to cover with the barf bag again. He did manage a thumbs-up.

"Bridget?"

"A-OK, Paul." Paul smiled as she gave her thumbs-up. The woman was a trooper.

"John?"

"A-OK, Paul."

"Alright, good. Bridget, you can start bringing the telescope online at your leisure," Paul told the occupant of seat 2B. After all, running the telescope was her job.

"Roger that, Paul. Bringing the ISR package online." Paul could see the icon for the system turn from red to green and could tell that it was being handled.

A few hours later, Thibodeau was still recovering while Wells and Graves were busily eating a snack and looking at the really awesome imagery coming through the telescope system as well as looking out the windows. Singer and Mbanta were drinking and playing with their water. Without gravity, any spilled water formed nearly perfect spheres and floated like little planets around those who were attempting to drink. Any of the foods or liquids not captured by the crew would hopefully be filtered and captured with the air-handling system. Drops of water or foodstuff might prove a problem if they were to seep into some of the ship's critical circuitry, but the ship was designed with sealed components to prevent just that from happening.

One by one the crew unstrapped and began bouncing around the cabin from wall to wall, chasing food globules and generally enjoying their weightlessness. For the most part the nausea had subsided—for the most part. Thibodeau still looked a little pale around the edges. To Gesling and the ground crew, who were watching the antics in the passenger cabin on closed-circuit television, they looked like a bunch of kids on the playground. But Paul had to admit that he had done the exact same thing on his first mission into microgravity. In fact, as far as he could tell, all the astronauts throughout history had done similar antics.

Paul believed they were all thoroughly enjoying their ride and was planning to remark to Childers that their customers were definitely getting their money's worth and the trip to the Moon hadn't yet even begun.

"Alright, everyone, strap in and prepare for docking with the refueling station." Paul waited until all the crew safety-restraint icons showed locked and in place before he toggled the automated docking-alignment thrusters routine. The thrusters fired and reoriented the ship so that it was still flying upside down, but now nose first.

"Extending refueling probe," he said as he tapped the controls. The probe extended from just under the nose of the little spacecraft to a point about twenty feet out in front of it.

"Control, this is *Dreamscape*. We've got the tanker's drogue in the crosshairs. Lidar shows we are right on target at three thousand feet and closing."

"Roger that, Paul. Telemetry tracking is good."

"Cycling the pumps and prop-tankage cryo."

"All systems look good to us, Paul. We show one thousand feet."

"Roger that, Control. Nine hundred seventy feet and closing. Still in the crosshairs." Paul gently placed his hand around the stick and prepared for the hand-off of the automated system's control of the ship's flight control. The smaller microthrusters on the end of the flexible probe tube were still on auto. The pilot would roughly guide the ship into the "basket" or "funnel" of the drogue on the refueling spacecraft. But the sensors would maneuver the end of the probe for precise corrections.

"*Dreamscape* has control of the probe and closing at five hundred feet."

"Roger that, *Dreamscape*. Looking good and go for refuel."

"Contact in ten seconds." Paul could feel sweat beading on his forehead, but he didn't have time to wipe it away. He maintained his focus as he guided the little proboscis into the refueling portal. Boom and drogue was how pilots had refueled aircraft for decades, and Paul had thousands of hours of practice in aircraft and several thousand hours in the simulator. He'd also actually docked with the refueling tank once during the orbital test flight. It was all well rehearsed, but he was still nervous as hell.

The boom clicked into place in the drogue, and the flex hose oscillated up and down slightly as the thrusters of the *Dreamscape* matched orbital velocity with the tank ship perfectly. The tube continued to jiggle only slightly.

"Bingo! We're hooked up and ready for refueling."

Gesling leaned back and took a moment to wipe his forehead with the back of his hand. He also let out a sigh of relief. One slight misjudgment on his part could have damaged the system and not allowed them to refuel—that would have ended the mission and sent them all home. A slightly worse than "slight" misjudgment could have sent a mechanical vibration down the tube that could buckle the tube and rupture the tank—that would have ended the mission in a fireball, and nobody would have made it home.

"*Dreamscape,* we show flow at one hundred gallons per minute nominal."

"Roger that, Control. We're refueling, and all systems are in the green."

Paul checked the crew's vitals and faces. They were all fine and appeared to be having the times of their lives.

"Ladies and gentlemen, this is your captain speaking. We have now passed through nine hundred eighty thousand feet, so feel free to unbuckle yourselves and move about the cabin." He added a little chuckle at the end to keep the mood light. Why not let them have their fun while the *Dreamscape* refilled its tanks at the orbiting depot to which it was now attached?

Maquita performed her mission then, which was to use external cameras to video all docking and landing procedures throughout the mission. She sat at her seat guiding the external cameras via the touch-screen panel at her station.

After the *Dreamscape's* tanks were full, Gesling set about the undocking process to detach from the depot and take up station a few kilometers away for the "night." He and the passengers would close the covers on their windows, darken the interior of *Dreamscape,* and try to get eight hours of sleep. He doubted that many would be able to sleep, but they'd been awake for almost eighteen hours and definitely needed a rest.

At Space Excursions' Nevada Spaceport, Gary Childers was jubilant. After the press conference, he granted no less than eight one-on-one interviews with various media outlets and was basking in the free and positive news coverage. Childers knew the value of free publicity, and he was definitely getting more than he had imagined possible. The *Dreamscape* and her passengers were in space and getting ready to go to the Moon.

In just a few hours, Gesling would awaken the passengers, run through his final checklist, and ignite the rocket engine that would take the *Dreamscape* out of Earth orbit and toward the Moon. The trip to the Moon would take a little more than three days.

Childers knew that once the main engine fired, they would be committed. The trajectory they would fly was called "free return" for a very good reason. Like Apollo 13, but hopefully without the peril, the spacecraft would fly by and around the Moon one time, not going into orbit, but rather looping behind the Moon and then coasting back to Earth. The main engine would fire again when the *Dreamscape* was ready to brake and again be captured into Earth orbit—after completing its historic journey around the Moon. The next flight, assuming there would be customers for it, would fire braking thrusters and enter orbit around the Moon. But that was the future. At the moment a "free return" was still a groundbreaking accomplishment for private industry.

Childers wasn't nervous about this aspect of the trip. He would only get nervous after Gesling brought the ship back to Earth orbit and prepared for landing. Getting from orbit to the ground was the part that haunted Childers. He remembered the *Columbia* space shuttle accident—he was at the Kennedy Space Center when STS-107 was supposed to land, and he would never forget the look on the faces of the ground crew when the ship didn't appear on schedule and they realized something must have gone horribly wrong. Their faces still haunted him, and the vision of his beloved *Dreamscape* breaking up high in the atmosphere was his nightmare. He was confident in his ship, his team, and in Paul Gesling—but he wouldn't really relax until the ship was safely home and the passengers giving their own interviews on all the news networks.

At his home in Houston, Bill Stetson watched the interview with Gary Childers as he sipped a cold Long Island iced tea. Sitting with his wife, during their last evening together before he was to leave for Florida, Stetson, too, was jubilant.

"That man ought to be running NASA," said Stetson.

Terry, his wife of twenty-two years, looked up from the image of Gary Childers centered on their television screen, placed her head in the crook of Stetson's outstretched arm, and said simply, "Oh?"

"He's got what most managers at NASA lost years ago—guts. This man risked his personal fortune to start a company and do something that even most governments couldn't do. He's sending people to the Moon. Now, granted, he's not landing, and that's a damned sight harder. But he is sending people to the Moon. If we had more leaders like him, I'd be going to Mars next week instead of the Moon."

"And how long would that take you away from me?" she asked.

"Well, about three years."

"I see," she said, wrinkling her nose in distaste and snuggling a little closer to her husband. "Bill Stetson, you will not be away from me for three years. Having you gone for a month will be too long as it is." She looked him in the eyes and moved her head forward until her lips were only a few inches from his.

"The kids won't be back for another two hours. Fred and Linda took them out to get dessert, and that means we have this great big house all to ourselves until they get back...." Her voice trailed off.

"Hmm. Well, Mrs. Stetson, whatever shall we do to keep ourselves occupied while the kids are away?"

Inching her way still closer to the husband she was about to lose for a month, the man who was about to be separated from her by a quarter of a million miles, she replied, "We'll think of something."

"Mission control, this is Stetson." He leaned in and kissed his wife softly but quickly. "We are go for launch."

Chapter 16

The three-day trip to the Moon passed quickly. Gesling observed that simply looking out the windows as the Earth diminished in size and the Moon grew ever larger was enough to keep most of the passengers mesmerized for hours at a time. Mealtime continued to be a mixture of eating and playing, though the personal aerial acrobatics had lost some of its luster after the initial thrill of their weightless experience had worn off.

Gesling also noted that, true to form, Mbanta did hit on both Bridget Wells and Maquita Singer. Wells was obviously offended and now did everything in her power to keep away from the Sudanese millionaire. Singer, who also refused Mr. Mbanta's advances, acted like nothing at all had happened. She chatted with him no differently than she did any other passenger. Mbanta also acted as if nothing had happened and even seemed somewhat puzzled by Wells's avoiding him. Gesling chalked that one up to the two being from radically different cultures. Mbanta was born to wealth and privilege and considered casual sex to be nothing more significant than a dinner date. Wells, on the other hand, had much more conservative moral views and wouldn't dream of having a casual relationship with anyone, let alone someone she hardly knew, and especially since she was married.

They were only about an hour away from passing within one hundred miles of the lunar surface as they began the looped trajectory that would take them behind the Moon to their closest view of ten miles up and then back around and toward the Earth. Gesling left the pilot's seat, pushing off from it like a swimmer in a competition, and floated back to be among the passengers.

"You'd better get your cameras ready. We're going to be passing close to the surface, and you are going to be able to get some awesome pictures. Bridget, keep the telescope running continuously."

"Roger that, Paul," Wells responded. "I'm not going to waste my precious few minutes looking at the Moon through a viewfinder. The telescope is on auto as planned. I'm going to be looking out the window."

"I'll get copies of pictures from *Dreamscape*'s sensors," Dr. Graves added.

To Gesling's surprise, the other passengers also decided to forgo taking pictures. They appeared to prefer savoring the moment.

"Sounds good to me. I'll be up front." Gesling pushed off and floated his way back to the command chair. Unfortunately, his sightseeing opportunities would be limited. He had to monitor the close-approach trajectory and make sure that they were where they were supposed to be. There wasn't much he could do if the ship was off course, but he might be able to do enough to avert catastrophe if he was paying attention and something did go wrong.

Gesling settled into his chair and affixed his earpiece in place. It was time for him to check in with the ground crew. After activating the voice link, he began speaking, "Rob? Are you on console? This is Paul."

The 1.3-second delay in hearing a response from home was short, but nonetheless maddening. Radio travels at the speed of light, and at the Earth-Moon distance it took 1.3 seconds for Gesling's voice to reach the ground and another 1.3 seconds for the return signal to get back to the Moon and Gesling's earpiece. It was enough of a delay for Gesling to consider it truly annoying.

"Got ya, Paul. Thanks for checking in. You're right on time." The response came from Rob Anderson, Gesling's longtime friend and colleague, who would be working console for fully one-third of the *Dreamscape*'s mission to the Moon.

"Control, you should see it. The Moon is an incredible place. We're coming up on our closest approach, and then we'll be in radio blackout. Anything in the telemetry that I should know about before then?" Gesling was starting to feel like a tourist, and he wasn't afraid to voice his own excitement at being this close to the Moon.

"Paul, the telemetry is clear. You should be fine for the time you'll be behind the Moon. We do have a request. Keep the radio on while you're out of line-of-sight. We got a request from some scientists in New York to look at how sharply the carrier signal cuts off as you pass behind the Moon—something about a theory that the Moon has a low-pressure atmosphere and that how the signal drops out will either confirm or disprove their theory. You know Gary. He's always eager to help out—especially if he gets some kind of credit for doing so."

"I'm sure there were dollar signs in his eyes," Gesling responded. "Sure thing. I'll turn up the squelch in my headset so I don't get blasted by the static."

"Enjoy the show," Anderson said.

"Right," Gesling said. "I intend to. *Dreamscape* out."

With that, Gesling settled back in his chair and took in the magnificent vista that was before him. He could clearly see the mountains and plains, as well as the craters and maria that made up the desolate lunar landscape.

"Nice view," he said to himself. "And from the crew of Apollo 8, we close with good night, good luck, a Merry Christmas, and God bless all of you on the good Earth." Paul muttered to himself the words of Frank Borman. He laughed. Hell, it was August.

Twenty minutes later, Gesling again rose from the command chair and pushed off to "swim" with the passengers. All five were looking out the windows, watching the surface of the Moon pass beneath them in stunned silence. Gesling didn't want to interrupt their ogling, but he did need to apprise them of their pending passage behind the Moon and the fact that they would soon be out of radio contact with the Earth.

"Ahem." Gesling cleared his throat to get their attention. "If I may interrupt you for just a moment, I need to tell you something."

Surprisingly, all five of the tourist astronauts looked away from the windows to hear what he had to say.

"We're about to fly behind the Moon. Since radio can't go through the Moon, we'll temporarily lose contact with ground control. So, if you need to send a message home or are expecting any messages, you'll have to wait until we regain radio contact."

They had been briefed about this before, of course, and, after hearing what he had to say, they one by one looked back out of the windows. Seeing this, Gesling decided it was time for him to do the same.

Moments later, the quietness, for Gesling at least, was interrupted by the sound of static from his earpiece.

"Shit!" said Gesling, realizing that he'd forgotten to turn up the squelch to mute the static resulting from the interrupted communications signal as the *Dreamscape* went behind the Moon. As his finger went to make the adjustment, he heard something in the static.

"Mumble mumble STATIC mumble STATIC **Emergency! Please help!** *Mumble mumble mumble"* came to his ear as he sat in stunned disbelief. Were they getting some weird bounce of radio signals off of Jupiter or something? Impossible. That would require a receiver antenna the size of the one in Arecibo, Puerto Rico.

Paul quickly looked around to see if one of passengers was calling him or playing some sort of obvious practical joke. They were all still intently looking at the Moon and totally unaware of what he'd just heard in his earpiece.

"Mumble STATIC **SOS! This is the crew of the Chinese exploration ship *Harmony* calling for help! We've crashed and are** *mumble mumble STATIC STATIC mumble mumble mumble..."* Gesling quickly came out of his surprised shock and sent the audio he was receiving to the main speakers so all aboard *Dreamscape* could hear and hopefully catch some of the words he was missing. He also made sure the data recorders were still functioning so there would be a record of what was happening.

From the speakers came *"Mumble STATIC* **crew of the *Harmony* calling** *mumble mumble* **crashed and we need assistance!"**

That got everyone's attention. Five heads turned toward the front of the *Dreamscape*. Singer was the first to ask, "What is that? Did someone just call for help?"

"Yes. Listen up. I can't make out everything that's being said, but it sounds like there are people down there."

"Ridiculous!" Thibodeau replied.

"Shh!" Wells scolded him, holding a finger to her lips.

"Mumble mumble mumble **can you hear us? Please, please,**

can you hear us?" The voice was unmistakably that of a woman with a Chinese accent.

Gesling made sure the microphone was open and replied, "Hello? This is the Space Excursions liner *Dreamscape*. What is the nature of your emergency? And who the hell are you?"

"*Mumble mumble.* **You do hear us! We're the crew of the Chinese exploration ship** *Harmony.* **We crash-landed seven days** *mumble mumble mumble* **air for another eight, maybe** *mumble* **days** *mumble mumble* **only this low-power transmitter and** *mumble mumble* **home** *mumble mumble mumble mumble STATIC.*"

"*Harmony*! This is *Dreamscape*. We lost some of that. Please repeat how many days of air you have remaining."

Gesling heard only static.

"Can we help them?" It was the voice of John Graves. Graves had floated to the front cabin and was positioned just behind Gesling.

"I don't see how we can do anything," replied Gesling, looking out the front window of the *Dreamscape*. "We're not designed to land on the Moon. Hell, we can't even brake into orbit to stay and look around for them. They didn't tell us where they landed, but it has to be somewhere either here on the far side or near the limb. We'd not have heard their signal otherwise. They must have been monitoring our transmissions and used our loss of signal as their window to try and reach us. That was a very low-power signal—almost totally lost in the noise."

"The telescope!" Bridget snapped her fingers and swam to her seat, buckling herself in. "Where do I look?"

"Who knows?" Gesling looked exasperated. He was used to *doing* something in a crisis, and there was absolutely nothing he could do about this one. He looked around the interior of the *Dreamscape* and at the five expectant faces staring back at him.

"We'll be out of radio blackout in a few minutes. I'll relay the news. The audio transmission will automatically downlink back to Nevada. I just need to tell them to listen to it."

"Captain Gesling," Thibodeau said gravely. "If there's nothing we can do, then who can?"

The question hung in the air for several minutes, sticking in everyone's ears like molasses.

"We can look for them!" Bridget said over her shoulder.

"Needle in a haystack," responded Gesling, audibly but in a

hushed tone. "I don't think there's a damn thing anyone can do. Those people are as good as dead."

"Yes, there is." Graves smiled and swam his way to his seat. "Captain. Could you relay all the radio signal-strength data to my seat plus our orbital ephemeris data?"

"Of course! Good thinking, John." Paul knew exactly what the engineer was on to. He swam to his pilot's seat and flashed through several screens of icons until he found the radio data, mission time down to the hundredth of a second, and the orbital data. "There, John. You should have it."

"Right," John replied. All Paul and the others could do was sit and wait. Well, mostly. Paul continued to broadcast, trying to get a response from the *Harmony*. Bridget had the telescope on maximum zoom, scanning across craters wildly. The others looked out the windows and through the ship's cameras at the monitors on their seats.

"Bridget." Mbanta swam up and interrupted her. Paul looked over his shoulder at the two to make certain there was no "friction" between them. But there was none. "Can you turn the gain of the telescope down to a minimum and reduce the brightness?"

"Uh, yes, I can."

"Okay, do that, and also go to a wide zoom angle," he told her.

"Wide zoom angle?"

"Zoom out," Dr. Graves added.

"Oh, alright. There. Now, why did I do that?" she asked.

"Because, my dear," Mbanta said, "if they are in the sun, then their ship will glint at us."

"I see. So, I'll scan and look for glints?"

"Great idea, Sharik," Maquita Singer agreed.

"Let me know if you find anything," Paul ordered.

"Roger that."

"Paul!" Graves called.

"Yes, John?" He swam his way to the fat engineer's seat. "Got something?"

"Well, I once made about seventy million dollars off of a video game that involved fighting aliens on a Moon base on the far side of the Moon. I put into the game a lot of detail regarding how to calculate orbits and such."

"Really? Had no idea about that."

"Well, at any rate, the signal was strongest when we were here."

Graves pulled up the time-of-flight view of their orbital location that each of them had as a screensaver at their respective stations. Graves pointed out their location and then continued. "The antenna-beam angle was simple to figure. I designed a satellite-phone network for communications in Africa once, made millions. So, our antenna was covering this footprint on the surface of the Moon, and from the signal strength we could narrow their location down to this spot here."

"Holy..." Paul looked at the map of the Moon where John had overlaid his calculated spot. "That's the size of a state!"

"Yes, but now we know which state. I'd suggest Bridget look there. We will be out of line-of-sight in a matter of minutes. We might also point our directional feeds that way as well. We might pick them up again." Graves looked neither proud of himself nor careless. Paul felt the man's expressionless explanations were just part of his personality. This was the kind of thing Graves did all his life. It was nothing unusual for him.

"Right. Good job, John." Paul pushed over to seat 3B. "Bridget, did you get the map coordinates from John?"

"I'm zooming out on that area now." Bridget worked feverishly at the touch screen. She had become proficient at the controls of the little spy telescope system over the past two years of training. Paul saw no need in taking over. By the time he managed to get into her seat or back to his, it might be too late. He pushed off and floated back to the pilot's seat. "Good, keep looking."

At the pilot's seat, Paul strapped down and started training the high-gain directional antenna across the general location that Graves had calculated, listening with the volume all the way up. Had there been an eleven on the controls, he'd have used it. He closed his eyes and listened hard.

"Paul!" Bridget shouted, followed by the others. It startled him. "What?"

"We have a glint! I'm zooming in now."

The spot was more than two hundred miles away. At that range, the telescope could resolve trashcan-sized objects. Bridget zoomed all the way in on the glint and then brought the contrast and brightness of the image back up to normal. And there it was.

"...*mumble mumble* **God, please! Do you hear us! This is** *Harmony*. **We crash-landed seven days ago. We only have air for another eight. We only have functioning this low-power** transmitter and have no means of getting home. Can you respond? *Dreamscape,* please reply!"

"*Harmony,* I read you. *Dreamscape* copies! Do you hear me?"

"**Dreamscape! Please help us. There are four of us . . . *static* . . . help, need air and evacuation . . . STATIC.**"

"*Harmony*! Do you copy? *Harmony, Dreamscape* heard you. If you hear us, we WILL relay this information back to Earth!"

"I got some nice video of their lander. If that is what you'd call it." Bridget Wells put the imagery data up on all the screens she had access to.

"Wow! Look at that there." Mbanta pointed at the large divot in the lunar surface that scratched out up to the lander. The Chinese spaceship appeared to be on its side, and there was a gaping hole near its bottom.

"Talk about being up a creek," Graves said.

"They'd need a lot more than a paddle," Thibodeau added.

"Right. Good work, everybody. There is nothing more we can do for them at this point." Paul looked out the window as they moved away from the Chinese crash site. They would be in radio contact with Earth in just a few minutes, and then all they could do was send the data they had taken. For now, Paul had a lump in his throat.

No one in the cabin of the small spaceship looping behind the Moon on the world's first space cruise uttered a word for the next several minutes. The crew of *Dreamscape* had turned out to be a fairly capable bunch, with hidden talents. Mbanta understood cameras, imagery, and finding needles in haystacks. That suggested to Paul that he might have some involvement with African military or intelligence groups, but he had no way of knowing that. Bridget Wells had followed her training and run the ISR telescope like a trained Air Force spy. But it was John Graves who had really stepped up. Paul had known the man was smart and a computer-savvy engineer just this side of Bill Gates, but he hadn't understood the depth of the man's knowledge. Paul had a new respect for his crew. Sure, they were all rich fat cats that sometimes seemed spoiled rotten. On the other hand, they had skill sets that enabled them to become those rich fat cats. Except perhaps Mbanta, who was born into it, and even he wasn't useless after all.

It wasn't until Paul heard the voice of his friend Rob Anderson in his headset that he moved away from the window and back toward the command chair. Suddenly the chair looked a whole lot smaller. In fact, the *Dreamscape* looked a whole lot smaller and much more fragile.

"Rob, you won't believe what I have to tell you. Get Caroline and Mr. Childers on the line ASAP. The *Dreamscape* is okay, but I'm not sure about the people on the Moon." Paul waited for his bombshell to drop, which it did a mere second later after the light-speed radio signal made it back to the Earth.

"Paul, say again. Did you say *people*?" Anderson sounded like someone had just told him that aliens had landed in Washington, D.C.

"Yes, I said *people*. How soon can you get Mr. Childers on the line? I believe I need to explain this to all of you at the same time. And get the audio and video portions of the engineering data that's coming down now from the flight computer. You need to hear it and see it." Gesling paused, waiting for Childers and, hopefully, Caroline O'Conner to get on the line. Bandwidth limitations would prevent the video images from making it for a few minutes, but the audio would be instantaneous, barring the speed-of-light limitation, of course.

Chapter 17

This was one press briefing for which Caroline O'Conner hadn't prepared Gary Childers. They had the speech ready for a fully successful mission. They had a speech ready for a disaster. In fact, they had five different speeches ready in case the worst happened and *Dreamscape* didn't make it back to Earth. They didn't have one prepared for telling the world that they'd discovered stranded Chinese astronauts calling for help from the surface of the Moon.

The hastily assembled press corps was expecting one of the five prepared speeches. It was, after all, too soon to declare the voyage a success, since the *Dreamscape* was still at the Moon and wouldn't be home for another few days.

"Hello." Childers began speaking. "A little over an hour ago, the pilot of the *Dreamscape,* Captain Paul Gesling, took the ship around the far side of the Moon and into radio blackout. The mass of the Moon blocked all radio transmissions to and from Earth. At this time, the *Dreamscape* picked up an SOS from the surface of the Moon." He paused.

The assembled press was truly surprised. Not a sound was uttered—other than one chuckle from a reporter who thought it was a joke—as they expectantly waited for Gary Childers to continue.

"The SOS apparently originated from the crew of a Chinese expedition that crash-landed on the Moon about a week ago.

We know there are four of them, but we don't know how they came to crash. All we know is that during the radio blackout, they, whoever they are, used a very low-power radio transmitter to signal *Dreamscape* and ask for help."

The men and women of the press corps quickly regained their composure. A few were already texting or twittering the information to their newsrooms, while others were preparing follow-up questions.

"Ahem." Gary Childers was not yet finished. "Captain Gesling spoke briefly with one of the Chinese, a woman, and she told him that they had enough air to last at least another eight days. The onboard telescope was able to zoom in on their crash site due to some amazing work by the crew of the *Dreamscape*. Who said they are space tourists? Those people are astronauts, if you ask me! And we have images of the crash site that will be available soon.

"We sent the information off to NASA and have no idea what they intend to do with it. I'm not even sure they knew we sent it. That is all I know. We weren't sure whom to call, and, given the urgency of the situation, we thought it best to let the world know about the crisis—so those who need to know can learn about it as soon as possible. That's why I'm here. And to be honest with you, I never expected I'd be up here saying anything remotely like this."

The reporter from ABC, recognizable to any space advocate as the "voice of all things space" from his almost cheerleading-like coverage of NASA and space flight in general, got the first question. "You're sure they are Chinese? Are you telling us that the Chinese test flight that launched recently wasn't a test flight but a real flight?"

"No, I'm not telling you that. You and I might infer that the Chinese actually launched people on their purported test flight, but I don't *know* any such thing. The woman told Paul they were Chinese. She called her ship *Harmony*. And no, I am not sure they are Chinese. I suggest you ask the Chinese about that."

"Mr. Childers!" shouted a CNN reporter. "Can your ship render any sort of aid?"

"Unfortunately not. And it's not my decision. *Dreamscape* is firmly in the hands of Newtonian physics and on its way back home. The ship's trajectory took it around the Moon, and now she's headed back toward the Earth. There isn't enough fuel on the ship to change course, and she isn't designed to land anywhere except here. That is, unfortunately, reality. I truly wish it weren't so. I would very much like to help these people. Perhaps merely detecting their signal was more help than we realize. I hope so."

"Mr. Childers!" The CNN reporter followed up with another question. "I assume you recorded the conversation. Can we hear it?"

"Absolutely. In fact, I'm being told through my earbud that the imagery data is ready now as well. Ms. O'Conner, please play the audio recording and post up the images."

Caroline started playing back the compressed recording on cue. The assembled media mob listened, spellbound, until the last burst of static. The images of the crashed Chinese spaceship cycled through on the large monitor behind him.

"We will provide a digital copy of the recording to everyone. Next question?"

"Mr. Childers!"

"Yes, Jason?" Gary pointed at the Fox News reporter.

"If they have been up there for a week already, why haven't the Chinese told us about it?"

"I guess you should ask the Chinese about that, but the implications disgust me to the very core."

The press was full of additional questions, but Gary Childers and Caroline O'Conner had only limited answers. The audio and imagery were all they had to offer.

"Bill! Bill! Get in here. You've gotta hear this!" It was the voice of Helen Menendez calling Stetson to the break room.

Stetson was in the hallway talking to Anthony Chow about the timeline of the second sortie that was planned for day three of their lunar mission. Chow's title was mission specialist, and that meant he and Helen were responsible for conducting the science operations while they were on the Moon. Stetson was learning of a small change that Chow wanted to make that would potentially shorten their time on the surface by as much as an hour. Given the urgency in Menendez's voice, the discussion would have to wait.

Stetson and Chow hurried down the hallway of the hotel-like building that housed them in the last few days before their historic launch. While they weren't isolated to the extent that the previous lunar-mission crews had experienced fifty years before, as much as possible they were still kept away from most sources of potential illness—other people. And, more importantly, they were kept away from the press.

Though it was a minor annoyance, Stetson fully supported the quasi-quarantine. He was known for saying that he didn't want to miss his chance of going to the Moon due to "a case of the damned measles" or, worse, "foot-in-mouth disease."

They entered the spartanly furnished break room just as the news commentator on the television began playing the *Dreamscape*'s recording.

"Emergency! Please help!... *STATIC* **SOS! This is the crew of the Chinese exploration ship** *Harmony* **calling for help! We've crashed and are...** *STATIC* **crew of the** *Harmony* **calling** *mumble mumble* **crashed and we need assistance!...** *STATIC*. **You do hear us! We're the crew of the Chinese exploration ship** *Harmony*. **We crash-landed seven days** *mumble mumble mumble* **air for another eight, maybe** *mumble* **days** *mumble mumble* **only this low-power transmitter and** *mumble mumble* **home** *STATIC*."

"Son of a bitch!" Stetson was the first to react. "You've got to be kidding me! The Chinese crashed on the Moon?" His mind was racing. His first thoughts were uncharitable toward those who had beaten him to the Moon. Getting there had driven his career, and his life, since he was a little boy listening to Gene Cernan say those final words before he and *his* crew left the Moon for home.

Only after he cursed them did he start thinking of how scared they must be—trapped on an airless world, waiting on their air supply to run out. He stood in silence, weighing the magnitude of the crisis with his personal sense of purpose.

Charles Leonard, the last of Stetson's crew, came into the break room and stood between Menendez and Chow as the television newscaster continued. "This is breaking news, and as yet there has been no reaction from the Chinese government or ours. What will the United States do in light of this new development? We will bring you up-to-the-minute information as we know it."

"That sucks" was Leonard's first comment after hearing the news. "They got all the way to the Moon, and now they're going to die there. I bet you they cancel our flight. You?"

Stetson didn't react. He'd had the very same thoughts shortly after hearing the news, but he quickly put them aside as counterproductive if not distastefully selfish. After all, there were humans about to die up there. Stetson's mind was racing, and he already had a plan that, if successful, would mean that most, if not all, of the trapped Chinese would get to see once again the blue sky of Earth. And they'd owe the United States space program their lives!

Calvin Ross wasn't accustomed to being summoned to the White House. Sure, he'd met the President there before his appointment, but all his other interactions with the administration had come through bureaucratic means—memos, budget blueprints, and a few phone calls from the White House Office of Management and Budget. This was a first, and it came just fifteen minutes after Ross had learned of the stranded Chinese. He had a desktop-computer application that tracked certain keywords such as *NASA*, *space*, *Moon*, etc. It was through an Internet alert that he became aware of the *Harmony* crew and their imminent death. He'd hardly had time to ponder the news before the call came to his BlackBerry and he was informed that a driver would be picking him up in three hours for a meeting with the Vice President and, perhaps, with the President himself.

Ross ran his fingers through his hair and picked up his cell phone to call his Associate Administrator for Space Flight. This AA was responsible for all of NASA's flights that involved sending people to space. There was a separate AA for robotic science missions, and another for aeronautics research. If anyone would know what was going on or if NASA could do anything to help, it would be *this* AA.

"The Chinese government denies this outrageous story about any of our taikonauts being stranded on the Moon. Our recent mission was a robotic rehearsal for our planned campaign of scientific exploration of the Moon and nothing more. Any story that contradicts these facts is simply not true."

The American lunar crew, minus Stetson, heard the vehement denial of the Chinese ambassador to the United Nations at the same time the rest of the country did—barely two hours after the news story broke.

"The video and audio all check out." Leonard spoke, his voice full of derision. "Sure, the guys over at Space Excursions made this all up as a publicity stunt. I know Paul Gesling, and he would not be party to any such thing. No, the Chinese ambassador is lying."

"What would they have to gain by lying?" Menendez responded.

"Stupidity," Leonard said. "Honor. Plain and simple. They only want to report success and not failure. They want the world to know that they are the next superpower, and you can't do that if you fail in something like this. Going to the Moon is the real deal, and if they have to admit they weren't up to the job, then they lose face. Unfortunately, it may mean that some brave people are going to die up there—and they won't get recognized as heroes by their own government, who are too afraid to admit they even exist."

"Craziness." Chow, visibly shaken added, "They're up there, alone, running out of air, stranded a quarter of a million miles from home. I doubt they've been able to eat anything, either. If they are trapped in their suits, as this imagery suggests they might be, then they have to keep them on to survive."

"Yeah, and better them than us," Leonard responded.

"Oh my God!" Chow, reliving his own personal nightmare in the privacy of his thoughts, could only nod his head.

Stetson called Calvin Ross as he was preparing for his upcoming meeting with the Vice President. Ross had a data book in his safe that described the entire Chinese rocket program in some detail. The files were classified top secret, meaning that not only were they a secret important to immediate national security, but no foreign nationals could be made aware of their contents even if they had the appropriate clearance level. Some of the data contained therein had been gathered using techniques that might be compromised if the contents were made known beyond only those Americans with a true "need to know."

Ross and Barbara Owen, the AA for Space Flight, were thumbing through the book, making notes, when Stetson's call came in. Stetson was among the very few to have Ross's cell-phone number. But Stetson was NASA's front man for the current generation. He was the new Captain Kirk.

"Calvin, we can save these people." Ross noted the sound of absolute certainty in Stetson's voice.

"Save them? How?" replied Ross. "Bill, are you serious?"

"Their message says they have air for another seven or eight days. For all practical purposes, that was yesterday. We're three days away from launch. It'll take three days for us to get to the Moon, leaving them with one day to spare. Maybe two, if we're lucky."

"Wait a minute, Bill," Ross said. "Let me put you on the speaker. Barbara is here with me." Ross leaned forward, touched the speakerphone button, and motioned for Owen to listen also.

"Go ahead, Bill."

"Hi, Barbara."

"Hi, Bill."

"We can save them." Stetson began to explain. "If we can find out where they are on the surface, and it looks like the *Dreamscape* crew did that for us for the most part, we can land there. Altair was intentionally overdesigned so we could land anywhere, anytime. That was one of the ways NASA originally sold the program. Apollo could only land near the equator—like we were planning to do on this trip. But we don't have to. We launch with enough fuel to do one of the missions we weren't planning to do for another few years. We can land anywhere on the Moon, as long as we know where to land before we launch."

"Wait a minute," Ross said. "Bill, you know I'm a politician, not a rocket scientist. Please explain why we've got to know before you go."

"It takes energy, and in our case, propellant, to change an orbit from being around the equator to being in a circle around the lunar poles. The same is true on the Earth. That's why it's easier to place satellites in geostationary orbit when we launch from the equator than when we launch from the Kennedy Space Center. You can get there from Kennedy, but it takes more fuel. You've got to crank your circular orbit down from 28.5 degrees to zero degrees, and that takes fuel. Now, if we need to land at the lunar south pole, then we need to launch at a time that minimizes the amount of fuel we need to burn in order to get there, and that's most easily accomplished if the rocket that originally puts us into space does part of the job. There is simply not enough fuel on the lander to do it by itself. Are you with me?"

"Yes, I think so." Ross didn't understand the details, but he did understand the overall concept. And he was certain Stetson and the other rocket scientists *did* understand it.

"Okay. Now, once I get there, I can land the Altair near their crash site, and we can cram them into the lander's ascent stage and bring them home."

"Bill." This time Barbara spoke up. "There isn't room on the ascent stage for your crew and their crew. Not only isn't there room, but the combined weight will be more than can be lifted from the surface with the Altair's engine—not enough thrust and probably not enough propellant even if there were."

"The rocket science part we understand, Barbara," Stetson said. "My crew won't be with me. This is a rescue mission, and I'll be going alone. That way we can fit all four of the Chinese in the ascent stage with me. We don't need to bring back any rocks, and that will save weight. And we can probably offload all of the science hardware—saving even more weight."

Ross didn't know if the plan was feasible; he would let his engineers tell him that. But he did know that this was just the kind of thing that, if successful, would be his ticket within the administration. And it might save some lives on the way. But more importantly, it would make him, NASA, the astronauts, and the space program heroes. Heroes got money and, more importantly, votes.

"Barbara, what do you think?"

"Well, I don't know. It sounds like it might work. But we'll have to run the numbers."

"Trust me, Barbara," Stetson said. "Hell, I ran the numbers! This *will* work. But we have to know where they are, and right now the Chinese aren't even admitting that the people Space Excursions talked to are theirs. It's my guess that the Chinese aren't sure exactly where they are. If we take their data and run it through a fine-tooth comb and a supercomputer, we'll have the crash position located close enough to do the job. We're taking the rover anyway, so if I miss them by a few miles, then I can go get them."

"Okay. I get it, Bill." Ross leaned toward the speakerphone, took a deep breath, and almost too eagerly replied, "Bill, you and Barbara get a team together and see if this will really work. Use whomever you need from Johnson, Kennedy, and Marshall. I'll carry this to the Vice President as an option, but he'll want to know yesterday whether or not we can really do it. That means I want to know for sure by tomorrow morning at eight o'clock.

And I don't like the idea of you going it alone. You're taking a copilot with you."

"Okay. I'll have to pick the right crew member, then. And we'll have to figure out something on the Altair that we can toss overboard to make up for the extra passenger."

"Do that. By eight a.m."

"Will do." Stetson wasn't quite finished. "Calvin. We must know exactly where they crashed. And that means the Chinese need to play ball yesterday. It takes time to run trajectories, and we need to know so we can tweak our launch window—before I launch. If we had their orbital-telemetry data that we could add in with the Space Excursions data, it would make life easier."

"I'll tell the Vice President," Ross said.

Chapter 18

The obscenely cheery voice of the news announcer blared from the alarm clock at exactly 5:00 a.m. the next morning, awakening Stetson from the three hours of sleep he had allowed himself the night before. "Good morning, Space Coast! It's time to get that pot of coffee brewing and for your five-day forecast."

Stetson groaned, rolled over, and quickly turned down the volume on the old-fashioned clock radio beside his bed. He'd been up until almost two o'clock meeting with Menendez, Chow, and Leonard, as well as a hastily assembled team of engineers from three NASA field centers. They were discussing all the options that might allow for a rescue of the stranded Chinese. In the course of the discussion, they had narrowed their choices to two: one with Stetson and Chow aboard and one totally robotic. Stetson had been emphatic about needing humans on board and in the loop. The NASA director had insisted it be a minimum two-man mission. So, Bill felt it only made sense that a rescue mission should have a medical doctor along for the ride. The decision was clear then that Anthony Chow, M.D., should be the crew member that joined him.

The engineers and bureaucrats at Marshall and Kennedy favored the robotic mission. There was less risk of losing a manned crew, and it was completely boring and unimaginative. Bill had argued until he was blue in the face that robots couldn't think on their feet, and with a potential communications delay of two or more seconds, that could be disastrous. It was clear that Stetson and his colleagues at the Johnson Space Center emphatically favored the manned mission.

Stetson had gone around and around with the engineers and was insistent that a person needed to be on board just in case something went wrong that only a person could fix. The counterargument favored not sending a person so as to allow one additional stranded Chinese crew member to return home without any modification to the Altair. It was too late to modify the spaceship now, since it was already packed away in the Ares V rocket on the launchpad. Any mods would have to take place either along the way or once they landed on the lunar surface. That was something robots could not do.

In Stetson's opinion, the discussion was somewhat moot, because they didn't know how many people were alive on the Moon. And what if medical attention could increase the number of survivors that made it home? And what if the Chinese survivors bumped the wrong control panel or accidentally changed some of the ship's control settings? What if? No, there were just too many "what ifs" to let the mission go without one or more of its intended crew members on board.

And without knowing how many, if any, of these "what ifs" would rear their ugly heads, how could anyone say having the ship fly up there robotically would make any sense at all? All the arguments for or against didn't matter anyway until safety signed off on it. Whatever the astronaut office said about mission success and mission safety was always considered to be the last word. If they said it was unsafe, then it was unsafe and would not fly. The converse was also true. And Stetson knew the rules of this game. He just had to make certain to convince them that it *was* safe and *should* fly.

As Stetson rushed through his morning routine and prepared to get his usual hot shower, he cranked up the volume on the radio and tuned it to a news station so he could keep one ear tuned in just in case. His interest and patience were soon rewarded.

"—And, in an unexpected turn of events, the Chinese government announced late last night that the astronauts on the Moon are, in fact, Chinese. The Chinese foreign minister made the announcement in a press conference while attending the World Energy Summit in Australia."

A man's voice, speaking Chinese, then came over the radio, followed seconds later by an English translation. "The four brave crew members of the moon ship *Harmony* are the pride of China. Our thoughts go out to their families as these heroes spend their last days making the ultimate sacrifice for their country."

"Joining us now is Eric Harris, author of many books about space and space exploration, and an aerospace consultant. Good morning, Mr. Harris. What can you tell us about the fate that awaits the Chinese astronauts? And is there anything we here on Earth can do to help them?"

Stetson stood outside his shower, the water not yet on, listening intently. He now knew that there were four people on the Moon to be rescued. Without any modification, the Altair could bring home a crew of four—him, Chow, and two of the Chinese. He was certain that enough weight could be off-loaded to allow another person aboard. Getting more than that on the ascent stage, that part of the rocket that would lift off from the lunar surface and take the astronauts back into space, would be a bit harder—but not impossible. No, he was sure they could come back with all four—though it would be tight. The radio program continued, this time with the self-proclaimed space expert, Eric Harris.

"Their fate is bleak. If they don't lose electrical power, which they shouldn't, since their lander has both solar arrays and hydrogen fuel cells, then they won't bake or freeze before their air runs out. Contrary to what you see in the movies, death by asphyxiation is fairly quick. In the absence of sufficient oxygen, people act normally until, and with no warning, they simply feel dizzy and then black out in a matter of seconds."

"Sounds gruesome," the newscaster commented.

"Well, yes. But at least it is quick. Well, in their case, not so quick, since they know it is coming."

"What about a rescue? Have the Chinese said anything about mounting a rescue mission?"

"No. A Chinese rescue is out of the question. They simply don't have the hardware—the rocket, the spaceship that takes them from the Earth to the Moon, the lander, and all that gear—they simply don't have spares ready to be launched on such short notice. They might be able to get something up in a couple of months, but by that time it will be a mission to bring home the bodies, not a rescue mission."

"I see. What a horrible situation." The newsman sounded ill.

"Yes, a bad situation," Harris continued. "But NASA might be able to do something. They have a rocket on the pad and are already scheduled to launch to the Moon in just a few days. It might be possible for them to rescue at least part of the crew. I certainly hope someone at the space agency is looking into it."

"Don't we all," said the newscaster. "And now, for all the sports action from last night. Boston looks like it's on its way to yet another victory in the—"

At this point, Stetson turned off the radio. Racing through his mind was what he was going to tell the NASA Administrator when they spoke in just a few hours. He was glad that the public, or at least the space wonks, were already talking about a possible rescue. That would mean the politicians would be less likely to nix the idea.

"We're going to bring those people home," he said aloud. "They're not going to die. Even if the SOBs deserve to die for beating me to the Moon."

The telecon began promptly at 8:00 a.m. On the line were Stetson and his crew, the NASA Administrator, the Associate Administrator for Space Flight, NASA's Chief Engineer, the Director of NASA's Safety and Mission Assurance, and a horde of bureaucrats who had either contributed something to the quick feasibility assessment or thought that they should have.

Stetson began by recounting his plan for the benefit of those hearing it for the first time. He described why the mission must have a trained crew aboard and why that crew must consist of Anthony Chow, M.D., and himself. He emphasized the M.D. part.

"Hold on just a minute." Administrator Ross confronted him bluntly. "Bill, if I were to tell the Vice President this morning that we can do this, can we really do it? Are you willing to bet your career on it? Or your life, for that matter. Because if we tell him that we can, then he'll ask the President to call the Chinese and make the offer. At that point, we're committed. And if we don't save those people, then your career, my career, and the future of our own lunar program might be toast."

"Calvin, I *know* we can do this. I've looked at the numbers, and I can bring back all four with me. It'll be a little crowded, and the air might be a little stale by the time we get home, but we can do it." Stetson held his emotions in check as much as he could, which was very little.

"And, sir, I'd like to add that there is a moral obligation here as well," Chow said. The Administrator didn't seem to have any response, but he did make a facial expression that suggested he didn't appreciate Chow's comment.

"Let's keep this on a technical-feasibility level," the NASA Chief Engineer, Tom Rowan, replied. "Calvin, I had a team looking at the numbers last night in parallel with Bill and his team. We agree with everything except for the reentry. We agree with his estimate of the propellant budget for getting Altair back into space and for getting Orion on a trajectory to bring it home—we ought to be able to off-load enough equipment plus some exterior panels to offset the extra weight of two more people for the Trans-Earth Injection burn. But we don't believe we can get you all safely to touchdown. We can cram everyone in the capsule, but it will simply weigh too much. We don't believe you can survive reentry and touchdown. Now, if we were landing in the ocean like we used to do, maybe, but that is still up for debate and moot. The capsule doesn't have flotation systems on it, since we're going to land on the ground like the Russians do. "

"Could they bail out at high altitude and parachute to safety?" another engineer in the room asked.

"Unlikely they would be in the right physical and mental state to accomplish such a thing. Who knows what kind of shape they'll be in when we find them?" the NASA Chief Engineer said.

"Wait." Stetson stopped them. "We don't have to bring them all down."

"What?" Ross asked.

"We won't all have to reenter in Orion. The plan we came up with last night is to transfer two or all of the Chinese passengers to the International Space Station before we come home."

If their microphones hadn't been muted, Stetson was sure he would have heard several engineers listening on the line pass out in their seats.

"Look. We're supposed to do a direct entry when we come home from the Moon in Orion. We leave the Moon and come screaming home, going directly into the Earth's atmosphere, using the atmospheric friction to slow down enough to pop our parachutes and get us to a dead stop. But we don't have to."

"Huh?" Ross's voice on the speakerphone sounded perplexed. "I don't understand."

"Just like in Apollo, we've designed Orion with a safe-abort maneuver in case something goes wrong on the trip home and the ship cannot reenter immediately. It's called aerocapture. We've never done it, but it should be relatively easy to do. Apollo was designed to do it, and so are we."

"Wait, wait, Bill." Ross, with a little agitation now apparent in his response, said again, "I don't understand."

"Of course." This time, Rowan answered the question. "Aerocapture. Instead of coming straight into the atmosphere and landing, with aerocapture you skim into the upper atmosphere just enough to slow down and enter orbit. It's sort of like skimming a rock on the surface of a pond. The capsule will dip into the atmosphere to slow it just enough to enter orbit. It can fire its retrorockets later to de-orbit and come home. But how will you get to the Space Station? It is at the wrong inclination."

"We thought of that," Bill said. "With aerocapture you can slow down *and* change your orbital inclination. We can aerocapture into an orbit that matches up with the station. Orion's been used to take astronauts to the station since the late teens. The docking hardware we use to mate with the lunar lander is the same hardware that is used when Orion carries astronauts to the station. We aerocapture, dock with the station, off-load our extra passengers, and then come home. I've got some engineers at Langley plotting the aerocapture maneuver right now."

"That leaves one big question," a nameless voice from among those listening on the telecon interjected. "How do they get home? The ones on the station, I mean."

"Well," said Stetson, "I haven't figured that one out yet. But there's plenty of air and water on the space station to keep them comfortable until we do."

"And, if some of them need medical attention, then they can come down in Orion. In that case, Bill and I will stay on ISS," Anthony Chow added. Bill liked the comment because it showed they had options.

The ten-second silence that followed seemed like an eternity to Bill Stetson. He'd given it his best shot, and now it was up to the NASA Administrator to give it a thumbs-up or thumbs-down.

"Bill, okay. I'll tell the Vice President that we can do it. Make it happen."

If this had been a videoconference, Bill Stetson might not have smiled. But since he was only in the presence of his friends and crewmates, that big Texas grin was painted from ear to ear.

"Yes, sir!" came through loud and clear.

Minutes later, the crew broke quarantine to meet face-to-face with the lead engineers who were going to make what modifications could be done on the launchpad, with only two days remaining until launch. And they had to go to the Altair simulator and practice taking it apart in spacesuits. The engineers had to have some specialty tools rapidly prototyped during the process. Fortunately, NASA astronauts and engineers had been learning how to do maintenance and construction in space for the last two decades as they had built the ISS and maintained it. Kluging tools for new jobs was old hat for them.

Gary Childers wanted to break the news to Gesling and his customers personally. He heard the news of the planned NASA rescue while he was at his desk, perusing once again the sponsorship agreements that would allow him to begin building his own lunar lander.

The media had been talking about a special announcement from the President being forthcoming, and when it was finally on the television, Gary Childers was watching.

The President, looking calm and in control as he did when he spoke to the nation about his plans for fixing the looming fiscal crisis, stood in front of the lectern in the White House briefing room with NASA Administrator Ross at his side.

He said, "I spoke directly with the President of China and made the offer to have NASA's upcoming flight to the Moon be a rescue mission. He accepted our offer, and now we, and the world, need to pray for the stranded astronauts and for the success of our planned rescue attempt. I'm going to turn it over to Mr. Calvin Ross, Administrator of NASA, to provide the details."

Childers listened to enough of the details to get at least some understanding of what was planned and then keyed in the access code on his workstation that would allow him to speak directly with the *Dreamscape*.

"Paul. This is Gary. How are things up there?" Childers asked.

"Mr. Childers. Thanks for asking. I think your passengers are having the time of their lives—or they would be, if they weren't thinking about those trapped Chinese astronauts. It's a mixture of elation and sadness up here. But I don't believe anyone will ask for a refund." Gesling sounded like he was trying to put the best possible face on what had become of their interplanetary vacation.

"Well, put me on the speaker. I have news."

"Go ahead."

"Hello!" Gary Childers greeted his customers, still about a hundred thousand miles from home. "I have good news. NASA is going to attempt to rescue the stranded Chinese astronauts that you found on your trip. It sounds risky, and it may not be successful, but if it weren't for you and the flight of the *Dreamscape,* these people would surely be dead and their deaths unknown until some future explorers found their bodies. The Chinese and the world owe you a word of thanks. Your vacation may have just saved the lives of four astronauts."

"Gary, thanks for telling us. You've got six smiling faces up here."

"Tell them I'm smiling, too. See you soon," Childers said.

Gary leaned back in his chair. He meant every damned word of what he'd said. He had just gotten the best publicity anyone could have imagined and perhaps saved some lives to boot. With that, Gary Childers was both a happy businessman and an elated human being. And he did have a big smile on his face to prove it.

Chapter 19

Not since Apollo 13 had so many NASA engineers been working with such urgency. Every room Stetson passed on his way to briefing room 1A was full of people poring over printouts and busily making calculations on their laptop computers. Normally, with launch only two days away, all the analysis would have been completed long ago—checked and rechecked weeks before. Now, with so many changes in the flight, many analyses were being performed for the first time. This wasn't in any of the simulations, so there was no backup plan to pull out and follow. This one was being created on the fly.

As he walked down the hall, he picked up snippets of conversation.

"...enough fuel for ascent if we remove another fifty kilograms, but..."

"We've never done an aerocapture! If we'd funded that flight experiment..."

"Shit! The lander can't do that! Look, here are the specs and I..."

Stetson smiled. These were good people. The best. They would figure it out. Stetson had flown combat missions, three shuttle missions, and two Orion flights to the space station. He knew what the hardware could do, and he knew the engineers would catch up with him eventually. Or so he hoped....

The first thing Stetson noticed when he walked into the briefing room was the presence of the four Chinese. They were standing together in the corner, conferring among themselves with their NASA liaison and translator standing a few feet away, looking anxious. Although Stetson didn't know any of them, he could immediately tell that one of the men—they were all men—was not an engineer. He was the tallest of the bunch, and he stood slightly back from the other three, apparently listening but really watching everyone else in the room. His eyes caught Stetson's as Bill entered the room, and then they quickly darted back to the conversation of the other three.

He's either a manager or a political officer or a spy, thought Stetson. And he didn't really care for any of the possibilities.

The conference room was long and broad, with windows that looked out at the distant launch towers at which both the pencil-like Ares I and the much larger Ares V were poised for takeoff. A simulated cherry table shaped into an ellipse sat in the middle of the room, equipped with individual power, network, and optical-fiber links at regular intervals to allow those in attendance to remain connected.

"Bill! Come on up here. We need to get started." It was the voice of NASA's Chief Engineer, Tom Rowan. Rowan, the man ultimately responsible for all the technical aspects of the mission, looked like he hadn't slept in days. His close-cropped hair was somehow matted to his head, and his clothes had that "day old with sweat" look. He also looked about ten years older than his forty-six years.

"Tom, good to see you." Stetson slapped him on the shoulder and shook his hand.

"You, too. You need to meet our Chinese counterparts. They flew in last night. That's also when we got their best data regarding the crash site. But we still don't know why they crashed. That's one of the items they are supposed to tell us this morning. I've got your coffee for you. Let's get this show on the road."

With that, Rowan convened the meeting, with more than two dozen people in the room scurrying for chairs and the four Chinese taking seats directly across from Stetson. After the introductions and obligatory handshakes, the Chinese lead designer, General Xiang Li, took the microphone.

Xiang, not looking a day over thirty-five but probably at least ten years older than that, gazed around the room, pausing briefly as he glanced at "the manager" from his group before moving on.

"Thank you for what you are doing. My country is deeply appreciative. I believe our engineers communicated to yours all that we know about the crash. The *Harmony* appeared to be in perfect health as it left lunar orbit and began its descent. And then something went horribly wrong. We believed the crew to be lost until your *Dreamscape* heard their distress call.

"We're still looking at the engineering data that was being transmitted to Earth autonomously by the spacecraft up until the point at which contact was lost. It's beginning to look like there was some sort of malfunction with its attitude-control system. The ship was beginning to rock back and forth, and it was building to a point at which the attitude-control thrusters would no longer have been able to compensate. We believe they, in fact, failed—causing the crash. We do not know why."

"What about communications? Did you hear from the crew?" one of the American engineers asked.

"At first, yes. We learned that the crew survived the crash and that the ship's hull was not breached. After only a few minutes, the link failed, and we heard nothing more. Until, of course, the *Dreamscape* made contact."

"Why didn't you tell anyone? Not just about the crash, but about the mission? The launch? Why did you keep it a secret?" A female NASA engineer that Bill didn't know by name asked the question that was on everyone's mind.

Xiang started to speak, but after he caught the eye of "the manager," he paused instead. Then he said reluctantly, "That was a decision made at the highest levels, and I am not at liberty to discuss it. Please let us remain focused on the technical issues— and the rescue of our taikonauts."

Stetson observed the nonverbal exchange between Xiang and what he now presumed was a Chinese political officer, and he didn't like it. He briefly fantasized about walking over to "the manager" and punching him out. At the moment, that would have to remain a fantasy... at the moment.

A flurry of questions followed. Most of them were about the status of the remaining supplies the stranded astronauts might have in their possession and how many days they could survive before rescue.

"Excuse me! Excuse me!" The voice calling out was from one of the few nonengineering members of the flight-support team,

Karen Williamson. Karen, who looked much like a suburban soccer mom, was the NASA psychiatrist. In her early forties, she'd worked with several crews on the International Space Station and spent time in Moscow studying the Russian cosmonauts.

"Uh, excuse me, EXCUSE ME!" After getting everyone's attention, she asked, "Did anyone tell the crew that a rescue attempt was being made? I mean, they are two hundred and fifty thousand miles away from home, facing—at least in their minds—certain death. Did anyone try to tell them that they shouldn't give up hope?"

Silence. In the room, all they could hear was the gentle hum of the air-conditioning system.

"From the lack of response, I'd guess the answer is no." She frowned at everyone in the room a bit dramatically. "I think someone needs to tell them that we're going to try a rescue. Otherwise they might just decide to not prolong what they believe is inevitable..."

The implications of her words began to sink in to those assembled.

"Damn. That didn't occur to me." Stetson was the first to respond. He turned to Xiang and added, "You said you tried to talk to them and failed, correct?"

"Yes."

"Well, *Dreamscape* managed to do it. Why is that?" Stetson asked.

"I've thought about that. There are two reasons. Based on the fact that their radio transmission wasn't heard until the *Dreamscape* was in the radio quiet of lunar farside, we think they were using their low-power radio designed for talking to the crew from the lander during EVA. The system doesn't have the power for us to pick up all the way back on Earth, but it did have the ability to reach the *Dreamscape* as it passed. And, most significantly, they are near the limb—they may barely be on the nearside after all. Direct radio communication to the Earth may be possible even without some sort of orbital relay."

"I see." Stetson said. "They were probably listening to *Dreamscape* as she chattered with Earth during her approach. Once the ship was cut off from any radio signals from home, they were able to get through. But if they are that close to the limb, they might hear something if we had a powerful enough transmission."

Xiang and many in the room nodded.

"Okay, then. Let's use the same frequency and the most powerful transmitter we've got to send them a message telling them that help is on the way."

Rowan asked, "But if they are on the far side, how will they even receive the message? And if they do, how will we know they did? For that matter, how do we know that they haven't already decided to kill themselves?"

"We have to try," Stetson answered. His face was grim. "I hope I don't land and find only bodies."

"Wait a minute," one of the communications engineers said. "We get weak signals from the Pioneers and Voyagers all the time. We *can* hear their low-power transmitters. You just have to know what frequency to listen to and when to point the Big Dish. If we need to, we could set up an interferometer out at the VLA. The SETI guys are probably all over this."

"What is the Big Dish?" Xiang asked.

"It's a nickname." Bill smiled. "Arecibo, Puerto Rico. That's where the National Science Foundation runs the largest single-dish radio receiver in the world. If they can get line-of-sight with even their low-power transmitter, then we will pick it up."

The engineer continued. "And Arecibo can also broadcast. They once sent a megawatt signal into deep space for Carl Sagan. The Moon is so close, if they've got a receiver and aren't totally blocked by the mass of the Moon, they'll hear it."

"That's right. I seem to recall that Sagan thing back when I was a kid," Stetson added as he thought about the problem. "Can't we also use the Deep Space Network? Arecibo will only work when the dish has line-of-sight with the Moon. As we rotate away from the Moon, we won't be able to listen or receive. By tying in the three DSN antennas—in California, Spain, and Australia—we should have coverage all the time."

"I dunno, Bill," Rowan replied, his face showing extreme skepticism. "So, we're going to listen for a message from people who may be dead, and if they aren't, their extremely weak radio signal will be blocked by the mass of the Moon, making it impossible for us to hear them? And while we're doing that at the Very Large Array and the Deep Space Network, we're going to blast a message to them with the Arecibo antenna telling them help is on the way. And, oh yes, they probably won't hear that message because the Moon is blocking our signal as well. Good plan, Bill."

"Right." Stetson leaned forward toward Rowan and smiled as best he could. "Yes, I think that summarizes it nicely."

"Bill, if it were anyone but you, I'd tell them where to shove this part of the plan. But I won't. We'll make it happen," Rowan said.

Damn right you will, Bill thought to himself.

"There's another problem." Xiang was speaking again. "By the time you get to the Moon, it will be night."

The implication of this statement was not lost to most of the space scientists and engineers in the room. Xiang continued.

"The Moon rotates more slowly than the Earth, completing one full revolution every twenty-eight Earth days. This means that the Moon's day is fourteen Earth days long, as is its night. Though surviving on the Moon anytime is a challenge, getting through the lunar night is particularly difficult. The temperature drops to minus three hundred eighty-seven degrees Fahrenheit at night, requiring a considerable amount of power to keep things, and people, warm. Batteries capable of providing the power needed to keep a crew alive during the fourteen-day darkness period are far too heavy to fly in space. Without sunlight, solar power is useless. That's why we didn't plan on them being on the Moon at night."

"That could be bad," Rowan commented. "What kind of power do they have? Will they have enough to keep from freezing until we arrive? Since they landed at the beginning of the lunar day, that'll mean they will have been in darkness for a little more than three days by the time we arrive. That is a long time."

"It is hard to say." Xiang replied. "If they are in their suits, and if the fuel cells survived the crash, then they could have found a way to use the various power systems on the spacecraft to keep themselves from freezing. Our engineers are quite well trained, and they know the systems of their spacecraft at least as well as your people know yours. There is a chance. Time is not on our side."

"Well, then," Stetson added, "I guess we'd better get off our butts and get busy."

Chapter 20

In the three days since Paul Gesling and the passengers of the
Dreamscape heard the plea for help from the stranded Chinese
taikonauts, the inescapable forces of gravity had been pulling them
back home toward Earth. The moment of their return was now
imminent, and they were busily preparing themselves for entry
into the atmosphere and a not-too-distant landing on the desert
runway in Nevada.

To most of the passengers, coming directly back home and landing on the same runway from which they left seemed like no big
deal. After all, didn't airplanes do that sort of thing all the time?

To Paul Gesling, who understood the complexities of orbital
mechanics, the relative rotation of the Earth, and the effects the
pull of gravity from the Moon had on his craft, it was simply
amazing. Here they were, coming back from a quarter-of-a-
million-mile journey to another world, and they were about to
enter the Earth's atmosphere at speeds beyond the human mind's
ability to imagine to pull off a pinpoint landing at the same spot
from which they had left several days ago. The timing had to be
perfect, and, from all indications, it likely would be. Nonetheless,
he was nervous and continuously checking for updates on their
position from the onboard computer.

In-space acrobatics behind them, the passengers were all buckled in their seats, running through the various checklists now

scrolling on the screens in front of them. True, many of their tasks were trivial and designed mostly to keep them busy and to make sure they didn't hurt themselves as the pull of Earth's gravity noticeably returned. But it worked.

Gesling was in the pilot's seat, running through his own, less trivial, checklist. One by one, the ship's systems were checked out and appeared to be in perfect operating condition.

Dreamscape would enter the outermost region of the Earth's atmosphere within the hour and be on the ground shortly thereafter.

The Honda minivan was back in place and ready to intercept as much data as possible during the landing. The same group of engineers that had been with the operation from the beginning were again in the van, as was their leader, Zeng Li.

Zeng was intently watching the televised coverage of the *Dreamscape*'s landing being broadcast live on most of the major American cable, satellite, and television news networks. The coverage was, of course, interrupted by frequent advertisements and "this just in" updates about some celebrity or another, but the clear focus was coverage of the landing of the *Dreamscape* and the emergence of the people who had just flown past the Moon. For a short while, most Americans would know the names of current astronauts and not just those they had read about in their history books.

The entire Chinese team had been as taken aback as the rest of the world at the news that their country had attempted a Moon landing. When that news broke, they had been resting at their Las Vegas hotel ("resting" was a relative term). All were shocked, and one of the team had subsequently become careless. In his excitement to learn more about the failed lunar landing and its crew, and especially since he had a brother who worked for the Chinese National Space Agency, he violated protocol and used Skype to call home and speak with his brother. Though he did not mention where he was or what he was doing, merely contacting his brother had been enough to set in motion the events that would soon lead to his capture and arrest.

His brother, like many other engineers working on China's military and civilian rocket programs—the two were almost indistinguishable—was on a CIA "watch list," and all of his communications were intercepted. This particular call was no exception.

The entire call was recorded and analyzed by the supercomputers at the National Security Agency (NSA). The call was flagged for follow-up by a human reviewer since it originated geographically near a recently reported act of espionage involving a certain private space company with compromised computer chips and now-stolen technical plans for a hypersonic rocket and potential global-strike weapons system. The fact that at least one of the participants on the call was a rocket scientist was the bit of data that ensured the message was flagged.

Within a few hours, an assessment team was poring over the transcript of the call, looking at its originating Internet service provider in the United States, and identifying the hotel on the Las Vegas strip from which it had originated. Shortly thereafter, they had the room number of the hotel and the name of the renter to whom the Internet service was being provided for a "nominal daily fee of $11.95." They were in the MGM Grand.

Taking a little longer, but not too long, voice-print-identification algorithms positively identified the brother of the Chinese rocket scientist and, based on other intelligence sources, had him firmly linked with his current employer—the Chinese equivalent of the Central Intelligence Agency. His photograph was now displayed on the NSA conference-room monitors as the assessment team again examined the intercepts and weighed what, if any, connection there might be between him and the recently stolen plans for the *Dreamscape*. According to the computer, and readily accepted by the team, the two must be linked. It was time to call the FBI.

By the time the *Dreamscape* was entering the atmosphere, and while Zeng was watching the event unfold on Fox News while his teammates intercepted telemetry from the Space Excursions facility only a few miles away, the FBI team was moving into place around them. High overhead, an unmanned surveillance drone had confirmed that the Honda was alone on the mesa. Twenty FBI agents in full-body armor were getting into position.

Gary Childers and Caroline O'Conner were waiting on the landing in the VIP viewing area near the end of the runway. Instead of the dozens of reporters that had been present at *Dreamscape*'s launch, the number of reporters was now well over two hundred. All of them were anxious to get the story from the people who had been to the Moon and found the stranded Chinese taikonauts. In addition to the reporters, there were at least fifteen book agents looking for an opportunity to speak with one or more of the passengers in the hopes of securing their stories for a sure-to-be-bestselling book. It was turning into a great day for commercial space exploration.

Glancing frequently at the overhead status boards, which showed a cartoonlike schematic of the *Dreamscape* and its reentry trajectory, Childers and O'Conner looked like expectant parents. Their baby, however, was returning from a journey to another world.

By squinting in the bright Nevada sun, it was O'Conner who first spotted the *Dreamscape* on its flight path back to the spaceport runway. She could not contain her excitement as she literally squealed and began to clap. Childers soon followed, as did all the VIPs and most of the assembled reporters. None had forgotten the *Columbia* space shuttle tragedy and all were relieved when they saw that *Dreamscape* had made it through its fiery reentry into the Earth's atmosphere. The ship was right where it was supposed to be and not a minute too soon or too late.

The *Dreamscape* grew in apparent size as it neared the runway. Like a glorious and noble bird it soared toward them, and, moments before touchdown, the landing gear sprang from within its body to provide the cushioning required for a soft landing.

"Three, two, one—touchdown!" came an anonymous voice from the PA system in the VIP area. The same voice was used as a voiceover by all the media broadcasting the landing, including the channel being watched in the Honda minivan just a few miles away.

"Three, two, one—touchdown!" said the voice of Space Excursions through the small speaker on the monitor that Zeng was watching intently while his colleagues were collecting telemetry from the *Dreamscape* as it rolled down the runway.

"Go! Go!" said the FBI team leader in charge of the raid. He spoke into the radio microphone wrapped around his head that allowed him to communicate with all twenty members of the team about to storm the van parked just ahead of them. The leader, Mike Brown, was a veteran of many drug raids and even a few counterterrorism raids. This was his first counterespionage raid, and he was not sure what to expect. His experience taught him that drug runners were the worst, often choosing to fight even when faced with overwhelming odds. The few terrorists he'd engaged hadn't suspected they were about to be raided, and they had simply rolled over without a fight. The drug runners, on the other hand, *always* had their guns at their side and seemed to relish using them.

Thanks to the drone flying directly overhead, the team determined that those in the van were alone and there was no sign of any remote-detection devices in the brush alongside the road leading up to it. With luck, the van's occupants would not have any warning of what was about to happen.

Like horses out of the gate at a racetrack, the highly trained members of the FBI's Southwestern Division counterterrorism squad moved toward the van from all directions. Each member of the team wore a helmet equipped with the latest communications system as well as the most advanced concussion protection available—should they be near a bomb blast. Head injuries from bombs were among the most difficult to prepare for. They all wore full-body armor, a hard lesson learned during their many drug raids over the years. More than one of this team had been saved from a bullet by their armor. And, of course, they had their guns out and ready for whatever might happen.

Simultaneously, the five SUVs that had carried them moved into position on the road in front and behind the van to block any chance of its escape.

The *Dreamscape* had been on the runway no more than five seconds when one of Zeng's team abruptly leapt from his seat near the front window of the van and began shouting in Chinese, "We have been discovered! Erase! Erase!" The man who shouted these words had just seen the FBI team swarm out of the brush, seemingly from nowhere. There was no other warning.

Though they were well trained in what to do in the event of discovery, there was simply not enough time to begin the process of erasing all of the data they were collecting—though

Zeng certainly tried. As soon as he heard the shouting and realized what was happening, he moved quickly to the console that would allow him, with just a few keystrokes, to begin erasing everything on the computers in the van. The erasure would be complete, randomly overwriting all the data multiple times in a process similar to that used by the Central Intelligence Agency for getting rid of information they didn't want exposed.

Zeng's hands were poised just above the console when the door to the van was thrown open.

Brown shouted, "*Raise your hands! Now!* This is the Federal Bureau of Investigation, and you are all under arrest!" Within seconds, Mike and three FBI men had entered the van with guns pointed at Zeng's team.

Zeng paused and looked Brown in the eye, his fingers just inches away from the keys that would delete everything. With his many years as an intelligence officer, he had learned to read people, including Westerners—whom he considered relatively easy to understand. He often told his team, "Westerners wear their intentions on their faces. They cannot help it." In this case, Zeng could tell that it was Mike Brown's intention to shoot him if he didn't immediately comply and raise his arms.

Though he momentarily considered performing his duty and lunging for the key that would erase the data, his instinct for self-preservation won out and he slowly raised his hands above his head. He never took his eyes from Brown's. Had he sensed a moment's hesitation, the data would have been erased. There was no such moment.

Within a single minute, the van was secure—not a shot was fired.

The *Dreamscape* rolled smoothly to the end of the runway and waited for the ground crew to bring the portable stairway that would allow Gesling, Thibodeau, Mbanta, Singer, Wells, and Graves to exit. For another few days, they would be the only American astronauts to venture beyond orbit since 1972.

After determining that the vehicle was safe for the passengers to exit, the door opened and the passengers slowly made their way down the stairs and onto a red carpet, where a jubilant Gary Childers met them. They had been in space for almost a week and were now in the middle of getting used to the tug of the

Earth's gravity. For some it was a welcome relief; for others, it was a reminder that their adventure was truly over.

With handshakes to the exiting men and hugs to the women, Gary Childers was again in his element. Speeches followed, and then the entire group awaited Paul Gesling's egress from the vehicle. As in the dress rehearsals, Gesling had to take care of his post-flight checklist before he could make his exit.

When Gesling appeared in the doorway, the crowd erupted into applause. And the applause was not limited to those in the VIP area. The throngs of people outside the gates that had turned out for the launch six days ago were back; they too clapped and cheered. And more than a few people watching on television did so as well.

Gesling, somewhat taken aback by the whole spectacle, raised a hesitant arm and waved back to the crowd. With a little more confidence in his land legs than the passengers who had exited before him, he made his way down the stairs and received an approving handshake and welcome from Childers when he arrived there.

"Well done, Paul," Gary exclaimed as he pumped his hand and patted him on the shoulder. "Well done!"

"Thanks" was all Paul could think of to say as he returned the handshake and smiled in Gary's general direction.

"Smile for the people, Paul. This is our payday."

"I knew you would do it!" Caroline O'Conner shouted and cheered as she brushed past Childers and threw her arms around Gesling, greeting him with a more than collegial "Welcome home, Paul." There wasn't time for the close contact to continue, but it was clear to all that neither O'Conner nor Gesling was quite ready for it to end.

"Payday? We lost money on this flight," Paul said under his breath to Childers.

"Did we, Paul? I'm not so sure." While the flight in particular lost money, Childers considered it an "investment." The book-ings on the next ten flights were firm, and by number eight he would be in the black. And he'd been thinking about the rescue mission. He'd heard one of the talking-head science experts on the news claim that all of the American and Chinese astronauts could reenter in the Orion space capsule and that they would likely be dropped off at the ISS. The wheels were turning in his dollars-oriented brain. Of course, his company could use the write-off provided by the first seven flights as "losses" if they needed to. And of course they would do that. With good accountants, losses could be a good thing. But Gary liked making money and planned on doing just that.

Chapter 21

Astronauts Bill Stetson and Anthony Chow were swiftly and accurately stepping through procedures and checking off items on their checklists. Their Orion space capsule sat roughly thirty stories atop more than a million pounds of highly explosive ammonium perchlorate composite propellant and another fairly large volume of liquid oxygen and liquid hydrogen. If things were to go awry, there would be plenty of fuel for that fire. But Bill and Tony were far too busy to ponder the ramifications of such an unlikely event when the solid rocket motors of the Ares I first stage ignited. Unlike the space shuttle, which sat lazily on the launch pad for the first few seconds after igniting its main engines, the Ares I leapt off the pad, the resulting acceleration pushing the two men solidly into their couches with more force than that experienced on any other human-rated rocket.

Selected for safety and not comfort, using solid rocket motors for a rocket carrying people had been controversial from the beginning. Many astronauts, including Stetson, had been skeptical. Unlike a liquid-fueled rocket, a solid-fueled rocket could not be shut off once lit. A solid rocket motor would burn until it ran out of fuel. And it was precisely because of this that the Von Braun team had designed the Saturn V rocket with liquid-fueled engines and refused to use solid rocket motors. But, being beholden to data, Stetson eventually became a fan of the approach when he reviewed the reports showing that solid rocket motors failed far less often than their liquid motor counterparts.

"T minus four minutes and holding." The voice of the launch director sounded deadpan and emotionless over the intercom, on television, radios, and inside Bill's helmet speakers. "This is a scheduled twenty-minute built-in hold. The countdown clock will resume in nineteen minutes and forty-seven seconds from now."

"Getting close, Tony!" Bill couldn't hide his excitement. "Put your game face on, buddy."

"Damn close, and put me in coach!" Tony replied, then keyed the com after looking at his checklist. "Launch control, we are starting the interior launch cameras and telemetry recorders."

"Roger that, *Mercy I*. Be advised that we've got launch weather verification, and it looks like all is go at this point."

"Control." Stetson added his checklist items to the conversation. "The launch computer is showing green and is configured for launch." Bill thought about the action taking place back in the launch control center or LCC. The director was probably polling the various console drivers to see if they were ready to continue with the launch. Were Bill a fly on the wall, he would have heard a query of "Launch Authority Team go, no-go?" Which would usually be followed by "Go for launch." And then "Guidance and Control go, no-go?" "Go for launch!" And the process would continue through all the Ares 1 launch systems until the launch director was assured that, indeed, the Ares 1 launch vehicle was cleared to leave Earth.

"Launch control shows first-stage igniter heater power removed. *Mercy I*, please verify."

"Uh, roger that, launch control. We show green light on first-stage igniter heater breakers," Stetson replied. Bill and Tony responded to what seemed like an endless list of items to be checked until the twenty-minute hold was complete. Finally, the word was given.

"This is launch control. We have final launch status verification and are now resuming the countdown. Start the clock now at T minus four minutes and counting."

"Roger that, control. *Mercy I* shows flight-termination system and solid rocket motors are armed." Bill looked over at his colleague and flashed him a grin. "We're almost there now!"

"Let's go, let's go!" Tony replied.

"T minus one minute and forty seconds. We show the rocket's flight-control system is enabled for launch. *Mercy I*, please verify."

"Flight-control system is green." Tony tapped the green icon on his computer screen to verify. At that moment the flight-control system software switched the entire flight-control system from land power over to internal rocket systems power and started counting off seconds to ignition.

"T minus one minute and counting."

"We ready, Tony?"

"A-OK, Bill."

"Roger that." Bill tapped another icon on his checklist. "Auxiliary power units are running, and *Mercy I* shows solid rocket motor thrust vector control gimbal test is good."

"T minus eighteen seconds. Ignition and hold-down bolts are armed and ready. We have sound suppression active and launcher flood is initiated."

"Roger that, control." Stetson pushed his body into his couch as best he could, preparing for the upcoming thrust.

"Launch inhibits are removed and vehicle is armed. Ten, nine, eight, seven, six, five, four, three, two, one, ignition!"

Bill and Tony held on and tried not to grit their teeth.

"We have liftoff! Start the clock as *Mercy I* clears the tower for America's return to the Moon!" The launch director's voice sounded excited and enthusiastic for a brief moment.

NASA was through simply sending astronauts around and around the Earth. It was finished sending only robots to explore beyond low Earth orbit. Americans were going into space, and they were on their way to the Moon.

As the Ares I cleared the launch tower, it began its ascent into Earth orbit, and its characteristic vibrations began shaking the teeth of the two astronauts perched on top. During its design, engineers had discovered that the vibrations caused by the firing of the solid rocket motors would be jarring enough to cause brain damage in its passengers. After considerable effort, a system was devised to dampen the vibrations, making them merely annoying rather than lethal. To those riding on the beast, the difference was a matter of academic debate.

The solid rocket motors had just burned out when eighteen mini-explosions occurred—jarring the veritable heck out of the astronauts and causing them to fall forward into their chairs. The explosive bolts connecting the rocket's first stage with its second stage had just fired. And the sequence was just as violent, as exciting, and as exhilarating as Bill had remembered from his previous two flights. Though still exciting, to Bill it was just another day at the office. To Tony, on the other hand, who had only participated in simulation flights thus far, it was all new and very scary. Very. Scary.

"Hang on there, Tony," Bill said. "Second-stage engines are about to kick in, and it is a kick in the pants!"

"I'm hanging!" Chow shouted back—welcoming the pause in the nerve-wracking launch vibrations.

"Going for second-stage ignition," Stetson radioed to mission control. The liquid engines of the second stage of the Ares I rocket fired, again forcing both Stetson and Chow back into their chairs at well over three gravities. There was very little piloting to be done in this phase of the flight. The computer controlled everything. Stetson monitored all the instruments just in case he disagreed with the computer and had to take over control. He was prepared, thanks to countless hours of training. But such an event was extremely unlikely. Bill kept an eye out anyway.

"Roger that, *Mercy I*. Telemetry shows second-stage ignition is good," mission control replied. *Mercy I* was the name given to the mission in the hours before launch. Rescuing the trapped Chinese would someday be considered to be the most technologically complex act of mercy in human history. It was likely the most risky and failure prone as well.

"What an incredible view," Chow exclaimed as he peered out the window to his right.

"I know it's a great view, Tony, but you will have time for sightseeing later. Let's keep an eye on the control panels. You and I are covering for Charles and Helen, and we've got to make sure we don't miss anything," Bill scolded the rookie astronaut. Though they were thoroughly cross-trained in the years prior to the flight, neither had really expected to be flying to the Moon performing the duties of their missing colleagues in addition to their own.

"Roger that" was all Chow could muster in response. Bill made a mental note to keep an eye over Tony's shoulder for the time being until he was certain he was going to be good to go. Just another precautionary measure.

The second stage of the Ares I lifted the Orion capsule into a circular orbit just above two hundred and fifty miles high. At that point, the second-stage separation pyrotechnics fired, blasting the liquid hydrogen and oxygen tanks away and allowing them to fall back to Earth and burn up on reentry. All that was left of the Ares I was the Orion spaceship and its two occupants. Thanks to the successful launch of the Ares V rocket, they were on track to rendezvous with the Earth Departure Stage carrying the lunar lander. After that, they would be on their way out of Earth orbit and moving toward the Moon.

Stetson had practiced the rendezvous with the lander several times in the last few days and thousands of times over the last few months. In about four orbits it would be showtime. Ignoring his own admonition, Stetson peered out the window to gaze on the beautiful blue planet beneath him. Scanning the surface to find a recognizable reference point, he quickly realized they were approaching the east coast of Africa and the Indian Ocean.

I never get tired of this, he thought to himself as he snapped out of his reverie and back into the reality of flying a spacecraft traveling at five miles each second. At these speeds, errors could be fatal and unforgiving. And he could not forget the error that had occurred in this stage of the mission during the test flight.

Four orbits passed a lot faster than Bill had expected. It seemed only moments ago that they were on the launchpad and now the LIDAR was beeping away at the Altair lander recently launched by the mighty Ares V rocket. NASA had come a long way from launching rockets separated in time by at least a month or more to doing it with only hours or days in between. Designing for relative simplicity had helped a lot.

"Houston, we have LIDAR confirmation that the range to target is twenty-five hundred meters and closing," Bill reported. "I am disengaging the automated rendezvous and docking system now."

"*Mercy I,* please repeat," said the monotone voice of the mission controller in faraway Houston, Texas.

"I said, I am disengaging the AR and D system and proceeding with a manual docking." Though choosing to turn off the automated rendezvous and docking system was within his purview as commander and pilot of the flight, it was still unusual to do so in the absence of any sort of in-flight anomaly or failure. To Stetson, the failure that had caused him to assume command of the rendezvous during the test flight was reason enough to take control now. Besides, what were they going to do about it? Abort and ask him to come home? Not likely.

"Roger that, *Mercy I*. We understand that you are proceeding with a manual docking. There are some curious folks down here who want to know why. I'm sure you'll fill them in."

"Will do, Houston," Stetson confirmed.

"All right, Bill, show me how a real astronaut flies a spaceship." Chow smiled, not at all worried that his colleague and friend might screw up as they moved around the Earth every ninety minutes or so, waiting to collide—dock—with the rest of their lunar-exploration vehicle.

"Just hold on, Tony. Help me keep an eye on that delta-vee," Bill replied matter-of-factly. "Two thousand meters to target," Bill said.

"Relative velocity one hundred meters per second," Chow told his pilot.

Stetson fired the forward thrusters to reduce the relative velocity between the vehicles. Stetson's actions were just like in the robotic mission weeks earlier, but this time there was no obvious failure. He had done it then, and, in his mind at least, he was sure to do it again. This was what Bill was born to do.

Stetson again fired the thrusters to slow the Orion. Like the previous firings, inside the capsule they heard the *BANG BANG* of the thrusters. The sound was loud and annoying, but also comforting. For Stetson, it was the sound of him being in control. And he liked being in control.

"One hundred and fifty meters to target," Chow said.

"One hundred meters."

"Twenty-five meters."

They both felt the bump as the Orion successfully mated with the Altair, making *Mercy I* a complete spacecraft. To Stetson, the resulting silence was deafening. His adrenaline was still pumping. Beads of perspiration were evident on his brow, and his ground-based physician was certainly monitoring his now-declining heart rate.

"Houston, this is *Mercy I*. We're docked and beginning the Earth departure checklist." Stetson was not about to take a break or relax while lives on the Moon were depending upon him.

"Tony, pull up the Earth departure checklist and let's get started."

"Roger that." Chow smiled, himself not completely relaxed, and replied in his most professional voice for the benefit of all those listening to the exchange back on Earth.

Chapter 22

A few orbits later, Stetson and Chow, with support from mission control in Houston, determined that all systems on *Mercy I* were operational and ready for Trans-Lunar Injection, or TLI. It was at this point that the liquid-fueled engines of the Ares V Earth Departure Stage, or EDS, would reignite and give them the kick they needed to get to the Moon. Using essentially the same engines that powered the second stage of the Ares I, the Ares V EDS had fired first to place the vehicle and its payload into Earth orbit. Now that the rest of the spaceship had arrived and docked, they were ready to be reignited.

As with all phases of the mission so far, with the exception of the docking maneuver, the TLI was controlled by the onboard computer. Stetson and Chow watched with excitement and trepidation as the clock counted down to engine start. They were excited about their journey to the Moon but simultaneously worried at what they might find there. The Chinese crew was now experiencing the very cold lunar night, and no one could be sure there would be anyone left to rescue once *Mercy I* arrived.

With only a few minutes to go before the engines were to ignite, Chow reached up and turned off the radio transmitter so as to keep cabin conversation from being broadcast home.

"Bill, have you thought about what we are going to do if we don't find anyone alive up there?"

"I try not to think about it. The Chinese ambassador requested that we bring the bodies home. But I'm not sure that would be the right thing to do. I think, if they are dead, that we should bury them on the Moon. They knew the risks, and if it were me, I would want to have the Moon be *my* final resting place. I'm not sure my wife would agree, but then again, she might. You?"

"I don't know. It's a shame we didn't have time to really plan for that contingency. I mean, if we bury them there, shouldn't they have some sort of marker or something?"

"Tony, these people are going to make it. We're going to get there, and we're going to get them home. No more of this dead and dying shit. We've got a rescue mission to make happen!"

"Right. I guess that's the only way to think about it until we get different data," Tony replied. "You got it." With that, he turned the cabin's transmitter back on.

The TLI burn was anticlimactic. Compared with launch and even the orbital-insertion burn, the boost that put them on a path to the Moon was fairly mild. The engines fired, changing the spacecraft's roughly circular orbit around the Earth to an elliptical one with its highest point at the radius of the Moon's orbit. If one were to look at the point in space at which the spacecraft would reach the Moon's orbit at that very moment, then all that would be found would be empty space. The Moon would not yet have arrived there in its own orbit about the Earth. The boost was timed so that the spaceship would arrive at a point in space at precisely the same time that the Moon would arrive, allowing them to rendezvous and then land. Orbital mechanics was all about where to arrive and when.

For the next few hours, Stetson and Chow performed various maintenance and preparatory jobs, finished their evening meal, and settled into their wall-mounted sleeping bags for a well-deserved night's rest. Neither felt the least little bit of space sickness. Stetson had experienced it on his previous flights, with less severity on each subsequent flight. For this flight, he hardly noticed it. Chow appeared to be one of those rare people who was unaffected by space sickness.

Chow struggled into his sleeping bag, taking comfort that the recirculating fans were humming in the background. He didn't want to fall asleep, have the fans fail, and suffocate on his own exhaled carbon dioxide. With no external forces or wind, it might be easy for an astronaut to suffocate during sleep, with a cloud of stationary carbon dioxide accumulating around his head. This, like many other "gotchas," was well understood by spacecraft designers. Chow did manage to get this thought out of his mind as he fell into a fitful sleep.

Gazing out onto the gray lunar surface, Chow was stranded in the lunar lander, waiting to die. He was alone. In his thoughts he was asking, Where is Stetson? Why isn't he here? *He knew that Bill had come to the Moon with him on the rescue mission, but he was nowhere to be found.* His panic began to increase until it finally reached a boiling point as he spoke to his wife, telling her goodbye from the Moon, when the alarm sounded and jolted him awake.

Momentarily disoriented, Chow looked around, trying to figure out where he was. For a moment he thought he was, like in his dream, on the Moon. He then concluded that he must be at home in his bed—*no, that wasn't right, either.* Now fully awake, hearing the blaring of the klaxon, he realized he was on the Orion spacecraft on his way to the Moon. He looked quickly over at Bill Stetson, who was also being jolted awake.

"Bill, what's going on?" he asked nervously.

"I have no idea." Stetson quickly unzipped his bag and didn't even bother to cover himself as he floated forward to check the status boards and find out why the alarm was sounding.

Chow unzipped and joined Stetson. Just as they arrived, the radio came to life.

"*Mercy I*, this is Houston. We're seeing a problem with one of your solar arrays. Are you seeing it as well?"

"Uh, checking it," Stetson relied. "Copy that, Houston—we see it. One appears to have stopped tracking the sun."

"That's what telemetry is showing us, over."

The solar arrays, mounted on the Orion near its base, provided most of the power required to run its systems. They were mounted on gimbals that allowed them to continuously track the sun so as to maintain the ability to generate a consistent amount of power. Since the Orion was moving toward the Moon while it was still orbiting the Earth, albeit on an ever-increasing altitude orbit, and since the whole spacecraft was slowly spinning to equalize the heat input from the sun in its so-called barbeque roll, the solar arrays were constantly moving to keep the sun in view.

"Batteries are kicking in," noted Chow as he looked at the status board. With the array not pointing at the Sun, the power generated would drop, requiring the onboard batteries to come online in order to maintain the ship's systems, including life support.

"Houston, one of the arrays appears to have seized and is not moving," Stetson said. He looked at Chow and then back at the status screen.

Chow could see that Stetson was concerned. Without maximum power from the arrays, the ship would have to rely on batteries to make up the difference. There was enough power from the batteries to allow the craft to swing by the Moon and return to Earth—this was one of the contingencies that the Disaster Team had noted and required them to train for. The Disaster Team were the guys who looked at all the possible failures and then wrote training scenarios for the astronauts to practice and learn from. This was one of them.

The problem with letting this real-life problem be resolved as it was during training was that they would not have enough power to go into lunar orbit and land. Without landing they could not rescue the stranded Chinese taikonauts. If they followed the book, the mission would be over. They would survive, and all the Chinese would die.

Chow momentarily imagined himself as one of the Chinese taikonauts, stranded, cold, and waiting to die. It was too much like his dream, and he quickly shook himself away from the daydream and said, "Bill, we can't let this happen. We can't let those people die."

"Damn right we can't. But right now I sure don't know what we can do about it. While I come up with something, let's run the drill."

"Makes sense to me," Tony agreed.

"Houston. We're going to power down the array-control system and restart. I'm pulling up the reboot procedure now. Do you concur?"

"We concur. Reboot will take approximately twenty minutes. We'll be running the simulations in parallel. If we come up with something you need to know, we'll be in touch."

"Roger that. *Mercy I* out." With that, Stetson began reviewing the manual restart procedure for the solar-array pointing system.

Chow hadn't trained for this, so he decided it would be best to step back—float back, as it were—and let Bill do his job. He went to the window and looked out into space. As the Orion spun, he caught sight of the Earth, which was still, by far, the largest object in view, and only fleeting glimpses of the Moon. He took a deep breath and waited.

Twenty minutes later, Chow watched Stetson complete the sequence that would completely power down the solar-array pointing system and then restart it. Anyone familiar with computers would have been in agreement with what he was trying to do—reboot.

Chow heard nothing to indicate that the reboot sequence was complete. He only heard his own breathing, some mumbled curses from Stetson, and a few status requests from the radio. He half-way expected to hear the sound of a large machine grinding to a halt and then restarting. Instead, there was just the silence of the crew compartment and the recirculating fans.

"Damn it!" Stetson said, pounding his fist against the console. The reacting force started him spinning in the opposite direction. He quickly stabilized himself with his other hand and planted a foot against his couch to hold him still. "Houston, the reboot is complete. No change. The array is not moving."

No sooner had those words left Stetson's lips than Chow's heart sank.

"We show the same on our boards down here, Bill. We're still looking at options."

Stetson pushed back from the console and floated to where Chow was perched.

"Tony, I have an idea. What if the gimbal just needs a good kick to get it moving again?"

"EVA?"

"Yes. I think I'm going to suit up, go out, and give it a kick. We've got to get it moving."

Stetson had that look that Tony recognized so well. It was that look that intimidated almost everyone who came into his presence. It was the *get out of my way, I have something important to do* look. And Chow didn't feel like getting in his way. He replied to his commander and friend, "I'll get the procedure pulled up, and then we'll get in our suits." Both men had to wear their suits, because the Orion didn't have an airlock. When the door opened to the vacuum of space, all the air in the crew cabin would vent.

That meant that everyone in the cabin had to wear their spacesuits for an EVA, even if they weren't the ones going outside.

Chow learned in his very early training that getting into his spacesuit wasn't like putting on a business suit. Each suit was specially designed or modified for a particular astronaut. Chow had his suit; Stetson had his own. The suits were kept aft and were at least readily accessible. Having only two people in a crew cabin designed to accommodate four was a plus—they had room to move around while they were getting their suits on.

Mission control had readily agreed with Stetson's EVA plan, though they didn't give the plan much chance of success. Some engineer quoted a thirty-five percent probability of success during the discussion, and Chow had to wonder how in the world they had come up with such a number. He thought to himself, *Why isn't it thirty percent? Or forty percent? Why thirty-five?* And then he concluded that they really didn't know. The engineer was just quoting some computer model that he probably didn't really understand anyway.

Forty minutes later, Stetson and Chow were suited up and ready to begin the EVA. Both men had checked and rechecked each other's suits, all according to procedure, and had "safed" any loose materials within the Orion. Once the atmosphere was removed from the Orion, Stetson would be able to open the door and begin his EVA. The last thing they wanted was for some vital piece of hardware to float out the door with him.

"Tony, we're down to minimum atmospheric pressure, and I am about to open the door. Are you ready?"

"I'm ready. I'll be here watching on the monitor. Just call if you need me."

"That's good to know." Stetson smiled. "But I think this'll be quick and easy. I should be back inside in just a few minutes."

With that, he reached down and forcefully pulled the door release, opening the cabin to space. Without so much as a swoosh, the door opened and both men were exposed to the vacuum. Glancing briefly back at Chow, Stetson pushed and gently eased himself out the door. Once his arms cleared the hatch, he attached the loose end of the tether from his spacesuit to the requisite attachment fitting on the hull of the ship. The tether would keep him from accidentally pushing off from the ship too forcefully and floating away into space.

Take it easy, Stetson told himself as he felt the reassuring snap of the tether to the fitting. Though the craft was traveling toward the Moon at over twenty thousand miles per hour, the motion was simply unobservable by Stetson as he began his spacewalk. Without a reference point, such as the ground whizzing by beneath him, and without any of the other side effects of rapid motion such as the wind caused by moving through it, his senses told him that he and the *Mercy I* craft were motionless in space. He could, however, directly sense the ship's rotation. With the starfield, sun, and Earth rotating around his field of view, he knew that the ship was spinning.

For a brief moment, he experienced a powerful sense of vertigo.

"It's so vast," Stetson said to no one in particular. With only his hand-sewn spacesuit between him and infinity, he continued pulling himself out of the Orion until he was totally exposed.

"I'm moving aft toward the arrays. I can see them clearly. One is at a dead stop," Stetson said.

Using the handholds placed on the Orion for just this type of contingency, Stetson pulled himself toward the malfunctioning array. As he got closer, he marveled at their scale. Unfurled to collect sunlight and extended outward from the ship on booms, they were simply beautiful. Each of the two arrays was also eighteen feet in diameter. Huge. As the sun rotated into a more direct view, the reflected light from the arrays varied in brightness, looking like a lighthouse beacon. Stetson was glad he had a sun visor built into the helmet. The sun was *bright*.

Breathing deeply now, Stetson could clearly see his objective. The gimbal at the base of the array boom was the most likely culprit. Putting hand over hand, Stetson moved closer until he was finally able to reach out and touch the malfunctioning piece of hardware.

"Tony, I don't see any sign of damage. It looks just like it did in the mockup and on the drawings." He inspected the gimbal motor so closely that he nearly touched it with his visor.

"Roger that, Bill," Chow responded from within the confines of the Orion. "Move your head to the right so I can get a better look." Chow was referring to the helmet camera built into each astronaut's spacesuit.

Stetson tilted his head, altering his vantage point so that the gimbal would no longer be quite as shadowed, giving his comrade a better view.

"Thanks. I can see it now. I've got the image on-screen next to the as-built image, and they look the same. No damage that I can tell, either."

"Roger that. I guess I'll see if I can kick it loose." Stetson was speaking figuratively. He had no intention of actually kicking the array. Instead, he looked for a convenient place to grab on to it, and then he began slowly twisting the boom, searching for a way to get it moving again. He encountered resistance. The boom didn't move.

Twisting harder in the clockwise direction, Stetson's entire body began to pivot counterclockwise, causing Stetson to momentarily lose his sense of balance just like before when he had pounded his fist against the console. He laughed to himself and said, "Newton got me. Hold on."

With that, he readjusted himself so as to get better footing on the handrail, wedging his boots to better anchor himself into position. Once he was satisfied that he wouldn't torque himself instead of the boom, he grasped the boom and tried again. Still nothing. This time he didn't slip, nor did he laugh.

After about ten minutes of twisting and turning without any success, he paused.

"Bill? May I make a suggestion?" Tony asked.

"Sure, go ahead," Stetson replied.

"Why don't I do another reboot while you are trying to work it loose? Maybe while the control system is not actively applying power to the gimbal's motor, you can get it to move. It might be locked in place electromechanically. If so, you'd be pushing against not only the gimbal, but the motor driving it."

"Great idea, Tony. Let's give it a try."

"On it."

Since Chow had never done the reboot, not even in training, it took him a little longer than it had taken Stetson.

While he was waiting, Stetson had time to contemplate the mission and where he was. He decided that no one, other than another astronaut, could even come close to understanding the emotions and feelings that one experienced in a spacesuit traveling through space. *God, I was meant for this.* Stetson said this to himself, not really to God. *My whole life led to this trip, and I love it.*

He was shaken from his reverie by Chow's voice on the speaker. "Bill, I'm ready. Are you?"

"Yes. I'll start flexing as soon as you cut the power and start the reboot sequence," Stetson replied.

"Okay. Here we go."

A few seconds passed, and then Chow's voice returned. "Now. The power is cycled down and getting ready to restart."

Stetson didn't hesitate. With boots still firmly wedged, he used both hands to grasp and twist the stuck array. Trying to move it first clockwise and then counterclockwise, Stetson jimmied the stubborn piece of hardware. He didn't believe he was getting anywhere, and then, abruptly, he felt a jolt and the whole gimbal began to move. Looking up at the array fan, he could see that it was starting to move under its own power. Moving his hands back from the boom and the gimbal so as to not interfere with its motion, Stetson watched as the array rotated and began again to track the sun.

"Bill, you did it. The board says the array is working, and I think I can see it moving in your helmet camera. Does it look okay to you?" Chow sounded ecstatic.

"Tony, it's moving. I'm coming back in." With those words, Stetson began his climb back toward the hatch.

After Stetson reentered the Orion, he repressurized the cabin, and then he and Chow removed their spacesuits. Even though the thermometer showed that the temperature of the cabin was where it should be, Stetson felt cold. He always felt cold after an EVA, and he attributed it to the psychology of having been floating in the endless frigid void of space. He knew he would warm up; it was just a matter of time. Of course, there was also a checklist to be completed after an EVA—it took them close to thirty minutes to complete it.

"Tony, we need to see what we can off-load from Altair. Have you got the latest list from mission control?" Stetson was referring to the fact that the range safety experts would not allow them to remove any items from the Altair or the Orion while the vehicle was on the pad in the days before launch. Having engineers mucking around with the cargo, messing up the mass distribution and balancing, not to mention being around during the final checkout, was just too much for the safety guys. Instead, the engineers in Texas and Alabama had come up with a list of items that could be thrown overboard to reduce the mass of the Altair's ascent stage so as to allow all six people to get off the surface of the Moon.

Chow, looking at the list as it scrolled across his personal view screen, replied, "Bill, they met the target with about ten kilograms of margin. We can get most of this off the Altair once we land. There's not much we can do until then. We don't want to mess with much of it until then—we don't want some of this to get loose until we're under gravity."

"I knew they'd come up with a plan. I'll look it over myself in a few minutes."

With that, Stetson and Chow were able to sit back and, for a few hours at least, enjoy their ride.

Chapter 23

The four-person crew of the Chinese ship *Harmony* huddled together in the near-complete darkness of their ship's crew cabin. The only light penetrating the blackness came from the LEDs on the instrument panel, showing which of the pitifully few systems were still powered on. Since the crash, the taikonauts had powered down virtually everything except the thermal-control system and, sometimes, the radio, in order to conserve power. The situation had been scary and uncomfortable, but not critical when the sun was in the sky, but now that the fourteen-day night had begun, every milliwatt of power translated directly into a few minutes of life. Power was heat, and in the unbelievably cold lunar night, heat was in short supply.

Harmony's captain, Hui Tian, surveyed the status of her crew by turning her head to look at each directly. Spacesuit helmets didn't allow for any peripheral vision, and in order to see something, she had to look at it directly.

To her immediate right was the ship's physician, Dr. Xu Guan. The relatively tall and gray-haired Xu had weathered the crash fairly well and was fully engaged in keeping everyone functioning. Though his dry sense of humor was greatly appreciated during the flight out, it didn't do much to boost morale after the crash. But that didn't stop him from trying. No matter what the situation, Xu seemed to have some pithy comment at the ready.

When they last spoke privately, Xu admitted that as a youth he had wanted to be a comedian but his father had disapproved. No doubt his patients back on Earth appreciated his humor more than the crew of the *Harmony*—at least at the present moment. Xu had propped himself against the wall with *Harmony*'s pilot, Ming Feng, leaning against him.

Ming had not weathered the crash well at all. In fact, he was failing both physically and mentally at a rapid rate. During their chaotic descent to the surface, when all the alarms had begun to sound, Ming had frozen and Hui had had to take control of the ship from him. If not for her rapid action, they might have all died upon impact—making a fairly sizable crater in the process. Upon impact, Ming was thrown into the control panel and, according to Dr. Xu, had fractured some ribs and perhaps suffered some internal injuries. He was now feverish and semicoherent. *That might be fortunate—under the circumstances,* Hui thought to herself.

To her left, rummaging again through the remains of one of the ship's computer consoles, was the *Harmony*'s engineer and political officer, Zhi Feng. He was not a big man, but his agile frame allowed him to gain access to parts of *Harmony* that would have been impossible for anyone else. He was also the youngest member of the crew. Hui guessed his age to be not more than thirty-five years. Zhi was at times a gift—he had used his engineering training and creativity to scavenge the parts required to keep the air and power functioning for far longer than she had thought possible. At other times, he was a curse—being the ship's political officer, he always made everyone feel like they were under a microscope and that any action of which he didn't approve would be used against them or their families upon the return home. If they returned home. Zhi had gone ballistic when Hui had used the radio to contact the American ship they'd been listening to as it approached the Moon. If it were not for the support she received from Dr. Xu, she suspected he would have smashed the radio rather than let her use it. They depended upon Zhi to keep them alive, but they were also very afraid of him.

Hui shivered in her spacesuit. The power in her suit was still at maximum; Zhi had been able to keep their individual suit batteries fully charged as he drained yet another fuel cell from within *Harmony*'s lander. To conserve power, however, the temperature in all their suits had been turned down to sixty degrees Fahrenheit, and even though every member of the crew prided themselves as being made of "the right stuff," they were all cold. Despite their status, and despite the actions taken by the now nearly useless pilot, she was proud of her crew. They were surviving and would likely last at least another day or so. Intellectually, she knew their situation was hopeless, but her nature didn't allow her to feel that in her gut. There was always hope. And it was her job as leader to instill that hope in her crew. So far it was working.

"I think," Hui said with a long pause, "I think I am going to turn on the radio again. Perhaps the American ship was able to alter course and is now in orbit or something. Please power it on, Zhi." She knew there was virtually no chance that any ship traveling to the Moon would be able to change course and rescue them, but she had to do something.

Hearing the conversation, Dr. Xu straightened up and placed the pilot's head against the bulkhead divider to keep him from falling completely over. Hui noticed and realized that the physician was positioning himself to provide the support she needed should this turn into a fight.

Zhi noticed the doctor's movements as well. He looked at Captain Hui with an expression of near-complete disregard—not anger or hatred—and said, "We will turn it on. But only for a few minutes. We do not have much power remaining, and I will not have my efforts at conserving it wasted in a foolish gesture."

Hui nodded her head, causing a strand of hair to fall annoyingly across her forehead to the middle of the field of view of her left eye. In a spacesuit, she could not simply brush it aside, and even moving her head to dislodge the hair was a major ordeal. She therefore ignored it.

"Hopefully, it will be more than a foolish gesture," she said cautiously to the political officer. "But only time will tell. Very good. Thank you."

Hui then walked over to the console and flipped the switch that would turn on the ship's low-power radio. It was designed to provide communication with taikonauts walking on the lunar surface and not more than a few hundred meters away from the lander. Fortunately, their weak signal had been heard by the *Dreamscape* as it passed nearby.

To her surprise, and to the surprise of everyone in the room, the radio immediately came to life with a voice of a man speaking in

Chinese. "Crew of the *Harmony*. Do not give up hope. Help is on the way. If you can hear this message, please reply." The message was followed by twenty seconds of silence, and it was then repeated.

"Unbelievable!" Zhi gasped. "How is that possible? We're near the limb, but for us to get a signal at this location would require enormous power!"

"Believe it or not, Zhi!" replied Hui, much more practical in her nature. "It does not matter how! Help is on the way! We must let them know we are alive." She moved the microphone to the open faceplate on her suit.

"This is Captain Hui of the *Harmony*. We hear you. We are alive, but just barely. How soon will help arrive? We cannot last much longer."

She stopped speaking and looked at the radio expectantly. Nothing happened for a few minutes, and then she again heard, "Crew of the *Harmony*. Do not give up hope. Help is on the way. If you can hear this message, please reply." It was a recorded broadcast.

"Ha." Zhi laughed pessimistically. "Of course they cannot hear you. The power on our transmitter is too low. They are broadcasting from Earth with who knows how much power. All we have is this miserable surface-to-surface radio."

"I propose a little patience," Dr. Xu interjected. "If it is from Earth, there will be a lag. So wait. Listen. And then respond again. You must try."

Hiu waited through the silence and couldn't contain her disappointment when the recording played yet again. As it stopped, she once again repeated her message, hoping that somehow it would get through.

Immediately following the meeting at which the idea of using Arecibo was first proposed, the Vice President of the United States contacted the Director of the National Science Foundation and secured the use of the dish. At first, the scientists who were told they'd lost their time at the observatory were quite upset—one even threatened to write his congressman. Once the situation was fully explained, however, they were unanimous in their support for suspending science operations and turning the big antenna into a radio station, broadcasting a message to the stranded Chinese taikonauts nearly a quarter million miles away.

At the same time the Vice President was making his call, NASA Administrator Ross directed that NASA's Deep Space Network (DSN) begin listening for any low-power radio transmission that might originate from the Moon. Freeing time on the DSN was a bit more complicated. The DSN was used to collect data from multiple deep-space missions and to send them critical commands and software updates. Focusing the network on the Moon meant that signals from the probes circling Jupiter, Mars, Venus, and elsewhere might not get their messages back when they called home. To meet all these competing needs was a matter of scheduling, scheduling, and scheduling.

That was several days ago, and the team running the Arecibo radio telescope had been sending their automated signals for nearly twenty-five hours when the Chinese taikonaut finally turned on her receiver and heard their message. The DSN's automated system picked up the extremely weak signal from Hui Tian and sent an alert to the operators monitoring the system. Less than six minutes after receiving Hui's message, human ears were listening and getting ready to send a response. For the operators at the DSN, this was an unimaginably fast response time.

For Hui Tian and the rest of the *Harmony's* crew, it seemed like an eternity.

Hui was staring expectantly at the radio when the automated message cut off and another voice inserted itself, in English. "Crew of the *Harmony*, this is Jeff Caldwell of the National Aeronautics and Space Administration. We hear you. Is this Ms. Hui? What is your status?"

"This is Hui Tian of the *Harmony*. We are so very glad to hear your voice. We are cold and very low on power. We have, at most, thirty-six hours remaining before we are entirely dependent upon our spacesuits. One of our crew is injured. The rest of us are okay."

After a brief lag Caldwell replied. "Understood. Ms. Hui, we are so glad to hear that. A representative of your government is here with us. Unfortunately, we don't know exactly where, and we are trying to track him down."

Caldwell's voice then faded a bit as he was obviously speaking to someone with him and not into the microphone. "I don't care if you have to personally search every bathroom in the building. Find him. What about the cafeteria? Okay, just go!"

"Ahem." Caldwell cleared his throat and collected himself before he spoke into the microphone again. "Ms. Hui, there is a rescue mission on its way to the Moon. They know where you are, and they will be landing very close to your location."

"A rescue mission?" said Hui. She was confused, knowing full well that China did not have another vehicle anywhere close to launch status. The transmission lag was quickly becoming intolerable.

"Yes. A NASA crew launched about two days ago. They are on the way to bring you home."

Hui and Dr. Xu were visibly relieved. *Help was on the way. They might just survive the wreck after all!* Hui looked from Dr. Xu to the wounded pilot and then to Zhi Feng. Zhi's expression was unreadable. It was clearly not the same one of relief that she was experiencing.

Moments later, a voice speaking Mandarin was heard through the radio. It was a voice Hui recognized. It was one of her fellow taikonauts, Gong Zheng. She and Gong had trained together, and she considered him to be a friend.

Gong said, "Hui. This is Gong Zheng. You sound well. Are you okay? You said someone was injured. Who?"

"Pilot Ming Feng was injured during landing. He needs medical attention." Hui's voice was firm, but she was very clearly tired.

"I understand," Gong replied. "How are Dr. Xu and Zhi Feng?"

"They were not injured. But we are all very cold and tired." She went on to explain their general situation.

After listening intently to the status of the crew, Gong said, "In order to help you, I need to know the status of the ship's system in detail." And so began a rather lengthy discussion of virtually every system on the *Harmony*—working and nonworking.

During the discussion, Hui once again glanced at the faces of her crewmates. Something was clearly bothering Zhi, and she had no idea what it might be. At the moment she needed to focus on keeping them all alive—and preferably warmer.

Chapter 24

"**H**ouston, this is *Mercy I*. All systems look good for LOI," Bill Stetson said calmly into the microphone. LOI, Lunar Orbit Insertion, would be the first time the Altair's engines would fire during the mission. In a few minutes, the modified Aerojet RL-10 rocket engines, burning liquid hydrogen and oxygen, would begin to slow the mated Orion/Altair *Mercy I* spacecraft so as to allow it to enter orbit around the Moon.

"Copy that, *Mercy I*. All systems look good on our end. How's the view up there?"

Stetson looked at Chow and then briefly out the window before replying, "Awesome. But it sure as hell would be a terrible place to spend eternity."

"Nice place to visit and all that ...," Chow added.

Stetson and Chow had been watching the Moon grow larger, and the Earth grow smaller, with each passing hour. As the Moon now dominated the view from their windows, so did its gravity dominate the little spaceship the astronauts inhabited.

"Couldn't agree more, *Mercy I*. Let's get you guys in orbit and down to the ground for that visit."

A few minutes later, the engines fired, and the *Mercy I* began to slow. At first, though Stetson could feel the engines firing and the resulting acceleration, it was not clear that it was having much of an effect. The Moon's apparent size was still changing—getting larger. Looking at the instruments to confirm that the engines were, in fact, working and slowing the vehicle, Stetson tried to hide his nervousness. He *knew* the engines were functioning and that they were slowing—but his innate Earth-evolved senses could not tell that anything was happening.

After the burn, the instruments confirmed that they had entered orbit, and Stetson breathed a sigh of relief. Looking out the window, Stetson could finally perceive that they were not going to fly by the Moon and off into deep space; rather, they were clearly circling the gray world for the first time. He thought again about Gene Cernan and his bittersweet departure from the Moon almost fifty years ago.

With that, Stetson and Chow once again had to run through their endless checklists. They were going to leave the Orion parked in lunar orbit while they went to the surface in the Altair. Unlike Apollo, there would not be anyone in the orbiting Orion while they were gone, and Stetson wanted to make certain everything was in perfect working order before he left. He looked at the solar-array status screen and saw that it was still working normally—to his great relief.

"*Mercy I*, do you copy?" asked one of the controllers in Houston. Chow replied, "We haven't gone anywhere. What's up?"

"According to the orbital-analysis guys, you should be in a good position to see the *Harmony* in about twelve minutes. Look aft, as you'll be flying almost directly over it, crossing from eleven o'clock to about four o'clock in your field of view. The sun angle will be favorable, and if you use the terrain imager you should get a good view. If the Lunar Mapper hadn't failed, we'd have some great pictures of the whole area for you. Unfortunately, all you'll have before descent are the images you get on the next two passes. You might say hello to the folks on the ground there while you're at it."

"Roger that. We'll make a phone call or two before dropping by." Bill looked at the surface and squinted, trying to see something, but eyeballs weren't anywhere near big enough to detect the downed spacecraft at the orbital distance of the Orion/Altair.

The terrain imager, on the other hand, was a different story. It was on the Orion to allow the crew to perform last-minute inspection of the planned landing site with ultrahigh resolution.

From lunar-orbital altitude, the terrain imager could capture the license number on the old Lunar Rover—if it had had one, and if the spaceship happened to pass over the Rover during the lunar day. Night imaging was still good, but not as good as what would be possible in full sun.

"Imager is coming online," Chow said. "Okay. Upload the targeting data and we'll see what she sees." Chow then used the touch-screen display to bring up what the terrain imager was viewing. With the imager tracking the ground, and with it set to nearly maximum magnification, the ground whizzed by dizzyingly fast. The onboard processors were able to extract still images from the video, making inspection of any particular spot relatively easy to accomplish.

Bill Stetson had been listening to the exchange in the background while he was checking out his suit for the surface EVA that would begin in just a few hours—once they were on the ground. He pushed off and floated over to Chow, stopping just behind him so that he could easily see the terrain-imager pictures as they came in. He also keyed at the microphone and tuned the digital transmitter across the band the Chinese were using while leaving the homeward-pointing communications links still in place.

Chow looked at the display, noting that mission control had synchronized a countdown clock to the time at which they should be able to see the *Harmony*. The camera would then lock on to the crashed ship and track it as they flew over, providing images from several viewing angles and giving the crew a good idea of where they should land the Altair. On the next pass, their orbital position would be different and provide yet another complete set of viewing angles. To complete their mission, they would leave the command capsule Orion and land on the surface in the Altair lunar surface access module. Then, if all went according to plan, they would bring the Chinese survivors back up in the Altair, dock with the Orion, and successfully complete their mission of mercy by getting everybody back to Earth safely.

"*Harmony*, this is NASA spacecraft *Mercy I*. Do you copy?" Bill and Tony kept their eyes focused on the imager screen. Still no sign of the downed vehicle.

"*Harmony*, this is NASA spacecraft *Mercy I* about to orbit over your position. Do you copy?"

"Not seeing it, Bill."

"Keep looking, Tony. It's there." Bill tried not to show any pessimism in his voice. "*Harmony,* this is NASA spacecraft *Mercy I.* Do you copy?"

At almost the same time that Stetson and Chow spotted the *Harmony* on the imager, a signal burst over the intercom.

"There it is!" Bill pointed at the screen.

"*Mercy I, Mercy I,* this is *Harmony*! It is great to hear your voice!"

Though the surface was in darkness, the camera's infrared augmentation and automated signal-processing algorithms were able to provide the two men with an image that was clearly identifiable as a manmade spacecraft sitting on a plain. It looked very small. As the camera locked on to the *Harmony* and tracked it, the image became relatively motionless as their ship flew overhead.

"*Harmony,* be advised that we are beginning our descent after the next orbital pass and will land as close to you as possible. Do you copy?"

"Copy that, *Mercy I.* We are eagerly awaiting you. Good luck with your landing procedure. Be aware that there are several crater rims to our north and west. There are boulders as large as automobiles scattered about to our east."

"Roger that, *Harmony.* Thanks for the advice. It's a little dark down there, so if y'all want to turn on the runway lights, it would help."

"If only we had the power to spare, *Mercy I.*" Bill wasn't sure the Chinese taikonaut understood his light levity. Rather than easing the mood, it might have been more unsettling to them. He made a mental note to forgo the jokes for the time being.

"We're moving quickly out of range, *Harmony.* We'll see you on the next orbit."

"Understood, *Mercy I. Harmony* out."

Chow looked at Stetson as they flew out of range and said, "Are we ready?"

"Damn right we're ready. Let's go get those people before they freeze to death. We're supposed to start descent just after the next pass. Suit up!"

On the surface, Hui and her crew were elated that the two American astronauts were directly overhead and looking down upon them. But they were too cold for that elation to help much.

It would take a couple of orbits for the Americans to land, and they might not land very close. Help was coming, but it would still be a little while.

They huddled together in the crew compartment watching the power indicator fade to nothingness. With the lander's last battery drained, and the fuel cells fully depleted, they were now totally dependent upon their spacesuits for warmth. If nothing were to go wrong, they should be able to survive in their suits for another eight hours.

"Americans. How are we supposed to light up the runway when we can't even heat our suits?" Hui asked Dr. Xu.

"I think that was an attempt to lighten the mood." Xu smiled at his captain.

"Humor? At a time like this? Americans." Hui shook her head. "How's Ming Feng?"

"Hard to say." The doctor peered through the listless pilot's faceplate and didn't look too happy. "He's still breathing. The breaths are rapid and fitful, but he's breathing. I don't know the extent of his injuries, and I fear that even if we get off the Moon, he might not survive the trip back to Earth. Hopefully, we can get him out of his suit and examine him better once the Americans are here."

"Carried home by the great Americans. Coming to the rescue of those poor, backward Chinese, saving us all and heaping shame and embarrassment on our country." It was the first time Zhi Feng had spoken in several hours, and the bitterness was impossible to escape.

"Zhi, we're going home. We're not going to die! And we got to the Moon ahead of all of them. Our countrymen will be proud— and it is better to come home to our families than to die here. I miss my family, and now that I have a chance to see them, I will not begrudge those who are coming to help us."

"I will. It is shameful. I will not be able to face my father—he served his country proudly and never had to bow before the Americans or anyone else."

"Would you rescue the Americans if they asked?" Dr. Xu joined the conversation. "My job is to save lives. Though it grieves me that our moment of glory is now one of humility, I will gladly accept help to save Ming's life as well as my own."

"We took China to the Moon!" Hui said, more than a bit

frustrated with the younger man. "Besides, we survived! We crash-landed on the Moon—two hundred and forty thousand miles from home—and have survived longer than we would have thought possible. And we owe that survival to you, Zhi. Without your engineering skills at keeping us warm, we would never have made it. *You* will be a hero!"

"Some hero. I kept us alive long enough for the Americans to get the glory. We would have been better off dead. At least then our countrymen could have come to get our bodies in a Chinese spaceship."

"You will be quiet now, engineer!" Hui, now clearly angry, asserted her command position. She calmed herself but left the edge to her tone. "Zhi. That is enough. We will not let misplaced pride stand in the way of doing what we must do to survive. We will not serve our country by being buried here. Enough! Need I remind you that I am in command of this mission? We will carry ourselves appropriately with the Americans and represent China with pride. That is an order."

Zhi did not appear to be impressed or affected by her order. But he did quiet and for that, Hui was grateful.

"It is not long now," she said. "They will be on the ground within the next three hours or less." Hui was reviewing the information provided from their last radio contact with Earth. Her colleague had stayed with her on the radio until she had to switch it off due their rapidly fading power. Had their counterpart on Earth not told them precisely when the American ship would arrive, they would not have had the power to communicate with them. She looked out the window and into the darkness.

"There are quite a few boulders out there. I hope they can avoid them on their way in." The thought of trying to pilot a lander in the lunar darkness terrified her. They had not been equipped for a night landing, and they had certainly not planned on staying until nightfall. She then thought about the American Apollo program and recalled that none of them had landed at night, either. The Apollo missions were carefully choreographed to occur during the day and at locations that would provide direct line-of-sight communication with the Earth. *Did their current lander even have landing lights?*

)   •   ●   ◖   (

Chow and Stetson were in their suits and in position for the Altair's separation from the Orion and their descent to the surface. All systems checked out, and they were ready to go.

Stetson was worried, but not about going down to the Moon. He was worried about the timing and the fact that the taikonauts had less than five hours of power left in their suits. He'd have to get the Altair on the ground close to the *Harmony,* walk to the Chinese lander, and help the four taikonauts get back to the Altair. While he was taking care of getting the stranded Chinese, Chow would begin off-loading the equipment from the Altair that would enable them to get off the Moon and back to Earth. Once he returned, they would have to break out some tools to remove a few panels on the exterior of the spacecraft. That was a two-man job at a minimum, and none of them had ever tried it. Stetson was worried about the timing and the actions. If everything went according to plan, they would have about an hour or two to spare to get to the downed Chinese. That wasn't much margin.

"Tony, separation in five seconds. Four. Three. Two. One. Separate!" called Stetson. The Altair jolted as it separated from the Orion. There was a slight roll as the two vehicles moved apart and then a low rumble—the Altair's engines were lit, and they were beginning their descent.

"How many times did you simulate landing in the dark?" asked Chow.

"This is my first," said Stetson. Unlike during any of their simulations, Stetson and Chow were descending to the surface in total darkness. "This was a mission scenario that was never supposed to happen," he said.

"You're kidding, right?"

"Nope. All the sims had us landing and taking off during the day. We don't have enough power to last through the night, and it's just too dangerous to land in the dark. Why on Earth would we simulate such a thing? It was never on anyone's mission plan!"

"So this will be your first time," said Chow.

"Yep! But, like I said, don't worry. We got pretty good pictures of the landing site from the Lunar Mapper before it crapped out, and now we can compare them with those we just took to make sure we don't put this monster down on any rocks or a crashed Chinese lander. We've also got the terrain-mapping radar and some pretty good lights that I am supposed to switch on now." Stetson paused long enough to activate four halogen lights pointing downward in their direction of travel.

Stetson continued, "The lights were put on here to help us avoid tripping on something in the shadow of the lander as we walk around. Depending upon the time of year and where you are on the Moon, the shadows can be rather long. We're going to use them to help us land instead. Can't talk anymore; I'd better pay attention to what I, er, the computer is doing as we land."

Stetson returned his attention to the view screen and the altimeter data. Though the lights were bright, the ship was still too far away for them to reflect from anything on the ground. The radar told him that they were five miles from the surface and descending rapidly. The automated system was taking them to a site about three hundred meters from the *Harmony*, in an area that was relatively free of boulders.

As the descent continued, Stetson closely watched the cameras for any sign of the ground beneath them. He was painfully aware of what had happened the first time an American astronaut descended to the surface of the Moon. That commander had been Neil Armstrong, and he had had to manually bring the lander down to avoid some boulders that weren't supposed to be in the way. They'd made it, but with far less fuel remaining than planned for. *That's why we have margin,* thought Stetson.

"I see the ground," said Stetson. And he saw it appear rather suddenly. One minute they were coming down through near-total darkness, and the next they could see the ground, and some boulders, just beneath and ahead of them.

"I don't see *Harmony*. Tony, look aft and see if you can find them." Stetson was hoping the computer had put them down in the right place.

The ship lunged upward as the engines further slowed their rate of descent. They were now dropping slowly toward the surface and, fortunately, the patch of ground they were headed toward looked wide open, with no boulders large enough to matter to the twenty-five-foot diameter Altair. Hopefully.

"Holy cow!" Chow exclaimed. "Look at the dirt we're kicking up. I don't see *Harmony*." The engines were now kicking up an ever-increasing amount of dust as the ship drew nearer and nearer to the surface. Some of the debris was undoubtedly being blown far enough to impact the walls of the *Harmony* only three hundred meters away.

With a thump, the Altair reached the surface and the engines shut off. The lights illuminated the area around the lander, and, over the next couple of minutes, most of the airborne dust and debris kicked up during descent settled to the surface. The Altair was on the Moon, and neither Chow nor Stetson said a word for at least thirty seconds.

"We're here." Chow exhaled and relaxed just a little.

"Right. Touchdown," Stetson replied. "We don't have much time. Let's go through checkout, and I'll get ready to get out of here and over to the *Harmony*—if we're in the right place. I never did see the ship as we were coming in."

"Houston, this is *Mercy I*. We're on the Moon." Stetson knew that history was being made, and he was being very careful in his choice of words. "We don't yet see *Harmony*, but I am preparing an EVA to find them."

"*Mercy I*, this is mission control. Good luck. You've got some very happy people back home who want to see you and your passengers get back home safe and sound."

"Roger that." Stetson reached forward and turned off the microphone. "Now that the perfunctory remarks are concluded, let's run through the checklist and make sure we don't screw anything up that will keep us from going home. See if you can contact *Harmony* on the radio again."

Chow adjusted some settings on the ship's transmitter and spoke into it. "This is *Mercy I*. Captain Hui, are you there? Can you hear me? Please respond."

The speaker remained silent. Chow repeated the message while gazing out the window at the lunar landscape. After another thirty seconds, he repeated it again.

"Bill, if they're still with us, then they're not able to respond for some reason. Their batteries and fuel cells must be totally out of power."

"I was afraid of that. According to what we saw when we flew over, we should be only about a thousand feet from them. Their ship should be just over there. Right?" Stetson said while pointing out the window toward an outcropping of rocks about one hundred and fifty feet away. "I guess I'll just have to go out there and find them."

For the next thirty minutes, Chow helped Bill Stetson check out his spacesuit. As during Apollo, spacesuits were custom designed to fit each astronaut. Each connection had to be secure and airtight; there was no room for error in the unforgiving lunar environment.

"Okay. I think I'm ready to go." Bill tapped a gloved hand against his sun shield, pushing it up and locking it out of the way. He certainly wouldn't be needing it. "Any issues with the airlock?" Unlike the Orion, from which the in-flight EVA had to commence, the living space in the Altair lander did not have to vent to vacuum for each EVA. Instead, the lander was equipped with an airlock.

"It's clear. Nothing but green lights on the panel."

With that, Stetson finished making the last suit connection and walked over to the airlock's inner door. It was barely large enough for him to enter fully encumbered, but he managed. Once inside, he closed the inner door and began preparations for opening the outer door—into the vacuum of space that was the Moon's natural environment.

"Alright," Stetson said as the door opened. "Tony, I'm on my way. While I'm gone, go ahead and start piling up the stuff we're throwing overboard. Just don't put any in the airlock yet. We may need to get our guests into the lander quickly, and I don't want any crap in the way. After we cycle them in, we can off-load. We'll assess their conditions, and then we'll do the mods to the skin of the ship."

"Sure thing. Good luck."

"Thanks."

With that, Stetson stepped out of the airlock. He had been totally ready for the outer door to open, but when it had, he reacted with a startle reflex. He carefully walked over to the door and peered out. But stepping out, on the other hand, was a whole different thing. As eager as was to step on the Moon, he felt a sense of hesitation, like looking down at a swimming pool below from the high dive and swallowing the butterflies in order to just dive in.

"Damn. What were those stupid-ass engineers at NASA thinking when they put the crew compartment on *top* of this monster?" Stetson said, forgetting that the live microphone was recording his words for posterity.

He was reminded by the voice of mission control. "Bill, is there a problem?"

Realizing what he'd just said into an open microphone, including the "damn" part, he replied, "No, there's no problem. Sorry about the chatter. I'm just looking out the door and down at the ground—the view surprised me is all."

But that was not what Bill Stetson was thinking. He was standing on the exit platform in front of the airlock and looking twenty feet straight down to the ground. *I told those jackasses that putting the crew compartment on top was a stupid idea, and they wouldn't listen. Falling twenty feet to the ground on Earth could kill you instantly. Falling twenty feet to the ground on the Moon in one-sixth of Earth's gravity would break bones, and, since you're three days from a hospital, it could still kill you. Dead would be dead. Stupid jackasses.*

Stetson moved across the platform to the elevator that would take him down to the surface. To call it an elevator was actually an undeserved flattery. It was more of a moving cage that would take astronauts from the crew compartment to the ground and back again. Though there was a ladder, the lander designers had realized the risks of a clumsy astronaut wearing a spacesuit attempting to use one on the Moon.

Stetson entered the elevator, closed the gate, and pushed the down button. With a clank, the elevator began to move slowly downward. After a painfully slow few minutes, which to Stetson seemed like an hour, he reached the surface.

A few minutes later, Bill Stetson became the first American to walk on the Moon since Gene Cernan. He tried not to think about the external cameras on the Altair recording his every move. He didn't make any pithy comments for posterity, nor did he think he needed to say anything. He was focused on his rescue mission.

He headed toward the boulders and, hopefully, the crew of the *Harmony*.

The boulders were farther away than they appeared. Without the usual reference points of houses, trees, or even clouds, it was very difficult to determine how far away an object on the Moon really was. The fact that it was nighttime further complicated gauging the distance.

Now acutely aware that he was potentially speaking to about six billion people listening back on Earth, he said, "It's not as dark as I thought it would be. The sun is not visible, and the Earth is only about one-tenth visible on the horizon here at the limb. But the reflected light from the Earth is more than enough for me to see. It's sort of like taking a midnight walk under a full Moon. It's tranquil. It's serene. It...it's beautiful."

Stetson had been walking for ten minutes, and he couldn't discern that he was any closer to the boulders than when he first left the Altair. He trudged on, alternating skipping and walking, depending upon how the mood struck him. Skipping along wearing a two-hundred-pound backpack was relatively easy on the Moon, where it weighed only thirty-three pounds. He managed to cover more ground that way to boot.

Approximately thirty minutes after leaving the lander, Stetson reached the outcropping of rocks on its left side. Now walking much more slowly due to the increased number of loose rocks near the base of the outcropping, Stetson moved around the boulders. As he made his way around, he saw the *Harmony*.

Clearly a copy of the Altair design, the lander was also, clearly, severely damaged. Instead of sitting proudly on the lunar surface as was the Altair, this lander looked like a silver wounded animal trying to get back on its feet while dragging a broken leg behind it. The front leg of the *Harmony* was crumpled; the remaining three legs were bent at impossible angles. What was once a hopeful symbol of China's emergence as a world power was instead a mangled mess on the lunar plain. Stetson was humbled, momentarily imagining that it was he and his crew similarly trapped so far from home.

"Tony, I see the lander. It is totally dark, and there is no external sign of life. I'm going forward. They're bound to be in the crew compartment. Camera working okay?"

Stetson tapped his helmet near where the camera was installed. The camera was broadcasting and recording everything he saw.

"Camera working fine. What a mess. Be careful." Chow kept his reply brief.

Stetson began walking toward the lander, and, as he got closer, he could see where the Chinese had run a hose from the ascent engine's propellant tanks to what appeared to be a small rocket test stand, complete with an improvised rocket engine, pointing straight toward the lower left wall of the crew compartment. The connections to the fuel tanks were crude and, from all appearances, leaky. Whoever had made the connection had found a way to puncture the tanks and insert what looked like aluminum air hoses into the openings. The hoses looked to be in pretty good shape as they snaked across the ground and connected to the bent metal of the improvised "engine." He couldn't tell from what the engine was made, but since it was so obviously charred, it couldn't have been aluminum. Aluminum would have melted during the resulting combustion.

The scorched sides of the compartment's outer wall were clearly visible just in front of the improvised engine's exhaust nozzle. Stetson immediately realized what they had done.

"Brilliant," he said. "Tony, do you see this?"

"Bill, I see something, but I can't tell what it is."

"It's a Bunsen burner. They built themselves a furnace to keep warm. A furnace! If their ship is like ours, and it clearly is, then they may not have had power, but they sure had fuel. The fuel they would have used to get back into space. Do you get it?"

"Um, no. I don't."

"Doctors," Bill muttered under his breath.

Not wasting any time, Stetson explained as he continued to navigate around the crashed lander, trying to find a way to get inside. "Like us, they used hypergolic fuel in their ascent stage because it has to be simple. Cryogenic fuel has to be kept cold, and it still boils off. They kept their system simple, and, from the looks of it, they used the same thing we do—N_2O_4. Mix it with hydrazine and, poof, it lights. Simple. Only instead of using the fuel to get off the Moon, they kludged it to make a Bunsen burner to keep warm. The flame was aimed at one wall of the crew compartment, and I bet I'll find them all huddled around that one wall. The flame is out now. And I can't tell from look-ing at it for how long. If it had been us, the flame might have burned right through the thin skin of the lander."

Stetson trudged forward and used his suit's built-in lamps to see the boot prints in the lunar dust leading around the lander to just the other side of the crumpled landing leg. Whoever made the burner had walked this way.

"Aha," Stetson blurted out without thinking first. "I see Mac-Gyver's boot prints leading back toward the crew cabin. And that's where I'm going now. I want to meet this guy."

Carefully avoiding the many shards of broken metal sticking

out from the damaged legs, Stetson made slow but steady progress toward the door of the cabin. Moving to his left to avoid a
rather large piece of metal, Stetson momentarily lost his balance.
Had he been on Earth in his ungainly suit he would have surely
fallen. As it was, he merely tipped to the side and then eased
himself back into an upright posture. As he did so, he bumped
into a strut that was, fortunately, not sharp.

"Careful, Bill," Chow spoke. "Those metal shards you are walking through look sharp enough to cut your suit. Is there another
path?"

"Maybe, but there's no time. I'm being careful. I have no intention of venting to vacuum when I'm this close." Stetson's reply
sounded confident, but his mental comment was not. *Please, God,
don't let me trip and cut my leg off....*

Inside the *Harmony,* as the crew huddled together looking at
their suits' power indicators drop mercilessly toward the red, they
felt the thump of Stetson's benign contact with the frame of the
lander. It wasn't much, but in a place where no wind has ever
blown, it was the first movement other than their own since the
crash. The large outcropping of boulders had effectively shielded
them from the dust and debris kicked up by the Altair as it
landed, and, since there was no atmosphere to carry sound, the
noise of a rocket engine descending to the surface only a few
hundred feet away was absent.

"Did you feel that?" asked Dr. Xu. His voice was muffled due
to the fact that their visors were closed to retain heat within the
suits and their suit radios were off to conserve power.

"Yes. Yes, I did. The lander is either settling or the Americans
are here," replied Hui Tian, her voice also muffled, as she rose
and moved toward the door. The crew compartment was crowded
and now very cold. Though her suit temperature was at the bare
minimum required to keep her alive and not hypothermic, she
was no longer aware of how cold she felt. Instead, she was focused
on finding out what had bumped the lander and at containing
her excitement at the thought that help had arrived.

She neared the cabin window and peered outside into the
near-darkness. At first she couldn't see anything, and then she
saw motion—and an American astronaut carefully climbing over

the remains of the lander legs toward the cabin door. She turned quickly to face her crewmates.

"They are here! The Americans are here!"

She moved to the cabin door and abruptly stopped. She stood motionless, staring at the metal door that separated her crew from the American astronaut.

"There's no power. We cannot open the door without power."

"Ha." Engineer Zhi grunted. "Of course we can. Just use the manual override. We trained for that a million times. Are you not thinking clearly?"

"Who is not thinking clearly?" Hui responded. "Zhi, did being in your spacesuit for so long make you forget that the cabin is pressurized? We've got close to one atmosphere of air in here pushing on the door. And there is no pressure on the other side. When we EVA, we have to vent the cabin first, and that requires power. The door opens inward. Without venting the air, the pressure is enough to keep the door from opening even if I use the manual override." Unlike the American lander, the Chinese did not have an airlock. When they exited for a surface EVA, the entire lander, like the Orion, vented to vacuum. The Chinese designers had not foreseen the need to design the door to open to vacuum when the cabin was still fully pressurized.

"Of course," Zhi chortled. "So, our American saviors arrive, and we cannot even go out and meet them with dignity." He lowered his head and appeared to stare at the floor in front of him.

"Let's get this door open." Dr. Xu gently moved the injured pilot to a resting position leaning against an instrument rack and rose to join his commander at the cabin door. "I am certain we can find a way."

Hui removed the latch from the door handle and grasped it in her right glove. Xu moved close to her, grabbed the handle next to where she had placed her hands, and began to pull.

Nothing happened. The door remained stuck.

"It is basic physics," Zhi said. "Atmospheric pressure is a little more than fourteen pounds per square inch. The door is about two thousand square inches. That means the total force pushing on the door is about thirty thousand pounds. Do you think the two of you can move thirty thousand pounds all by yourselves?"

Hui and Dr. Xu responded by trying again to move the door. Again, nothing happened.

"Enough." Hui and Dr. Xu turned to face Zhi. Clearly frustrated, Hui spoke, "Zhi, do you have any ideas? What can we do to open the door?"

"Hmm." Zhi looked up at his commander. His response bordered on insubordination. "Captain Hui, if I knew, I am not sure I would tell you. Who will recall what we did to get home when it will be the triumphant American heroes who get the credit? It is better to die than to let them have the glory that should have been ours."

"I do not understand you, Zhi. You are the one who figured out how to keep the ship warm using the rocket fuel. You are the one who kept the fuel cells working far longer than they should have. You are the one who will get much of the credit for keeping this crew alive long enough for the Americans to give us a ride home. You are a hero of China! Do you not see that? Are you giving up? Why? You've done so much already!"

"Because it was pointless. It would have been better if we had died in the crash. This was supposed to be our day. China's day." He averted his gaze from Hui back to the cabin floor and said nothing more.

It was at that moment that they heard a banging sound come from the other side of the door. It sounded like whoever was on the other side had picked up a piece of metal and was using it to signal them.

Dr. Xu responded by banging his glove on the door.

"Without air, he won't hear that." Hui was frustrated with their predicament as well. She wanted to go home. "But he might feel it."

"Or he might not," Zhi added.

"We've got to let him know we are here and what our problem is. I'll turn on my radio." She raised her hand and turned on the power to the transmitter within her spacesuit.

"Hello? Can you hear me? This is Captain Hui of the *Harmony*. Can you hear me? Please respond if you can hear me!"

The banging on the other side of the door continued.

Standing on the other side of the door, Bill Stetson couldn't tell if there was anyone alive or dead within the ship. The door was closed, and the ship was completely dark. He couldn't get to the window to look in due to the fact that he was now a good fifteen feet off the ground, standing in what looked like the remains of a construction site after an earthquake, and if he were to try and reach the window, he would almost certainly fall to his death by being skewered on one of the many sharp edges of mangled metal that used to be the *Harmony* lunar lander.

He grasped the small aluminum rod that he'd picked up during his climb to the door and banged again.

Anthony Chow was sweating. It was a cold sweat, and it wasn't caused by his work dismantling an experiment rack to be thrown overboard. Nor did the temperature within the Altair cause it. It was the cold sweat of fear.

Left alone in the lander for over an hour, Chow at first didn't think much about anything other than getting the weight of the lander down to the point that would allow them to take on passengers. He'd already moved the easy stuff like the sleeping hammocks, the food rations that would have sustained the crew for an extended surface stay, and the containers that were to safely store the rocks and core samples they would have collected and returned to the Earth. There was still a lot to be done in order to get the lander off the Moon, even some modifications to the structure, but Chow couldn't do those on his own. That would have to come later when Bill got the survivors back to the ship and they had a chance to assess and think on their situation a bit longer.

It wasn't until he began to review the service manual for the experiment rack—so as to figure out how to disassemble it for throwing overboard instead of fixing—that he began to consider his situation. There was a little bit of tightness in his throat, and Tony could tell that he was starting to sweat.

What if Bill didn't come back? What if his friend were to have an accident and never return? What if the engines don't start on the lander, making the trip home impossible? He really didn't want to die on the Moon.

Alone. Trapped. Facing death. No way out. It was his nightmare, and at that moment, Chow stopped working and stared out the window at the dimly lit lunar landscape. Fortunately for him, it was very dimly lit and he could only see the area immediately around the ship due to the lights. Being inside the lit ship, his eyes were dilated and couldn't gather enough light to really see how vast the lunar wasteland around him truly was. Tony leaned forward and pulling himself closer to the window.

He was letting himself go unchecked in a downward spiral of despair and fear without having other tasks to keep his mind occupied. He was so absorbed in his fear that he almost didn't hear the voice on the ship's radio. Slowly, his mental faculties overcame the fear, and he was able to focus. He did hear a voice. It was the voice of the *Harmony*'s captain.

The female voice was weak and barely audible as it came over one of the radio frequencies that the Altair was monitoring. "...hear me? Please respond if you can hear me!" The only reason Chow could hear her was because the Chinese engineers had told their NASA counterparts what channels the taikonauts would be using in their systems. This was the reason they'd heard them before while orbiting. After losing them following the first orbit, they had left the system on autosearch mode. The Altair's radio was programmed to scan these frequencies and to stop on whichever one was active. This was the Chinese suit-to-suit communications channel.

Chow didn't react quickly, but he did react. He slowly pulled himself together and moved toward the radio. At one point he even shook his head and took a couple of deep breaths.

"Get it together," he told himself out loud.

"Please respond..."

"Captain Hui. This is Anthony Chow of the *Mercy I*. Can you hear me?"

"Yes, yes! I hear you! Thank God you can hear me. My suit is almost out of power. Are you the one banging on our door?"

"No, that would be Commander Stetson. I'm back in the lander getting the ship ready to carry you and your crew home."

"Can you tell your commander that we hear him, but we cannot open the door. We have no power to run the depressurization system and evacuate the cabin. And with the cabin pressurized, there is no way to open the door for us to get out."

"Uh, I think I understand. I'll relay that to Bill. Hang on. His suit won't work at this frequency, so I will have to be the middleman and relay information between the two of you."

"Understood," Hui answered. "Thank you."

Chow was now sufficiently recovered from his lapse to relay the information to Stetson, whose reply was classic. "Damn!"

"Bill. You mentioned that there is a lot of debris. Can you use something to smash their window or to puncture the skin of the lander? If we can get the pressure down, then they can open the door."

"Uh, let me look around," Stetson replied. "There is no way I can even get close to the window. It is too dangerous. And I doubt that I can get sufficient force to puncture the skin of the lander. I'm fifteen feet in the air, bouncing around like a beach ball in this pressurized suit, and I can barely keep myself from falling every time I bang on the door. There is no way I can get this can to open from out here. Wish I'd brought some tools with me. We didn't plan this well."

"Unfortunately, they are saying the same thing on the inside. They tried breaking the glass, but it didn't work. That stuff is almost as strong as steel. They're still looking around for something they might be able to use to puncture the skin from the inside."

"Well, then I'll just come back and get the power tools we brought with us. That'll take some time." Bill grunted.

"It's worse, Bill," Tony continued. "You may have time and power left, but they don't. Captain Hui told me that they have less than an hour before their suits run out of power and they start to freeze. And at minus two hundred degrees, that'll happen quickly."

"That's not enough time for me to get back to Altair, find the right tools, get back here, then figure out how to cut through the hull, and then get them safely back to Altair. Not enough time."

"We have to do something, Bill."

"I know, I know. Tony, do they have any ideas?"

"Not so far as I can tell. Sounds like they've tried everything and used up their last drops of extra power," Tony explained.

"Come on, let's think on this. You might toss it back to Houston and see if anybody there has any ideas."

"Done. But they aren't sure what to do without power, either. Or tools. Picking up some of the stuff around their crashed ship puts you at more risk than Houston wants."

"I don't disagree with them on that." Then it hit him. "Power is the key! Tony, I've got an idea."

"We need one."

"Well, I've got one, and it's because of something you said. You said I've got power and they don't. But they do. If they have enough power to run heaters in their suits for another hour, then surely they have enough power to run a pump long enough to get the air out of the cabin. They can use the power from one of their suits to vent the air, and then they can open the door."

"I'll relay the message."

Hui listened intently to Anthony Chow relay Stetson's suggestion. Her excitement and optimism grew. She looked around the room at her crew and settled her gaze on the engineer—the political officer who, in her mind, was suddenly being more of a political officer than an engineer.

"Zhi, can it be done? she asked.

"Yes." Without removing his gaze from the floor, he replied, "It can be done."

"Will you help? We can't do this without you. I don't know the lander systems and where the control circuits are for the pump. I could look it up if the computer had power and I could pull up the manual. But then, if we had power for the computer, then we could open the door. You're the engineer. Do the job for which you were trained. *Be an engineer.*"

Zhi looked up from the floor and gazed directly into Hui's eyes. Like two dogs trying to decide which was alpha, they stared at each other long and hard. Finally, Zhi averted his gaze.

"I'll help. First I need to open this access panel." Zhi pointed to Hui's right at one of the instrumentation panels that ran along the wall of the lander. He rose from the floor, picked up a screwdriver from where he'd left it after a previous power-scavenging activity, and moved toward the panel.

"And one of you will have to give me access to the batteries in your backpack. There isn't much time, and whichever battery I use will have even less power remaining—perhaps none."

"I understand." Hui didn't hesitate. "You will, of course, use mine."

"Of course."

Hui at that moment realized what she was committing to. Without power, not only would the temperature in the suit start to drop, but also the air would stop circulating. Unlike deep-water suits, spacesuits didn't just let compressed air from the tanks in the backpack diffuse into the suit. That would have been too wasteful and would severely limit how long astronauts could remain in them. Spacesuits had fans and carbon-dioxide scrubbers that required continuous airflow—and power. Without power, the air in her suit would slowly become poisoned by carbon dioxide, and she would suffocate. That is, if she didn't freeze to death first.

"Dr. Xu, get Ming ready to travel. We will need to move quickly."

Zhi was good. In less than ten minutes he had the access panel open, some insulation removed from the wires providing power to the pump that would vent the cabin's air, and had found the connectors and wires he would need to send power from Captain Hui's spacesuit battery to the pump.

"Captain Hui. Step over here and face away from me. I need to connect your batteries to the pump."

"Understood." She complied, and he continued his work.

"I'm first going to shut off the power to the rest of your suit. Once I've done that, I'll connect the pump, and we'll see if it works. Are you ready?"

"Yes."

The next thing Hui heard was the sound of silence. She'd been hearing the spacesuit fans since sealing herself in as the *Harmony*'s cabin began to freeze, and she'd gotten quite used to their reassuring white noise. Now there was silence. The suit was well insulated, so she did not yet feel any colder. It was too soon for that.

Behind her was the rustling of the engineer as he scrambled to make the necessary connections. When he was on a technical task, it was easy to forget that he was also the ship's political officer. All signs of his previous defeatist demeanor were now absent.

"Here goes," the engineer said. The next thing they all heard was the whirring sound of the vent pump. As the air pressure began to drop, the crew could see some of the lighter objects in the cabin flutter in the ensuing wind. After just a few moments, the sound began to drop in frequency as the pump slowed and the air pressure dropped to the point that sounds would no longer propagate. The cabin pressure was now essentially the same as that of the lunar surface—zero.

Hui felt the engineer fiddling with something in her backpack. Then he tapped her on the shoulder and said something she could not hear.

"I can't hear you! The air is gone, and we'll have to use our suit radios." She tried to turn on her radio, the one she'd used to speak with Tony Chow, and nothing happened. She was completely out of power. Her heart sank. Her life had only tens of minutes remaining unless she could either get more power or out of her spacesuit.

Hui moved quickly to the door and once again tried the emergency exit handle. This time it moved, and after just a few seconds the door was open. Standing on the other side was an American astronaut wearing a grin that only an American could possibly have conjured up under the circumstances.

He said something she could not hear. He then said it again, emphatically.

Not knowing the specifics, but understanding what he was probably saying, she turned and pointed toward Dr. Xu and the wounded pilot. She then made the universal hand motion indicating that they should leave first.

Not waiting for additional prompting, Stetson moved toward the doctor and the wounded pilot. He reached down and helped Dr. Xu lift Ming so that they could carry him out the door. With some effort, and guidance from Captain Hui, they were able to get him outside the cabin for the first time since they landed.

Captain Hui looked out and down at the remains of her beautiful lander and sighed. *We will be back,* she thought. *But for now, we will get home!* She shivered, and then she realized that her fingers and toes were starting to get cold.

She followed Stetson out and around the side of the lander and down what remained of the stairs to the lunar surface. This was the path she and Zhi had taken when they had built the makeshift furnace. This time it was much more difficult because Dr. Xu and the American astronaut were burdened by the limp mass of Ming Feng. Taking care to not drag Ming's deadweight across anything sharp enough to puncture his suit, they finally reached the ground.

Hui's feet were getting very, very cold, and she could no longer feel her fingers. Her head was also noticeably colder. She realized that her entire body was cooling rapidly, but the relatively poorly insulated extremities were the first things she noticed. In her mind, the pace was on one hand too slow—she would surely freeze to death or suffocate before getting to the American lander at this rate. On the other hand, if they were to rush and injure someone, then it could be a death sentence. She would have to be patient.

It was then that she noticed that Zhi was not with them. He was still in the lander. She ran up and tapped Dr. Xu on the shoulder to get his attention. He looked back at her as she pointed up to the lander's now-open door and waved her arms. Xu looked back at her and grimaced. She could tell that he understood. There was nothing they could do. He could not go back because of his need to help carry Ming. If she went back, it would be a death sentence—she simply did not have time to spare.

"If he wishes to remain here and die, then that is *his* choice," she said aloud to herself.

The group of four made their way around the boulders that separated them from the Altair and began their march across the lunar desert toward it.

In the distance sat the Altair, dimly illuminated from above by the reflected Earthlight and brightly lit from below by its own floodlights. To Hui, it was beautiful. It looked safe and warm. It was how they were going to get home. It was also intact. The four legs were upright, and there were no signs of any of the problems experienced by the *Harmony*.

Hui was now very cold. She was also getting light-headed. For a brief moment, she even forgot where she was. *Hypoxia,* she thought. *Oxygen deprivation.* But she was too relaxed to panic.

"Help!" she said aloud. "I'm starting to poison myself on my own carbon dioxide."

No one could hear her.

Still, she trudged on toward the lander. Consciously putting one foot in front of the other, she kept up with the group. Left foot, right foot, left foot, right foot, right foot..." *A nap about now would be nice.* Darkness overcame her.

"Tony! We've got a problem. Captain Hui just collapsed. I'm about one hundred feet away, helping to carry one of their injured, and now we've got two down. I'm going back to see what happened," Stetson said into his radio.

Stetson released his hold on the wounded pilot, forcing Dr. Xu to stop moving and simply hold him. Even on the Moon, carrying a limp deadweight like a person was almost impossible without help. This was especially true if the deadweight was encumbered with a two-hundred-pound spacesuit. Stetson cautiously quickly moved back toward the fallen Chinese captain, wondering what had happened.

He reached her and bent over to see if she was conscious. He then tried to figure out what might be the problem. Using his headlamp, he peered through her visor and saw that she was not conscious. She looked very pale. It was then that he noticed the status lights on her suit—they were not powered on.

"Tony! I'm with Captain Hui, and her suit is completely out of power. I don't know how long it's been that way, but long enough for her to pass out from oxygen deprivation. She has to be getting pretty damn cold. I've got to get her into the ship now. Can you talk to the other Chinese on the radio?"

"I don't know. She's been the only one to answer up until now. I'll try. Stand by." The signal went blank as Tony switched channels back in the lander.

Stetson left the fallen Hui and went back over to Dr. Xu. He grasped the shoulder of the only other person standing on the lunar surface and began to motion toward his fallen comrade. Looking into Xu's face, Stetson realized he was talking to someone—it had to be Tony. Xu said something and then nodded his head in understanding.

Stetson helped lower the pilot to the cold and gray lunar surface. As he did so, he realized that the fallen Chinese would likely lie there, losing heat through his suit into the cold lunar surface for at least the thirty minutes it would take to get Hui to the Altair and into the airlock. He'd hoped to cycle two at a time into the Altair, but clearly Hui would not live long enough to get both her and the other stricken Chinese through the airlock at the same time. This was getting complicated.

Stetson and Xu quickly bounded back to Captain Hui, using a combination run and skipping motion. Once there, they picked her up, one man under each of her arms, and began carrying her toward the Altair. They passed the other injured man on their way, causing Stetson to wonder if they would be able to get back to him before his suit went dead.

After what seemed like an eternity, they reached the Altair and the lift that would carry Stetson and Hui up twenty feet to the airlock.

"Tony, tell the other taikonaut that the lift will only carry two people at a time and that I need to get Hui up and into the airlock as soon as possible. He needs to wait here for me to come back so we can get his other colleague. Okay?"

"Roger that." Tony's reply was brief. "I'm on it."

Stetson eased Hui from Xu's shoulders and dragged her onto the lift. He then gently pushed Xu away and closed the gate. It was clear from looking at Xu that the doctor understood, though he was starting to look worried.

Knowing that the man would not hear him, Stetson nonetheless said, "I'll be back."

With the push of a button, the lift moved upward toward the Altair's airlock. Stetson took that brief moment to look back toward the man they'd left on the surface. He was lying there, unmoving—a silent testament to the frailty of man.

Stetson, with a scant few seconds available for self-reflection, thought to himself, *For all this hardware and technology, it all still comes down to this. People. With all our frailties and weaknesses, we still come and do the hard things. Let's see those damned robotic probes do this! Thank God for our manned program.*

The lift jolted and abruptly stopped.

Stetson was startled out of his introspection. He quickly pressed the start button. Nothing happened. The lift didn't budge. He pressed the stop button and then the start button. Nothing.

"Come on! Does nothing work on this damn ship!" Bill slapped the wall of the lift in frustration. "Tony! The lift stopped. We're almost to the top, perhaps eight feet from the platform. I messed with the buttons and nothing happens. It's stuck."

"Can you get the captain to the platform? Do I need to suit up and come help?"

"There's no time for that. I'll have to figure something out. Stand by." He looked around him on the platform and didn't immediately see any way to get the elevator working again. The eight feet between him and the platform that led to the airlock wouldn't have been a huge problem if it had just been him stuck. He could easily jump up, grasp the platform's ledge, and then pull himself up. But it wasn't himself he was trying to save. It was the unconscious and likely suffocating Captain Hui that he was trying to save, and she was, at this point, no different than a three-hundred-and-fifty-pound sandbag.

"Tony, I'm going to try to hoist Hui up on the platform. In one-sixth gravity, she won't really weigh all that much, maybe sixty pounds, but it'll be a bulky sixty pounds to push up. Here goes."

Stetson leaned forward and pulled Hui upright. He lifted her apparently lifeless body over his shoulder and maneuvered himself toward the side of the elevator closest to the platform above. He then took a deep breath and shoved. As he was lifting, his right foot slipped suddenly backward, causing him to lose his balance. He and Hui's body wavered and slipped to one side, running into the wire wall of the elevator and then tumbling to its floor.

"That didn't work so well," Stetson muttered under his breath.

Without any more hesitation, he grabbed Hui and tried again. This time neither foot slipped and Hui's upper body did land on the platform. But it didn't stay there. As Stetson shifted his hands to push on her lower body, she slipped off and fell back on top of Stetson, once again causing him to lose his footing and fall backward into the wire wall.

"There's got to be a better way. I need a rope or something."

"A rope? We've got a rope. It's with the surface-exploration kit that we're throwing overboard. I can get it in the airlock in just a few minutes. Leave her on the platform and come on up. I'll cycle the airlock so you can come in and get it."

"I don't see another way." Stetson was already lowering Hui gently to the elevator floor. "On my way."

Looking like a comic-book character, Stetson bent his knees and sprang upward toward the platform in a maneuver that would have been simply impossible to achieve under normal gravity conditions. The upper two-thirds of his body landed on the platform and bounced almost a foot in the air. He had to quickly reach out and grab one of the crisscrossed diagonal beams on the walkway next to where he landed to keep from falling back down to the elevator.

"I feel like the Michelin Man. Somebody's got to invent a better damned spacesuit!"

Stetson pulled himself up and walked quickly toward the closed airlock door. Just as he arrived, the door opened slightly, and he saw a cloud of dust poof outward around the edges. Tony had vented the airlock so Stetson could quickly get the tether he needed to save Captain Hui. He reached down, grabbed the tether, and started back toward the stuck elevator.

"Bill, I just lost communication with Dr. Xu. He just lost power in his suit while we were talking. I bet that probably means that the injured pilot has lost power also."

"Great. Just great. Thanks for telling me. We've got to move faster."

While talking, Stetson maneuvered himself back to the upper portion of the platform and clipped one end of the tether to a support strut. He tossed the other end down onto the elevator platform next to Hui's body. Taking a pose that would appear very awkward on the live television feed from the external cameras, Stetson dropped onto his stomach with his legs dangling in the open space above the elevator platform. He then lowered himself back down. It was not graceful, but it worked.

He quickly secured the tether to Hui's suit and attached it to where he thought its Chinese equivalent tether would be designed to attach. Though he was tempted to peer again through the visor to assess Hui's condition, he did not. There was simply no time.

He again hoisted himself up from the elevator and onto the platform. This time, he was not so ungainly. Once there, he looped the tether around a nearby strut to provide some mechanical advantage, and began to pull. It was not the smoothest of ascents—Hui's body dangled to and fro and even banged into the sides of the elevator cage as it rose toward the open top and to within Stetson's reach. Once she was just below the platform, he secured the tether.

Since she was now tied into position, he didn't have to worry about dropping her, and he could concentrate on grabbing her suit in the right place to hoist her up and to safety. After a few unsuccessful attempts, he was able to get her up and on the platform with him. He was out of breath.

He disconnected her from the tether and carried her to the airlock. Once she was inside, propped against the inner door like a rag doll, he quickly backed out and closed the outer door. He then said into his radio, "Tony. She's in the airlock. Get her inside as quickly as you can."

"Roger."

Stetson grabbed the tether and moved quickly to the ladder that led to the ground. Looking down and wondering how he and Dr. Xu were going to get the pilot up to the top deck, he again cursed the engineers who designed the lander with the crew compartment so far off the ground, this time with the microphone off. "Jackasses."

By the time Stetson reached Dr. Xu and the motionless pilot, they had been without power for about twenty minutes.

Tony's voice coming through the radio startled him. "Bill, I believe the captain is going to be okay. I put her on oxygen the minute I could get to her, and her color is starting to return. It was close. She's still out cold, though."

"That's good news, Tony. I wish we could tell her friend here. Let's hope we are as lucky with these two. I don't know how long she was without power, but it can't have been very long or she would have been dead."

Not wasting any time, Stetson had been working with the doctor in pulling Ming Feng up from the lunar surface and placing his bulky spacesuit arms over their shoulders. He looked over at the Chinese doctor and saw from the look on his face through the suit's visor that he was ready to go.

Hearing only his breathing, Stetson and Dr. Xu walked across the dimly lit lunar surface toward the Altair lander. The walk seemed to be taking a long time to Stetson; he could only imagine how long it seemed to the doctor. Finally, they reached the base of the lander.

"Tony. I'm trying to tell the doctor to take the end of the tether and to start climbing the ladder. But without a radio, I'm not sure how to explain it."

"Bill! Touch your faceplates and scream!"

"Think that'll work?"

"Try it."

"Okay." Bill faced the Chinese astronaut and leaned his faceshield over until they touched. At first Dr. Xu started to back away, but Stetson shouted as they came into contact, and the man paused. "Can you hear me?"

"Yes, but barely."

"Damn, Tony, it works."

"How about that."

"Listen!" Bill shouted again. "Take this up the ladder! Then I'll attach the other end to him. Once on top, loop it over a strut and start pulling while I push him up from underneath. Understand?"

"Understand! Will do!" was Xu's reply.

Moments later, Dr. Xu, holding the tether in one hand, began climbing. The first five feet went smoothly, but then he abruptly stopped. After pausing, he resumed his ascent, but at a slower and more clumsy-appearing gait.

"Tony, can you see him? What is going on?"

"He looks to be confused as best I can tell, Bill," Tony said.

"He stopped being much help and has become real damn clumsy."

"His extremities must be getting very cold, Bill. He probably has to watch his hands and feet on each and every step since he isn't getting any feedback from them. One misstep near the top and we may lose him." Bill was beginning to be glad he had brought Anthony Chow, M.D. along.

Dr. Xu was moving very slowly at this point. He was only slightly more than halfway up and Stetson was starting to doubt that he could make it. Stetson looked around, trying to come up with plan B.

"He's taking too long," said Stetson.

Painfully slowly, the doctor climbed to within the last few rungs of the ladder from the top. He swayed, and Stetson steeled himself for what seemed inevitable—a twenty-foot fall to the lunar surface. The swaying stopped and the doctor reached for the next rung. Finally, he made it to the top and the relative safety of the platform, upon which he collapsed. Miraculously, he did not drop the tether.

Stetson paused, not sure of what he should do next. Without the Chinese doctor pulling while he pushed, it would be impossible to get the unconscious pilot to the top of the ladder.

The tether moved, slowly at first, and then it rapidly became taut. Looking up, Stetson was surprised to see Tony Chow's faceplate looking down at him. Chow gave him the thumbs-up sign.

"Bill, let's get your guy up here, and then one of us can go through the airlock with him. If you're ready, then let's get this done." Tony's voice sounded fresh, enthusiastic, and very, very good.

Stetson grabbed and lifted the limp pilot's body as Tony pulled it from above using the rope. Slowly they lifted him up to the platform that surrounded the habitat.

Once on top, they carried the two Chinese to the ship's airlock and stuffed them inside. The airlock was designed to hold two fully suited astronauts who were standing under their own power. Getting two limp bodies upright and into a room that was only slightly larger than a broom closet with a third astronaut was quite a challenge.

As he waited for the airlock to cycle and his turn to enter,

Stetson looked out over the lunar surface toward the boulders that obscured the damaged Chinese lander. *It is so beautiful,* he thought.

At first Stetson thought his eyes were playing tricks on him, but he soon realized that the motion in the distance was real. The shape of another spacesuited human was now clearly visible as it walked toward the American lander.

"What the...?" Stetson said. "Tony, I think the fourth taikonaut has decided to join us. He's walking toward us now."

"I wonder what took him so long. Does he look like he'll need help? He's bound to be out of power like these guys."

"Don't know," Stetson said. "I can't tell. He doesn't look like he needs help. When you get inside, give him a shout."

Another five minutes went by before Stetson heard anything from Chow. In the meantime, the Chinese taikonaut had gotten much closer. From what Stetson could tell, he didn't look like he was going to need any help.

"Bill. I'm in. I've got three unconscious Chinese in here. They are all breathing, but it's too early to tell if there has been any brain damage. But everywhere I step, there's people."

"Good work, Tony." This drew a smile from Stetson and was really the first good news he'd had in an hour or two. "That's a good problem to have. There'll soon be two more of us in there. Hopefully, we will be able to stand under our own power."

"That's a good thing. It's getting pretty crowded in here," Chow replied.

"Hey, how'd you know we could touch helmets and talk like that?" Bill asked Chow.

"I read it in a science fiction novel once when I was a kid. *Have Spacesuit, Will Travel* or something like that."

"I'll be damned."

"Well, if you are, it'll be standing room only."

Stetson figured it must be very crowded at maximum capacity inside the Altair now. The simple fact of the matter being that the Altair's ascent stage was designed to hold four people under very Spartan conditions. To sleep, the astronauts would string hammocks and sleep two on each side with one directly above another. There was not enough room to have four cots on the floor. For getting back into space, it was assumed that the four astronauts would be standing. Six standing astronauts would be a tight fit, but doable. Having one or more of their number lying on the ground could make things complicated. Having three on the floor was something he hadn't planned on.

"Agreed, Tony," Stetson replied. "That's a good problem to have. I'm just glad that we'll be coming home with all of them."

Stetson walked to the ladder and looked down as taikonaut number four approached. The Chinese astronaut looked briefly upward and began to climb the ladder toward Stetson.

A few minutes later, Bill Stetson and Chinese Political Officer Zhi Feng cycled through the airlock and into the Altair.

Chapter 25

Everybody except the injured pilot seemed to have strong vitals. Bill rummaged through some of the last-minute supplies that had been stored aboard the Orion and then transferred into the Altair after launch. The key supplies were replacement power packs for the Chinese spacesuits. Bill pulled them from a storage bin Velcroed to the rear wall and started to examine how to install them. The Chinese engineer, the only conscious member of the *Harmony* crew at the moment, saw what Bill had and moved carefully around his limp crewmates strewn about to get a closer look.

"I can do this." He looked at Bill and held out a hand to take the power cells. "Do you have a regular screwdriver?"

"I have two." Bill handed the man half of the cargo and reached in a sleeve pocket for a screwdriver. Both of the men had removed their helmets and gloves but were still in their suits.

"Why do we need these? There is air in here." The Chinese taikonaut seemed confused and a bit more than concerned to Bill. But Stetson was going to cut the man some slack since he had been practically left for dead for several days now.

"We're all too heavy. This ship's engines are a precursor to the ones that Altair will eventually have. This one just wasn't ready for a big, bulky sample-return mission. We're gonna have to go outside and remove some exterior panels in order to be light enough to get us all up to lunar orbit." Bill pointed at two of the panels that would have to go. The two panels alone were three hundred kilograms.

"I see. China was not the only country with technical constraints."

"More like political." Bill shrugged. "The on-again, off-again, on-again nature of politics and the American space program left Altair as the last vehicle to be finished, and at a third of the originally planned budget."

"Ha, the American might is not so great after all." Bill didn't know how to respond to the man, so he didn't.

"We've got to get these suits back up and running." He nodded to the suits and started to work. Stetson wasn't sure that he liked the man's attitude and wasn't all that happy about talking with him at the moment.

"Mission control, we're all suited up and ready to begin the exterior skin modifications." Tony scanned the interior of the ship and made certain that all of the passengers had their suits sealed off. Three were still unconscious, so he had to check them each himself. Bill had recruited the coherent engineer fellow to go outside and do the work on the spacecraft. Tony wasn't sure if Bill didn't like leaving the Chinese inside all by themselves with them locked outside or if he just thought that the doctor in the bunch should stay inside with his patients.

"Roger that, *Mercy I*. Pipe Bill through, and we'll walk him through the mods."

"The line is open, Houston."

"Roger that, *Mercy I*. Begin decompressing the cabin."

Tony stood with his back against the wall, leaning a bit to take the weight off as he cycled the interior-pressure vents. He was tired. It had taken him and Bill and Zhi nearly two hours to cycle all of their superfluous supplies and whatnot out to the lunar surface. Now there was deconstruction work to be done. Sure, all six of them could stand inside the vehicle, very closely. Very. Closely. But they were still too heavy to get off the surface. The mission had been planned to take four American astronauts to the lunar surface and back on a shoestring budget and a very compressed schedule. This version of the Altair was only a limited prototype and not the final design of the vehicle that would fly on future flights, if there were any. The politics of the Constellation program to send Americans back to the Moon had been quite a battle. The program had used a majority of NASA's budget since 2011.

The Apollo-era program had about the same amount of money, sixteen or so billion dollars per year, between the mid-1960s and early 1970s. Extrapolating the Apollo budget to modern-day dollars, taking into account inflation, would be about one hundred and two billion dollars per year. So, it was clear that the NASA budget was about six to seven times underfunded. It was ridiculous how low the funding for the American space program had become while any number of entitlement programs were running at hundreds of billions of dollars per year with no public debate on shutting them down. And, to top all that off, the robotic-probe planetary scientists had a powerful lobby on Capitol Hill literally able to force NASA to use up about a quarter of its budget for unmanned probes to the outer planets, comets, asteroids, and other places like Pluto. The science return on those missions versus the science return on manned missions was often the subject of heated debate.

Needless to say, the Altair, being the last of the vehicles to be constructed in the project, was built on a fraction of the planned budget. It was slimmed down, and every corner that could have been cut on its design and construction *was* cut. The engine was smaller, the frame bulkier, than it should have been, and the fuel tanks were smaller. There was very little margin left for extra weight with four occupants. With six, they were way overweight, and even throwing everything overboard was a couple hundred kilograms short, with no margin for error. The engineers back at NASA had figured out a work-around, but that meant some major modifications to the vehicle's exterior structure.

Tony could faintly hear some whirring, more like buzzing noises, vibrating through the structure of the ship and into his helmet that was propped against the wall. His guess was that it was from the cordless power tools being used outside. It took another hour for the engineers at Johnson Space Center to talk Bill and Zhi through which bolts to remove. Where to pry at a panel. When and where to hit something with a hammer. And then all of a sudden a large screwdriver blade poked through the wall from the outside. Tony listened, only half paying attention, and nearly dozed off at one point, but the vibration of a saw blade cutting through a metal panel fastener startled him to attention. Then all of a sudden he heard Bill.

"There, Zhi. Hold it there." Then there was a pause. "Step out of the way and hold on to something."

"Okay, Tony," the engineer at Houston said. "Very carefully, hold on to the pilot-station panel and kick the skin panel with the bottom of your boot."

"Uh, roger that, Houston." Tony carefully found himself a handhold. He didn't want to bounce out with the panel and go flying onto the surface some twenty or more feet below. Once he assured himself he was secure, he prepared to kick. "Kicking in three, two, one." *Clank.* The vibration of the kick resounded through the structure of the cabin.

"It didn't come free," Bill pointed out.

"We expected that, Bill," Houston responded. "Our models show it will take a minimum of three kicks. Tony, when you're ready, kick it again."

"Roger that," Tony replied and steadied himself again. "Kicking in three, two, one." This time the panel surprised Tony and the engineers at Houston since it let go and sailed out across the lunar surface quietly until it skidded to a stop somewhere out there in the darkness.

"Great, Tony!" Stetson exclaimed.

"Houston, it came free," Tony acknowledged. There was some chatter behind the engineer's voice that sounded almost like bickering. "Either your models were wrong, or I can kick harder than you guys thought."

"Good job, *Mercy I*. Be alert that the guys down here have made several wisecracks about always knowing that you were stubborn as a mule, but they didn't realize you could kick like one, too."

"Copy that, Houston," Tony said with a bit of an unenthusiastic laugh.

"Get ready to repeat that process," Stetson instructed.

"Roger that, Bill."

"We are go for second panel removal," Houston said.

"No rest for the wicked, hey, boys?" Tony added.

"Let's get to work, Zhi." Stetson didn't waste time in moving on to the second panel. "Maybe this one will be easier since we've got experience now."

It wasn't.

)　●　●　●　(

It took a total of five hours and thirteen minutes for Stetson and Chow and Zhi to completely prepare the Altair for its return to space. For the first two and a half hours, Tony, Bill, and Zhi had tossed supplies out of the airlock. The remainder of the time was pulling the exterior panels. Only moments after the first panel came off, both Hui and Dr. Xu regained consciousness and were able to help. Once they were all six back inside the Altair, it was still crowded but at least now they had an entire wall out, so the view was fantastic. Well, it would have been fantastic had it been daytime and they could have seen anything. Actually, the view was extremely limited and very low light, but it was still the Moon. So, as far as the astronauts were concerned, the view was fantastic. It didn't hurt that they could just see the Earth on the horizon shimmering blue and white and begging them to come home.

At least at this point any extra baggage could just be tossed through the open hole in the ship. They were careful to cover the edges of any rough pieces of metal with special tape that they had brought along for just that purpose. Dr. Xu and Hui made themselves busy covering the opening rough spots very carefully. It would have been very bad to tear a suit on a jagged edge during the three-hour ascent to the Orion capsule in orbit.

"Houston, this is *Mercy I*. We just chucked the last of the ballast overboard, and we're almost through the prelaunch checklist. Have you uploaded the ascent trajectory yet?" Chow was the one speaking to ground control while Stetson continued locking things down for the ride to space. They had added some extra strapping in order to tie themselves to the wall panels during ascent. Nobody at Houston liked this part of the mission, but it had to be done.

"*Mercy I,* this is Houston. Yes, the trajectory was just uploaded. If you go on time, you'll be on an optimized return to Orion for the trip home. Medical wants to know your assessment of your passengers' conditions."

"Well," Chow began, "Captain Hui is in good spirits and seems fine. Dr. Xu is also okay. He's been at the pilot's side since he awoke. The pilot is still out cold. They said he's been that way for days. And the engineer, Zhi, he's, well, he's here. He hasn't said much since he came aboard, even when he was helping Bill with the modifications."

Chow turned to face Captain Hui and said, "Captain, are you and your people ready to go home?"

"Absolutely." Hui smiled.

"Houston, her smile said it all. We'll be ready at T minus zero."

Before returning to his own business, Chow looked at Zhi one more time. Zhi looked back; his gaze was more of a stare than polite eye contact. Chow thought, *Geez, you'd think he didn't want to be rescued. Why'd he help us if he doesn't want to go home? I've seen that look before. He must be in shock or, worse, experiencing Post-Traumatic Stress Disorder.*

An hour and fifteen minutes later, the six-person crew of the Altair was ready to leave the Moon. Unlike when Gene Cernan had departed those many years before, there were no lofty words or promises of a peaceful return. There was simply the business of getting ready to launch and the perfunctory exchanges with the control center back home.

The countdown clock counted backward toward zero as five of the six astronauts stood side by side, with Hui and Xu sharing handholds intended for use by only one astronaut during this phase of the mission. The fallen pilot, Ming Feng, was propped against one wall, and both Captain Hui and Dr. Xu had to stand against him, wedging him in place. He was strapped against the handholds. There was simply no room to stand elsewhere. Zhi Feng stood against one wall, motionless and still quiet.

"*Mercy I*, the clock is ticking," Houston announced.

"Alright, everybody brace for lift-off!" Stetson ordered his crewman and passengers. "Tony, we've got a green light on the thruster-pump valve."

"Roger that, TPV is go."

"Here it comes!" Stetson held fast and did his best to scan the screens and the occupants of the little ship as the burn kicked in. It was clear that they all felt the initial lunge. The Altair's main engine ignited, and they rose from the surface quickly at first. Due to the jolt, everyone in the cabin had to readjust their footing to keep from falling.

"Houston, this is Bill. Present velocity is one point eight

kilometers per second and increasing." Bill did his best to hold on and keep up with the instruments.

"Roger that, *Mercy I.*"

"Approaching two point four kilometers per second!" Bill shouted as they reached the lunar escape velocity. Moving rapidly, the Altair rose to rejoin the now-empty Orion in lunar orbit.

"Did you feel that?" Tony asked Bill.

"Yes, I did!" Bill reached up and tapped the attitude-control algorithm screen, bringing it to the front. The thrusters started firing rapidly, and the ship started rocking back and forth.

"Ahhh!" Hui shouted as she lost her handhold and slipped. "I'm falling!"

"Tony! Grab her!" Bill shouted. But Tony couldn't react fast enough to do anything. Fortunately for Hui, her tether pulled taut and stopped her from falling farther than just an arm's length outside into the lunar night. But she was dangling against the already rocking ship and throwing off the center of mass for the control algorithms to adjust correctly. Tony and Xu did their best to pull her back up and steady her.

"Houston! We've got rapid bang-bang corrections going on, forcing us to precess and rock like mad. Any suggestions?"

"We're working on it, *Mercy I*, but it might take longer than it will take to get up to the Orion. Are the manual controls an option?"

"Roger that!" Bill replied. *Are the manual controls an option, hell!* "Manual systems online. Pilot taking over in three, two, one!" Bill took the controls and fought against the rocking and bucking ship. *Bang, bang! Bang, bang, Bang, bang!* went the manual corrections he initiated through the joystick. For several moments it seemed as though Bill wouldn't be able to overcome the wild ride that the computer had generated for them. But finally he got the ship settled down enough that he could control it completely.

"Houston, I'm gonna have to fly her up to Orion. There are orange and red lights popping up nonstop on my screens."

"Roger that, *Mercy I*. Good luck."

"Did we do something to the ship that we shouldn't have?" Tony asked.

"Sure we did, but it didn't cause this. We've got either some software or electronics issues going on here," Bill said.

It was a long three hours of constant course correction and

slipping and holding on and slipping again all the way up to the Orion. But Bill knew that he was just the man for the job. He had hours and hours of training time on this vehicle. Granted he'd never simulated flying it with holes in the sides and six passengers aboard, but he was the most experienced at flying the ship.

After the second time that Hui had been tossed sideways and nearly out of the ship, she managed to use her tether to lash her left arm to a handhold.

It was a *long* three hours.

The rendezvous with the Orion capsule went exactly as planned. The crew then transferred from the Altair to the capsule that would return them home.

Stetson surveyed the five-person crew that he would be responsible for bringing home. They were alive, but tired and dirty. This was the first time he noticed the stench coming from the open suits worn by the Chinese. They'd been living in their suits for days, and they reeked of body odor, urine, and fecal matter. They'd been able to vent the worst of the mess from their suits while the air in their lander had been kept warm by the makeshift Bunsen burner, but when the air got unbearably cold, they'd just "vented" into their suits.

Everyone's suits, except for Anthony Chow's, were covered with a layer of lunar dust, turning their previously pristine white appearance to dark gray.

"What a mess," Stetson told them as he surveyed the situation. "Okay. We all need to shed these suits and bag them quickly." He didn't want to offend the Chinese, who might not be aware of just how bad they really smelled, so he decided to use a plausible sounding, and totally accurate, alternate reason for asking them to remove their suits.

"You're all covered with lunar dust. We can't risk letting the dust get into Orion's systems, so we need to get them sealed up as soon as possible. Please strip them off and secure them as best you can against the aft wall." Lunar dust was formed from eons of meteorite impacts, and each piece was more like a multi-spiked ball than its well-weathered Earthly cousins. It stuck to everything, and letting much get into the Orion's cabin simply posed too great a risk to its electronic systems.

The first to enter the Orion was Bill Stetson. After checking the ship's onboard systems, he went back into the Altair and scanned the rest of his crew. He cycled them in and then pressurized the cabin. They each began getting out of their suits.

"Captain Hui, we brought one change of clothes for you and each member of your crew. This is one case where knowing a little about each of you ahead of time came in handy. Here are packages with your names on them. They contain the clothing and a few other items your people thought you would need. Also, there are antiseptic wipes available."

Hui smiled and then replied, "I am not by nature a very modest person, Captain Stetson, but I understand the indelicate situation in which we find ourselves, and I will, of course, efficiently work the problem." With that, she and the rest proceeded to strip. They then placed the filthy suits in garment bags, sealed them, and stowed them as best they could.

Hui looked like a different person without her bulky spacesuit and dressed in a fresh flight suit. Chow had changed into his flight suit, and both Xu and Zhi were clad in clean undergarments provided. They'd also managed to get Ming into his fresh flight suit. Each of them had bathed with the wipes as best they could.

"Gentlemen and lady, welcome aboard the Orion."

Stetson helped Dr. Xu transfer the limp body of Ming Feng into one of the four chairs anchored to the floor of the capsule that would return them home. The chairs were arranged two on each side, one above the other with an aluminum deck below each of the top two seats. Open space separated each pair of seats, allowing movement between them.

Stetson buckled Ming into a seat on the lower deck.

The four remaining astronauts pulled themselves through the ring and floated into whatever open space they could find available in the very cramped interior of the Orion.

Zhi, still mostly keeping to himself, managed to be the last person to enter the Orion from the Altair. Immediately after passing through the airlock, he launched himself like a torpedo toward the lower decking and the chair into which the pilot had been strapped, narrowly missing a collision with Dr. Xu in the process. His rapid movement distracted everyone from seeing what he had curled in his hands that he then rapidly tucked away behind the Orion's lower right seat: a .45 caliber revolver.

"Ming's got one seat," Bill said. "I need one during the Trans-Earth Injection burn and reentry. Each of you two will have to share one. After TEI, we can take turns with two people hanging around until they get a chance to buckle in for a while."

Hui looked at Chow, shrugged her shoulders, and motioned to one of the available seats. Taking the cue, Chow moved to the seat and motioned for Hui to take it. She pulled her weightless self into the seat. He then followed by wedging himself next to her and using the seat belt to fasten them both down.

Dr. Xu and the still-silent Zhi moved to the only remaining seat and rather awkwardly buckled themselves in as well.

About thirty minutes later, there was another countdown and then the engine on the service module ignited, giving them the impulse required to return the ship to Earth. The maneuver was short, lasting only long enough to give the ship the speed required for them to be on a course for home.

Stetson spoke just after the engines shut down. "It's been a long day. Unless anyone objects, I'm going to dim the lights and take a nap."

No one objected. Though they all peered out the window at the Moon one long, last time.

The rest of that day was uneventful. Though they were restless and crowded, the mood was generally upbeat. After all, they had all gone to the Moon, and it looked like everyone was going to make it home. There was good reason to be upbeat.

Hui chatted frequently with her Chinese colleagues back on Earth, speculating on what might have gone wrong with the *Harmony* and caused it to crash. She repeatedly tried to engage Zhi in the discussions—without success.

Dr. Xu almost never left the side of Ming, fretting constantly about his condition and speculating on why he had not regained consciousness. He, too, engaged in protracted discussions on the radio; his were mainly with Chinese physicians who were monitoring Ming's condition from afar. Chow was often right there with him, checking Ming's vital signs and engaging in similar discussions with his American counterparts in Houston.

Stetson purposefully remained somewhat aloof, watching the crew with interest and silently assessing them. His conversations with mission control were strictly business, and he never missed an opportunity to speak with his wife and children.

Chapter 26

The alarm sounded but didn't exactly jolt him awake. Bill was strapped into the commander's seat, his seat, and had been out for more than three hours. He was in the midst of a very good dream about his wife on a beach, and there were very few clothes involved. Then the alarms sounded and men came in and pulled him away to respond to some emergency. The alarm continued to sound.

"What's that?" He finally snapped awake and immediately started scanning the screen in front of him. He had to squint, because he was extremely tired and hadn't slept much since the whole mission began. Now they were more than a half day into their journey back to Earth.

Momentarily disoriented, Chow stirred himself awake in the adjacent couch. He looked around, and Bill figured he was doing the same thing he had done. He was probably trying to figure out where the heck he was.

"Rise and shine. Looks like another day, er, night at the office," Bill said.

"Huh?" Bill could see that his colleague finally realized he was on the Orion spacecraft somewhere in the depths of space between the Moon and Earth and that an alarm was blaring at them. And in some way or other, that alarm probably meant something was trying to kill them in some form or fashion. Chow looked quickly over at Bill, who was smiling right back at him.

"Bill, what's going on?" he asked nervously.

"I'm not sure yet," Stetson said. "Won't be long for Houston chimes in, I guess."

Right on cue, the communication icon flashed and chimed.

"*Mercy I*, this is Houston. We're seeing a problem with one of your solar arrays. Are you seeing it as well?"

"Uh, checking it," Stetson replied.

"Something wrong?" Hui floated up next to them.

"Not sure yet, Hui," Tony said to her.

"Might as well rest until we figure it out, Hui. Nothing you can do right now," Bill added. "Though my guess is that we've got an EVA coming up."

"*Mercy I*, any word on that solar array?"

"Copy that, Houston. We see it. It's the same one we had trouble with on the way out."

"That's what telemetry is showing us, over."

"Damn. And I was having a good dream, too." Bill stretched as best he could and pulled up the diagnostics for the solar array. "At least we've got experience with the thing this time."

"Right. I can do the EVA," Tony offered.

"Don't jump the gun. Maybe we can get her started up."

"Batteries are kicking in, just like on the way out," Chow grunted.

Bill continued to scan through the diagnostics while Tony kept his eyes on the status board. With the array not pointing at the sun, the onboard batteries had to come online in order to maintain the ship's systems, including life support. With six crew members in the Orion now, that would tax the batteries far more quickly than they were designed for. The carbon-dioxide scrubbers were already running full bore.

"Houston, the same array appears to have seized and is not moving," Stetson said. He looked at Chow and then back at the diagnostics screen.

Chow could see that Stetson was concerned. Without maximum power from the arrays, the ship would have to rely on batteries to make up the difference. There was probably enough power from the batteries to allow the craft to return all six of them back to Earth. Probably. Bill didn't like "probably."

When the panel stuck on the way to the Moon, the concern had been that they would not have enough power to go into lunar orbit and land. Without landing they could not have rescued the stranded Chinese taikonauts. If they had followed the book, the mission would have been over; they would've survived, flown around the Moon, and all the Chinese would've died a cold, lonely death on the lunar surface.

Now the problem wasn't to rescue the Chinese from the Moon. It was how to get them and Tony and himself back to Earth safely. And to do that, they had to have those solar panels working.

"Tony, let's run it by the numbers just like last time," Stetson ordered. "We know how well that worked."

"Makes sense to me," Tony agreed. "Who knows, maybe it'll work this time."

"Houston. We're going to power down the array-control system and restart. I'm pulling up the reboot procedure now. Do you concur?"

"We concur. Reboot will take approximately twenty minutes. We'll be running the simulations in parallel. If we come up with something else you need to know, we'll be in touch."

"Roger that. *Mercy I* out." With that, Stetson began reviewing the manual restart procedure for the solar-array pointing system. "You know, I'll bet there's one of them damned Chinese circuit boards in that thing that screwed us on the test flight."

"No way to know that," Tony said.

"Well, when we get home I'm looking into it."

Twenty minutes later, Stetson went about the motions to complete the sequence that would completely power down the solar-array pointing system and then restart it. The system rebooted, and the drivers started reloading.

On the way out, Bill had managed to flub several key entries and had to redo them. This time it went smoothly. Bill entered the last keystrokes and then leaned back.

"Nothing to do now but wait a minute or two." There was just the silence of the crew compartment and the recirculating fans.

"Any luck?" Hui floated quietly up between Bill and Tony unexpectedly. The two of them nearly jumped out of their skins. "Sorry to have startled you."

"I thought you were going back to sleep." Bill's statement sounded like an order.

"Sounded like too much excitement up here to miss out on."

"Dang." Stetson hung his head. Same result as on the way out to the Moon. Nothing happened. "Houston, the reboot is complete. No change. I'm afraid we're gonna have to go out and kick the tires."

"It looks the same down here, Bill. Be advised that we've run the simulation down to the milliwatt. With the six of you in there, you need that pane working. You are still a long way from home."

"Understood, Houston." Bill sighed. "Looks like we're gonna start suiting up for an EVA in here."

"What seems to be the problem?" Dr. Xu floated up behind Hui.

"A solar panel is stuck and not generating enough power," Hui explained to the Chinese doctor. "We must all get in our spacesuits so Captain Stetson can go outside and fix it."

"That's right. Everybody has to button up so I can go outside and fix this thing. Tony, we'll do it the same as before." Stetson pushed away from the console and leaned back in his couch. He was still strapped in.

"Bill, I can go this time," Tony interjected.

"No. Not because I don't think you can do it, Tony." Bill paused so he would get his words right. "The first time I kicked at the thing, I almost fell off. I know where to stand now and how to do it right the first time without as much risk. I'm now trained to do this. You aren't."

Stetson gave Tony a look that meant the debate was over. He was certain Tony understood why. It was the look that intimidated almost everyone who came into his presence. Bill never really even understood how effective that look was on people. He was just Bill Stetson. The look was just his *I'm serious here* look. But to anybody else, it meant *Get out of my way. I have something important to do, and you ain't gonna keep me from doing it, because I'm Bill Stetson.*

"Roger that. I'll get the procedure pulled up while y'all get in your suits. Then I'll get suited up." They all had to wear their suits because the Orion didn't have an airlock. When either the main hatch or the docking hatch opened, it exposed the ship to the vacuum of space and all the air in the crew cabin would vent. That meant that everyone in the cabin had to wear their spacesuits for an EVA, even if they weren't the ones going outside. Had they not had to modify the Altair, which was still docked with them, the passengers could have just gone into the Altair during this EVA. But that option was out, as there were two one-meter-long by half-meter-wide holes in one of its walls.

One of the big issues was the status of the Chinese spacesuits. They were a mess. It took them fifteen or so minutes just to get them out of the bags and cleaned up to a level that was tolerable for use. And *tolerable* was a word with a very broad definition. They were tolerable in that if the Chinese taikonauts didn't put them on, they were all going to die. Funny how the definition of *tolerable* changed when one's life depended upon it. . . .

Forty minutes later, Hui, Xu, and Zhi were in their suits and had manhandled their injured colleague into his. Stetson and Chow were ready to begin the EVA. Once Bill was certain that everyone had checked and rechecked each other's suits, all according to procedure, and had "safed" any loose materials within the Orion, he gave the order to move out with the plan. Once the atmosphere was removed from the Orion, Stetson would be able to open the door and begin his EVA. The last thing they wanted was for some vital piece of hardware to float out the door with him.

"Tony, we're down to minimum atmospheric pressure, and I am about to open the door. Are you ready?"

"Roger that, Bill. Just call if you need me."

"Will do." Stetson smiled and gave a thumbs-up. "But I think this'll be quick and easy. I should be back inside in just a few minutes."

"The dashboard shows decompression and a green light for opening the hatch," Tony acknowledged.

"Good." Bill reached down and forcefully pulled the door release, opening the cabin to space. Without so much as a swoosh, the door opened and they were all exposed to vacuum. Stetson pushed and gently eased himself out the door, careful not to bang his pack against the hatch-seal ring. Once his arms cleared the hatch, he snapped the loose end of the safety tether from his spacesuit into place on the hull of the ship.

Been there and bought the T-shirt, Stetson told himself as he felt the reassuring snap of the tether to the fitting. On his previous EVA to fix the solar array, he recalled that he had experienced, albeit very briefly, a slight bout of vertigo. With the star field, sun, and Earth rotating around his field of view, he knew that the ship was spinning. This time, he didn't take the time to look around and managed to avoid being disoriented.

"I'm moving aft toward the arrays. I can see them clearly. Our buddy is at a dead stop," Stetson said. "Once again, for posterity, I don't see any sign of damage. It looks just like it did in the mockup and on the drawings and when I came out here and looked at it last time."

"Roger that, Bill. Looks the same as before," Chow responded from within the confines of the Orion. "Just tell me when you're in place to kick the thing."

"Give me a minute."

"Roger that. Getting in place to kick it loose." Stetson actually had no intention of kicking the array at all. Just as before, he planned to pull like the devil against the thing, hoping to break it free of whatever was sticking it in place. He placed his feet sturdily against the hull of the ship, with the toe of one of his boots wedged up underneath the handrail as far as he could get it. Then he grabbed hold to the panel with both gloved hands.

"Bill, I'm ready to cycle the reboot sequence whenever you give me the word," Tony announced over the radio.

"Roger that, Tony. I'm in place and ready when you are," Stetson replied.

"Okay. Cycling the reboot now." Bill waited a few seconds, and then Chow chimed in again. "Now. The power is cycled down and getting ready to restart."

Stetson didn't hesitate. With boots still firmly wedged, he used both hands to grasp and twist the stuck array. Trying to move it first clockwise and then counterclockwise, Stetson jimmied the stubborn piece of hardware. Quickly he felt a jolt, and the whole gimbal began to move. Just as before, the array fan was starting to move under its own power. Stetson watched as the array rotated and began to again track the sun.

"Best damned solar-panel repair team in the galaxy," Bill chortled through a sigh of relief.

"The board says the array is working once again." Chow sounded ecstatic.

"Tony, it's moving. I'm coming back in." Stetson began his climb back toward the hatch. "Let's hope it holds for the next two and half days to get us home."

"Roger that."

Chapter 27

They were one day out from Earth when they received a message that the President would like to speak with them.

Painfully aware that the conversation would be broadcast on television and the Net, Bill Stetson arranged his multinational crew to make sure that Captain Hui and Dr. Xu were front and center. The aloof Zhi remained to one side while he and Chow each stood on the other.

It was actually a joint call from the President and Chairman Jiantao of China. After the expected congratulatory remarks by both leaders and a brief exchange of pleasantries from both the American and Chinese astronauts on board, followed by both leaders reciting a renewed commitment to working together in the peaceful exploration of space, the televised visit began drawing to a close.

Making his concluding remarks, the President said, "Captain Stetson, Dr. Chow, you are American heroes. Your bravery in making this trip to secure the safe return of our Chinese friends and explorers will go down in the history books as one of the greatest acts of heroism in the history of humanity. A grateful world thanks you."

Knowing he was expected to respond, Stetson replied, "Thank you, sir. We are honored and proud to have been able to serve our country and help bring these, our new friends, home."

The call ended, and a clearly relieved group of tired and dirty astronauts breathed a sigh of relief. Stetson returned to his seat and immediately began to once again review the procedures for their upcoming aerocapture. The maneuver had never before been used, and he wanted to make sure he knew what to expect.

Everyone else more or less returned to what they'd been doing before the call, except for Zhi. Purposefully he moved to the lower deck and toward the seat in which the stricken pilot was sleeping. Dr. Xu was also moving toward the pilot and, as a consequence, was the first to see Zhi remove the handgun from behind the seat. He let out a cry of protest.

Zhi's eyes were on fire. He said to Xu, speaking in Chinese and for the first time, "I will not allow us to be demeaned and rescued like we are helpless children. *We* were to be the heroes. *We* were to return home to the parades. *We* were to be the symbols of the new China. Not them!"

Stetson and Chow did not understand the words, but they could tell from the tone and the gun that Zhi had gone over the edge. As he watched Zhi wave the deadly weapon, Stetson momentarily wondered why an engineer on a Moon mission would have a handgun. More urgently, he wondered what he planned to do with it.

"Captain Hui! What's going on? What does he want? And please tell him that firing a gun in this ship could kill us all."

Hui said something to the engineer in Chinese that immediately drew an angry response. Zhi lashed out with the gun and hit Dr. Xu across the cheek, sending the doctor tumbling toward the outer edge of the ship's interior. Small red droplets were now floating in the air around Dr. Xu.

Zhi spat while he steadied his motion and spoke, this time in English. "I will not be humiliated. I will not allow our great country to be humiliated. We should have just died a hero's death on the Moon. Now the world will bestow upon you the honor that should have been ours! You failed us, Captain!" Zhi turned to face Captain Hui and said, "You never had the courage to do what was required."

Stetson could tell from Zhi's countenance and posture that he was not bluffing. While he was looking at the Chinese taikonaut, Stetson moved his hands behind his back and slightly to the right, skimming over the control panel until they found one of the few actual switches still used on human spaceflight—the one that would turn off the automatic pilot.

When the system beeped, acknowledging that the command had been received, Zhi abruptly turned toward Stetson and shouted something as his fingers tightened on the trigger of the handgun.

Before he was able to fire the gun, the ship's attitude-control thrusters fired in rapid bang-bang succession, causing the entire ship to begin tumbling.

The gun discharged, and the bullet barely missed hitting Stetson. Instead, it struck the floor beneath his feet. As Zhi moved to reorient himself and brought the gun up to fire again, Stetson launched himself across the room directly toward him. Simultaneously, Dr. Xu threw himself at Zhi, striking him on the side opposite his gun hand. With Stetson and Xu trying to disarm him, Zhi simply began rapidly pulling the trigger.

A bullet struck Dr. Xu in the leg, causing him to convulse and curl into a ball. The next bullet went wild and struck the floor like the first one. Before he could fire it again, Stetson cold-cocked him on the jaw, causing the enraged Zhi to let go of the gun and rebound toward the opposite wall.

Before Zhi could recover and reorient himself in the weightlessness of the Orion's cabin, Hui had him in a choke hold.

Stetson quickly assessed the situation in the ship. The immediate threat posed by the Chinese engineer was neutralized—Hui had him pinned almost to the point of losing consciousnesses. Based on the amount of blood spheres floating through the cabin, Dr. Xu was severely injured. Tony Chow was already with Xu and working to stop the bleeding. The injured Chinese pilot was still out cold. The ship was tumbling, thanks to the distraction of the autopilot being turned off and Stetson's engaging the attitude-control thrusters. The ship's radio was signaling that mission control wanted to speak with them. And then there was the matter of the three gunshots.

Like we needed this bullshit! Stetson said to himself. "Tony, you take care of the doctor while I stop us from tumbling." Stetson moved to the control panel and reengaged the automatic pilot. At that moment, orange and red lights began popping up across the ship's status screens.

He said, "Captain Hui. Use some duct tape from the mechanical kit to tie up your friend. It ought to hold him. I've got to figure out what's happened and why the screen looks like a Christmas tree."

"Bill! You need to see this." Chow looked up from Dr. Xu's injured leg and motioned toward the hundreds of perfectly spherical red balls of blood circling in the air near the center of the crew cabin.

Stetson looked toward the blood and didn't like what he saw. The spheres were moving toward the center of the Orion and swirling slowly around each other as they also moved toward the floor. As they neared the floor, they swirled around each other in a tighter circle, moving faster and faster, until they finally disappeared. A miniature funnel cloud had formed in the Orion, with the tip of the funnel being a hole in the floor made by one of Zhi's bullets. They were losing air.

Stetson quipped, "That explains one of the alarms." He moved toward the hole to get a closer look.

"I'll use the patch kit. We have it aboard in case of a micrometeor strike." He moved to one of the storage bins along the outside wall of the capsule and opened a compartment. Inside the compartment was a small container filled with what looked like Silly Putty. The kit was standard issue aboard the Orion and designed for the purpose of repairing damage caused by a tiny meteor or orbital debris. Space was filled with small meteors, and, over time, the probability of a spacecraft getting hit was large enough to consider it a serious threat. The sealant could patch a small hole and keep the Orion from losing atmosphere.

"This patch ought to work." Stetson carefully removed the putty from the container and filled the hole. The remaining blood spheres slowly dispersed after the airflow out of the cabin stopped.

"Zhi is secure. How may I help?" asked Hui.

Stetson looked toward the Chinese captain and saw that she had not only securely bound the renegade engineer but had taped his mouth shut as well.

"Uh..." Stetson thought for a second. "Why don't you answer the radio while I tend to the rest of the alerts? The headset is on the control panel."

Hui moved out from her position on the upper deck toward the control panel, eased on the headset, and activated the radio.

"This is Captain Hui, speaking for Captain Stetson. Umm, how may I be of assistance?"

Stetson had to laugh and then said, "I bet they didn't expect her to answer."

He moved to the control panel and positioned himself only a few inches from his Chinese counterpart as she described the violence that had transpired aboard the ship to the ground crew back in Texas.

Stetson looked at the myriad of ship-status alerts and slowly turned them off, one by one, until only a few orange lights remained. None of them were still red, which meant the ship was not in imminent danger.

"Captain Stetson, your mission controllers wish to speak with you." Hui slipped the headset from her head and handed it to him.

Stetson declined the headset, switched the audio to the loudspeaker, and said, "This is Stetson."

"Bill, we were more than a little surprised to hear Captain Hui answer our call. We've been trying to reach you for quite some time. She says that you have everything under control and that the hole in the floor is sealed. Is that correct?"

"Yes, that is correct."

"How is Dr. Xu?"

Stetson looked toward Tony and Xu. Though he was obviously in pain, Xu gave a thumbs-up sign. Tony, after only a brief moment of hesitation, also gave a thumbs-up.

"He'll make it."

"Glad to hear it." The mission controller then hesitated before he said, "Bill, there's another problem you need to know about. The hole that you patched probably pierced the heat shield. The patch you put in place will keep you from losing atmosphere, but it will never survive the heat of reentry. Our models indicate that the hole on the outside of the ship is probably two or three times larger than what you see on the inside. The energy of the bullet was mostly deposited in the outer skin. If you don't patch it on the outside with the heat-shield repair kit, then you might not survive the aerocapture."

"EVA?" Stetson said.

"I'm afraid you'll have to. Are you up for it?"

"Well, I am certainly okay with going out, but I am not sure about what to do with the rest of my crew. Their suits are a mess. It'll take us some time to clean them for reuse. How much time do I have before we have to jettison the lander and begin reentry procedures?" The lander was not designed to return home to Earth. Before the Orion made its final entry into the Earth's atmosphere for the upcoming aerocapture maneuver, the lander would have to be jettisoned. The big kicker would be if they had time to get in their suits and to complete an EVA before the aerocapture procedures began.

"Six hours."

Not much time, Stetson thought. Then he replied, "That's plenty of time. Stetson out."

"Okay, folks, we've got to get suited up quickly. I've got to go outside and play."

"You have another patch kit?" Hui asked.

"Yes. After the *Columbia* accident back in 2003, NASA developed a technique for patching damage to the shuttle's heat shields so that similar accidents could be prevented. The requirement applied to the Orion as well—here we are. The heat-shield patch kit is stored near the one I just used. Without it, that hole will allow hot gases inside the ship and act like a blowtorch. We would never survive that."

It took twenty minutes to get the injured Dr. Xu into his suit. Another thirty-five to get the unconscious pilot back into his suit. At first Zhi acted as if he were going to refuse to put his suit on, so Hui asked Stetson to hold the pistol on him while she and Tony supervised his suiting up. They then proceeded to duct tape him back down. That took another thirty minutes.

Chow opened up a secure radio channel to Stetson. "Bill, can we repressurize the Orion while you are on the EVA so I can have access to my patients? If one of them were to need attention, I'd like to be able to get to them quickly."

"I don't see why not. That way you can monitor the ship and run through the checklists again also. We know the damage that was caused by one of the bullets, but not the other two. I'd rather find out now than during aerocapture. How is Dr. Xu, really?"

"He's lost a lot of blood, and the bullet severed his fibula—one of the bones in the lower leg. He's stable but in a lot of pain. He should be okay if we can get him to a hospital soon. Putting him back in the suit was very painful for him. I gave him some morphine."

)   ●   ●   ●   (

"Okay, we've got just a little more than five hours to fix the ship, get back in, and get ready for aerocapture," Stetson said. "Everybody has masks down and is ready for depressurization. Then Hui and I go outside and look for the damage on the ship. Once we find the damage, she comes back inside while I do the repair. It's a one-person job anyway. While I'm outside, you repressurize the cabin. When I want back in, you do it all again in reverse order. That's the plan. Got it?"

"Got it, Bill." Tony nodded.

Hui would look at the top portion of the ship while Bill looked at the underside. Stetson communicated over the suit radio to Hui.

"Captain Hui. I won't ask why one of your crew had a gun. Quite frankly, I don't care. But I do want to know if I need to worry about anything else from you and your crew that might endanger me, my crew, or my ship."

"Commander Stetson, please know that I am so sorry about what happened. I knew that Zhi had a gun with him on the trip. He was our—how do you say—political officer. But I did not know he had brought it with him from the lander to your ship. I believe we might have used it on ourselves had your ship not come to our rescue."

Stetson looked around the empty Altair and out the hole in her side. He could see the constellation Orion as plain as he ever had. *That's fitting,* he thought. "I never imagined my trip to the Moon would be anything like this."

"Nor did I."

"It'll go in the history books." Stetson could see the concern and slight smile on Hui's face.

"In ours, too."

Chapter 28

"I have completely covered the upper portion of the ship's hull and found no other holes," Hui radioed to Stetson. "I am not sure where those other bullets went, but they did not penetrate the hull on the upper half."

"That's good news," Bill replied. He had worked his way around the bottom half of the Orion twice and had found only the one major hole that he had already patched from the inside. "Something on the inside must've stopped the bullets, then. One of them likely being Dr. Xu's leg."

"Yes, you are most likely correct on that one," Hui agreed. "I can work my way down to you and offer a hand."

The damage assessment done, Hui offered once again to stay outside and help, but Bill patted the kit attached to his side and smiled.

"You go on and get back inside. I can handle this." He motioned for her to go back into the Orion so they could close the main hatch.

"Very well, Captain." She complied reluctantly, as far as he could tell.

Stetson watched as she made her way back to and then through the hatch. Once Tony had assured him that she was safely back inside and that the hatch was closed, he was ready to begin making the repair.

Outside and on the bottom of the Orion he studied the hole in the heat shield. Bill found the damage just below the handholds he'd used on the previous EVA, and he was now in a position to repair the damaged heat shield. Looking momentarily out into space, he could see the beautiful blue planet that was the Earth looming ahead of them. Stetson thought of his wife and children back home worrying about him, and he felt guilty. He was sure they now knew about the shooting, and he didn't like the fact that in addition to all the fears that were normal when an astronaut went into space, they would now have to worry about a crazy person shooting him.

Pulling himself back to the present, he continued moving around the periphery of the hole on the bottom of the Orion. The damage from the bullet was obvious. In the otherwise per-fectly smooth dark gray surface of the heat shield was a jagged hole at least three inches in diameter. He hoped the patch kit worked as planned.

"Houston, I see the damage. Can you see it with the suit camera?"

"Bill, we see it. It looks nasty from here. Can you repair it?"

"I think so. But it will use up the kit."

"Understood. Our engineers here agree."

"Stetson out."

Bill then used a clip to fasten his tether to an anchor point close to where he needed to make the repair so that he would not waste valuable time inadvertently floating away.

In the Orion, the air pressure was restored. Chow maneuvered through the cabin and toward the primary control panel, noting that there were still far too many orange alerts.

"Interesting." Hui popped her faceshield up and scanned the control panels. "Dr. Chow, what do all the orange indicators mean?"

"Well, uh, hmm . . ." Chow wasn't one hundred percent certain himself, so he took a closer look. "Those are systems the computer has flagged as being not quite right or in need of monitoring by the crew. They would be red if there was a serious malfunction. Orange just means that they need checking and monitoring. Personally, I like green."

"Green is a *nice* color." Hui smiled.

Chow began checking each system just as he had been trained

while Hui watched the video feed from Stetson's spacesuit as he repaired the damage caused by the bullet piercing the ship's heat shield. Chow occasionally glanced up from his work to note Stetson's progress as well.

Repairing the damage took Stetson a little over an hour. It wasn't as simple as taking a caulking gun and squirting goop into the hole and letting it dry. Back in the space shuttle days, it was discovered that leaving a "bump" on the surface of the heat shield that protruded more than three millimeters above the surface could cause extreme frictional forces that would rip the patch right off or cause it to superheat and therefore burn off. The heat shield on the Orion was a bit more forgiving, as it was a reentry capsule and not a flying surface, but the models had shown that large bumps on the surface would increase the heating and might be detrimental to the patch materials. In other words, rough patch jobs could be bad. Bill did his best to be meticulous about the process, but it wasn't easy in an EVA suit with those bulky gloves. On more than three occasions during the patching process, he cursed the spacesuit designers and muttered that mankind would never make it to Mars if they didn't invent a better suit.

"Tony, this is Bill." Stetson's voice came over the ship-to-ship radio channel.

"Bill, this is Tony. Go ahead."

"I've done all I can do out here. According to my watch, we haven't got that long before we have to jettison the Altair and start our aerocapture checklists and procedures. I'm on my way in."

"Okay, Bill. I'll get everybody's faceshields down and buttoned up so we can depressurize and get you back inside."

"Roger that. I'll just hang out here until you give me the word."

"Got it. Preparing to cycle the hatch."

Turning away from the control panel, Chow motioned for Captain Hui to button up and help Bill.

He followed Hui to the hatch and showed her how to open it once the depressurization was complete. With his spacesuit donned, and confident that Hui could handle opening a hatch,

Chow turned back to the command console and rapidly completed the checklist. He had just initiated the cabin depressurization when one of the many orange warning lights turned bright red. Chow noted the warning and touched the screen to bring up more information about the alarm. He didn't like what he read.

He went back to the beginning of the depressurization sequence and began again—much more rapidly this time. The result was the same. The red warning light remained stubbornly lit, and the cabin did not depressurize.

Chow was beginning to sweat in his suit, and his heart rate began to rise. *No, no, no, this can't happen now!* he thought to himself.

"Bill, this is Tony. We've got another problem."

"Our luck, huh?" Stetson replied. "I was starting to wonder. I've been at the door for a few minutes waiting on you to open her up. What's the problem?"

"I can't open the door. I started the depressurization sequence, and then the status board lit up like a Christmas tree. I've been through it twice now, and all I can tell from the fault tree is that we can't depressurize to let you in. I don't know if the problem is mechanical or if it's just a sensor somewhere."

"How much time do we have before you have to separate from the lander?"

"A little more than an hour."

"Well, that's just great. I sure as hell don't want to ride out an aerocapture from here."

"Bill, unless we get this door open within the next thirty minutes or so, you won't be able to come inside at all."

Chow activated the voice link to mission control and brought them into the discussion, hoping against hope that one of the many NASA engineers would come up with something that would allow them to bring his friend inside before it was too late.

Chow ran through the entire procedure one more time with the same result—the red light would simply not go away.

"Houston, there has to be something else we can try," Tony said and tried not to sound desperate.

"Okay, *Mercy I*. We've got another fix we want you to give a go."

"Roger that, Houston. Let's have it." Tony had high hopes that the engineers back at NASA would figure this out. They always did.

"It looks like we've got several circuits interrupted, probably due to damaged systems, but, nonetheless, we aren't going to trick the computers to depressurize the cabin. So, what we need to try is to cycle the inner docking hatch of the Orion. And then blow the Altair hatch out."

"Can we do that with the Altair attached to the Orion?" Bill interjected.

"No, Bill, we can't. So, we'll have to attempt this when we jettison the Altair for the aerocapture maneuver. The timeline will be tight," Houston responded.

"Hang in there, Bill. We'll start prepping for this procedure." Tony did his best to assure his commander, but he wasn't all that confident himself.

"Tony," Hui said vocally and not through the radio. "If the computer will not let us open the hatch because we're not depressurized, then why will it let us undock the Altair?"

"The engineers down at Houston want us to give it a try. And, frankly, I'm not giving up on Bill without trying something."

"Understood. Whatever I can do to help, just let me know." Hui nodded sincerely at Tony, but he could see the concern, fear, and lack of optimism in her face.

"Bill, this is Tony. I've got to start the entry procedure checklists, and the engineers have a mile-long sequence of breaker flipping that I have to do before we undock."

"Roger that, Tony. Do what needs to be done." Stetson, not sounding at all like a man who had just been handed a death sentence, added, "Tony, one more thing I want you to understand."

"What's that, Bill?"

"No matter what happens out here, our first obligation is to get this crew and this ship safely home. Understood?"

"Understood." Tony didn't like the sound of that.

"Good. Get to it."

"Yes, sir."

Chapter 29

The mood in the Orion was morose. With two crewmembers injured, one incapacitated, and another trapped outside the ship, Anthony Chow was in command, and he didn't like it. At least he wasn't stranded on the surface of the Moon and left to die, as had been his biggest fear right up until they had actually left the Moon. Now, who knew? The likelihood of the aerocapture maneuver failing was pretty high, but Tony never had any fear of that part of the mission. Besides, he had way too many things going on to let his mind dwell on such negative things.

The Altair was about to be separated from the Orion on schedule, and they were less than two hours away from entering the outer portion of the Earth's atmosphere. Chow was putting all his faith in those wizard engineers back home in mission control to come up with a magic spell that would save his ship's captain, his friend. And that magic spell was a tedious one. It had taken him more than fifteen minutes of changing commands, throwing toggles, tapping icons, and physically flipping switches.

"That's the last breaker. Check!" Tony reported.

"Roger that, *Mercy I*. Now, we need to do all this in very rapid succession, so make certain Bill is in the safe location and be prepared for rapid depressurization."

"Roger that." Tony looked around the cabin and saw that

everybody was strapped in or tied off to something. "Bill, are you clear out there?"

"Roger that, Tony. I'm in the predetermined safe spot. It's just me and my old solar-panel buddy out here. Let's get on with this."

"You got it, Captain." Tony readied himself for typing in a rapid sequence of commands and for tapping toggle icons. "Everybody button up. We start rapid depressurization in ten seconds." He waited until he got a thumbs-up from Hui and then tapped the first icon. Then he followed the sequence as the engineer at Houston called out the commands.

"That's the last one, Tony. Now cycle the docking-ring hatch." The engineer sounded confident that the sequence would work.

"Roger that. Cycling the hatch." Tony nodded to Hui to hold on and hit the hatch cycle. The icon flashed green for a brief second and then orange. Then it cycled to red and popped up a window explaining that the exterior hatch was depressurized and that they couldn't open the interior hatch without pressurizing the Altair first.

"Shit." Tony's heart sank. "Houston. I hope you have a plan C."

"Uh, it didn't work?" The engineer's voice sounded surprised. "*Mercy I*, what is the status of the hatch? Our feeds show it as closed."

"Roger that, Houston." Tony hung his head as best he could in a spacesuit. "The hatch is closed and locked out."

"Be advised that the Altair jettison sequence is in place and will continue."

"Roger that, Houston. The Altair sequence is still green."

"Sorry, *Mercy I*. Be advised that at this time there is no plan C."

"Come on! Can't you guys come up with something?"

"Sorry, *Mercy I*. The Altair has to jettison now in order for the proper orbital energy to be achieved following the aerobraking maneuver. We can't postpone the Altair jettison any further."

"Listen, Houston. Bill's outside, thinking God only knows what, and you're sitting down there giving me a lecture about the physics of aerocapture? I want to know what we can do to help him survive. Can he ride this thing out there? Can he tie down to the nose or something?"

Chow watched as the Altair jettison cycle completed, and he felt a slight shift as the Altair released from dock.

"Tony, I wish there was something we could do. In a few minutes, you're going to skim the outer part of the Earth's atmosphere at more than twenty thousand miles per hour. Let me put that another way; the relative wind velocity around the outside of the Orion will be twenty thousand miles per hour. And as you begin to enter the atmosphere, the atmospheric friction will superheat much of the atmosphere around the Orion to many thousands of degrees. There is simply no way an astronaut in a spacesuit can survive that. Even if Bill could find a way to anchor himself to the ship, he would be fried. I want him to come home, too, but there is simply no way we can find a quick fix to make that happen. If we can't get the cabin to depressurize, we can't open that hatch." The voice on the other end of the radio connection was professional, with an appropriate amount of empathy thrown in. The combination angered Chow, who would have responded better to more anger and less sympathy.

Chow struck the control panel with his right fist and turned off the radio. He briefly looked up at the ever-present video camera and then toward Captain Hui.

"Dammit all to hell," Chow said.

"We have to tell him." Hui frowned.

"No, we don't. He knows what it meant when the Altair drifted away and the hatch didn't cycle."

"Tony, this is Bill."

"Bill?"

"You did your best. Now focus on the mission goal."

"Roger that, Bill." Tony had tears starting at the corners of his eyes. "It's been an honor, Captain Stetson."

"Honor's all mine. I would like to talk to my wife if that could be arranged."

"Hang on. Oh, and Bill, be advised that the solar arrays are about to start cycling in, so you might want to steer clear of that."

"Right."

Gary Childers was in his Lexington, Kentucky, headquarters building with Paul Gesling and Caroline O'Conner watching the press coverage of the *Mercy I*'s flight. Like most of the world, they'd been mesmerized by the saga of the rescue mission. They'd been elated when the Chinese crew was found alive, on the edge of their seats when they learned that the crew had almost not survived the hike from their crashed ship to the American lander, and shocked when the broadcast had been abruptly cut off not long after the crew had spoken with the President and Chinese Premier. They were now grieving over the pending death of Mission Commander Stetson.

For what seemed like the thousandth time, the newscaster began to describe the aerocapture maneuver that the *Mercy I* was about to attempt. "In just under twenty minutes, the Orion's heat shield will begin to get hot as its friction with the Earth's atmosphere is used as a brake to both slow the ship and change its flight path so that it can subsequently dock with the International Space Station. Under normal circumstances, the Orion would simply enter directly into the atmosphere, like the Apollo missions, and come straight home to the surface. But these are hardly normal circumstances. The ship, occupied by a crew of six—before the unfortunate absence of Commander Stetson—is simply too heavy for a safe landing here on Earth. Instead of coming directly home, they will be docking at the International Space Station. Once there, the two wounded crew members plus another astronaut can return to the Earth in the Russian Soyuz spacecraft that is docked to the station as a lifeboat. At this time, NASA has not decided how to bring the remaining crew back home to Earth. Neither the U.S. nor the Russians have any ships ready to fly, and it could be months before this situation changes. Back to you, Jane."

Childers picked up the remote and muted the sound before he had to endure more inane comments from the empty-headed newscaster in the studio.

"Paul, I have an idea. We use the same docking ring that NASA uses, right? Didn't we standardize on that after we won the space station robotic resupply missions contract back in 2012?"

"Why, now that you mention it"—Gesling leaned forward— "yes, yes, we did. It was too expensive to do anything else. NASA had spent hundreds of millions of dollars developing the docking ring, and it didn't make sense for us to reinvent the wheel. Though there are some things about the design that really need to be changed."

"Good, good," Childers said. "Tell me if I'm wrong about this. There's nothing that's keeping us from flying *Dreamscape* again, right? I mean, the ship is supposed to be able to turn around and fly again in just under two weeks after an orbital flight. Is there anything unique about your trip around the Moon that would make this turnaround time any different?"

"No, not that I am aware of."

"Good. Go out to Nevada and see to it that the *Dreamscape* is ready to fly as soon as it is safe. You're going to the Space Station and bringing home some real God-damned American heroes. We found these people, and now, by God, we're going to help bring them home."

Gesling and O'Conner rose from their chairs and began to move toward the door. Gesling, as usual, took the lead just ahead of O'Conner so he could open the door for her.

"Caroline." Childers stopped her. "Please stay here. After I call our illustrious senator, I suspect I will be not only speaking with the NASA Administrator, but I'll also be holding a press conference. I need your help to put together the talking points and the not-so-subtle message that Space Excursions is not only about joyrides but also search and rescue. If we pull this off, we'll have customers beating down our doors for the next quarter of a century!"

Caroline looked momentarily at Gesling, offered him a smile, and then returned to her seat in front of Gary Childers. Gesling paused, left the room, and closed the door.

"Don't worry." Childers leaned forward toward Caroline. "He'll be all right. He's leading a charmed life, and I suspect that you are making it even more so. Let's get this plan together so you can get out to Nevada yourself as soon as possible."

"Yes, sir!"

Bill sat straddle-legged as best he could on the capsule, keeping one hand on the handhold and staring off into space. Earth was filling up a good portion of his field of view now. There was nothing he could do but sit there and contemplate. He contemplated his childhood, his life before NASA, then when he became an astronaut. He thought about his wife and kids. It made him happy to think of them and sad that he might be leaving them to fend for themselves in the world. Then he wondered if he should have done anything different. His final conclusion was no. If he ended up making the ultimate sacrifice, that would be okay with him. His mission had saved several lives and showed everyone that humans could work in the vast emptiness of space. Humanity could now go to the Moon to perform rescue missions. And, eventually, his mission would show that, even though space was a tough place to survive, humanity had what it took to do it. He was certain every other astronaut felt the same. He was pretty sure that even the Chinese taikonauts felt that way or they wouldn't have taken the risks they did to beat the Americans to the Moon.

Bill was pretty sure that if things went bad, there would be a bit of backlash from the public. There might be that knee-jerk reaction to resist spending more resources on such a risky thing as space travel. But he also knew that everybody wanted to see Captain Kirk. Since before he was born humanity had wanted to explore space. Granted, for the most part, everyone wanted somebody else to do it and somebody else to pay for it. Well, Bill *was* that somebody else to do it. He had no regrets. He would do it all over again even if it meant that he would end up in exactly the same predicament, or even worse.

"Bill, are you still with us?" Chow said into the radio.

"I'm here. Where else would I be?" Stetson responded, sounding not at all like a man about to die.

"They've got your wife and kids on the private line. Do you want to speak with her now?"

"That's a stupid question. Put them on."

"Right. Here she is." Chow changed the setting to channel five, the private line that would allow Stetson and his wife to speak without anyone aboard, in the press, or even in mission control listening. The call would be recorded, but it, like other private-line calls before it, would not be made public without consent of the astronaut. Long ago, NASA had decided that everyone was entitled to private conversations with their loved ones, even astronauts.

Bill Stetson had wanted to go to the Moon since he had been old enough to remember. It was his main goal in life. Well, he had gone to the Moon. In fact, he had done more than go to the Moon. He had gone to the Moon and rescued a ship full of stranded astronauts and done his best to get them home. And, as far as he could tell, it looked like they were going to get home. He sat on the lower half of the Orion space capsule just beneath the solar arrays staring aimlessly the beautiful starry space. He didn't really wonder about the afterlife, because he felt at one with the universe right then and there. The problem wasn't fulfilling lifelong dreams and goals. The problem was leaving behind the ones that he loved. And he loved his wife with all his mind, body, soul, and heart. Then there were his two kids. His daughter was fourteen going on twenty-three and looked just like her mother—acted like her, too. And his son was eleven and every bit as bullheaded as his old man. It tore at Bill's insides thinking of them growing up without him there to see it. He indeed felt he was making the ultimate sacrifice to push humanity into space and was proud of what he had done, but right then and there he just wished he could hug and kiss his family.

"Bill? Do you hear me?" He could hear his wife biting back the tears.

"Terry? I hear you, gorgeous!" Bill paused long enough to swallow the lump in his throat. "Sally and Neil there, too?"

"We're here, Daddy. We love you!"

"I love you, too, kiddos. Listen to me now. Things have gotten away from me up here, and it doesn't look like I'm gonna be coming home. It was worth it, though, because we saved four lives." Bill gulped and wasn't certain what his tear ducts would do in microgravity.

"No, Daddy! You have to come home," Sally cried.

"Baby, you've got to be there for your mother and your little brother. You have to promise me to keep him out of trouble. And you have to promise me to always be great and do your best, just like you always have."

"I promise, Daddy." Sally sobbed deeply. "No, Daddy. I love you!"

"I love you, too." Bill really wasn't sure what to say, but this was his last time to ever leave his son with any man-to-man wisdom. He didn't have any, but he wished he did. "Neil."

"Dad."

"You know your mother took a lot of coercing to get her to name you after Neil Armstrong, but in the end she caved."

"I know, Dad. You've told me that story before." The boy kept his voice strong and held up like a little man.

"Well, son, I want you to promise me to be as great as your namesake. Can you do that for me?" Bill was beginning to learn that tears just balled up in the corner of your eyes in no gravity.

"No, Dad. I won't," his son told him.

"Now, don't give me any sass, son."

"I don't want to be as great as the first man to walk on the Moon. I want to be as great as you, Dad!" Neil said through sobs.

"I love you, son." *What can I say to that?* Bill thought. He had to pause for a second or two as he almost lost control of himself. He managed to hold back from breaking down completely. "You will be the man of the house now. You take care of your mother and your sister, you hear me?"

"Yes, sir."

"Now, kids, I love you both. I love you more than anything in the universe, and I hate that this is how things turned out. I'm not going to say goodbye, because I'll always be right there with you, looking out for you. I'll always be a part of everything you are and everything you do. I will always be there. I love you."

"Daddy!"

"Now let me have a private word with your mother, please." Bill wished he could just hold them one more time. See their faces and laugh with them just once more. He couldn't even stand having to tell them goodbye. He was pretty certain that those were the last words he'd ever say to his children. He hoped they were good enough.

"Bill?"

"Terry, honey. You are and have always been the absolute love of my life," he started but really didn't know what else to say. It was the truth that he felt in his heart, so that is what he decided to go with. "I'm so sorry that I'm not going to be there to help with the kids and to grow old with you."

"Bill, you are the love of my life, too. Oh God, Bill, what have you gone and done? I'm trying to be strong, but—"

"You go ahead and cry if you need to, baby."

"Bill . . ."

"Hey, listen, you remember that time we were down at the Cape and had that little convertible rental car." Bill wasn't sure where he was going with this, but he wanted to be happy with his wife just one more time. He wanted to relive a happy memory with her just once more.

"Yeah, the Ford Mustang. It was red."

"Yeah, that was it. I remember telling you that I was gonna go to the Moon then, and do you remember what you told me?" Bill bit at his lower lip to steady it from quivering.

"Yes, I do."

"What did you tell me?"

"I said, *Bill Stetson, if you're gonna go running off into space, you better have the decency to be here in nine months when I have your baby!*" That had been nearly fifteen years ago. And he had been there for the delivery, for both of them.

"Took me a long time to get to the Moon, huh?"

"Uh-huh."

"Well, I just want you to remember how happy we were that day and how much in love we were. I still love you that much right this second. More."

"Me, too, Bill. Oh God, I'm going to miss you."

"I love you."

"I love you, too."

Stetson's conversation wasn't extremely long. Only a few minutes, actually. Just a few short minutes later he was back on the line with Chow. There wasn't much to talk about, but he felt like talking to somebody.

"We'll be entering the uppermost part of the atmosphere in about fifteen minutes, Bill. The computer is running the show, and, well, I just wanted to say thanks for picking me to go to the Moon with you."

"Tony, you're welcome. Let's not drag this out, shall we? Give the ship your full attention and get these people home."

"But, Bill," Chow replied, close to crying.

"Tony, you did your best."

"If we could've just got the damned cabin to depressurize." Tony slapped his hand against the couch's armrest. "Damned computer. Back in the Apollo days, they'd probably have been able to manually blow the hatch or something."

"Naw, I think after the Grissom incident that they actually took off the explosive bolt—wait a minute!" Bill stopped midsentence. "Tony, get Houston on the line and get that pistol out and make sure it has a round in it!"

"Bill?"

"Not much time, Tony! Do it! And tell them to keep my wife and kids there."

"You got it!"

) ● ◉ ◖ (

"That might just work, Bill!" mission control replied. "Give us a minute to determine the safest place to implement the plan."

"Go ahead, but we don't have a whole bunch of minutes left," Bill said. "Tony, I want you practicing putting your glove on and off while Houston is figuring this out. If you need help, get Hui to back you up."

"Bill?"

"Well, you can't fire the pistol with your suit gloves on. If you need Hui standing by with them to help you get them on quickly, then do so," Bill explained.

"Oh, I see." Where the engineers back at NASA hadn't figured out the problem, Bill just might have. Another reason that he had been the right man for the job all along. "But, Bill, it will take a few minutes for the cabin to depressurize, so I'll be in no danger."

"I still want you sealed up as quickly as possible, just in case. And have the putty standing by."

"Roger that." Tony slipped the seal ring on his right glove and twisted it. It took him a few seconds, but it came off fairly easily. Getting it back on took him almost a minute and a half. It almost startled him when mission control chimed in.

"*Mercy I*, mission control."

"Go ahead, Houston."

"We've done a quick analysis and believe that this is a workable plan. The best location to create a leak will be as far into the nose as possible, just to the right of the docking-ring hatch. It is likely that the boundary-layer plasma will not damage the ship critically if there is a structural-integrity breach there. The plasma should flow past any damage up there."

"Alright, then—let's do it." Tony slipped his glove off again and handed it to Hui. "Hang on to this for me, please."

"I've got it." Hui nodded to him.

"Bill, are you clear of the nose out there?"

"Roger that, Tony. I'm still hanging out with my old pal the solar panel." Bill paused, slightly wondering if his need to use levity in the current situation was his subconscious helping him deal with the fact that he was teetering on the edge of dying. He shook that nonsense from his mind. "Good luck."

"Right." Tony glanced at the countdown clock on the screen,

noting that they had less than fifteen minutes until it would start getting bumpy. "Houston, let's get on with this. Give me the breaker sequence now."

Tony had both gloves off and started flipping icon toggles on the computer touch screen. He had to have all the right breakers thrown so that the pressurization system wouldn't just increase the oxygen flow into the cabin to make up for a leak. That took a couple of minutes. Then he was ready.

"Alright, everybody clear!" He scanned the cabin for an all clear from Xu, and then Hui. "Bill, here goes."

Tony gripped the pistol in his hands. He raised his arms as best he could in his suit and took aim just to the right of the apex of the cone where the docking hatch was located.

"Firing in three, two, one, *no shot.*" Tony instinctively pulled at the trigger again. "What the . . . ?"

"You didn't disengage the safety," Hui pointed out.

"Oh. I see." Tony used his thumb to push the safety off and then raised the weapon again. "Once more. Firing in three, two, one!"

The pistol fired and tossed an empty casing across the cabin. The casing ricocheted off a couple of panels, making a clinking noise as it did so, and then began a slow-drifting trajectory about the cabin. The bullet, on the other hand, slammed against the interior wall panel a good half meter from where Tony thought he had been aiming. But it didn't really matter as long as it worked.

"*Mercy I*, mission control."

"Go ahead, Houston," Tony answered.

"We show you've sprung a leak and are losing cabin pressure."

"Hold on, Houston. I'll check it out."

"Before you do, put these on." Hui handed Tony his suit gloves. Tony waved them off, handed her the pistol, and tapped at the control screen. He could have sworn he was hearing a faint hissing sound, but his ears were ringing from the pistol report, so he wasn't certain.

"We've got a red light on the pressure panel. The question is, are we leaking fast enough, Houston?" Tony held his breath while he waited on mission control's response. It seemed like forever before he got it.

"Hold on, *Mercy I*. We're running the numbers now."

"It's gonna work," Tony said to nobody in particular, but everybody heard it.

"Negative, *Mercy I.* Looks like at your current leakage rate, it will take about twenty minutes before the cabin is empty." Tony felt his heart sink again.

"What!?"

"It was a good try, Tony. I knew it was risky."

"Bill, are you still clear?"

"Yes, but why do—?"

Tony grabbed the pistol from Hui unexpectedly, took aim, and fired two quick rounds just to the top and right of the docking-hatch door. The sound of the reports rang like a bell inside the cabin, hurting his ears. He hadn't balanced himself as well this time, and the pistol firing pushed him hard enough to make him tumble over. Newton's law of reciprocal force, action and reaction, got him. He quickly grabbed on to a handhold and righted himself. He held the pistol up once more, considering firing it again.

"Tony! Stop it before you endanger the entire mission!" Bill shouted back at him.

"That ought to do it." Tony thumbed the safety on the pistol and handed it to Hui. "Put that thing away for me, will ya?"

"Yes." Hui looked nervously at Tony. "I think I should."

Tony went to check the status panel. He looked at the reentry countdown to see where they stood. There were about nine minutes remaining before things started getting too close for comfort.

"*Mercy I,* we show an increase in the depressurization. What's going on?"

"I made two more leaks," Tony said nonchalantly and half expecting Houston to respond with a *"You did what?"*—but they didn't.

"Understood, *Mercy I.* Be advised that the engineers don't recommend adding any more."

"Uh-huh." Tony sat down and began working his gloves. He watched the countdown clock continue getting closer to the aerocapture. "Bill, I suggest you get to the main hatch and stand by."

"Well, I'm ahead of you, Tony. I'm already on my way," Bill said.

"Should we start trying to cycle the hatch?" Hui asked. Tony hadn't bothered to ask where she had put the pistol. He didn't care. He didn't need the thing any longer.

"Good idea. Let me finish with this glove. You got the patch kit ready?"

"Here." Hui held up the kit.

"Great." Tony put the hatch on cycle, but the icon went red and didn't open.

The ship was beginning to have a noticeable vibration. Tony gripped the console to shore himself up.

"Hey, do you guys feel that?"

"What?" Hui gripped the console's edge with her glove. From the look in her eyes, Tony knew the answer before she said it. "Yes. What is that?"

"I can feel it out here, Tony," Bill answered. "Ignore it and keep focusing on the job at hand."

"Roger that, Bill," Tony replied. Bill was right. They had to focus and get Bill inside the cabin before it was too late.

The ship had penetrated far enough into the exosphere to begin experiencing turbulence. The exosphere of Earth extended out as far as ten thousand kilometers. The Orion was traveling over fifteen kilometers per second. It would take the ship less than ten minutes to travel into the denser portions of the thermosphere, where the real turbulence would start. They had less than five to seven minutes, depending on the computer model used, to get Stetson inside.

Chapter 30

"**C**ome on, dammit!" Tony watched the hatch icon still showing red. The countdown clock gave them three minutes left. The NASA engineers at mission control didn't like cutting it so close. Tony liked it even less. He could just imagine how much Stetson liked it. "Bill, hang on out there."

The vibration of the ship had continued to grow to the point where it was no longer a subtle thing that could barely be felt with a tight grip. Tony was pretty sure he could see things starting to vibrate.

"What's taking us so long in there, Tony? Not to be antsy or anything, but Earth is looking really big!"

"Just be ready!"

"Roger that!"

"Hui, be ready with that patch kit. As soon as the hatch icon goes green, you start patching the holes!" Tony hit the hatch-cycle routine again. It went red. "Come on!"

"Yes, Tony. I will." Hui held the kit at the ready, looking like a lioness ready to pounce on a gazelle. Tony thought that the Chinese had made a good decision in picking her as their first Moon mission commander.

"God, if you can hear me, now would be a good time to help us out!" Tony hit the hatch icon again. For the millisecond it took for the electrons to travel from the screen to the central processor of the computer, the processor to understand and process the signal, and send a response, Tony held his breath for what seemed like an eternity.

"Green light! Go, Hui! Go!" Tony shouted, not quite gleefully but close enough, as Orion's main hatch started to cycle open. Tony yanked on the handle and pulled the latch until he could see space outside. Hui pushed herself up to the apex of the cabin, and Tony turned to help his captain. "Bill, get your butt in here!" He held a handhold as close to the hatch door as he could manage. The door slid open, and as soon as it did, Bill's hand poked through.

"Grab my hand, Tony!"

"Got it! Come on, Bill!" Tony grabbed at Bill's arm and pulled as best he could. The ship lurched very gently, but just enough to give them concern. "We're getting close!"

"Hui, how's it look?" Bill asked as he crawled his way through the hatch. He reached back, disconnected the tether, and pulled the rope inside.

"I've got one hole patched."

"I'm in, Tony. You can let go now. And cycle the hatch!" It was clear that the Orion had gotten its captain back.

"Roger that!" Tony pushed to the console and tapped the hatch icon until it cycled shut. Bill tugged the handle just to help it along. The icon went from red to orange to green, and then Bill tugged at it again. It was closed and sealed. He was inside. And, by God, it was good!

"Hot damn," Bill shouted. "Houston, this is Stetson. All members of the *Mercy I* crew are inside, present, and accounted for."

"Great news, *Mercy I*. We recommend you cycle the repressurization as soon as possible so the patch sealant will cure quicker. And y'all need to buckle up."

"Understood, mission control."

"You heard the man, Tony. Get us some air in here." Bill looked up at Hui. "You need any help?"

"Done!"

"Awesome. Now get down and get buckled in."

"*Mercy I*, mission control."

"Go, Houston."

"Looks like the skin temperature is starting to build up. You came in just in time, Bill."

"I like to make an entrance," Bill said. "Somebody tell my family I'm coming home!"

"Roger that, *Mercy I*. Bill, your family heard the whole thing." There was a brief pause and some static. "Be advised that you are about to go through an ionization radio blackout."

"We understand, Houston. We'll talk to you after aerocapture." With that, Bill pushed himself into the captain's seat and started buckling in. He glanced over at Tony, who was also buckling in. "Thanks, buddy." He gave Tony a smile and elbowed him slightly.

"Couldn't have seen going home without you, Bill."

"Well, let's hope my patch job on the bottom of the ship holds and your target practice on top of the ship isn't a problem."

"We're gonna make it."

"Damn right we are."

The vibration within the ship ratcheted up to the point that the computer panels in front of them became nearly unreadable. Bill held on to his armrests and tried to relax. He was mostly blissfully happy as just a few minutes ago he was pretty sure he was going to die. But now it seemed that if he were to die, it would be because the heat shield failed, not because he was trapped outside. The Orion was a good ship. He was confident that it would get them home.

The Orion capsule jerked forward and lurched backward in a way that seemed like it happened at the same time. The side-to-side vibrations grew in amplitude. Bill looked up at the top of the ship, where Tony had shot it three times with the pistol. He hoped the damage was far enough forward that the hot atmospheric plasma wouldn't vent into the cabin and cook them. He also hoped that hot plasma didn't vent through the bullet holes of the outer hull and weaken some beam or strut that would compromise the structural integrity of the ship, the end result being the ship flying apart and killing them all.

"Seven gees!" Tony shouted.

"Hang in there!" Bill gripped at his seat harder and flexed every muscle in his body to prevent passing out.

"Ten gees!" Tony said, more gutturally this time.

"We should top out in a minute or so. Just hang in!" Bill grunted and flexed and breathed and grunted and flexed. He sounded a lot like a woman in labor. "Aaahhh wooo wooo!"

The vibration grew louder, harder, and faster—shaking all the astronauts to the point that their teeth rattled. No amount of training in a centrifuge or even launches on the really shaky Ares I rocket could prepare a person for that type of skeleton-jarring ride.

BANG! SCREEEEEEECH! BANG!

An even more extreme noise resounded throughout the ship, their suits, and their bones. It startled Bill, but there was nothing he could do. He would have sworn it came from the top of the Orion near where Tony had shot it up. He wasn't certain, but he was also pretty sure he could hear a much louder roaring sound than he had before.

SCREEEEEEEEEECH! ROAR!

"What the hell is that?" Tony shouted.

"I don't know, but there's nothing we can do about it! Just hang in and pray!" Bill shouted.

"Fifteen gees!" Tony shouted over the jarring, rattling, screeching, and roaring.

The ship rocked back and forth so hard that Bill was worried the injured and otherwise incapacitated crew members might not be faring so well. The air inside the cabin had reached one atmosphere, so the sound of the ship being buffeted was getting extremely loud. It sounded like he had stuck his head inside a jet engine while it was at full throttle. Bill managed to glance at Tony and could see that his body had gone limp.

"Tony!" Bill had the notion that he would tap at the console in front of him and check Tony's vital signs, but that would require him to raise his arm—and he couldn't. It weighed more than two hundred pounds at the moment. "Everybody hang on back there! Come on, baby! Hold together! We're gonna make it!"

Bill's vision started to tunnel in, and he grunted and fought against blacking out. He fought like a world-champion boxer tied up in the twelfth round. In the end he went down swinging, but he lost the fight.

Chapter 31

"Go, baby, go!" was once again all that Paul Gesling could utter as he alternated looking out the window at the landscape of Earth receding below him and the LCD display that showed the status of *Dreamscape*'s onboard systems. All the systems were reading in the green, and the ship was cruising past Mach 2—twice the speed of sound—at the moment. He held the flight-control stick gently with his left hand and went through a continuous ballet of tapping the control screen with his right.

It had only been a little more than a week since the *Dreamscape* was rushed through refurbishment, refueled, and rolled out on the runway in Nevada before they had restarted the countdown for the launch. It all seemed rather quick to Paul, but Gary Childers had given him the last say. Had Paul said "no-go," then Gary would have abided by that decision. At least that is what Paul liked to believe.

Just less than two weeks ago, the little ship had flown a crew of space tourists around the Moon and done so flawlessly. In fact, they had done more than just fly around the Moon on the most expensive and dangerous vacation ever. They had also acted as a search-and-rescue mission. They had detected Chinese taikonauts stranded on the Moon and had been instrumental in saving their lives. It was clear that the Chinese government had had no intention of telling the public of the stranded taikonauts and had *Dreamscape*'s crew not found them, the world might have never known they were ever there. But they did find them, and that was the first step. NASA did the hardest part of going to the Moon and getting them. But Paul was in the process of flying the *Dreamscape* back into space to help bring them home. The final part. It was fitting in Paul's mind that the rescue started with the *Dreamscape* and would likely end with it. Of course, they had yet to run any of this by NASA or the Chinese, but drowning sailors will swim to the nearest lifeboat. Besides, once the *Dreamscape* made it to the right orbital altitude, it would take a day or more to crank the inclination to the same angle as the space station. After you added another a day or so to chase it down, it just made sense to get into space as soon as possible.

"Control, we're go for scramjet separation." Paul could talk through the procedures in his sleep by this point, but he wasn't about to give it a try. He kept his focus on the job at hand.

"Roger that, Paul. Go for first-stage sep." Then the stage-separation icon flashed and the Bitchin' Betty chimed at him.

"Prepare for stage separation in five, four, three, two, one."

Paul felt his pulse quicken in anticipation of the stage separation as he waited for the five explosions that would soon sever the bolts holding the two parts of *Dreamscape* together. This portion of the flight always scared the living daylights out of him. But he also knew that the technology for such accurate pyrotechnic timing was well understood. It always amazed him how it never sounded like five explosions at all. It simply went bang, and that was that.

Bang!

"We've got good separation," he radioed to control.

"Copy that, *Dreamscape*. Scramjet separation is complete."

"Now preparing for main-engine ignition in twenty seconds." Gesling was nearing the point at which the powerful main rocket engines would fire, giving him the final acceleration needed to attain the seventeen thousand miles per hour required for orbit. Escape velocity was just that one stage away. Orbital altitude and velocity were one main rocket burn away.

"Roger that, Paul. Main burn in fifteen . . . ten . . . five, four, three, two, one."

"We've got good burn on the main engine, and all systems are go."

Never in the history of aerospace, or humanity for that matter, had a single spaceship flown an orbital mission, a month or so later flown around the Moon, and then just a few short days later flown back to orbit. The *Dreamscape* was truly being pushed to the limits of space-technology capabilities and reliabilities. Paul tried not to think about quality control, workmanship, parts and materials fatigue. After all, *Dreamscape* had been designed to fly with a rapid turnaround. Paul wasn't quite sure if this was the *type* of rapid turnaround planned, especially while the rocket was fresh off its first mission and practically just out of the test-flight phase.

"Just fly the plane," he told himself. The first and foremost thing all pilots trained themselves to do was to learn to fly the plane no matter what the instruments were saying or whatever else was going on around them. Fly the plane. He gripped the controls and swallowed the lump in his throat, forcing it back into his stomach. It amazed him that he still got that lump. He was now quite the space veteran. But flying in space on a screaming, highly volatile, explosive rocket engine was indeed scary. Paul had every right to be at least a little bit nervous. He also had every need to overcome that nervousness and do his job.

The first stage, then fully separated from the rocket-powered *Dreamscape*, began its glide back to the Nevada desert. Operated by onboard automatic pilot and with constant monitoring by engineers in the Space Excursions control room back at the launch site, the first stage was on target for a landing back at the location from which its voyage began. So far the *Dreamscape* was doing everything just right.

The acceleration from the main burn continuously pushed Paul back into the webbing that secured him to his seat. He could feel the skin on his cheekbones being pulled back toward his ears. He could hear his heartbeat and feel the kick to his abdomen as the *Dreamscape*'s engine engaged at a little over twenty thousand feet. The whine of the engines was only momentarily loud before the cabin's active soundproofing kicked in and diminished it to something just short of a deafening dull roar. The sound may have diminished a bit, but the g-forces slamming Paul into the seat were far from over. At the moment he was feeling over five gravities and would endure it for a few moments more. Paul grunted against the crushing weight of his chest and forced himself to breathe through it.

He was on his way to orbit. Once he got there, he'd circularize his orbit and then crank his inclination up to match the International Space Station. Then he would chase the ISS until he docked with it. Upon docking with the space station, he'd offer the rescued astronauts a ride home. At least that was the plan with which he'd started.

Chapter 32

"**M**ercy I, this is mission control, copy?

"*Mercy I*, this is mission control, do you copy?

"Come on, guys, this is Houston, come in?"

Bill would have sworn he was having a bad dream. No, a nightmare would have been more like it. He'd been stranded outside a spaceship for hours, only to make it inside the thing just in time to go careening through the Earth's atmosphere at over fifteen kilometers per second. The ship had shaken him to his bones. His teeth and jawbone ached from having clenched so tightly. Somewhere in there he had passed out. That had probably been for the best. He imagined that the ride may have even been worse after he'd passed out.

"Uh, roger...*ahem*...roger, Houston," he said weakly. Bill shook his head and squinted his eyes as best he could in his suit. He reached up and tapped the control screen and brought up the ship diagnostics. Cabin pressure was good, so he popped his faceplate. Just doing that nearly exhausted him. He let his arms fall back down beside him, and they actually fell. He had a bit of a dizzy sensation also. "Uh-oh. That can't be good.

"Houston, this is *Mercy I*, over." Bill reached up and switched on the internal microphone. "Hey, anybody with me in here?"

"Zhi and myself are awake, Bill," Hui answered. "Xu and Ming are alive but still out."

"Tony?"

"Huh, what, hey?" Tony startled as he awoke.

"Easy, Tony."

"Bill, I feel like I'm gonna throw up," Tony said.

"Yeah, me, too. I think we're spinning or tumbling. I'm try-ing to figure it out." Bill carefully moved one hand and tapped the commands to bring up the flight-command suite. The digital direction gyroscopes, Global Positioning System, and attitude determination and control systems seemed to be all functional and online. The gyro was rolling counterclockwise. And that meant that the Orion was spinning like a top.

"Good to hear your voice, Bill," mission control replied. "We need to assess the ship and telemetry data. We show an induced roll?"

"Roger that, Houston. We're rolling pretty darn quickly. My guess is we're pulling about three gees." Bill worked his hands out of the gloves and did his best to stow the gloves out of the way without getting sick on himself. Then he eased his left hand around the stick.

"Copy that, *Mercy I*. We show your rate of spin to be conducive to a three point two one gravity load."

"Why hasn't the automated attitude control and stabilization system kicked in?" Tony asked.

"Good question, Tony." Bill tapped the screen. "Holy crap. Uh, Houston, I'm looking at the boards for the attitude control and stabilization system, and it is all orange and red across the board. I've got alarms on the ACS PROP, Main Guidance Processing, and a P&P Alert on RP. Any advice there?"

"Copy that, *Mercy I*. Hold one for that."

Bill considered just taking the manual controls and trying to straighten out the ship. The problem with that would be that if they had suffered some damage during the aerocapture maneu-ver, or Tony's target practice, then putting power to the thrusters could start a fire, cause an explosion, or do nothing. They could withstand the merry-go-round for another minute or two. But not much longer than that.

"Hey, didn't something like this happen to Neil Armstrong?" Tony asked.

"Gemini 8. Neil and David Scott docked with the Agena target vehicle, and apparently the attitude-control systems for the Gemini capsule and the Agena kept firing, and they couldn't seem to get them to stop. They ended up aborting the mission and using the Gemini capsule's reentry thrusters to straighten them out, if I recall. But I think they were spinning head over heels, not round and round like we are." Bill squinted his eyes. The roll rate was getting worse. Maybe it just felt worse.

"Okay, *Mercy I*, we believe that the P & P alert is the key. The pressurants and pressurization algorithm is telling us that we've got either an ACS roll thruster stuck open or there is a leak in the propellant line that is rapidly venting. But since the thrust appears to be very stable and directional, our best guess is the thruster."

"Uh, okay, Houston. What is our work-around?" Bill inched his hand closer to the manual-control switch.

"Bill, you need to see if you can reboot the ACS. The PROP team thinks that there might be a valve stuck open, and the reboot will close it."

"Okay. Roger that. Start with the reboot sequence."

"Roger that, *Mercy I*. Here we go. ACS SEQ 999GGH3..."

It took Stetson more than seven or eight very long minutes to type in the commands. During that time Tony Chow began retching and heaving into a barf bag as best he could manage. The Chinese crew members seemed to be handling the situation a little better.

"Alright, Houston, hitting reboot now." Bill tapped in the final command code. When he did, everything went black. "Jesus!"

"What the...?" Tony forgot his barf bag when the lights flickered out.

"Houston, we've had a complete power failure here. All my boards are out." Bill started tapping at reset switches and breakers, but nothing seemed to happen. For some reason, the communications system was still up.

"*Mercy I*, we've lost all feeds but the Ku-band links. No telemetry whatsoever is making it to us. We are looking into it."

"Roger that, but we are still spinning up here." Bill was beginning to think that the ship was about to come apart at the seams. They had comm-system power. That meant something. They needed the ACS back online if he was going to stop the spin.

"Bill, my screen is coming on!" Tony shouted.

"What does it say?" Bill tried his best to move his head in that direction, but the spin kept him from doing so.

"It's a hard reset! I think the entire system shut down and is now starting to boot back up." Tony reached up and tapped the enter key on the console, and his screen lit completely up and started loading the operating system. Then the lights flickered back on, and Bill could hear the carbon dioxide scrubber fans start up again.

"Houston, be advised that we've got systems coming back online." Bill's screen blinked back on and began loading the mix of drivers loaded onto it to command the spacecraft. "Any idea what just happened?"

"Uh, we're working on that, *Mercy I*. Right now we believe we had a main power-bus failure and back-up power has kicked in," Houston replied.

"Roger that. Now we need to stop this rolling." Bill waited as the system came completely back up. "Houston, I have an initial idea that will help."

"Go ahead, Bill."

"I want to redeploy the solar arrays." Bill understood that they were spinning about the roll axis just like a figure skater on ice doing an axel. When figure skaters let out their arms, it slowed their rate of spin due to the law of conservation of angular momentum. Extending the solar arrays should have the same effect. It probably wouldn't stop the spin, but it would slow it to something a little more tolerable.

"We agree with that, Bill. Go ahead and cycle the solar arrays, over."

"Roger that, Houston. I'm making my way through the procedure now." Bill tapped several commands, and then the graphic of the exterior view of the ship showed the solar panels extending. Bill could feel some vibrations from the gimbal motors. The lights turned green for both arrays, showing that they had been fully extended. He held up his arms. They didn't feel as weird as they had before.

"Did it work, Bill?" Tony asked.

"Don't know. I feel different, but we'll have to wait until the gyro is fully back online. Another minute will tell." So they waited.

And waited.

When the Orion completely rebooted itself and all systems were back online, the directional gyro showed that the ship was still spinning, but at about half the speed it had been before. That was a little more tolerable.

"Okay, Houston, we show that our roll rate has dropped to a constant speed. Also note that the roll thruster appears to have turned itself off during the reboot." Bill hit the auto ACS icon and activated the automated-control system.

Bang! Bang! Bang, bang, bang!

Several attitude-correction thrusts were initiated by the computer, and then the roll rate showed zero on the directional gyroscope. The ship had stopped spinning. And not a moment too soon, as Tony Chow was reaching for his barf bag once again.

"Houston! That worked. We've stopped spinning, and now I believe we are back in business. I'm setting up a full diagnostic run now to see what shape we are in. That should only take a few minutes." Bill tapped in several key sequences and then leaned back to look out the docking windows. Earth filled the view, and it was awesome. From the look of things, Bill was guessing that they were somewhere over China at the present moment.

"Hey, everyone. Take a look out the window." Chow, Hui, and Stetson each took a turn unbuckling and floating up to the windows and peering out at Earth—at home.

Bill watched as his home planet rotated beneath them. From the looks of the size of things, it seemed about right. He'd been in low Earth orbit many, many times now and knew what it looked like. One thing didn't seem to add up, though. If he had his bearings straight, then it appeared to him that they were flying much closer to an equatorial orbit than the orbit of the International Space Station.

"Uh, Houston, is there something else you need to tell us?"

Chapter 33

"**M**ercy I, something went wrong on aerocapture." Mission control started in with the bad news. "You might have figured out by now that you aren't at a fifty-two degree inclination in your orbit."

"I was beginning to wonder about that, Houston." Bill replied. "So, where are we?"

BANG! Bang, bang, bang! A big jolt resounded through the ship, followed by three ACS bursts. Then there were more ACS burns. *Bang, bang, bang. Bang, bang.*

"Holy crap!" Bill grabbed at his armrest with one hand to steady himself. With the other he tapped at the attitude-control diagnostics and the directional-gyro screen. "Houston, we've got something going on here. We're rocking and rolling like crazy, and the ACS is trying to keep up with it."

Bang. Bang, bang, bang, bang. Bang, bang. All the ACS thrusters seemed to be firing to correct for something, and the ship continued to rock with each bang.

"*Mercy I*, we show P & P PROP warning again, and the fuel level in ACS is dropping rapidly."

"Roger that, Houston. The ACS is firing almost continuously now." Bill considered taking control, but he had no idea what the ship was doing and why the computer felt it needed the ACS control thrusters to fire. Something was pushing them. "Tony, can you see anything out your window? I've got nothing on this side."

"Bill! There's something spewing sparkly stuff in a jet out the side over here." Tony sounded upset.

"Alright. Take it easy, Tony." Bill didn't like the sound of that. It was never a good idea to be spewing anything out of the ship if you didn't have to. "Houston, we've got something leaking out of the capsule near the starboard side up at the nose." He didn't have to remind anybody that that was the location where Tony had taken up target practice before the aerocapture. That big noise they heard during the capture process might have been something coming loose up there.

"Copy that, *Mercy I*."

Bang, bang. Bang, bang, bang.

"Houston, be advised that the P & P PROP warning light is not resetting. Also, it looks like we're gonna run out of fuel in the ACS thrusters if we don't do something soon." Bill was getting concerned. They were off their orbit and running out of fuel. They didn't die on the Moon, or on the way back to Earth orbit, and he hoped they wouldn't get stranded in Earth orbit just to die before they could get back to the space station. Home was just a few hundred miles beneath them. Somehow, they had to survive long enough to cover those last few hundred miles. Those last ones were just as deadly as the first half million.

"Sorry, *Mercy I*. We haven't come up with a solution yet. Keep trying to reset the flow system and get that warning light back to green."

"Roger that, Houston." Bill didn't like it. Houston always came up with something to at least try. "Tony. We're on our own. We've got to fix this."

"Bill, we don't even know what is wrong."

Bang, bang. Bang. The attitude-control system continued to fire correction burns.

"Everybody, faceplates on. I'm going outside to see what is going on," Bill ordered the crew.

"Bill, shouldn't we run that by Houston first?"

"They don't have any idea what is going on, Tony." He hadn't come this far to fail now.

"We're not even sure the hatch will cycle, Bill."

"Well, I sure as heck don't want to get stuck outside again. If it cycles, we'll leave the hatch open until I come back in."

"Makes sense," Tony agreed.

"You still see that stream of stuff on your side?" Bill stretched to look out his window but didn't see anything.

"It's still going strong."

"Figures."

Bang. Bang.

Bang. Bang. Bang, bang.

The hatch had opened without a glitch this time. Resetting it before the aerocapture maneuver must have fixed the software problems, at least temporarily. With the ship rocking back and forth, Bill thought it would be wise to stay in intimate contact with it. Had he let himself float freely about it, one of the ACS burns might rock the ship into him and knock him out, damage his suit, or damage the ship even further.

"Whoa! Are you seeing this, Tony?" Bill moved his head back and forth so the camera in his helmet could see all the damage.

"It's amazing we made it through aerocapture," Tony replied.

Bill surveyed the damage as he held on to the bucking bronco. Each time there was an ACS burn, which was now about one every couple of seconds, he would nearly lose his handhold on the ship. A section of the multilayered insulation (MLI) blankets was charred black and peeled away from the hull, exposing an aluminum panel that had been superheated and flexed outward. The nose of the spacecraft on that side looked a little bit like a partially peeled banana. The bent panel was no longer than a piece of printer paper, but it was angled outward enough from the ship that it must have been causing all sorts of drag during the aerocapture. The bent panel had likely acted just like a flap on an airplane wing. Bill understood why their orbit was wrong. It dawned on him that he never did get the rest of the information from Houston as to how wrong it was.

"Look at that." Bill whistled as he reached the forward-roll thrusters. The stream of sparkling stuff was fuel jetting out of the plumbing that fed one of the little rocket engines. One of Tony's bullets had loosened the exterior panel enough so that it moved around during the aerocapture maneuver. Apparently it moved enough to bang into the little metal tube that carried the propellants to the thruster. The tube was spewing around randomly like a high-pressure water hose with no one holding on to it. It really wasn't quite that bad, but the little metal tube, no bigger than a drinking straw in diameter, vibrated around several inches in any direction. That was the culprit imparting random thrust to the spacecraft and totally messing around with the ship's attitude control.

"Can we clamp that off?" Tony asked.

"I'm gonna try, Tony." Bill reached down into the panel and slid his fingers in behind the tube. "I'll see if I can bend it over shut."

Bang. Bang. Bang, bang. He paused to adjust his hand- and footholds a bit better. Instinctively, he double-checked his tether. He was strapped on to the ship just fine.

Confident he wasn't going to get thrown from the ship, he set back to work. He did his best to work his gloves into the crevice between the tube and the ship's structure. It was a tight fit, but he managed. First he tried to squeeze the tube between his thumb and forefinger, but that didn't work at all. Then he tried bending the tube over with the strength of his fingers, but there just wasn't enough dexterity with his spacesuit gloves on. He cursed the spacesuit technology for about the millionth time on the mission.

Not having much luck here, he said to himself just as he felt the tube give. Then the little tube bent at the tip of his thumb, and he managed to get both hands down to bend the tube the rest of the way over. When he did, the spewing gas slowed to a small trickle out the end of the tube. Bill continued to bend the tube back on itself until there was no more visible sign of the gas leaking. "I think I got it stopped."

"Permanently?" Tony's voice sounded in Bill's helmet.

"I doubt it. Sooner or later the pipe is going to give out. But I don't see any other fix at the moment. Maybe Houston can think of something before that happens." Bill looked up and toward the Earth. It seemed farther away than it had earlier. He was sure that if that was the case, then something had gone *way wrong* on the aerocapture procedure. He really needed to get back on the horn with Houston.

"Well, Bill, we're ready for you to come in whenever you are," Tony told him. Bill could sense the anxiety in Tony's voice.

"Tony, have you noticed anything different?' Bill asked.

"Sure have. The ACS thrusters haven't kicked in for the past couple of minutes."

"Right. There's nothing more I can do out here. Let's cycle the hatch," Bill ordered after he climbed in and untethered himself.

"Roger that, Bill," Tony replied. "Cycling the hatch."

Nothing.

"Uh, Tony. Cycle the hatch." Bill put a glove on it and prepared to help out with a tug.

"Roger that, Bill. Cycling the hatch." Tony tapped the icons on the screen for the hatch software to activate. Again, nothing happened. The door remained wide open.

"What else can go wrong?" Bill muttered to himself—hoping he hadn't jinxed the mission as soon as he said that. He made his way over to his couch and in front of the command consoles.

"Is there a problem, Captain Stetson?" Hui asked.

"Looks like there might be. We'll work it." Bill tried to focus his mind. So much had happened in the last few hours that it would have been too much for most normal people. Fortunately, Bill was far above the average—even for an astronaut.

"Bill, there is no power getting to the door. The circuits must've gone dead when we cycled it open." Tony continued to look at the diagnostics screen that was almost all orange and red.

"Houston, this is *Mercy I*. We've got our leak stopped, but now our main hatch door is frozen in the open position," Bill communicated back to Earth.

"Copy that, *Mercy I*."

"And, Houston, you might as well give me the rest of the bad news, because it looks to me like we are presently farther away from Earth than I expected us to be." Bill almost held his breath waiting for the answer.

"Roger that, *Mercy I*. Bill, here is the problem. Something went wrong on aerocapture, and you came out in a forty-four degree inclination. Plus, your orbit is fairly elliptical. The orbital guys tell me you're tracking with a perigee of about one hundred and ninety-four miles and an apogee of about three hundred and sixty-seven miles." Bill listened and tried to work some of the math in his head. He couldn't. But that was what Houston was for.

"Okay, Houston, what does that mean?"

"You don't have enough fuel to crank your inclination enough to make it to the space station. You'd also need to circularize your orbit some. There just isn't enough fuel for both maneuvers." Mission control got quiet for a second.

"What do we do, Houston?" Bill asked.

"First thing we need to do is get that door closed. We think we have a workaround."

"Roger that," Bill replied. "What do we do?"

Chapter 34

"**P**ull harder, Hui!" Tony urged the Chinese taikonaut. "Bill, I don't feel it budging at all."

"Yeah, I think the motors are seized up, and I haven't cut the right interlock cable yet," Bill replied. "Houston. That didn't work."

"Roger that, *Mercy I*. There is a mechanism behind the panel you just pulled off on the right side and underneath the door's track. You see it?"

"Roger that, Houston. I see it." Bill reached in the hole they had made in the ship's interior panel to feel the track-alignment mechanism. The door looked like it was in the right place, and nothing was wrong mechanically. It had to be software or a seized-up motor.

"Okay, Bill, pop the breaker-box lid open with the regular screwdriver," the mission control engineer directed.

"Roger that." Bill reached in with the long-length screwdriver and loosened the spring-loaded screw mechanism holding the breaker box in place. When he got it loose, it flipped up easily. "Okay, Houston. Got it open."

"Now, there is a single throw breaker on the bottom right-hand side of that circuit box. Do you see it?"

Bill reached up with a finger poised to push it if that was the order.

"Okay, Bill, don't touch it yet, because it may only let loose for a second or two. Make certain that Tony and Hui are pulling on the door when you do," Houston directed.

"Understood, Houston." Bill looked over at Tony and Hui. "Are you guys ready to pull?"

"Yes," they replied in unison.

"Well, then, in three, two, one, go!" Bill depressed the button. It clicked on, and the hatch sprang to life. The release and close mechanism activated and started cycling the door closed. Then there was a *snap* he could feel in the panel box as the breaker threw open again. "Don't stop! Keep pulling!" he shouted.

Tony and Hui had gained enough momentum with the door before the breaker clicked again that it actually slammed closed. Bill depressed the switch once more, and the lock seal popped into place just as the breaker threw again. Tony and Bill both tugged at the latching mechanism and agreed it was closed.

"Houston, I believe that worked." Bill swam his way back to his console and scanned the screen. "Looks like the interior is sealed off. Tony, start repressurization."

"Roger that, Bill." Tony sounded relieved.

"Now, while the cabin comes back up to pressure, why don't you folks down there start talking to me about how we're gonna get home."

"Well, Bill, we've got a solution. It's an unexpected one. But we've got one," mission control started. "We're working an orbit circularization burn calculation based on the fuel you've got left. We'll give you the procedure in a few minutes."

"Yeah, and we circularize our orbit. Then what?" Tony asked.

"At that point, we'll be in a wait mode as the Space Excursions ship *Dreamscape* plays chase with you. Once it catches you, you'll dock with it, all of you will transfer over, and then the captain of that ship is going to bring you home. Over."

"*Dreamscape*?" Bill and Tony said almost simultaneously.

"Houston, would you repeat that?" Bill asked.

"Uh, roger that, *Mercy I*. The *Dreamscape* is in LEO right now and starting to crank up to your orbital inclination," Houston explained.

"But they just got back from the Moon a week ago! They're flying again already?" Tony said, completely flabbergasted.

"Roger that, *Mercy I*. It appears they have a short turnaround. Good thing for us. At this point we wouldn't have a workaround for getting you back down." Bill waited for the reality of that last statement to sink into everybody on the ship.

"Understood, Houston. From the looks of things outside, we couldn't attempt any type of reentry even if we weren't too heavy." Bill thought for a bit about what they needed to do exactly.

"Captain," Hui interjected.

"Yes, Hui, what is it?"

"If this *Dreamscape* has to adjust its inclination and then catch us to dock, how long will that take?" Hui asked.

"Don't know." Bill had no clue. He did know that on several of the times he flew the Ares 1 and the Orion capsule to the ISS, it usually took about three days to get up, change to the station inclination angle, and then chase down the station and dock. "If I had my guess, we're talking a couple of days."

"I see." Hui grimaced noticeably. Bill figured that the taikonaut was ready to get out of her nasty spacesuit for good. But they could manage a couple more days.

"Houston, *Mercy I*." Bill had other concerns as well. Maybe Hui did, too. "Before we do any circularization burn and before *Dreamscape* starts orbit matching, we should do a quick status check. We'll probably need to minimize our O_2 usage."

"We've been looking at that, *Mercy I*," Houston replied. "We want you to run a quick systems diagnostic on the propellants and pressurants. That P & P PROP warning earlier needs to be fully assessed."

"Understood, Houston. We're already on it." Bill turned to Tony and off-mic said, "Tony, let's get that started."

"On it." Tony was already tapping at the screen. With the cabin pressurized and the immediate dangers somewhat benign, he placed his suit gloves in the box near his seat, and his helmet came off. The rest of the crew had done the same.

Bill didn't want to bring it up, but he was pretty sure that it was starting to smell in the cabin. There was an air filter, but it hadn't been designed for six. Bill unbuckled himself and decided to float around the cabin and check on morale. The Chinese pilot was still out, but his vitals seemed to be a little better. The stimulants, antibiotics, and other injections that Tony and Dr. Xu had administered to him seemed to be improving his condition.

Xu, on the other hand, was having a lot of pain with his leg. Bill and Hui had to order him to take a pain injection. He resisted, arguing that he needed to keep an eye on Ming. Xu then made a comment about possibly losing his leg. Bill hoped that wouldn't be the case.

Then there was Zhi. The engineer and political officer had caused a lot of their troubles. He was in his suit with his gloves off and helmet tethered to him but was otherwise immobile. Hui had his arms duct-taped to his torso and his legs taped to his couch. She fed him and gave him water if he asked for it. But Hui was not about to let him loose. Bill agreed and let her handle it. She seemed capable of controlling the situation. There were a few times when he got loud and mouthy at first, but when he did, Hui had Xu or Tony sedate him.

"Captain Stetson." Hui floated beside him while Bill was taking the time for a snack. Bill wasn't sure, but he thought he was eating yogurt. He chased it with some orange juice.

"Yes, Hui?"

"I'm concerned about our oxygen and carbon-dioxide levels." Hui frowned slightly.

"I know. Tony and Houston are running the numbers right now. CO_2 shouldn't be a problem, though, because we've got plenty of extra lithium-hydride scrubber canisters." Bill pushed over to a bin, turned and pulled the locking mechanism, and slid it out to show Hui a stash of scrubber filters. "See?"

"Good. What about oxygen?"

"Don't know. We should know soon enough." Bill finished off his juice with a final squeeze and then kicked back over to his station. "Tony?"

"You'd better talk to Houston, Bill."

"Alright." Bill buckled himself in so he wouldn't be floating around. He had always found he could concentrate on what he was doing better that way. Then he put his headset back on. "Houston, this is *Mercy I*. Any word on our status and burn calculations?"

"Uh, roger that, *Mercy I*." There was a brief pause. "Bill, we are optimizing the burn for the Orion as well as calculations for the *Dreamscape*. Your rendezvous is critical. It looks like Orion will have enough oxygen to sustain you until *Dreamscape* can get there, but just barely. You're going to have to drop to a third of an atmosphere to maximize your O_2."

"Just under five pounds per square inch shouldn't be a problem, Houston, right? After all, that's what we do for an hour or more before a long-term EVA." Bill wasn't too concerned. He had spent hours at four and half pounds per square inch atmospheric pressure during some of the EVAs he'd done on the ISS. And there were people who climbed Mount Everest and spent many days at a comparable pressure or less. They'd be weak and light-headed, but they'd be alive. Some people responded poorly to the low pressure after a while and had blood form in their lungs, but astronauts would be weeded out if they showed any such symptoms. Bill hoped the Chinese picked their crew as stringently.

"Roger that, *Mercy I*. All of you should be able to handle the low pressure, but it will likely be uncomfortable for you."

"We'll make do, Houston. We'll make do. Now, how about those burn calculations, over?" Bill was ready to do something. Anything.

"Roger that, Houston. Thanks for the numbers." Paul Gesling had been on an open channel through Space Excursions' mission control and NASA's mission control since he had reached low Earth orbit. NASA had finally figured out exactly where the Orion space capsule had ended up and had worked out a complex series of burns for the Orion and *Dreamscape* to perform. Paul worked as cooperatively with the NASA engineers as he could.

"Thanks to you, *Dreamscape*. Let's hope this works so we can bring our people home," Houston responded. "Now, do you have any further questions before you initiate the burn, over?"

"Negative, Houston. We've got it under control." Paul double-checked the computer screens to make certain the data for the burns had been entered correctly. Mission control had repeated it several times as he entered it, reread it, and then checked it again. NASA was nothing if not thorough. Paul almost took their cautiousness as a sign that they didn't trust him. But he did his best to put those types of thoughts out of his head. They didn't help anybody, and those poor folks in that space capsule stranded in orbit, the wrong orbit, needed all the help they could get.

"Roger that, *Dreamscape*. We're here if you need us," Houston replied.

"Control, could you get Gary on the line?" Paul addressed

Space Excursions' own mission-control team, which consisted of two to four people depending on the time of day and the day of the week. He had them switch over to their own private and encrypted channel.

"Roger that, Paul. Give us a minute," they responded. A few minutes later, Gary was on the line.

"What's up, Paul?" Childers asked. Paul could see his face on the videocam screen.

"We are almost go for this burn, Gary. It just dawned on me that we've never tried the airlock docking mechanism out before. We've never done an EVA from *Dreamscape*. And we've never actually docked with the International Space Station yet," Paul said. His voice had more concern in it than usual.

"Do you have any reason to believe it will not function properly, Paul?" Childers raised an eyebrow, looking almost annoyed. "We shouldn't have led these people on if we don't think we can do this."

"No, no. I'm just saying. We've never done this type of thing before. When it works flawlessly, we should have some camera footage of it for future customers to see." Paul smiled at his boss.

"Now, that's the kind of entrepreneurial spirit I've been wanting to hear from you! Great idea. You think you can figure out how to set up the internal and external cams to give us decent shots?"

"Once I make this burn I'll have about two days with nothing else to do. I'll figure it out. Uh, don't take this wrong. I want to save these people with all my heart. But it just dawned on me that nobody was paying us for this flight, and it is going to eat into our budget." Paul had other test flights in mind that this rescue mission would remove from the schedule. *Dreamscape* had a very tight and very fixed budget. Rescue missions hadn't been figured into it.

"Don't worry about the business end right now, Paul. Just do your thing up there. That will be worth billions in the long run," Gary assured him.

"Right. When we've got more time in a few hours, we could talk more on the subject." The burn countdown clock turned yellow, showing five minutes and counting. "Getting close. Better let you go and get NASA back on."

"Understood. And Paul..." Gary paused and smiled. "Good luck."

"Thanks."

Chapter 35

"Thanks." Dr. Xu took the water bottle from Tony and took a long draw from it.

"You're welcome. How's the leg feeling?" Tony looked at the bandaged area around the taikonaut's tibia. It had been a day and a half since they had done their last orbit-correction burn and would be another day more before they could dock with the *Dreamscape*. There appeared to be no more leaks, bursting pipes, randomly firing thrusters, or sticky solar panels, so they had all taken off their suits. As far as Tony was concerned, doing so might help him save Xu's leg.

"It hurts, but not as badly as it did yesterday," he told Tony.

"Well, I'm going to redo this dressing and put you in a boot," Tony explained. Xu nodded in understanding. "In America, we have these big football players break a leg completely into two pieces, get some surgery and wear one of these boots, and then they'll be playing again by the end of the season."

"I've seen the same, Tony." Xu smiled. "I fear that I've lost a lot of bone material there. It will in the least make the bone shorter on that side."

"I've seen that fixed, too." Tony swabbed an antibacterial wipe over the wound and then filled it with triple antibiotic ointment before he rewrapped it. He noticed that Xu took a big whiff through his nose, as if trying to smell it. "Dr. Xu, I can assure you that there is no infection. You are not going to lose your leg to thrombosis or *Clostridium perfringens*. The antibiotic injections we've been giving you have worked just fine."

"Thank you, Tony. This all is..." Xu paused nervously. "Unsettling to me."

"As well it should be! It ain't everyday that a man gets his leg nearly blown off by a forty-five caliber pistol round." Tony gripped his shoulder and nodded to the man. "You're doing great. Don't worry."

"Very good then."

"Now, let's get you into this boot." Tony slipped the inflatable plastic cast gently around Xu's foot and then slid it up his leg like a sock. Then he pulled the tab on the inflation cartridge. The cast instantly filled with air pressure and held Xu's leg in place. "There. That should do it. You should try to rest."

Tony drifted by Zhi and looked at him. The man was out of his suit, but he was still taped up. Certainly he had to be uncomfortable being all bound up like that. Tony nodded to him, but Zhi just stared off into space.

"Are you doing alright?" he asked. Tony reached over and felt his pulse. He was fine.

"I am not in need of your assistance, Doctor," Zhi grunted.

"If you change your mind, let me know." Tony pushed away from him and over to Ming, who was still unconscious. Before they had reduced the air pressure in the cabin, he had seemed to be getting stronger. But for the last day or so there had been no change in his condition. Tony checked the pressurized intravenous-fluid bag, and it seemed to be functioning without any problems. He checked his other vitals, including his heart rate, temperature, and blood pressure. He then did a pupil-response test and seemed to see some improvement there.

Once Tony was sure he couldn't do anything else for the patient, he moved on to the command area, where he and Bill sat. Hui was in his seat, talking with Bill.

"Am I interrupting something?" he asked.

"Oh, Tony, excuse me." Hui started to unbuckle herself from his seat.

"No, no. Don't get up. I'm gonna float around awhile," Tony told her. "Anything new happening?"

"No," Bill answered. "We were just chatting about what we say happened up here."

"What do you mean?" Tony was confused.

"We cannot tell the world that a taikonaut fired a handgun aboard the spaceship, nearly killing us all and at least severely wounding one of us," Hui answered. "It would not only be bad for the Chinese space program, but it would be bad for everybody."

"I agree with Hui on this, Tony. We need to get our story straight with NASA and the Chinese ambassador before we get on the ground and there are video cameras on us from every which way." Bill sipped something that appeared to be coffee from his squeeze bottle and let out a sigh. "This is a mess, and I'm sure mission control will support our story. And any video that exists showing the, um, *outburst* will be kept locked up and away from the press."

"I see," Tony said. "Well, it is my opinion that Zhi has PTSD. I've seen the look before. Were he and Ming close?"

"PTSD?" Hui asked.

"Post-Traumatic Stress Disorder," Tony explained.

"Yes. I agree," Hui said.

"None of that matters. The story must be that we had systems malfunctions or there was an accident from the modifications we did on the Altair that caused our problems." Bill was adamant about the fact that astronauts didn't cause the problem. That had been a philosophy of NASA's since the Apollo era. The astronauts were heroes and couldn't do anything wrong. Oh, there had been a few glitches here and there that were hard to overlook, but for the most part the astronaut image was protected as best it could be.

"Xu might want to press charges. I might myself, but I understand what you're saying." Tony steadied himself against the console and stretched as best he could. "Above my pay grade. I think I'll Velcro myself to a bulkhead and take a nap. If you two figure out my story, let me know."

"Good night, then." Hui smiled at him. "I'm certain those above our pay grade, as you say, will tell us what to say."

"Let me know if you need me," Tony said.

There was only about thirty minutes left before the *Dreamscape* and the Orion would be in docking range. Bill had been in constant conversation with Houston and Captain Gesling for a good while. The systems checks had been plodded through twice already. There was very little to do but wait. Bill hated waiting. He'd been doing enough waiting on this mission. They needed to get hooked up and get the injured crew members in a hospital. He also had a few reservations about the docking hatch on top of the Orion. It wasn't all that far from where the aerocapture damage was. Bill tried not to think about that. He hoped they wouldn't need to suit up again, but if the docking hatch wouldn't open, they'd all have to suit up and go out the main hatch, if they could get it open, and EVA to the *Dreamscape*. Whatever they had to do, Bill assured himself that they would do it.

"*Mercy I*, Houston, over."

"Go ahead, Houston," Bill replied.

"We're looking good, and we need to start bringing the pressure up slowly," Houston said.

"Roger that, Houston. Time to start the pressure recovery." Bill started up the sequence to bring the air back up to a full atmospheric pressure level within the cabin. Otherwise, there would be too big of a pressure differential between the two spaceships when they docked, and they wouldn't be able to get the doors open.

There was just enough air left in the Orion for a day at low pressure or about eight hours at full pressure. The plan that NASA had come up with to keep enough oxygen in the cabin until help could arrive had worked out with a little margin to spare. Fortunately for all of them, America had spawned a private space program that could be ready as quickly as it had been.

"*Mercy I*, this is *Dreamscape*, over."

"Go ahead, *Dreamscape*," Bill replied.

"I've got a visual on you, *Mercy I*," Paul Gesling announced. "My clock shows twenty minutes and counting. Do you see me?"

"Tony?" Bill nudged Tony awake with an elbow. "We're on, buddy. Look out your side for the *Dreamscape*."

"I'm looking," Tony said as he wiped the sleep from his eyes. "I don't see anything yet."

"Wait, there it is. I see a glint over there." Bill pointed out his window. "*Dreamscape*, we see you." Bill said that loud enough for everybody to hear. There wasn't a sound made in the cabin. He was sure he could hear six hearts pounding with anxiety.

The next twenty-six minutes went by very slowly as the crew of Orion watched. The *Dreamscape* docking mechanism was on the starboard side just aft of the wings and on top of the fuselage of the vehicle. The docking ring of the Orion was on the nose. The two ships inched closer and closer together, nose to midsection. Finally, the onboard lidar locked the two spacecraft docking rings in the computer control system and the automated program took over the thrusters.

"*Mercy I*, this is *Dreamscape* showing ten seconds to dock. Delta-vee at three meters per second," Gesling announced.

"Roger that, *Dreamscape*," Bill replied. "*Mercy I* shows two meters per second...one point seven...one point three...zero point eight...zero point four...and three, two, one, dock!"

Clank, clank, kathunk!

"Docking ring activated. *Dreamscape* shows good seal!" Gesling said.

"*Mercy I* shows lock and good seal. Houston, this is *Mercy I*. Docking maneuver complete!" Bill said. There were cheers inside the cabin as well as around the world. There was a banging on the airlock door.

"Captain Stetson, this is Paul Gesling. If you folks want to open up in there we'll see what we can do about getting you home," Paul said over the radio.

"Roger that," Bill replied. "Tony, cycle the docking hatch."

"Yes, sir!" Tony tapped in the commands, and the lights all stayed in the green. The docking ring appeared to be one system that was still in functioning order. "It's working!"

Bill kicked up to the ring and pulled the hatch. It opened, and he found himself staring at the smiling face of the *Dreamscape*'s captain. He held a hand out, and Paul Gesling took it.

"Bill Stetson."

"Paul Gesling. Nice to meet you."

"Believe me, Paul, the pleasure is all ours." Bill smiled back at him. "Now, we've got two incapacitated and one walking wounded. We should move them first."

"Understood."

They set about moving Ming and Zhi into the *Dreamscape* and buckling them in. Zhi didn't put up a fight at all. Ming, on the other hand, pushed away Bill's hand when he tried to drag him up through the docking ring. Both Tony and Xu rushed to him to check his vitals and pupil response. Testing the waters again by squeezing Ming's hand resulted in a similar response. Ming appeared to be trying to pull away from the stimulus.

"Is that involuntary, you think?" Bill asked the two doctors.

"Can't say for sure, but it is a good sign. Some coma patients do that and some don't. Some do it before they wake up." Tony sounded very enthusiastic.

"Good news." Bill nodded. "Let's get this done and get home."

It took about thirty minutes to get everybody into the *Dreamscape* and strapped in. There was one more astronaut than there were chairs, and Hui argued that she would sit on the floor. Bill shut her down quickly and said he would do it.

"Ladies and gentlemen. If you will, this is my ship, and I am her captain. From the duration, here to the ground, I am the one calling the shots, if you don't mind." Paul took charge. "Captain Hui, while I've no doubt that you can handle the ride back not in a couch, you have been in distress far longer than Captain Stetson. Therefore, it is my decision that he will be the odd man out."

Hui didn't like the order, but she followed it.

"Now, Captain Stetson."

"Call me Bill."

"Very well, Bill. I have this figured out." Paul led Bill to the toilet room. The little room was larger than the toilet on a 767 and had a window in it. "Sit there. Here are some straps that I want you to buckle yourself in with." The toilet had connection rings in the wall for use during zero gravity.

"Who'd ever thought I'd be riding back home while sitting on the pot?" Bill laughed.

"Best seat in the house, Bill. Hold on and good luck." Paul winked at him.

"God speed, Captain," Bill told Paul as he closed the restroom door. "Now, why don't we have one of these on the Orion capsules?" Bill laughed to himself.

"Lady and gentlemen, this is the captain speaking. Be prepared for reentry burns in ten seconds," Paul said gleefully. "Let's go home."

Epilogue

The first thing that Bill Stetson did after they stepped out of the *Dreamscape* onto the landing pad in Nevada was to grab his wife and kids, who were waiting at the bottom of the stairs of the vehicle, and hug them to him and kiss each of them with all his heart. An ambulance rushed Xu, Ming, and Zhi off to a hospital for "treatment and evaluation," according to the official story.

Gary Childers had made certain that the original crew of the *Dreamscape* was there to meet the remaining Chinese crew members—on camera, of course. After all, had it not been for them, the Chinese taikonauts would have never been found. And there was Paul Gesling waving and shaking every hand thrust at him. The *Dreamscape,* her crew, and her captain were definitely heroes of the rescue.

Bill, Tony, and Hui stuck around for debriefing and then interviews. Gary Childers had catered food trucked in and a live orchestra. The gala was nothing short of a black-tie event. Senators and members of Congress were there to pump the flesh and ride the media wave. The NASA Administrator made a speech, and at one point there was a joint phone call from the President of the United States and the Paramount Leader of China. Space hadn't been so on the forefront of the world's mind since the first Moon landing.

Later that evening, Bill Stetson stepped out to look at the *Dreamscape* one more time. It was a good little ship. He liked the design and actually wondered if it could be redesigned with the docking ring on the nose so an Altair lander could be mated there. He liked the little ship better than the Orion. Perhaps future missions might marry up the NASA and private space-industry technology to a single, better system.

Bill wasn't sure about any of that, but he did plan to work on it in the future. He looked up at the full Moon glistening in the clear, star-filled night sky. After taking a few minutes to let his eyes get adjusted to the darkness, and his mind clear from all of the events of the day, Bill had a smile on his face as big as the one he'd gotten when he was five years old.

"We did return, and not only did we get there, but on a rescue mission—maybe there's hope for us after all," he said aloud. Bill thought about his aging mother and that first night that he had seen Gene Cernan leave the Moon. "I told you, Mom. I told you I was gonna go to the Moon someday."

Afterword

When Les Johnson and I started writing this book, both of us were very excited about the progress of the plan for America to go back to the Moon before 2018. I had actually been working on the flight-testing plan for the Ares I test vehicles and Les had been working on the Altair lunar surface access module a bit. The ideas were solid. The progress was happening. We were going back to the Moon!

Well, we were...

Then something bad happened. Politics.

Now, I'm not going to get into Republican versus Democrat or vice versa in this Afterword. This is not the place for that. But what it is the place for is to talk about what is wrong with how America approaches space exploration.

Before we can get into why we aren't going back to the Moon now, we have to talk a little bit about money. Back in the 1960s when President John F. Kennedy pledged that America would go to the Moon in one decade, NASA had a budget of about fifteen billion dollars per year. That is $15,000,000,000 per year. That budget remained steady throughout the Mercury, Gemini, and Apollo programs, seeing man walk on the Moon a year or more ahead of schedule.

Following the Apollo era, NASA's budget continued to remain the same give or take a billion dollars or so each year. Throughout the 1970s and 1980s, when the space shuttle was being designed and tested, throughout the 1990s, when the shuttle was flying and taking pieces of the International Space Station up to orbit, and throughout the construction of the space station itself, NASA's budget remained constant at around fifteen billion dollars per year give or take a billion or two. Even when President George W. Bush issued the goal to go back to the Moon by 2018, the budget was only increased about two billion dollars per year, and NASA was still expected to complete the space station, continue flying the shuttles for another decade, do all the science missions to planets and such, while building the rockets to go back to the Moon. During the Apollo era, NASA's budget was to go to the Moon, not all that other stuff too!

Oh, and by the way, did you catch that I said that for the past forty-five years NASA's budget remained at fifteen billion dollars per year or so? Let's think about that. In 1965, fifteen billion dollars was a heck of a lot of money. Then we had the extreme inflation era of the 1970s and steady inflation even in the good economic decades. I found six different calculators on the Internet to convert yesterday dollars into today dollars. I inputted the year of 1965 (right smack in the middle of the space-race era), fifteen billion dollars, and the told the calculators to convert that to 2010 dollars. The average value was $152,000,000,000, or one hundred fifty-two billion dollars. Ten times more than the current NASA budget. Ten! Times!

So, get this straight. NASA was given the goal around 2001 to figure out how to go back to the Moon with ten times less money than was used before. And, oh by the way, also use about six billion dollars a year for the International Space Station, another four or five for the shuttle, and one or so for science missions. The back-to-the-Moon plan, called the Constellation Program, had to figure out how to do this with about four to six billion dollars a year until the station was complete and the shuttles were retired. Then they could ramp up spending on just the Constellation Program. But it would still be at ten times less money than was used to go to the Moon in the first place. NASA's solution was to take longer to build the rockets. Where the original space race took Americans only a decade to get to the Moon, it would have to take two decades to go back based on the budget.

So why didn't President Bush just ask Congress to give NASA

more money if he really wanted us to go back to the Moon? The answer is simple. He probably didn't really care, or at the very least didn't think American voters thought it mattered if we went back or not. Oh, there is a small-but-large-enough-to-not-ignore voting bloc that has continuously lobbied to go back to the Moon and then to Mars for decades. This was the Bush administration's way of throwing them a bone and winning a few votes. Pushing the goal date out to 2018 meant that his administration would have long been out of office, and he could always blame the next administration for not continuing with the plan.

Well, it is time to start that blame game now.

Now, don't get me wrong, at least there was a plan for us to go back to the Moon under Bush. Granted, the plan was thin in dollars and stretched way too far out on the calendar, but it was a plan. The key here is that it was Bush's plan. And Obama killed it.

President Obama killed the Constellation Program. After nearly a decade of designing the rockets and spacecraft, testing them, launching an Ares I test vehicle, building test models of the Orion and the Altair, developing the mission timelines, scenarios, and schedules, after a decade of training a new cadre of astronauts, after having spent tens of billions of American taxpayers' dollars, President Obama simply killed the plan, quite likely because it wasn't his. And then he said, "But I just have to say pretty bluntly here: We've been there before."

Well, it seems clear that the President doesn't understand how little of the Moon we have visited up close, and just how little we know about the Moon. Twelve men have walked on the Moon. Six missions carried two men each time to the lunar surface. A few times they took a buggy that was limited in range by about six miles from the landing site. So the maximum area each mission could have observed up close was about one hundred square miles. That is roughly the square miles enclosed by the Interstate 495 "Beltway" that encompasses Washington D.C. If we add up all six missions and assumed each surveyed the maximum area of the Moon they could, which they didn't, then we get a total area of about six hundred square miles. That is not even a fraction as big as Hawaii. The surface area of the Moon is about 14.6 million square miles. So, we have actually looked at about 0.000004 percent of the surface of the Moon! We truly haven't "been there before."

It's bad enough that Bush didn't have enough gumption to truly make a return to the Moon happen, or at least get the ball rolling downhill so fast and with enough momentum that the following administration had no choice but to keep it going. Now Obama has followed the same blueprint as Bush: he has set the goal of a manned mission to an asteroid by 2025, to be followed with a manned mission to Mars sometime in the 2030s. By setting goals that are so far off, and not providing significant funds to reach them, he makes a token gesture toward space exploration while providing that he, like Bush, will have long since left office if we haven't reached those goals.

But why should it take twice as long for us to relearn how to go back to the Moon? It shouldn't. We've been flying in space for decades now and have technologies that would boggle the minds of the smartest scientists during the Apollo era. Given a similar budget as the Apollo program (adjusted for inflation), we should be able to go back to the Moon in a few years to a decade, certainly not two decades. It all boils down to silly politics.

Think about the so-called bailout packages that both Bush and Obama were involved with. In a period of two or three years, over a trillion dollars was spent on welfare, entitlement, and government-involvement efforts to fix our broken economy. Had we taken just one hundred billion dollars of that money and marked by law as the money to be used to go to the Moon within the next ten years not only would we have gone back to the Moon, but we would have seeded the space industry and sparked it into a thriving job maker in an economic down cycle that hasn't been seen since the Jimmy Carter years. Millions of jobs would be created by such an effort, and the spinoff technologies and businesses would be tremendous. And it would have only been a fraction of the total bailout money. I'm not saying that this would be a fix to the economy, but it sure couldn't hurt, and America's pride would receive a well-needed shot in the arm.

So right now we're all back to being stuck on the planet with no hopes of getting back to the Moon anytime soon. Our only hopes of getting there are for you, the voting masses, to tell your senators and congressmen and -women that we need to create a space plan, set it in stone, and stick to it! Even if it is lowballed on the money end and stretched out on the calendar like the Constellation Program, it would still be a plan with a goal and a schedule. But we can't keep starting and stopping all the time simply because of politics.

We need to go back to the Moon. If we can't even go back to the Moon, then what would happen one day if that dreaded planet-killing comet or asteroid is headed for us and we want to knock it out before it gets us? If we can't even make it to the Moon we surely can't do that. And if we can't even go back to the Moon, which is right there just a quarter million miles away, we surely can't make it to Mars, which is about a hundred million miles away (sometimes closer sometimes farther). If we populated the Moon and Mars and maybe some other places in the solar system, we wouldn't be as likely to be wiped out by a rogue asteroid or comet. We simply must go back to the Moon, not just for curiosity, adventure, or even science: we need to go back for humanity's sake.

We shouldn't just want to go back to the Moon. Humanity, in order to survive and to show that we belong in this universe, must go *Back to the Moon!*

Travis S. Taylor, Ph.D.
August 1, 2010